Maxim Jakubowski has written and edited ~~more~~ a wide variety of subjects including science fiction, fantasy, rock music, film and humour. He is the editor of the Blue Murder crime series and created the cult imprint Black Box Thrillers; co-owner of Murder One, England's premier crime bookshop; and a noted authority on the genre.

New
CRIMES

New CRIMES

edited by
Maxim Jakubowski

Robinson Publishing
London

First published in the UK by Robinson Publishing 1989

Collection copyright © 1989 by Robinson Publishing
Introduction copyright © 1989 by Maxim Jakubowski
Cover illustration © 1989 by David Wyatt

ISBN 1 85487 037 8

10 9 8 7 6 5 4 3 2 1

Typeset by Selectmove Ltd, London
Printed by The Guernsey Press Co. Ltd., Guernsey, Channel Islands

Acknowledgments

January 1953. A different version appeared in ARGOSY in 1939 as
DEATH IN THE YOSHIWARA.

'Professional Man' by David Goodis. © 1953 by the Estate of David
Goodis. First appeared in MANHUNT, October 1953.

'An Interview with Patricia Highsmith' by John Williams. © 1989 by John
Williams.

'The Making of Trouble is Their Business' by John Conquest. © 1989 by
John Conquest.

Contents

Features

INTRODUCTION

Welcome to *New Crimes*, the first of what we hope will become a regular series of anthologies of new crime and mystery writing dedicated to the healthy proposal that crime pays. . . At any rate, for authors, editors and publishers!

I strongly feel that crime and mystery writing is currently going through a golden age. The field displays an unparalleled vigour and not a month goes by without yet another remarkable novel or author breaking through to a larger public. This, happily, encompasses all the many sub-categories that make up today's crime and mystery landscape: the hardboiled P.I. genre, the classic "cozy" English mystery, the gritty police procedural, the feminist sleuths, the dark psychological tales of murk and menace and, even, the Sherlockian pastiche.

I'm particularly pleased that this inaugural volume of *New Crimes* succeeds in offering samplings of all the above categories, with a variety of stories by some of my favourite authors. Here, you will find splendid new tales from Britain, the United States and the past (with our Vintage Corner, which will be devoted to stories never previously published in book form).

So, who are the cuplrits, this time around?

Ed Gorman lives in Iowa where he works in media consultancy, edits the field's fast becoming indispensable news and comment magazine *Mystery Scene* and writes the popular Jack Dwyer P.I. novels. He writes "Two diverse elements went into my story, the first being my discovery lately of the American literary minimalist writers Raymond Carver and Richard Ford. I wanted to try a crime story in that form. The second is the fact that an employee of mine has a husband in prison and on the day she goes to see him her life is shattered. For a long afternoon we talked of what life's like for the wife of a prisoner."

Margaret Yorke, one of the finest exponents of the classic school of English mysteries, lives in Buckinghamshire. The author of 31 novels (*Crime In Question*, 1989, is her latest) she is an ex-Chairman of the Crime Writers' Association.

Derek Raymond's real name is Robin Cook. Which is what he is known as in Europe. Because of an American author with a similar name, he is obliged to use a pseudonym in England and the USA. A larger than life character, he now lives in France where he has seldom been seen in public without his black beret. He is currently writing his memoirs, and odds are that they will be as fast-moving as his novels. . . His long-awaited new novel '*I Was Dora Suarez*' was published in 1989.

The Burke novels of **Andrew Vachss** are increasing in popularity, making him one the shining new stars of crime writing in the 1980s. A New York attorney specialising in cases of child abuse, his latest novel is *Hard Candy*, 1989.

Paul Buck's only crime novel is his curious novelisation of *The Honeymoon Killers*, but he is well-known as a poet, translator and avant-garde exponent. His story here is his first crime tale in many years and marks his return to the genre. Several novels are already on the way.

The elegant **Peter Lovesey** is another of Britain's prominent mystery writers. His latest novel *The Edge* (1989) is a dark tale of love and treachery set in the aftermath of WW2, but the story he has written for us is a clever and unsettling puzzler.

Creator of the Nameless Detective, **Bill Pronzini** is one of the great American specialists of the hardboiled genre. A prolific anthologist and author, no new magazine could be without him.

Mike Ripley with his first two humorous novels featuring the trumpet-playing detective, Angel, has quickly carved a unique niche for himself in British detective fiction. A senior public relations officer in the beer industry, his story stems from his professional background.

Based in Somerset, expatriate US author **Michael Z. Lewin** usually prefers to be categorised as soft-boiled rather than hardboiled. He has written eleven novels and shares his affections between three characters: Private Eye Albert Samson, Lt. Leroy Powder of the Indianapolis Missing Persons Bureau and his latest creation, social worker Adele Buffington.

Born in Guyana and now a lecturer in London, **Mike Phillips** has written two novels featuring the wily black journalist Sam Dean. This is the first short story Dean, a British 'tec with a difference, appears in.

How do you present **John le Carré**? Well, I don't think a clever form of introduction is really needed. *George Smiley Goes Home* was initially published in 1979 a small anthology, celebrating the anniversary of the literary agency which then represented him. It's a rarely-known piece, which I thought was worth reprinting.

The truculent Inspector Lestrade novels of **Mike Trow** have been a cult success at my bookshop, London's Murder One. I'm delighted that my invitation to join the crowd at *New Crimes* has inspired this jovial Isle of Wight school teacher to pen his first Lestrade short story.

Now on the committee of the Crime Writers' Association, **Liza Cody** is at the forefront of a new wave of young British crime and mystery writers. The creator of a delightful sleuth, Anna Lee, Liza lives in Somerset with her husband and daughter.

Barry Gifford lives in California where he edits the acclaimed Black Lizard crime line. His last book was a collection of revisionist film reviews *The Devil Thumbs a Ride*. He is also the author of a definitive biography of Jack Kerouac. David Lynch, the director of *Blue Velvet*, is currently filming his new novel *Wild at Heart*, with Nicolas Cage, Isabella Rossellini, Harry Dean Stanton and Laura Dern.

Well-known in England as a cartoonist and astrologer, **Barry Fantoni** wrote two wonderfully tongue-in-cheek excursions into Chandler territory, featuring Mike Dime, in the early 1980s. His story Hopper and Pink, is the first of a new series of Mike Dime tales after a long interruption.

While the mystery world eagerly awaits a new novel (bring delivered to his publishers chapter by chapter!), **James Crumley** shares his time between Montana and scriptwriting duties in Hollywood (a recent effort was the immortal *Women With No Shirts But Machine Guns*). Since a recent foray into Europe in October 1988 for the Grenoble Crime Festival, Hemingway-like Crumley has become even more of a legend in his own time.

Stephen Gallagher is one the rising stars of the British horror field. Much of his work has operated on the borderline of crime and horror, but his short story for us is his first specifically in our area. Two of his novels are being filmed.

Prolific and popular **Robert Barnard** is nearing the top of the league of British detective fiction. He lives in Yorkshire, sports a delightful sense of humour and his latest novel is *Death and the Chaste Apprentice*.

Founder of Sisters in Crime and today's prime practitioner of the female Private Eye adventure with her heroine Vic Varshawski, **Sara Paretsky** goes from strength to strength, and I'm particularly proud to present a major new novelette by her, featuring her eponymous hardboiled lady sleuth.

Our Vintage Corner this issue takes its opening bow with previously uncollected stories by two of my favourite writers, Cornell Woolrich and David Goodis. Enjoy their dark and obsessive worlds as I never fail to do.

British journalist John Williams is completing a book of interviews with all the major American noir writers of the 1980s (Vachss, Crumley, James Lee Burke, Michael Malone, James Hall, etc. . .). Many of his interviews appear in British magazines *The Face, Arena and NME*. His conversation with Patricia Highsmith appears here first.

Once the mainstay of London's *Time Out* agitprop pages, and a consummate expert on all things noir and country and western, **John Conquest** is now living in Texas. He has recently completed a monumental book on the private eye genre. In his article, he talks about its writing and makes some intriguing observations about the field he knows so well.

I've tried to make the menu as varied as possible and hope you'll all come back to the table again. Happy dirty deeds.

                                                      Maxim Jakubowski

PRISONERS

by Ed Gorman

I am in my sister's small room with its posters of Madonna and
Tiffany. Sis is fourteen. Already tall, already pretty. Dressed in
jeans and a blue t-shirt. Boys call and come over constantly. She
wants nothing to do with boys.

Her back is to me. She will not turn around. I sit on the edge of
her bed, touching my hand to her shoulder. She smells warm, of
sleep. I say, "Sis listen to me."

She says nothing. She almost always says nothing.

"He wants to see you Sis."

Nothing.

"When he called last weekend—you were all he talked about. He
even started crying when you wouldn't come to the phone Sis. He
really did."

Nothing.

"Please, Sis. Please put on some good clothes and get ready 'cause
we've got to leave in ten minutes. We've got to get there on time and
you know it." I lean over so I can see her face.

She tucks her face into her pillow.

She doesn't want me to see that she is crying.

"Now you go and get ready, Sis. You go and get ready, all right?"

"I don't know who she thinks she is," Ma says when I go downstairs. "Too good to go and see her own father."

As she talks Ma is packing a big brown grocery sack. Into it go a
cornucopia of goodies—three cartons of Lucky Strike filters, three

packages of Hershey bars, two bottles of Ban roll-on deodorant, three Louis L'Amour paperbacks as well as all the stuff that's in there already.

Ma looks up at me. I've seen pictures of her when she was a young woman. She was a beauty. But that was before she started putting on weight and her hair started thinning and she stopped caring about how she dressed and all. "She going to go with us?"

"She says not."

"Just who does she think she is?"

"Calm down Ma. If she doesn't want to go, we'll just go ahead without her."

"What do we tell your Dad?"

"Tell him she's got the flu."

"The way she had the flu the last six times?"

"She's gone a few times."

"Yeah twice out of the whole year he's been there."

"Well."

"How do you think he feels? He gets all excited thinking he's going to see her and then she doesn't show up. How do you think he feels? She's his own flesh and blood."

I sigh. Ma's none too healthy and getting worked up this way doesn't do her any good. "I better go and call Riley."

"That's it. Go call Riley. Leave me here alone to worry about what we're going to tell your Dad."

"You know how Riley is. He appreciates a call."

"You don't care about me no more than your selfish sister does."

I go out to the living room where the phone sits on the end table I picked up at Goodwill last Christmastime. A lot of people don't like to shop at Goodwill, embarassed about going in there and all. The only thing I don't like is the smell. All those old clothes hanging. Sometimes I wonder if you opened up a grave if it wouldn't smell like Goodwill.

I call K-Mart, which is where I work as a manager trainee while I'm finishing off my retail degree at the junior college. My girlfriend Karen works at K-Mart, too. "Riley?"

"Hey, Tom."

"How're things going in my department?" A couple months ago Riley, who is the assistant manager over the whole store, put me in charge of the automotive department.

"Good, great."

"Good. I was worried." Karen always says she's proud 'cause I worry so much about my job. Karen says it proves I'm responsible. Karen says one of the reasons she loves me so much is 'cause I'm responsible. I guess I'd rather have her love me for my blue eyes or something but of course I don't say anything because Karen can get crabby about strange things sometimes.

"You go and see your old man today, huh?" Riley says.

"Yeah."

"Hell of a way to spend your day off."

"It's not so bad. You get used to it."

"Any word on when he gets out?"

"Be a year or so yet. Being his second time in and all."

"You're a hell of a kid, Tom, I ever tell you that before?"

"Yeah you did Riley and I appreciate it." Riley is a year older than me but sometimes he likes to pretend he's my uncle or something. But he means well and, like I told him, I appreciate it. Like when Dad's name was in the paper for the burglary and everything. The people at K-Mart all saw it and started treating me funny. But not Tom. He'd walk up and down the aisles with me and even put his arm on my shoulder like we were the best buddies in the whole world or something. In the coffee room this fat woman made a crack about it and Tom got mad and said "Why don't you shut your fucking fat mouth Shirley?" Nobody said anything more about my Dad after that. Of course poor Sis had it a lot worse than me at Catholic school. She had it real bad. Some of those kids really got vicious. A lot of nights I'd lay awake thinking of all the things I wanted to do to those kids. I'd do it with my hands too, wouldn't even use weapons.

"Well say hi to your mom."

"Thanks Riley. I'll be sure to."

"She's a hell of a nice lady." Riley and his girl came over one night when Ma'd had about three beers and was in a really good mood. They got along really well. He had her laughing at his jokes all night. Riley knows a lot of jokes. A lot of them.

"I sure hope we make our goal today."

"You just relax Tom and forget about the store. OK?"

"I'll try."

"Don't try Tom. Do it." He laughs, being my uncle again. "That's an order."

In the kitchen, done with packing her paper bag, Ma says, "I shouldn't have said that."

"Said what?" I say.

"About you being like your sister."

"Aw Ma. I didn't take that seriously."

"We couldn't've afforded to stay in this house if you hadn't been promoted to assistant manager. Not many boys would turn over their whole paychecks to their Ma." She doesn't mention her sister who is married to a banker who is what bankers aren't supposed to be, generous. I help but he helps a lot.

She starts crying.

I take her to me, hold her. Ma needs to cry a lot. Like she fills up with tears and will drown if she can't get rid of them. When I hold her I always think of the pictures of her as a young woman, of all the terrible things that have cost her her beauty.

When she's settled down some I say, "I'll go talk to Sis."

But just as I say that I hear the old boards of the house creak and there in the doorway, dressed in a white blouse and a blue skirt and blue hose and the blue flats I bought her for her last birthday, is Sis.

Ma sees her too and starts crying all over again. "Oh God hon thanks so much for changing your mind."

Then Ma puts her arms out wide and she goes over to Sis and throws her arms around her and gets her locked inside this big hug.

I can see Sis' blue eyes staring at me over Ma's shoulder.

In the soft fog of the April morning I see watercolor brown cows on the curve of the green hills and red barns faint in the rain. I used to want to be a farmer till I took a two week job summer of junior year where I cleaned out dairy barns and it took me weeks to get the odor of wet hay and cowshit and hot pissy milk from my nostrils and then I didn't want to be a farmer ever again.

"You all right hon?" Ma asks Sis.

But Sis doesn't answer. Just stares out the window at the watercolor brown cows.

"Ungrateful little brat" Ma says under her breath.

If Sis hears this she doesn't let on. She just stares out the window.

"Hon slow down" Ma says to me. "This road'z got a lot of curves in it."

And so it does.

Twenty-three curves—I've counted them many times— and you're on top of a hill looking down into a valley where the prison lies.

Curious, I once went to the library and read up on the prison. According to the historical society it's the oldest prison still standing in the Midwest, built of limestone dragged by prisoners from a nearby quarry. In 1948 the west wing had a fire that killed 18 blacks (they were segregated in those days) and in 1957 there was a riot that got a guard castrated with a busted pop bottle and two inmates shot dead in the back by other guards who were never brought to trial.

From the two-lane asphalt road that winds into the prison you see the steep limestone walls and the towers where uniformed guards toting riot guns look down at you as you sweep west to park in the visitors' parking lot.

As we walk through the rain to the prison, hurrying as the fat drops splatter on our heads, Ma says "I forgot. Don't say anything about your cousin Bessie."

"Oh. Right."

"Stuff about cancer always makes your Dad depressed. You know it runs in his family a lot."

She glances over her shoulder at Sis shambling along. Sis had not worn a coat. The rain doesn't seem to bother her. She is staring out at something still as if her face was nothing more than a mask which hides her real self. "You hear me?" Ma asks Sis.

If Sis hears she doesn't say anything.

"How're you doing this morning Jimmy?" Ma asks the fat guard who lets us into the waiting room.

His stomach wriggles beneath his threadbare uniform shirt like something troubled struggling to be born.

He grunts something none of us can understand. He obviously doesn't believe in being nice to Ma no matter how nice Ma is to him. Would break prison decorum apparently the sonofabitch. But if you think he's cold to us—and most people in the prison are—you should see how they are to the families of queers or with men who did things with children.

The cold is in my bones already. Except for July and August prison is always cold to me. The bars are cold. The walls are cold. When you go into the bathroom and run the water your fingers tingle. The prisoners are always sneezing and coughing. Ma always brings Dad lots of Contac and Listerine even though I told her about this article that said Listerine isn't anything except a mouthwash.

In the waiting room—which is nothing more than the yellow-painted room with battered old wooden chairs—a turnkey named Stan comes in and leads you right up to the visiting room, the only problem being that separating you from the visiting room is a set of bars. Stan turns the key that raises these bars and then you get inside and he lowers the bars behind you. For a minute or so you're locked in between two walls and two sets of bars. You get a sense of what it's like to be in a cell. The first couple times this happened I got scared. My chest started heaving and

I couldn't catch my breath, sort of like the nightmares I have sometimes.

Stan then raises the second set of bars and you're one room away from the visiting room or VR as the prisoners call it. In prison you always lower the first set of bars before you raise the next one. That way nobody escapes.

In this second room, not much bigger than a closet with a stand-up clumsy metal detector near the door leading to the VR, Stan asks Ma and Sis for their purses and me for my wallet. He asks if any of us have got any open packs of cigarettes and if so to hand them over. Prisoners and visitors alike can carry only full packs of cigarettes into the VR. Open packs are easy to hide stuff in.

You pass through the metal detector and straight into the VR room.

The first thing you notice is how all the furniture is in color coded sets—loungers and vinyl molded chairs makes up a set—orange green blue or red. Like that. This is so Mona the guard in here can tell you where to sit just by saying a color such as "Blue" which means you go sit in the blue set. Mona makes Stan look like a real friendly guy. She's fat with hair cut man short and a voice man deep. She wears her holster and gun with real obvious pleasure. One time Ma didn't understand what color she said and Mona's hand dropped to her service revolver like she was going to whip it out or something. Mona doesn't like to repeat herself. Mona is the one the black prisoner knocked unconscious a year ago. The black guy is married to this white girl which right away you can imagine Mona not liking at all so she's looking for any excuse to hassle him so the black guy one time gets down on his hands and knees to play with his little baby and Mona comes over and says you can only play with kids in the Toy Room (TR) and he says can't you make an exception and Mona sly like bumps him hard on the shoulder and he just flashes the way prisoners sometimes do and jumps up from the floor and not caring that she's a woman or not just drops her with a right hand and the way the story is told now anyway by prisoners and their families, everybody in TR instead of rushing to help her break out into applause just like it's a movie or something. Standing ovation. The black guy was in the hole for six months but was quoted afterward as saying it was worth it.

Most of the time it's not like that at all. Nothing exciting I mean. Most of the time it's just depressing.

Mostly it's women here to see husbands. They usually bring their kids so there's a lot of noise. Crying laughing chasing around. You can tell if there's trouble with a parole—the guy not getting out when he's supposed to—because that's when the arguments always start, the wife having built her hopes up and then the husband saying there's nothing he can do I'm sorry honey nothing I can do and sometimes the woman will really start crying or arguing, I even saw a woman slap her husband once, the worst being of course when some little kid starts crying and says "Daddy I want you to come home!" That's usually when the prisoner himself starts crying.

As for touching or fondling, there's none of it. You can kiss your husband for thirty seconds and most guards will hassle you even before your time's up if you try it open mouth or anything. Mona in particular is a real bitch about something like this. Apparently Mona doesn't like the idea of men and women kissing.

Another story you hear a lot up here is how this one prisoner cut a hole in his pocket so he could stand by the Coke machine and have his wife put her hand down his pocket and jack him off while they just appeared to be innocently standing there, though that may be one of those of stories the prisoners just like to tell.

The people who really have it worst are those who are in the hole or some other kind of solitary. On the west wall there's this long screen for them. They have to sit behind the screen the whole time. They can't touch their kids or anything. All they can do is look.

I can hear Ma's breath take up sharp when they bring Dad in.

He's still a handsome man—thin, dark curly hair with no gray, and more solid than ever since he works out in the prison weight room all the time. He always walks jaunty as if to say that wearing a gray uniform and living in an interlocking set of cages has not yet broken him. But you can see in his blue eyes that they broke him a long long time ago.

"Hiya everybody" he says trying to sound real happy.

Ma throws her arms around him and they hold each other. Sis and I sit down on the two chairs. I look at Sis. She stares at the floor.

Dad comes over then and says "You too sure look great."

"So do you" I say. "You must be still lifting those weights."

"Bench pressed two-twenty-five this week."

"Man" I say and look at Sis again. I nudge her with my elbow. She won't look up.

Dad stares at her. You can see how sad he is about her not looking up. Soft he says "It's all right."

Ma and Dad sit down then and we go through the usual stuff, how things are going at home and at my job and in junior college, and how things are going in prison. When he first got here, they put Dad in with this colored guy—he was Jamaican—but then they found out he had Aids so they moved Dad out right away. Now the guy he's with is this guy who was in Viet Nam and got one side of his face burned. Dad says once you get used to looking at him he's a nice guy with two kids of his own and not queer in any way or into drugs at all. In prison the drugs get pretty bad.

We talk a half hour before Dad looks at Sis again. "So how's my little girl."

She still won't look up.

"Ellen" Ma says "you talk to your Dad and right now."

Sis raises her head. She looks right at Dad but doesn't seem to see him at all. Ellen can do that. It's real spooky.

Dad puts his hand out and touches her.

Sis jerks her hand away. It's the most animated I've seen her in weeks.

"You give your Dad a hug and you give him a hug right now" Ma says to Sis.

Sis, still staring at Dad, shakes her head.

"It's all right" Dad says. "It's all right. She just doesn't like to come up here and I don't blame her at all. This isn't a nice place to visit at all." He smiles. "Believe me I wouldn't be here if they didn't make me."

Ma asks "Any word on your parole?"

"My lawyer says two years away. Maybe three, 'cause it's a second offense and all." Dad sighs and takes Ma's hand. "I know it's hard for you to believe hon—I mean practically every guy in here says the same thing—but I didn't break into that store that night. I really didn't. I was just walkin' along the river."

"I do believe you hon" Ma says "and so does Tom and so does Sis. Right kids?"

I nod. Sis has gone back to staring at the floor.

"'cause I served time before for breaking and entering the cops just automatically assumed it was me." Dad says. He shakes his head. The sadness is back in his eyes. "I don't have no idea how my billfold got on the floor of that place." He sounds miserable and now he doesn't look jaunty or young. He looks old and gray.

He looks back at Sis. "You still gettin' straight As hon?"

She looks up at him. But doesn't nod or anything.

"She sure is" Ma says. "Sister Rosemary says Ellen is the best student she's got. Imagine that."

Dad starts to reach out to Sis again but then takes his hand back.

Over in the red section this couple start arguing. The woman is crying and this little girl maybe six is holding real tight to her Dad who looks like he's going to start crying too. That bitch Mona has put on her mirror sunglasses again so you can't tell what she's thinking but you can see from the angle of her face that she's watching the three of them in the red section. Probably enjoying herself.

"Your lawyer sure it'll be two years?" Ma says.

"Or three."

"I sure do miss you hon" Ma says.

"I sure do miss you too hon."

"Don't know what I'd do without Tom to lean on." She makes a point of not mentioning Sis who she's obviously still mad at because Sis won't speak to Dad.

"He's sure a fine young man" Dad says. "Wish I woulda been that responsible when I was his age. Wouldn't be in here today if I'da been."

Sis gets up and leaves the room. Says nothing. Doesn't even look at anybody exactly. Just leaves. Mona directs her to the ladies room.

"I'm sorry hon she treats you this way" Ma says. "She thinks she'd too good to come see her Dad in prison."

"It's all right" Dad says looking sad again. He watches Sis leave the visiting room.

"I'm gonna have a good talk with her when we leave here hon" Ma says.

"Oh don't be too hard on her. Tough for a proud girl her age to come up here."

"Not too hard for Tom."

"Tom's different. Tom's mature. Tom's responsible. When Ellen gets Tom's age I'm sure she'll be mature and responsible too."

Half hour goes back before Sis comes. Almost time to leave. She walks over and sits down.

"You give your Dad a hug now." Ma says.

Sis looks at Dad. She stands up then and goes over and puts her arms out. Dad stands up grinning and takes her to him and hugs her tighter than I've ever seen him hug anybody. It's funny because right then and there he starts crying. Just holding Sis so tight. Crying.

"I love you hon" Dad says to her. "I love you hon and I'm sorry for all the mistakes I've made and I'll never make them again I promise you."

Ma starts crying too.

Sis says nothing.

When Dad lets her go I look at her eyes. They're the same as they were before. She's staring right at him but she doesn't seem to see him somehow.

Mona picks up the microphone that blasts through the speakers hung from the ceiling. She doesn't need a speaker in a room this size but she obviously likes how loud it is and how it hurts your ears.

"Visiting hours are over. You've got fifteen seconds to say good-bye and then the inmates have to start filing over to the door."

"I miss you so much hon" Ma says and throws her arms around Dad.

He hugs Ma but over his shoulder he's looking at Sis. She is standing up. She has her head down again.

Dad looks so sad so sad.

"I'd like to know just who the hell you think you are treatin' your own father that way" Ma says on the way back to town.

The rain and the fog are real bad now so I have to concentrate on my driving. On the opposite side of the road cars appear quickly in the fog and then vanish. It's almost unreal.

The wipers are slapping loud and everything smells damp, the rubber of the car and the vinyl seat covers and the ashtray from Ma's menthol cigarettes. Damp.

"You hear me young lady?" Ma says.

Sis is in the back seat again alone. Staring out the window. At the fog I guess.

"Come on Ma, she hugged him" I say.

"Yeah when I practically had to twist her arm to do it." Ma shakes her head. "Her own flesh and blood."

Sometimes I want to get mad and really let it out but I know it would just hurt Ma to remind her what Dad was doing to Ellen those years after he came out of prison the first time. I know for a fact he was doing it because I walked in on them one day little eleven year old Ellen there on the bed underneath my naked dad, staring off as he grunted and moved around inside her, staring off just the way she does now.

Staring off.

Ma knew about it all along of course but she wouldn't do anything about it. Wouldn't admit it probably not even to herself. In psychology, which I took last year at the junior college, that's called denial. I even brought it up a couple times but she just said I had a filthy mind and don't ever say nothing like that again.

Which is why I broke into that store that night and left Dad's billfold behind. Because I knew they'd arrest him and then he couldn't force Ellen into the bed anymore. Not that I blame Dad entirely. Prison makes you crazy no doubt about it and he was in there four years the first time. But even so I love Sis too much.

"Own flesh and blood" Ma says again lighting up one of her menthols and shaking her head.

I look into the rearview mirror at Sis's eyes. "Wish I could make you smile" I say to her. "Wish I could make you smile."

But she just stares out the window.

Sis hasn't smiled for a long time of course.

Not for a long time.

THE BREASTS OF APHRODITE

by Margaret Yorke

A group of tamarisk trees clustered together in the coarse grass between the bungalow block and the sea, which today was whipped into small stiff waves with narrow white crests. At sunset, the sturdy pollarded trunks of the trees stood out black against the pinky-gold sky and the shining water, their branches entwined like interwoven limbs topped with feathery foliage. Several hundred yards from the grey pebbled shore a fishing boat trawled its nets, the vessel pitching and tossing among the hollows of the vivid blue sea. There was not a cloud in the wide pale sky, and today the humped outline of the Turkish coast, only ten miles distant, was just a grey haze on the horizon.

On loungers outside the low white building where each apartment tapered off from its neighbour to give an illusion of privacy, Lionel and Eileen Blunt lay toasting in the sun, Lionel in shorts, Eileen in a trim one-piece suit which to some extent restrained her generous curves. Behind them their bungalow was orderly, all trace of their picnic lunch tidied away, no clutter of possessions strewn about the cool bedroom where the twin beds reposed pristine, their fresh white sheets undisturbed since the maid's earlier attentions.

"Fancy! No blankets!" Eileen had marvelled when they arrived two days ago.

"Too hot, dear. You'll not need one," said Lionel in a worldly way.

Before making the reservation he'd closely questioned colleagues at work, taking every precaution against booking them into an unsuitable hotel: you heard dire tales of holiday disaster, and Eileen would not take in her stride any imperfection in the arrangements. Why should she? A holiday was for pleasure and refreshment.

The Blunts usually went to the Lake District or Cornwall each September. As their circumstances improved over the years, with Lionel secure though no longer rising in the hierarchy at the bank, and Eileen safe in the county planning office, they had progressed from the bed-and-breakfast accommodation of early years to comfortable three-star hotels with bathrooms en suite and usually tea-making facilities too. Eileen had resisted the lure of foreign travel: something to do with their honeymoon in Majorca where she had not liked the plumbing nor the night-club in their hotel, which on their one visit after dinner had given her a headache.

They'd married late, both thirty-five at the time. Lionel until then, had been the support of a widowed and delicate mother, and Eileen, one way and the other, had somehow missed out on marriage. They'd met, prosaically enough, when Eileen had enquired about opening a high interest deposit account at the bank and Lionel had taken immense pains to advise her wisely.

Now they had been married ten years, and Lionel, to surprise her, had come home one February day with a bundle of brochures and a tentative booking made for two weeks in a Greek holiday paradise where, in your own private bungalow, you cold forget the world amid palm trees and bougainvillea. The hotel had been recommended by the assistant branch manager at the bank, who had been there the year before and had allayed Lionel's fears about any defects Eileen might not enjoy.

"I'd thought St Mawes this year," had been Eileen's response. There were palm trees there, if Lionel was so set on them.

"We should go abroad, while we're in our prime," said Lionel stoutly. "One day we'll be too old." And won't have been anywhere, he added, silently. "We'd be sure of the sun," he told her. "That would set you up before winter, dear. You know you've been peaky lately."

They'd both had flu, a nasty variety leaving them coughing and aching for weeks afterwards.

"Well, if you'd like it, dear, then of course we'll go," said Eileen. She was fond of Lionel, who had caused her not a moment's anxiety since he rescued her from spinsterhood.

The decision made, she applied herself to preparations for their expedition with her usual efficiency, laying in extra supplies of anti-mosquito lotion, antiseptic cream, sting remedies and bismuth mixture.

"You'd think we were going to Timbuctoo," said Lionel at work, feeling a trifle disloyal as he revealed that the spare room bed at

3, The Crescent was already neatly covered in travel necessities laid out for packing. Eileen had made herself two new sundresses; she liked sewing and did *gros point* tapestry in the evenings while Lionel watched television. His mother had knitted a lot; he liked to see a woman work creatively with her hands.

There were no little Blunts. None had arrived, and since Eileen never referred to the matter, Lionel concealed his own disappointment. They never discussed such subjects and even now, after moments of intimacy, were both embarrassed by the inevitable loss of dignity involved. Eileen, in particular, attached great importance to outward appearances and was always so neat; there was never a thing out of place at home, everything washed up immediately after use and put away, cushions plumbed up and newspaper tidily folded. So that now even the holiday bungalow was in apple-pie trim.

It wasn't like that at the Dawsons.

You could have knocked Lionel down with a feather when there, in the queue at Gatwick, stood Bill and June Dawson, he in jeans and anorak, she in a pink cotton jumpsuit, her unruly mane of curly, copper-coloured hair cascading down her back.

The Dawsons, with their three children, had moved to The Crescent two years ago. Their furniture was a hotch-potch collection acquired from junk shops over the years; watching them unload if from a self-drive hired van one Saturday, Eileen had felt quite ashamed on their behalf of its shoddiness. The children, who usually had dirty faces and often snivelling noses, were plump, happy and confident; never shy.

"Their manners are atrocious," Eileen had said when, after debating the matter because the newcomers were so shabby and down-at-heel in appearance, she had gone over to speak words of welcome as became the senior wife in the group of six identical houses. She found the children all sitting round the kitchen table eating bread and jam with no plates, just in their fingers, which were grubby to say the least.

Lionel, an only child, thought it sounded rather fun. As time went on he had made friends with the young Dawsons, mended their bicycles—all bought third, fourth, of fifth hand and not checked for safety before use—and, when they went on holiday or to see their grandparents, he went over to tend their hamsters and rabbits. The Dawsons had gone camping in France every year since their marriage, sheer folly, Eileen thought, when they still lacked a decent three-piece suite and the children wore clothes bought at jumble sales. Eileen was an excellent cook and she often baked jam tarts or gingerbread men especially for the Dawson children whom she suspected of being fed solely on chips and baked beans. She had wondered if June would be offended if she were to make the small girl a dress as a Christmas present; the child, who was four, always wore her brothers' outgrown and patched trousers and old felted sweaters. Lionel's main recreation was making models of men o'war throughout the ages, and both the small boys were intrigued by his work though their sister was too young to show much interest. They often came round to examine the construction in progress, leaving behind a considerable trail of dropped sweet papers and, it seemed to Lionel, an echo of laughter.

But now here the Dawsons stood, in line for the flight the Blunts were catching, and alone, without their children!

"That is who I think it is, isn't it?" Eileen whispered, fumbling for her spectacles.

"Oh yes," Lionel said. No one but June could have hair that colour, tumbling in such sweet disorder down her back.

"They never said!" Eileen's tone was accusing.

"Where are the children?" wondered Lionel.

"Well, they won't be going to the Bella Vista," said Eileen dismissively. It was far too expensive for the impecunious Dawsons. Bill was a free-lance photographer and how they managed to keep up their payments on the house in The Crescent Eileen did not know.

But indeed they were! Lionel could make out the labels hung on Bill's camera bag.

"Surprise, surprise!" said June, who detected no reservation in the tone of either Blunt neighbour as they uttered cries of greeting and recognition.

It seemed that her father had won the holiday in a sweepstake on the Derby and had presented it to them for a second honeymoon. By coincidence, the hotel allotted as the prize was this one so carefully researched by Lionel months before, and the only date for which it was available was now.

"We can lose each other out there," Eileen decided as they checked in their luggage and were given adjacent seats across the aisle of the plane.

But it hadn't worked out like that. Their bungalows adjoined, and much time was spent spread out among the oleanders and hibiscus bushes soaking up the sun within a few yards of one another.

And June lay there topless!

Eileen was appalled. Apart from themselves, there was the gnarled old gardener who moved about adjusting the range of the sprinklers which daily soaked all the vegetation. Even Lionel did not know where to look when she spoke to him, as she often did. He tried not to notice her small, high breasts with the amazing, huge dark nipples. You'd think with all those kids they'd be different, somehow. He began dreaming about them at night, even moaning once in his sleep.

Eileen woke him at once.

"Sh, Lionel," she admonished. "You were making a noise. Bill and June will think —" but she would not say what they would think if they heard these abandoned sounds through their wide open windows. She pressed her own lips tightly together when Lionel was overwhelmed with ardour. It would never do for Bill and June even to think they'd heard anything remotely "like that", and she hid her own head in the pillow when it became clear that the other couple were turning to good account June's father's gift.

"There'll be another mouth to feed next year, you mark my words," Eileen declared, and even Lionel thought that would be excessive, costs being what they were.

"Why don't you strip off too?" said June on the third morning.

"I'd be ashamed," said Eileen austerely.

"Why be coy about your body?" said June. "You'll feel so free, and it's only natural, after all."

Eileen blushed furiously.

"I'm not slim like you," she answered.

It was true. Looking at them, you would think Eileen was the mother of three, not the lithe young woman whose skin was already the colour of honey. Eileen suspected she lay about half-naked in their untidy garden whenever the summer sun shone instead of cleaning the house or preparing a wholesome meal. Still, in spite of her disapproval, even Eileen could not help warming to the girl whose fecklessness was in such sharp contrast to her own capability.

That first night the two couples entered the restaurant together and were placed at neighbouring tables by wide windows which were open to the terrace on these balmy nights. Subsequently, the Blunts ate early after a drink in the bar which overlooked the huge blue-tiled swimming-pool. The Dawsons had brought their own duty-free liquor which they consumed on their bungalow verandah. The Blunts had usually almost finished their meal by the time the younger couple arrived, both rather tiddly by this time and with June's appearance drawing warm smiles of welcome from Spiro, their waiter.

It was Bill who suggested that for part of the holiday they should share the hire of a car. In that way they could explore the island properly without being herded along on a tour. There were archaelogical sites to inspect and natural beauties too, valleys and gorges of renown; and they could seek out hidden isolated beaches. Lionel, who was apprehensive about driving on the wrong side of the road since he had never done it, leaped at the idea, aware of how such freedom could enlarge their explorations. The costs for a week, shared out, would not be enormous, and Bill could do all the driving.

In their rented Fiat they visited an ancient excavated city set on a hill amid pines and fragrant herbs. They entered tiny white-washed churches whose ornate interiors were redolent with the scent of incense. In one village an old lady beckoned them into her house and displayed photographs of seaman sons and indicated her own bed, high against one wall. She gave them sprigs of myrtle and offered them bottles of oil, and they left her three crumpled fifty drachmae notes, Lionel wondering if they had given her enough. They ate at tavernas by the sea or had picnic lunches on the beach, buying huge tomatoes, fresh cucumbers and fruit and rather dry rolls, drinking the rough local wine. And they found deserted coves where June stripped off all her clothes and hedonistically bathed naked in the warm sea.

Eileen, by this time, had begun to slip the straps of her bathing dress over her broad, fleshy shoulders as she lay on the sand, a straw hat over her face, sleeping off the wine which seemed to pack a hidden punch, or perhaps it was the air that made her feel as if she was floating away; she hadn't slept so much and so deeply for years. When the others were all in the sea, she at last daringly pulled her top right down and June was correct: she did feel a sense of liberation. She intended to restore herself to decency before the swimmers returned, but she dozed off. Waking, blushing, she heard Bills' camera click.

"You shouldn't, Bill," Lionel rebuked.

"Why not? Eileen's got breasts like Aphrodite," said Bill. "What's it matter between friends?"

But Lionel was worried and fell silent. He was sure that Bill would display his holidays snaps around The Crescent when they returned; Eileen's nakedness would be revealed to all their neighbours. What he did about June was own affairs; she was a pagan soul, and shameless; but Eileen was different.

She altered, however, after that episode, and in the evening suggested they should invite June and Bill to drinks on their patio before dinner. She made Lionel go with her to the small supermarket near the hotel and they bought beer, ouzo and cheese biscuits, although until now she had refused even to sample ouzo.

"Aphrodite was the goddess of love, you know," Bill said, toasting her.

Eileen simpered. Yes, that was the word; and Lionel shuddered as he drank his beer—he liked to know where he was with his drinks—and proffered peanuts.

They all dined at the same time that night, and afterwards strolled on the shingly beach. June led Lionel down to the water's edge and began throwing stones out to sea, shaking back her mane after each toss, dabbling her toes in the phosphorescent at the water's edge, her sandals kicked off and abandoned, bare feet impervious to the pebbles. When they turned at last the other pair were nowhere to be seen.

"Bill's seducing Eileen," June said, giggling. "He fancies her something rotten you know. He'll be calling on Bacchus for help."

"You shouldn't talk like that," Lionel reproved, "I know you're only joking, but some people might think you meant it."

"Believe me, it's true," said June. "Why shouldn't they have some fun? And why shouldn't we?"

Lionel knew about wife-swapping, of course; it had even been alleged to take place on the estate where The Crescent was situated; keys were flung into some central pool and general post was played. But such activities were not for him and Eileen and he was shocked.

"What nonsense you talk," he said, and walked off along the beach. "Come on, June," he called.

He was anxious to return to his wife in case June's incredible words should somehow prove to be true, but he did not want to leave her alone and it took him some time to persuade her. She was in a silly mood and clung to him, pressing her slim shape against him, hanging on to his arm. Her hair floated against his face and across his mouth; it smelled fragrantly of lemon shampoo. When at last they reached the bungalow block and he left her on her own verandah, she still clung to him and fastened her mouth to his; she was insatiable. Lionel hoped he had no grass stains on his trousers; they had moved off the hard stony beach into the shelter of a clump of hibiscus. He had to unwind her arms from around his neck and push her towards her own room. Where the light was on, no doubt attracting mosquitoes.

Eileen, more sensibly, had turned theirs off; he could hear her evenly breathing as, freshly showered, she lay beneath the sheet. He showered too; June's scent was all over him.

He did not see the footprints until the next morning. Clear and sharp, in talcum powder, they led one way, from the Dawsons' verandah on to his and Eileen's, and they were made by his wife's size six feet; June's feet were several sizes smaller.

Lionel did not, at first, accept the message. He knew that June spread chaos wherever she went and no doubt talcum powder too: but Eileen didn't. He brooded about the trail as they drove to Lindos after breakfast. Bill's camera lay on the back seat of the car; what other exposures had he made?

They parked as near to the beach as they could, then trudged through the busy streets of the small town to the citadel. June toyed with the idea of riding a donkey but it cost money, and Eileen, who would have liked to avoid the climb, felt she could not be the only one to do so.

"We'll swim later," Bill said. The beach was already filling with exposed bodies beneath umbrellas. They'd have lunch, they decided, at one of the tavernas where vines shaded the tables.

The ascent was steep, past white-washed buildings and importunate shop-keepers, and, higher up, vendors of embroidered table cloths and lace mats whose wares were spread at the side of the high, narrow path. Eileen stopped to admire some fine examples and was subjected to a tirade of sales patter in Greek and fragmented English.

"Your work is as fine as that," Lionel declared loyally. His own lapse had to be erased, and so must all evidence of anything Eileen had done, which would not be easy since proof lay in Bill's expensive camera. His mind closed on a vision of what might have passed between the pair while June kept him occupied; had the Dawsons colluded to lead him and Eileen astray or was June just seeking vengeance of her own? And what about Eileen herself? How to account for her actions? Of course, she was drunk on not only ouzo and wine but also the diet of myth and legend they had absorbed, and it was all his fault, for it was he who had wished to forsake safe St Mawes and seek the Aegean sun.

At the entrance to the site they paid their fee, took their tickets and began the final climb. June went first, her long slim legs, tanned brown now, scissoring their way. Eileen, panting a little in the heat, followed, and then Bill, who wore his camera slung round his neck. Lionel came last in the file of modern pilgrims.

"Be careful," called Lionel, for the steps were steep and there was no barrier to protect you from the sheer drop at the side.

As he spoke, Bill unhooked his camera to fiddle with some adjustment of the lens. He was going to use it, snap poor Eileen's fat rump as she lumbered upwards.

Lionel spoke to him sharply, distracting him, and the moment passed, but in that instant he made a plan and his chance to carry it out came when they descended. Bill had taken several exposures on the acropolis; he had photographed the bay where allegedly St Paul had landed, and the town below. As they went down the path again, in the same order, Bill, as if to plan, was holding the camera in his hands. Lionel reached out to jerk it from his grasp; one twitch was all it would need to send the thing hurting down to the rocks below, where it would smash and the film inside would destroyed.

But Bill's reactions were quick to protect his precious possession. Saving it, he stumbled, and his left hand shot out towards Eileen. She lost her balance straight away, gave one shrill cry and, in a second, had taken the fall Bill had intended for the camera.

"Oh, my God!" Bill was the first to scramble down the rest of the stairs and make his way to the mewing heap that was Eileen as she lay, legs twisted beneath her, in the shadow of the citadel.

The shock was too much for her. She died of that, not her injuries.

After the funeral Bill gave Lionel the photographs he had taken of her that last night, a sheet draped round her like a chiton, Aphrodite garbed.

Was that all that had happened between them? Now Lionel would never know. He hoped that decency alone would prevent Bill from showing any of the other exposures round The Crescent, but in any case, as soon as it was possible, he sold the house and asked the bank to arrange a transfer.

He moved to Manchester, where two years later he married a widow he met in a cruise.

EVERY DAY IS A DAY IN AUGUST

by Derek Raymond

I am very thin: so thin that I can slide through anything. A long time ago my girl laughed and said she was sure that if I never turned sideways on to her I would disappear like a postcard.

But it was the opposite that occurred.

When I ask how it occurred, when I ask why, the answer is only a dark confusion chikka chikka chikka chikka, nineteen whole times.

I seldom dream. The last dream I had was of my mother. "I must get up somehow so I can get at you!" she screamed in it—and she did, gripping the edges of her grave.

I don't think I was ever a particularly unquiet person to begin with, although it's true that I could never prevent myself speculating on what women really do to themselves with their fingers in private, once they feel sure that they're not being observed. In the tube, on my way to work, I could never help my gaze sliding to watch their fingers gripping the bright chrome rails of the carriage, the eyes of the women apparently separate from their motionless fingers, the eyes absent in a book or newspaper. But in other places, in a different time, light and situation, I know the objectives towards which the same fingers work;

then they are detectives to their owners. But under the glittering public lights such women, like my woman, are demurely reading a paperback which is invariably about perfect love in America.

But they radiate the same sly guilt that any criminal has.

I know I can never keep my own fingers still. They are as thin as the rest of me and rush away from my arms on the slightest excuse; then, like children in a garden, if I am not watching, they get up to any kind of mischief, scampering with a pianist's touch towards secret matters in the evening light: *chikka.*

But now I must go and say my nightly prayer, as I have always done at this time.

I have no real need to reread what I wrote—I already know it—only it is the pattern that determines me that I must do it, as I must perform all my gestures. I know the words by heart:

> "My name is Martin Shingle;
> I do not know my age."

This is crossed out, and replaced by:

> "My name is Martin Shingle;
> I don't know who I am."

To be replaced, in turn, by:

> "My name is Martin Shingle;
> I am not of my own age."

To what extent is existence nothing but commerce, until the time comes?

The walls of the flat are yellow, particularly in the sitting-room. Everything is yellow in this room, (which I may visit only on occasions), except in the case of one broad bare wall. This last is spattered right across with reddish-brown, rust-coloured stains, such as you see in the photographic enlargements of a sick man's cellular structure. These stains are the colour of blood—in fact, they may very well actually *be* blood. After all, stupidity, coldness, resignation, are sometimes not sufficient, when it comes to the point, to protect a person, and then there are incidents between people that occur in a final manner. I can't on my conscience, sir, affirm that these stains *are* blood *though of course I am anxious to assist your enquiries in any way I can, and although there are large vague patches in my memory I will let you know the minute I clear them up because I would like that; I would like to get shot of it.*

That's between you and yourself, they said. *We can't help you there. All we want is to get at the facts.*

The facts.

And nobody can ever help you *there*. People are always too busy when it comes to helping you *there*.

Yet it's there that we live, and how we live: that secret spot.

The stains are thick and clotted, such that you could pick them off the wall with your nail, if you wanted.

But in any case the stains, whatever they are, are not recent.

But what in existence is recent? What is distant? Something that happened years ago can seem as fresh as yesterday, or seen for tomorrow!

They treat us as hard as logic, seeking only facts, but never seeking to know why such facts are.

Your name is Martin Shingle?

Yes.

Whatever else I am, I am at least my own name.

It is time for me to leave my mind for my heart, for the light in my room has changed, so that I know it is time for me to say my prayer before I begin.

My heart: I know I left it in this flat somewhere.

I suppose I shall find what I believe I had to begin with, in the end, wherever those two ends of life may truly be.

The date, August 7th, 1928, means something. It was the evening I came back from the doctor's, a chilly night, to be greeted by her in our flat standing hand in hand with a stout young man, totally unknown to me, her saying: *This is Willy. Willy, this is Martin.* I instantly took in the silly, yet bestial look this young red-faced fool in his loud suit had for her and knew that it had happened between them while I was at the doctor's as I was most nights after leaving the office, the doctor saying, *The enlarged lesion on the left part of the glans is of venereal origin,* at the same time looking away from me in a way that my pride could not stand, *sir.*

Doctors call that a lesion. To me it was agony of both flesh and spirit, attacking me both in feebleness and my strength and manifesting itself as shame a scarlet, brilliant red pimple two and a half millimetres tall with a white tip too painful to pinch, even touch; and no women or any other being would look at it except from the safe side of a bedroom. And I a clerk! A clerk, with my self-containment, my dignity, my position in the company: and, at home—the envy of my neighbours—my Mother, my Flat, my Woman!

Yet my pimple could have been caused by only one woman—because she was, and always had been, the only woman.

I remember I had my mouth open to speak in peace, coldness and fury together; the colours of the room and the people in it blurring, and it was then that she felt it safe to laugh with the young man beside her and refer to my extreme frailty and thinness which after all was the way I was born, but she enjoyed the flat and my safe position in life; but while she laughed on the young man stole a look at my face and made an excuse to leave quickly, and then we were, except for Mother in the next room, to all intents and purposes alone *and I tell you again that some of the stains are very thick and clotted and if you wanted to you could pick them off the wall like scabs with your nail as they are extremely old and I have always been very clean and particularly in my habits,* and that the only refuge I had from her contemptuous laughter was retreat, as I did each night and hold my secret self in my hand behind the locked door of the freezing lavatory.

I was no longer a man, if I had ever been one: just a being frozen in his low rank, shame of his social disease, and misery: pressed, at this limit into doing anything if it came to it—any gestures whatever that might affirm me, open any door at all that might get me out to the freedom that must, must exist.

I am only a concert platform, only a scene that represents many. The paying audience eagerly anticipates our suffering and, with a quiet "ah!" as the suffering performers arrive, instrument in hand, settles back to listen to what we discordantly have to tell or even, at the top, the limit of our voices, yell.

I clearly remember the night I took action towards freedom and finally alter my situation. Though I have many blanks in my mind, I remember being pressed between the positions of two fears: what I was and was becoming, and had become, and what had to be done by me if I was to change that, and become different from that being who, each night, removed his lower underwear to examine the discharge in them, which told me in the two colours of purulent red and yellow that I was as good as grave-dust even before my time was out. All I could do at the day's end was find something clean to cover my lower limbs till morning came, and sleep alone in the bed to which I had been consigned, and consigned myself, saying my prayer as I had been taught before I fell asleep to bad dreams as I had been taught, which consisted, perhaps, of:

Deliver me.

My name is *Tractatus* (I don't know yet all that it entails or means); but it is a position from which all being can objectively be seen. Such a king as Tractatus, (and his realm), is rarely permitted to exist for long on earth: yet such suppression explains the disorders that teem on the face of the prostitute that we have made of human territory. It was innocent before, which is why the whole northern sector of my kingdom is in revolt. The responsibilities of any prince are great, in no matter what domain, and it may, in certain cases, have been necessary for him to be deformed, and so transformed, by pain, shame, evil, disease and fear such as his people know, in order for him to accede to the true crown.

I describe my interior life, and there is no one to listen; but I know now that it takes the very greatest experience imaginable to be able to govern by consent a village of no more than a hundred men; for they wish to know that you are able to govern yourself before they will allow you to take their decisions, and it is now sure to me, that if you insist against their will, then you will have collapsed with your ambition, and can forget the crown which, in our old lands at least, was voted to you, never sought or seized.

I, Tractatus, have been rendered invisible. Yet I exist. I will, by the same laws that governed me before, be recreated by an inversion of the same laws, if only in order to show that what seems invisible is actually indivisible, as such states have always been, and will always be.

My windows are so thick with dust that the daylight penetrates only as a dull orange colour. But that makes no difference to me. To me the light and shadow are as they were when the windows were clear—moving as exact as clock-hands across the furniture, across the floors. Thus I know to the second when I am compelled to move—when to get up: when to hear the two voices, when to put on my black office suit and coldly comb my hair, revolving carefully in the mirror, and then leave my room, turning left along the narrow passage encumbered with books, passing the kitchen on the right, pausing to grip the already sharpened weapon in there I continue, no louder than a whisper, past the bathroom, its tiles bathed in the light of the August afternoon, very hot: this light glances off the while tiles across the passage through the half open door; then I got past what Mother always referred to as The Smallest Room In The House with its funny smell that we never talked about and that no plumber could quite cure—and so, on time, as ever, to the second, into the broad living-room where the situation is.

Everything is utterly clear, blindingly so, up till then; it's only after that the gaps and blanks begin.

I perform it all, everything, down to the last detail, every day, between sunrise and sunset.

Always an August day. Every single day is a day in August. What happened before, or in between, I can't tell, *although I am doing my utmost to cooperate with you, gentlemen*. I may have been in bed, as I always find myself, getting up as the action begins, my decision taken. Before, I may have been absent, asleep. Blank. *I can't tell you; I have absolutely no references, gentlemen: no memory, though I know there's something I ought to tell you that would relieve me, make me feel better.*

Nobody ever comes. Only once a woman came to the flat with a man; I heard their voices through my bedroom door. I was terrified; it was an intrusion from another world: a complete shock, like ghosts; they didn't belong. I shrank in the stride that I had to continue; the woman's tread disturbed me—she has very heavy legs and struck the floor with her high heels in a way I didn't like, besides being terrified by it. The man meantime started up some patter about the flat being in a desirable neighbourhood. But the woman shut him up with a snap before she was ten paces indoors; I may have acted in some way to her, carrying out my prescribed walk, so that she may have seen or felt—in any case her heel ground into the boards of the room as she turned and left, saying that she didn't care for the atmosphere of the place, no matter how nice the view was. She told the man she had wasted her time for nothing and they left, slamming the door heavily behind them and double-locking it.

But that was many years ago.

You simply cannot know how terrible it is to live in a single time as well as beyond it, simultaneously:

The true terror, to me, is that.

Far more terrible even than my looking into Mother's eyes when she finally died next door, still laughing at me as she had done ever since I was eleven years old, the year my father left her and so supposedly, I imagine, escaped intact. Her sarcasm removed by death, I remember, her eyes were just colourless jelly.

Yes, like that:

Just jelly, the kind children could eat if they didn't know what it was.

Half asleep renews nothing—Mother is still standing opposite me as I am on the point of waking; she is in black, wagging her great forefinger at me, screaming in my face. Then, with no warning whatever, her square white black-eyes face dissolves into a molten rash and she falls back bubbling like hot rain in a bucket, ripping her tight two-piece costume against some nail in a chair as she falls, revealing her excellent legs up to the border of her stockings.

I touched her legs once as a child and drew back even before she lashed out; they were hard as steel.

I thought that the meaning of existence was that it had an end. But I was wrong; mine hasn't any. Each repeated moment is as painful as the poisoned blood a man squeezes from a wound or disease—evil cannot be said to be the fault of its host but of the innocence by which he contracted it, until the host is so invaded by the spread of his disease, born of his curiosity, that he can finally no longer by any means feel his way back through his damage—and so the burnt, wingless angel falls, and becomes Tractatus, crowned to the vast misery and squealing disorder that is Tractatus' kingdom.

So I have become a treatise, an object for analysis, abhorrence and suspicion, without ever having been the man that my distant, yet accompanying body told me I was. I had the desire to be what Nature had made me, but was caught in a heavy door slamming between two states, and so never became one. I have seen half-crushed beetles still trying to run away from the boot. I clung to my facade of normality until my accelerating interior chaos exploded like a star, reducing me to a few curled-up newspaper cutting burned by decades of the same sun, forgotten with the rest of man's general catastrophe.

Once a word sounds abstract I no longer know what it means; I told the visiting priest that. Abstractions obscure everything to a mind that is generally very clear. I don't think the man understood.

I recall the strident woman saying to the agent: *There isn't even any water or light on in this filthy, smelly dump!*

I was angry at that; it made me radiate. I was born in this place, and live out my time in with Her, Mother and my sickness, and the strident woman must have felt something, as she very quickly went away, slamming the front door, and I still feel the blast of August heat that the closing of the door sent from outdoors into the flat's environment.

I don't know why I remember so clearly that it was that particular day in August—I just do. I am back in the office where I am in that tearing hurry to clear up an account so that I can get away from the everyday iron bands of discipline also, that afternoon, the pain in the little wrinkled sheath of my trousered secret became so sharp behind the stripes of the material suddenly, that I broke the nib of my pen against the paper, ruining my copperplate. Interiorly, while mending the pen hastily, I was already back at the flat, where my lovely girl was stored, ringing with endless laughter. I looked at the office clock to see if I could finish earlier than usual if I hurried; it was already seventeen minutes past five. I told all the people who asked me that question, over and over, exactly the same thing: I know, because at the same time that I looked at the clock, I was aware of my painful little secret that had got crushed in my haste between my crossed legs and so got stuck by her discharge to my thigh and black trousers, and I explained to the endlessly questioning people how she throbbed to the same rhythm as my own hope, doubt and terror: how my poor little Miss Rosie implored me, on each of her pulsations, to do something about her that would make us both well again.

How easily reality can slip into imagination; and then, at a stroke, what you imagine becomes the real thing!

People aren't shot because they want to be, but because they have to be. People don't drink because the want to, but because they must. Murders and self-murders are committed because, in the circumstances, there is no alternative whatever. Those who control the climate of public speech ensure that such people, already being well rained on, are thoroughly drowned. All these screaming, dying people, the people of Tractatus' kingdom, know that they have got to be destroyed because chance, which men once called God, has decided that they must be. They die, as men do in any war, to satisfy someone else's ambition, *which expresses herself as a desire for the general good*.

I tell you, you must be the victim before you can become the true and trusted king of this strange realm. It is a place where the endurance of shame, of the pointed finger of cowards—the endurance of this is the only hope of sailing away again on your original pride. Or at least, it is the only hope of most people.

I tell you: if there could have been one day, just one, when I could truly have said that I was not in pain, that I hurt nowhere, and for that single moment was as open towards others and as happy as some declare that it is possible for people to be—then at last I could be what I am sure I was designed for, and need no longer reign, a black and occult king over this land.

It was a short time, but we were so happy when we first met. It was too good. It was like the false few days of intense heat that introduce a bad summer; you know that it must break in thunder. It was too easy to capture her, and be captured by her. Did you know that it is possible for two devils to be happy together for a glancing time, eyes, sheets on a bed, the breathlessness of passion, at the counter of a pub. Evil can be courteous, like mine, or broad and laughing, like hers; it can manifest itself in extremely good manners and a thin, distant smile, like mine—which I realised intrigued her, just as her fat thighs, cold look and chubby, pretty face intrigued me. Thin as I am, I was the quarrel, the bolt to have her: and I did.

I seriously studied the gestures that I had seen real people make in the direction of love up to the point where I could judge that it was safe and even wise to send her a tangled mass of wild roses bound with a white ribbon and my gilt-edged card, given away by the florist, on which I wrote, with great pleasure and passion in my cramped hand: "My heart lies at the heart of these." I remember taking great pleasure, too in paying—counting out the money coin by coin and placing it on the counter, at the same time glancing at myself in a convenient mirror.

It was only later, in the course of one of our furious rows in the flat, when we had discovered that neither of us really possessed the other in the way that we had each separately believed, that she told me my careful flowers had ended up in next morning's garbage. She added: *I kept your silly little card for fun, though: look!*

That was sick knowledge brought home to me that grew and burst: it most certainly was! My small, elegant bottom, the posed position of my thin legs laughed at me, and she laughed at them.

Well, now it is my time, and I must get up, dress, carefully comb my hair, then pass soundlessly out of my bedroom door to turn left, passing the kitchen where I pick up what I need in the hot sunlight. Then, as in the gestures of a rite, monastically, passing as a cold, graven image through an instant of fire, I continue on past the smell of the lavatory which the plumber hasn't yet come to repair, to the living room.

The drawing-room, as Mother, yelling with laughter at us both as she always did from her prostrate position in her room next door, would have said.

The end started between us as another silliness. We always described what had happened between us as a silliness when we made up. I know it always started or ended with the time when I got home one evening early from the office and found her in the living-room hand in hand with the stout young man, and I knew by instinct that they had had it off together and she said imperturbably, smiling: "Well, Martin, this is Willy. Willy, this is Martin." Willy was German. Though a big man, he took one look at the dense glare in my face and made an excuse, coughing, to leave hurriedly.

"Did you give him what you've given me?" I said.

"I don't know," she said, shrugging. "I suppose so. At least I may have done."

I hit her straight across the face. She didn't care. There was some sort of a blank period, and then the next thing was, we were in bed together, busy making up—and Mother next door was going through paroxysms of laughter and giggling at us all the time. I was glad the day she died slowly in a series of fits; I sat over her and said softly: "Die, die, die, you old bitch, go on, do it!"

"Stay as long as you like, darling," she mumbled among her last curses, "I'm loving it," and so she went.

Her mirth used to come right through her wall into the sitting-room; it used to destroy us until suddenly she was gone. I sent her body off to the nearest undertaker, and neither of us went anywhere near the funeral, though someone informed me that the stink of diesel in the chapel as she slid though and burned was overpowering—the witness had to go out and look across the wild terrain of West London and look at the brambles in the churchyard and the distant high-rise blocks, to recover.

I think I was in the office at the time, sir, catching up with my accounts; I'm doing my very best to help you in your questions and remember. But I'm afraid it's no more good just now, though of course if I do come up with anything else I'll tell you straight away; I'm most anxious to be all the help I can with your enquiries.

I know I had to go and see Mr Boggis in the office at a quarter past five before I could leave. But that was nothing. I was in a hurry to get back to our home, and everything important happened well after that. *Yes, well I know you're aware of that, sir.*

What the silliness was is too powerful for me to remember; all I know is that I end my ever repeated journey in front of the sitting-room wall. Willy had been while I slept; but I knew that he had been and left even while I slept: my little Miss Rosie and what is wrong with her never truly allows me to sleep. For the first time my girl backed off from me, her laughter shut off and out: for the first time, and the last time, I saw her revealed as afraid. Then there was what I call this silliness. You have got to try and understand that after the silliness—as we always called our rows—there was, according to the enquirers, nineteen times over no one there afterwards any more except myself. For an uncountable time there was just the abreaction in me that followed my ritual gestures—the necessary silenced laughter of the others that had caused, and now eased, the grief of the sick lie person I nursed and examined in my hand, and my own sadness. It can be very hard to know whether or not you've behaved correctly when you're under pressure in a certain state: *I should have been glad to have the view of*

my old chief, Mr Boggis, sitting apart from us all in his glass cubicle
up at the office in Oxford Street on the fifth floor, yes sir. I try
over and over to remember what happened by, or rather against,
the sitting-room wall, but it's no good—at the last moment it goes
dark and the next thing I know is, I'm back in my little bedroom again.
The light falls across the floor in its "get set" position, but I am already
stirring on the mattress, ready to start out to reach her and explain.

I was taken away to a medium-sized bare room painted green by a
good many uniformed men, and there men in correct suits shouted
at me and hit me across the face at times when I couldn't answer their
questions—though I was trying hard so that I could be left alone to
come to terms with what I was, must be, and what had become of me
and my world. Then, I don't know how long after, there was a quiet,
seeking voice, asking the same questions as the others had asked with
their fists. I clearly remember that I shrieked at the other voice: how
can one planet understand another?

But at the last minute everything went dark, and I was back in my
room again.

Then, later—I don't know how much later—I found myself faced
by even further unpleasantness in a really big room absolutely packed
with people presided over by a vicious-looking old man in black and
red robes while a team of men in dark gowns tried to force me to
explain how an entire self had expressed itself in less than two minutes
and ended in front of them—a phenomenon that they had no intellec-
tual or other means whatever of understanding themselves, but they
were being well paid just the same, if their clothes and watch-chains
under their obligatory dress in that room were anything to go by.

They were a dream to me, whatever they did or proved or said. The
difference between themselves and I was that they were dishonestly
sick. Whatever happened to me now, in public, I was dreaming; I was
already different, in the sky, beating my white wings along a solitary
shore before turning towards my new kingdom. How can you, and
why should you, murder, make love, and wish you could play the
violin?

But at least my poor little sick Miss Rosie, whom I coaxed out of my
clothes as I always did when we were alone together and examined for
new blisters, new wounds seemed to hurt less once all the people had
taken me back to my room and let me be—once they had all gone and
stopped shouting and proving.

Proof needs no theatre: theatre exists to reveal, on the contrary,
false proof.

Once I was back in my bare room, nursing my little friend quietly
that was myself, after all the shouting, I remember that the people that

came seemed kinder, changed towards me as they approached, bringing us my food, dulling all that sharpness of the past by suggesting a game of whist, or chess, in quiet tones. I was happy with them in a long-ago way as I proceeded to change my wings and my skin and my state.

Last was the big place, the tall right-angled structure in the middle. In a series of frozen gestures I underwent what I was instructed was necessary for me to undergo there, blindfolded and bound so that I might in no way be able to seize the wooden edges of the dark and so upset the eyeless balance of the witnessing officials.

After the quick, vast challenge of falling, after the sharpness, there was a nameless long darkness before at last I found myself back in the flat again.

Why did the young man scream when he broke into the flat and caught me half way in my journey? Why did he fall and remain at the end of the long sitting-room, interrupting my passage? His rucksack and the saucepan that has rolled across from it into the middle of the floor are totally wrong elements.

I would have talked to him! If I could have talked to him he might have saved us! Me, she, Mother and my little secret self! Was I not presentable? I look decent in my black suit, dressed for the office; my thinness hardly shows.

It is time for me to comb my hair before I leave my lonely bedroom. I see now that if I ever truly want the young man to talk to me I must try to hide the rope that I carry round my neck; and I must correct this terrible tilt to my head.

EXIT

Andrew Vachss

The black Corvette glided into a waiting spot behind the smog-gray windowless building. Gene turned off the ignition. Sat listening to the quiet. He took a rectangular leather case from the compartment behind the seats, climbed out, flicking the door closed behind him. He didn't lock the car.

Gene walked slowly through the rat-maze corridors. The door at the end was unmarked, a heavyset man in an army jacket watched him approach, eyes never leaving Gene's hands.

"I want to see Monroe."

"Sorry, kid. He's backing a game now."

"I'm the one."

The heavyset man's eyes shifted to Gene's face. "He's been waiting over an hour for you."

Gene walked past the guard into a long narrow room. One green felt pool table under a string of hanging lights. Men on benches lining the walls. He could see the sign on the far wall—the large arrow indicating that *EXIT* was just beyond Monroe. They were all there: Irish, nervously stroking balls around the green felt surface, waiting. And Monroe. A grossly corpulent thing, parasite-surrounded. Boneless. Only his eyes betraying life. They glittered greedily from deep within the fleshy rolls of his face. His eight hundred dollar black suit fluttered against his body like it didn't want to touch his flesh. His thin hair was flat-black, enameled patient-leather plastered onto a low forehead with a veneer of sweat. His large head rested on the puddle of his neck. His hands were mounds of doughy pink flesh at the tips of his short arms. His smile was a scar and the fear-aura coming off him was jailhouse-sharp.

"You were almost too late, kid."

"I'm here now."

"I'll let it go, Gene. You don't get a cut this time." The watchers grinned, taking their cue. "Three large when you win," Monroe said.

They advanced to the low clean table. Gene ran his hand gently over the tightly-woven surface, feeling the calm come into him the way it always did. He opened his leather case, assembled his cue.

Irish won the lag. Gene carefully roughened the tip of his cue, applied the blue chalk. Stepped to the table, holding the white cue ball in his left hand, bouncing it softly, waiting.

"Don't even think about losing." Monroe's voice, strangely thin.

Gene broke perfectly, leaving nothing. Irish walked once around the table, seeing what wasn't there. He played safe. The room was still.

"Seven ball in the corner."

Gene broke with that shot and quickly ran off the remaining balls. He watched Monroe's face gleaming wetly in the dimness as the balls were racked. He slammed the break-ball home, shattering the rack. And he sent the rest of the balls into pockets gaping their eagerness to serve him. The brightly-colored balls were his: he nursed some along the rail, sliced others laser-thin, finessed combinations. Brought them home.

Irish watched for a while. Then he sat down and looked at the floor. Lit a cigarette.

The room darkened. Gene smiled and missed his next shot. Irish sprang to the table. He worked slowly and too carefully for a long time. When he was finished, he was twelve balls ahead with twenty-five to go. But it was Gene's turn.

And Gene smiled again, deep into Monroe's face. Watched the man neatly place a cigarette into the precise center of his mouth, waving away a weasel-in-attendance who leaped to light it for him. And missed again . . . by a wider margin.

Irish blasted the balls off the table, waited impatiently for the rack. He smelled the pressure and didn't want to lose the wave. Irish broke correctly, ran the remaining balls and finished the game. *EXIT* was glowing in the background. As the last ball went down, he turned:

"You owe me money, Monroe."

His voice trembled. One of Monroe's men put money in his hand. The fat man spoke, soft and cold: "Would you like to play again?"

"No, I won't play again. I must of been crazy. You would of gone through with it. Yes. You fat, dirty, evil sonofabitch . . ."

One of the calmly waiting men hit him sharply under the heart. Others stepped forward to drag him from the room.

"Let him keep the money," Monroe told them.

Gene turned to gaze silently at the fat man. Almost home . . .

"You going to kill me, Monroe?"

"No, Gene. I don't want to kill you."

"Then I'm leaving."

A man grabbed Gene from each side and walked him toward the fat man's chair.

"You won't do anything like that. Ever again."

Monroe ground the hungry tip of his bright-red cigarette deep into the boy's face, directly beneath the eye. Just before he lost consciousness, Gene remembered that Monroe didn't smoke.

He awoke in a grassy plain, face down. He started to rise and the earth stuck to his torn face.

His screams were triumph.

BACK DOOR MAN

by Paul Buck

I should've gone in the front way, then I wouldn't have tripped over the mess of empty spirit bottles jumbled behind the kitchen door. That was only the beginning. The acrid stench partially braced me for what my eyes were about to witness. I gasped for air as I stumbled across the kitchen and reached for the switch. It was dangling away from the wall and I was lucky not to fry myself as I groped to light the place. The whole scene was such a disaster I wouldn't know where or how to start describing its state. I could only ask myself what had happened in my absence, and how had my home been transformed into a slag heap?

I stepped through to the hall and barged into the lounge, pushing whatever impeded the door backwards into the room.

Belinda was slumped on the sofa, clutching a bottle of gin, some quiz show blabbing inanely on the TV.

"Hello, sis," I started, holding back the flood of words and feelings dying to burst forth.

She looked up at me, trying to focus. "You back already," she blurted, finally. I couldn't be sure whether she'd recognized me, or whether she'd just seen the shape of a person in front of her. She looked well passed the point of comprehension, and it was barely coming up to noon. Perhaps she hadn't straightened out from the effects of the previous day before plunging in for another day's dosage. I didn't much care. I just wanted to know one thing before I tossed her out with the garbage.

"Where is she, Bel?" I wanted to start civil, even if I knew it'd be short-lived.

"Where's who?" I guessed she did know it was me.

"Where is she, Bel? You know who I'm talking about."

"Oh, you mean your precious little Sally," she said, then belched.

"Yes, I mean Sally, you disgusting bag of shit." Shit mightn't be the right word. But she was gross, dirty and despicable. When a woman of under thirty can pass for over fifty then something's amiss.

"High and mighty, ain't we?" She lifted the bottle and tried to pour it into her mouth while she laughed. It missed, mainly. It poured down her apology for clothing.

I snatched away the bottle and hurled it towards the corner. It struck the wall with a dull thud, didn't break. It bounced to the floor and gurgled its contents onto the carpet.

"You didn't oughta do that, Dick. You didn't oughta . . ." Her words tried to flow out, but they were slurping, just like the bottle.

"Shut up and listen," I said, leaning across, grabbing a handful of soggy cardigan and blouse, and dragging her to her feet. It was as much as I could stand to hold her before me. Her vile breath, the reeking smell of her clothes, all of it turned my action into an endurance test. I gulped some air and turned back.

"Where is she, Bel? Where's Sally?"

"She ain't here, that's for sure." Her eyes weren't afraid. They were nothing, just blank.

"That's obvious," I said. I glanced around the room. "She wouldn't let this happen to her home."

"Home, call this home." She tried to laugh, but her throat clogged instead, produced a rattling gurgle. I tightened my grip.

"Not after you've been in it, not now." I felt bitter. Though how to express it when the other is void, is no more than a series of pat responses.

"Not ever."

"I ain't gonna spend much time, here, you understand?" I shook her. "Just tell me, how long's she been gone?"

"Dunno." Her eyes fixed on mine. She wasn't there. She smiled, from nowhere. "She just went," she added.

"How long?"

"How should I know? I'm not a diary."

"Just a soak."

"She was just gone one day. Some months ago." Her voice faded away.

"Last year?" I asked. My arm was tiring as quickly as my patience.

There was a long pause before she answered. "Hell, I can't remember. Yeah, last year. 'Fore Xmas. She didn't come and give me no present or nothing."

"Hard cheese," I offered.

"After five years of looking after her, for you . . ." She paused, looked in my direction, if not at me, then continued. "For you, she ups and goes. What a way to show her grat . . . her gratitude." She closed her eyes. I wanted to punch them open, my fist was begging.

"That figures," I said, more to myself. "She stopped visiting around then. Not that she . . ." I let it drop.

"Thank God the slut's gone," she declared.

I reacted instinctively before the words had died on her lips. No one calls my daughter names. I cuffed the wreck of a woman across the cheek. Her face jerked across. The skin was so loose, it took on a new shape for a moment. Then I saw her throat retch. I let her go and she toppled back to the sofa and started vomiting.

I watched her heave a half dozen times. There was no point in preventing the outpouring, redirecting it to a container. I couldn't recognize my home anyway. It would require a bunch of exterminators to strip the place bare and start afresh. If I had been planning to stay, which I hadn't.

When she'd finished she wiped her mouth on her sleeve, slipped to the floor and leaned back against the seat, looking even more depleted. Slowly, she looked up at me and laughed weakly.

"I should kill you for this," I said. I didn't have the emotion or the venom any longer. They were just words. "You deserve it."

"High and mighty, you'll never change." Her words were clearer, though her voice was weaker.

"I left her with you, Bel. You were to look after her."

"I tried, but she changed."

"She's just a kid."

"Oh yeah. That kid's seventeen now. She's a woman. Or didn't you notice on her visits?"

"Sure she was growing. But she was still a kid. Your responsibility."

"Yeah, so you say."

"And this, this is how you drove her out." I looked around. A face on the TV laughed at me. I turned back.

"This is what that slut drove me to," she stammered.

I couldn't take this. She knew how I felt about my one and only. I clenched my fist. She laughed and leaned away. I responded with a foot instead, swung it hard into her body, caught her right side below the ribs. Her hand went to the pain and she straightened. I swung again, caught her breast. She grabbed the foot, tried to pull me over. I shook my foot free.

"You bastard, you," she screamed, only there was no energy in it.

"Just tell me where she went," I demanded.

"I've no idea, you go find her."

"Where?"

"Not heard a word from her."

"Nothing?"

"Go try your mates up west, that's about her mark."

"Who?"

"Dunno."

"Who?"

"Dunno, d'I?"

"You must have some idea?"

"Just know she was taking up with some people you knew."

"Who?"

"Remember a blonde woman. Bit stuck up, a classy broad."

"Rita Roberts?"

"Could be. Sounds right." She wiped her nose on her sleeve.

"What did she want with her?"

"Dunno. Perhaps it wasn't her."

"And you didn't stop her?"

"You can't stop a rat once it's in the sewer."

I wanted to leave the room before I lost control of myself. I turned back and swung my boot. It clipped her jaw, sent her backwards into the pool of her vomit on the seat.

"I want you out," I spat at her. "Go where the hell you want, just get out of my life. For ever."

"That's all the gratitude I get. Your own sister." She remained sprawled. There were no tears. She might as well be dead.

"You're lucky to get out of here alive. Family or no." I kicked at her arse and she slithered further into the puke. I could have killed her, but prison was only a few hours behind me. And that's the way I wanted it to remain. Behind me.

I guessed Rita still lived in the same place. I wasn't sure of the number but I knew the street. Mayfair was expensive, even though the buildings didn't always look it from outside. I recognized the block and entered. The porter directed me and I took the lift.

The door opened. Six years hadn't changed her. Her friends provided her with enough finance to buy everything that keeps one's looks in shape. I called them her friends. I was being polite. They were her clients, would always be that, nothing more. No matter how she viewed the relationships. I didn't understand why Sally should befriend her. I didn't want to understand was more to the point, I didn't want to consider the possibilities.

"I guessed you'd come by, sooner or later," she said, letting me enter. She reeked of an orchid-based perfume.

"Why?" I said and moved into the lounge.

"Oh, you know."

"No I don't."

"One thing and another."

I turned to look at her. She wore a smile on her face that made me feel sick. I tried words rather than a fist.

"Stop hedging, Rita. Where's Sally?"

She shrugged. "She's a grown woman now, she can. . ."

"She's a child, Rita," I cut in. "She's seventeen, for chrissakes. A child."

"As I said," Rita added, resuming her quiet manner. "She's all grown up, she wants to go her own way."

I stepped closer, grabbed her round the throat.

"I oughta strangle you. I will if I find you've done anything to spoil my child."

"Let me go, and. . . and I'll explain." She was keeping her cool, unreasonably I thought. I could sense a smirk behind her mask and her words.

"You bet you will," I spat out and pushed her backwards until she struck an armchair and fell back into it. Her gown parted and I saw she was naked beneath. Prison does things to a man's libido, but I was more concerned with my daughter's interests, tried to stem the upsurge of blood in my groins.

"Look, Dick. I don't know where she is now." She rubbed her neck. "Yes, I did see her, some months back. She was desperate, she wanted money."

"Why did she come to you?"

"Haven't a clue."

"Who sent her?"

"I thought you might have mentioned me to her. She said you were her father. That's why I helped."

"Helped? How?"

"I gave her some money. She said you had some owed you. I knew, though I didn't let on."

"Where'd she go?" I was standing before her just asking for straight answers.

"I don't know. Not seen her around since."

"You just gave her money and let her go?"

"Yes. No. Well, she stayed a day or two. Holed up here. Came to a party or two. She's very attractive." She realized the way she said it was stupid. I wasn't a prospective client. She caught the anger that flared in my eyes and added: "She was straight. I looked after her, okay? Better than I hear that sister of yours did."

"And that's it?" I continued, ploughing forward.

"Yeah, couple of days, then she was off."

"No idea where?"

"None. But she ain't round here no more. I'd know if she was."

"You sure?"

"Sure, I'm sure. Look, Dick, ain't you got no other relatives she might go to?"

"No, none."

"Pity. I'd like to help you."

"You better be giving this to me straight, Rita. If I find you've anything, anything at all to do with her, when I find her, your life will be nothing." I stared hard at her.

"Big shot, ain't you? You think I'm scared?"

"You'd better be. Your fancy men can't protect you every minute of the day."

"Look, Dick. Calm down. She'll be okay, you see." She stood and came up close to me. My groins started to stir again. I kept them in check, despite her bidding. "You just need to relax a bit."

"I'm relaxed enough, babe. So quit the smooth talk."

I placed my hand square on her face and pushed her backwards, as hard as I could. She staggered a few paces, then tripped over the edge of the fur rug and fell, grabbing at a resplendent 20s Lalique glass lamp, sweeping it over with a crash into the hearth.

I didn't stop to catch her curses.

Who was I to be contemptuous of Rita, for I was doing precisely the same thing, being at the beck and call of the wealthy. Though I hadn't been so smart, I hadn't collected my payment up front. If I had it would have been earning solid interest in some account whilst I served out the sentence. But it had all taken place so quickly. I had seized the chance and decided that at last I could change the direction of my life, and more importantly, the direction of my daughter's life.

Harry Osborne was all smiles. If smiles and bonhomie could be equated in monetary terms then Harry would be very rich. Harry was very rich. His fortune was invested and most days he spent a few hours controlling his interests from an office not far from Rita's place. Harry had plenty of time on his hands. Time to indulge himself. It was indulging his fancies that revealed his foibles. And

it was as a result of one of his foibles that I had first encountered
him. I had stepped swiftly into his place to take a fall for him. I
wasn't exactly versed in all his interests, perhaps I should say his
fancies, but I had a pretty shrewd idea about them. Yet what did I
care of his perversions? I had only one care where Harry Osborne
was concerned. He owed me money, I'd come to collect.

"You've come for your money, I expect," he stated as his assistant
showed me in.

"That's right, Harry," I said, briefly following her legs as she
exited.

"How much did we agree?" he asked, once I had turned my attention back to him.

"One hundred grand."

"Oh, yes."

"But that was some years ago. Six to be precise," I added. "What
about interest?"

Harry laughed. "You'll make a businessman yet, Dick. However,
I'm afraid I can't oblige. It wasn't my fault you didn't collect in
advance."

"Things moved too quickly, right?"

"Precisely."

"Lucky old you."

Harry ignored my comment. He opened a cheque book on the
desk. "Cheque okay?"

"Cash, if you don't mind."

"Cheque, cash, whichever. My cheques don't bounce."

"Sure they don't, but. . ."

"You don't trust me." He straightened and replaced his pen in his
pocket.

"Cheques can be stopped so easily."

"And you think if I give you cash I can't stop you as easily?" He
laughed.

"I'll take my chance." I crossed to the desk.

"I don't have it here now. I'm sorry."

"I'll give you a few hours. Will four be okay?"

"Four sounds fine."

"I'll be off."

I moved towards the door. He intercepted me, took hold of my
shoulder, though he didn't apply pressure. I stopped.

"Out of curiosity, dear boy. What are you going to do with the
money?"

"Just that you said, become a businessman." I looked round at
him. "Build a solid future for those dear to me."

"I thought your wife was dead?"

"She is, but my daughter isn't."

"Oh yes, your daughter. How is she?"

"Fine."

"Good. She was taken care of while you were away, I trust?"

"Yes, she was." I looked at his hand. He removed it from my shoulder. "Now if you excuse me I'll go and leave you plenty of time to assemble the necessaries for my return. Wouldn't want you to miss the bank before it closes."

I smiled at Harry. He smiled back, a glint in his eye that I didn't fully understand. Or perhaps I did. The rich stay rich because they don't let go of their money unless they've no option. Harry had plenty of options as I would undoubtedly discover.

I sat in a bar, pondering my next steps. Though I had had plenty of time in prison to plan my every move, since my confrontation at home, all my scenarios had suddenly turned arsy-versy. I had gathered something was wrong when Sally's visits stopped six months ago, but I hadn't sensed my world had sunk so low. I would find Sally. My only lead appeared to be Rita. I vowed to return and gently persuade her to remember further details. Meanwhile I had to focus on the money, make sure I wouldn't be tricked out of it.

Four o'clock came. And went. I took my time. I returned to Harry's office just off Piccadilly, near Green Park, and took up a position in a doorway opposite. I waited, biding my time. I wanted him to leave. I wanted so see if he'd invited any other friends to the office to add weight to his desire to keep hold of the money. I knew he would try to double-cross me, but not by what means. I had never seen men around Harry. He always seemed to be surrounded by pretty women. Money at work again.

I heard a clock chime the half hour in the building behind me, and then I saw Rita come out from Harry's. She glanced around, but didn't see me as I retreated into the shadows. For a moment I was surprised by her presence, then I reasoned that Harry was just her type. I didn't think much further on the connection, I was waiting for a man to depart.

A few minutes later, a man emerged. It was Harry. Perhaps I'd misjudged him. Somehow I didn't think so. He was carrying a briefcase. I guessed it contained the money, though it didn't appear large enough.

I crossed the street and followed the big man. He disappeared into a private underground car park. I slipped in behind him, avoiding the gatekeeper. As Harry turned the key in his BMW I came alongside him.

"There you are," I said. "I just missed you."

"This isn't four o'clock," he replied and continued to open the door.

"I got held up in the traffic," I offered.

"Come tomorrow, dear boy."

"Why bother? You've got it all there."

"Have I? You sure?"

"Haven't you?"

"Some of it." He leaned against the back door and looked at me.

"What about the rest?" I asked.

"It's in a safe, a time lock safe. So, dear boy, I can't touch it till tomorrow."

"I'll take this for now." I held out my right hand and he dropped the case handle into it.

"As you wish."

"Get in the car," I said.

I went round and climbed in beside him.

He was very cool. "You've the case. But I'd like my papers from it, please."

I opened it slightly and saw various papers. I had a better idea. "Take me to your home," I said.

"I can't do that."

"Why not?"

"It's against the rules."

"Whose rules?"

"My rules."

"You're being stupid."

"Dear boy, I only ever allow women into my home. It's a rule."

"You'll have to break it, for once."

"As you wish."

We drove in silence and I tried to figure out why he had such a strange rule. Was he that afraid of men?

His house in Belgravia was grand. The gates opened and shut automatically at his command. We stepped out into the garage and went through to a lift in the basement. A maid dressed in frilly French fineries rushed from the kitchen to greet Harry. The degree of shock that swept her face when she saw me. . . I jumped forward, afraid she would collapse. Harry hadn't been kidding. Obviously men did not come to his home. After she'd recovered sufficiently, she became flustered, didn't know what to do. Harry calmed her and we took the lift up to the lounge.

I had never seen such a lavishly decorated residence. It was more than just the splendour, it was the very nature of all the furniture and furnishings. Everything had a sexual aspect to it. Everyday things had become sexual art objects. I had heard that Catherine the Great had had furniture designed with erotic embellishments, I had seen photos of Indian temples adorned with erotic couplings, but I had never seen or imagined that one person could decorate their home exclusively with such sexual explicitness. I wouldn't have been surprised to find erotic paintings and drawings on the walls, or a library or erotic books, but I was staggered as I discovered everything was shaped and moulded as a tribute to one end: the Holy Grail of sex. Or perhaps I should say, desire. Or, lust. For it was far beyond a temple to the fair sex. The place reeked of depravity.

I was visibly taken aback. Now I could understand the rule for the exclusion of men. This was a paradise of women. This was Harry's paradise of women. For women? I didn't really think so. I couldn't see that women would willingly stay here. There was that pervading atmosphere of degradation that I felt sure would turn them off. Offers of money would confuse that viewpoint.

I didn't know what to say. All thought of my business at hand vanished. I set down the case and walked about.

Harry had overcome his uncomfortableness and now took pride in my behaviour. He was like a school kid, showing me one thing after another, explaining to me the various histories of the pieces, for not only had he collected many of the objects from far and wide, but he had designed new ones, and had replicas made of the lost trophies he had read about or seen illustrated in books.

I wanted to see more, even though deep down I despised the total concept of his pleasure. I asked to go from one room to the next. He refused. I insisted. He capitulated, resigned to the situation. He obviously knew how to control women better than his own sex.

Each room had a different décor, a different angle to it. We climbed the staircase and entered the master bedroom. I had expected it to be a room of mirrors. In fact it was more a tomb, laden in black. I tried to be enthusiastic while I looked for another way through to the next room. I noticed a door that blended with the wall. I crossed to it.

"No, not that door," he said firmly.

"Why not?"

"It goes nowhere interesting."

I ran my fingers down the jamb. I felt a button and pushed. The door opened and I stepped in.

The room was decked out as a torture chamber. Hooks, pulleys, chains and manacles hung from the walls and ceiling. A rack stretched along one wall. An array of weapons from various centuries and countries lined the other walls. And a couple of suspect thrones sat squarely in the centre, inviting occupation. I declined their offer and carried on around the room, halting momentarily against what looked like an elaborate upright coffin, before returning to face Harry. He had pushed the door shut. Suddenly I was afraid of him. He was bigger than me, although not as agile. Our means of exercise were undoubtedly different. I could reach a weapon as easily as him I reckoned. Thus my fear subsided.

There was a further click behind my right shoulder. I glanced round. A young woman had entered via another door. It was not the same young woman as before. This one was dressed as a slave, not a maid. She was encased in a black latex suit that hugged her body contours, all except for her pubic region, and her breasts, areas which protruded through the outfit. On her feet, she wore black patent with high heels. And her face was masked, her hair flowing behind. She carried two goblets of wine on a silver tray.

Harry's eyes, that had a few moments ago fired with anger, now transformed themselves into gleams of joy. I couldn't understand him once again.

The slave was silent. Her head was bowed. I could see she showed no shock at the sight of another man, even though her eyes were downbent. The maid had plainly instructed her as to the company. She offered her master a goblet, he accepted. She turned to me. I accepted, then set it down on the side. I distrusted its contents. She stood by the rack with her back to her master. He clicked his fingers and she bent forward, presenting her arse and her sex to his eyes and hands. Harry ran his fingers over the firm skin and down into the crevice.

I didn't like what I was seeing.

"What do you think of her?" he asked, as if making small talk of just another object around one's house.

"I don't know as it's to my taste," I replied, finding myself responding in a like tone, though I added an edge of sarcasm upon hearing my first words issue forth.

"Surely, she is?"

"I mean the room and your attitude with women," I said with obvious irritation.

The young woman's head turned slightly as if she had picked up on the sound of my voice, rather than what I was saying. She recoiled. She had broken a rule, that was apparent, though Harry didn't raise any objections. Rather, he smiled further.

"Would you like to avail yourself of the goods," he suggested.

I declined.

"Pity. She's very good."

"I'm sure she is."

He removed his hand from his fondlings, then slapped her firmly, not hard. "Turn around," he commanded.

She turned to face Harry.

"Face our guest, my dear."

She hesitated.

"I'm ordering you," he said, raising his voice a fraction.

She lifted her face.

"Raise your eyes."

She looked at me through the mask. I was embarrassed for her. I looked away. Harry laughed. I looked back at him, then at her. I had imagined her eyes would display her embarrassment. I was wrong. They were hard, hard as nails.

"I think it's time I left," I said.

"No, not yet. You wanted to look around. You brought this upon yourself. Take off your mask, child."

She hesitated, then took the step.

It was my turn to recoil. I stepped back on seeing Sally. Everything hit me at once. I wanted to lash out. I couldn't. Her eyes fixed me to the spot. I didn't need to look at Harry, he was laughing. I could hear him, laughing, laughing at me, laughing at his little game.

"You forced me to break my rule," he said, "but I think I'm having the last laugh."

"You perverted bugger," I said to him, though my eyes were still riveted to hers.

"Shut up, dad," Sally snapped.

My mouth dropped open. She sounded so cold and callous. Was this my daughter? How she had changed in half a dozen months.

"It's your fault I'm here," she said. A smile flickered across her face and she continued: "I'm glad I'm here. I like it here. Harry knows how to treat me." The naughty girl smile that she ended with dissolved to a stone-hard stare.

"My fault, I don't understand?"

"Auntie Bel sent me to Rita to discover just what type of person you were. And Rita introduced me to Harry, because you had connections with him. How can you object when you're involved in this world up to your neck?"

"I wanted to take you away from it. That's why I was connected, did time. For you. For the money to take you away." The more sincere I tried to be the more I felt I was treading on quicksand.

"Oh sure. You never cared."

"Don't say that," I retaliated.

"If you'd cared, you'd never have left me with that ogre of a sister of yours. I hated her. I hate women, don't you understand anything?"

I didn't. But this was leading nowhere. I had to change tack. "Why don't you and me leave this place and forget it ever happened?"

"Sorry, dad. I'm happy here. I've everything I want."

"I've money to buy you what you want."

"But yours will run out, eventually."

"And what if yours does too?"

"It won't."

I felt the impulse to make it happen. I turned and looked to the wall. I noticed a studded ball connected by a chain to a staff on the side. Later I discovered it was known as a morning star, for some unknown reason. I picked it up.

"Don't be stupid, Dick," Harry said, stepping forward.

I brandished the weapon. It was heavier than I thought. I knew it was lethal, immediately.

"Just keep coming you pervert," I provoked.

"What would you hope to gain from this, dear boy? You kill me and you'll place yourself back in prison."

"But I'll free Sally in the process."

"True." Harry paused and pondered, stroking his chin.

Sally looked from one to the other of us, then jumped between. "Oh no, you won't," she exclaimed. "You'll have to get me first."

"Out of the way, Sally," I instructed. I should have repeated it, been firmer. I was still seeing her as a child, despite all, a child who irritatingly got in the way.

"No, dad. I mean it. Kill me, if that's what will make you happy."

Sally started backing away, making Harry back away behind her. I edged forward. We were moving round the room. I watched closely, watched to see that no other weapons came within their reach.

"Stop," I ordered. I was more decisive this time.

"Make us," Sally spat back.

She stopped anyway. There were no weapons at hand, only the large coffin object to her right. Sally glanced at it, slid her hand along one edge and found a catch or something. It swung open. It was like a coffin stood on end, its door was fitted with spikes from top to bottom, except for the slit where the eyes of the entrapped could look through. I'd seen a similar torture instrument before in a film, or in a still from a film. It was called an Iron Maiden. I knew what it would do.

Sally jumped into the box. She glared at me, her hatred holding me rigid.

"Get out of there," I said firmly.

"No. Try and make me."

I stepped closer.

"Harry," she said sharply. "If he steps closer, close the door."

"I can't do that child," he replied, his voice breaking apart.

"You can if I tell you you can," she told him. I was beginning to understand their relationship.

Harry was in a real quandary. He wore his weakness like the spare tyre around his waist. His mask was crumbling. Not only was I, the one who had taken the fall for him earlier, putting him on the spot, but it was my own daughter conducting the overall state of affairs.

"Don't you close that," I barked at him.

Her eyes blazed at me.

"Your lovely little daughter. You wanted to do so much for me. I spit on you. I spit on your love." The words rolled out across layers of anger.

"You don't know what you're saying," I tried, to console her.

"I don't want your love. I want to control my own life."

"And your death?" I said, wishing immediately to retract it.

"And yes, my death. My destiny."

"Okay, but not now. Come out of there." I was scared for her. She took after me, impulsive. Now I sensed she was worse than me.

She turned to Harry. "Harry, close the door," she demanded.

Harry stood there, holding the door. "I can't child," he whispered.

"Harry, close the door," she yelled.

"I can't child. I just can't."

"I'll close it if that's what you want," I snapped, and moved towards it.

"No, you won't," she snarled, turning on me. "I don't want you to interfere. You've done enough damage."

I grabbed hold of the door.

"Let it go. Don't you dare," she shouted.

Harry grabbed for me, tried to stop me. I pushed him back without any difficulty. He stumbled and fell against the rack, banged his head and sunk to the floor.

I stood with the door in my hand, moving it to and fro slightly.

"Right, come out of there," I ordered loudly.

"Never," she screamed back.

"Come out, Sally." As I said her name, my daughter's name, it became distant. Her name. Her. She became divorced from me. Sally, who was she? She was a stranger. This wasn't my child. Not any longer. The thought was brief, an instant, nothing longer. I was shaken from it by her demands.

"Just go."

"No, you come out."

"No, you go."

"Come out, I said."

"Go away."

"Listen to me."

"Just go, you hear."

"I won't," I shouted again. I was almost hoarse.

Her eyes had seemed to harden with each curse, as if they were being notched up on the rack. I saw then, through those eyes, that she was contaminated. Nothing but contaminated. And she would never lose that dirtiness. She would never be pure again, nothing could be done to restore her virginity. Nothing would remove those indelible stains. Soiled. She was soiled. No longer mine. She was the world's. Not mine. She deserved to be treated by the rules of the world, the rules of the jungle. Her eyes and her screams had driven me half out of my mind. "Just go. Just go. Just go and forget me," the words came pouring out at me, battering at my body.

"I'll forget you," I returned. "I'll forget you alright, my girl," I repeated and cut the cord.

The door swung to, almost as if I had been preventing its closure. I saw her hands move upwards as she tried to stop the inevitable. I saw it slam, saw it slam again. And again. Again. As if reinforcing the point of closure. I saw her eyes open in amazement as the spikes pierced her body.

Death was not instant. There was still enough time for that look of hatred to crawl back into those eyes, those eyes that came out to pierce me, screaming their hatred into my nerve ends. I doubt if I'll ever forget that moment, those eyes of hatred . . . those eyes at death.

I was too confused to know what to do. Her eyes were coating mine as I turned to flee. I tripped over Harry's body, he was coming round, and I looked for the catch to let myself out. I felt sorry for Harry, though not for any true reason. But he was the real victim. He was the fall guy. Any other time, I would have laughed.

Downstairs I turned back to the lounge to grab the case. As I walked away from the house I wondered why I'd taken the money. I didn't want it. I would give it away. I opened it, extracted a bundle and shoved it in the face of the first down and out I stumbled across. I'd do it again, and again, I told myself. I found myself drifting towards Rita's. I decided I had another score to settle. Then I thought of Belinda. I had mistreated her badly. Yes, probably. Now I could hazard why she was as she was on my return. Perhaps money would help to buy a tonic of whatever she wanted to mend the scars. I clung onto the case. I hailed a taxi and had it drive me home. Bel hadn't departed yet, the lights were still blazing everywhere. I went to the back door and forced my way in.

I took a breath and crossed the kitchen. I came to the lounge. The door was ajar. There was a rope tied to the handle. It went straight up and over the door. It looked taut. I pushed the door, pushed harder to clear what was impeding it. I pretended I didn't know. I knew. I had been in prison. I edged into the room. Belinda was dangling on the other side of the door. She had been dead for some hours.

YOUDUNNIT

by Peter Lovesey

Y ou.

Yes, you, reading this.

How would you like to be a character in this story? Take a deep breath. It's a murder mystery. If you suffer from nightmares, nervous rashes, or have a dicky heart, better turn to something less dangerous. But if you think you can take it, read on.

Now step into the story.

Someone speaks your name.

Cautiously you answer, "Yes?"

You find yourself in an office furnished simply with a desk and two chairs, the sort of room universally used for interviewing purposes. It might seem totally impersonal were it not for the glass-fronted case mounted on the wall in front of you. Inside is a large stuffed fish.

"You may sit down. This will take a little time." Although the bearded man behind the desk isn't wearing a uniform, authority is implicit in his voice and manner. He is broad-shouldered, with a thick neck. His head is bald at the crown, with a crop of grizzled hair at the sides and back as compensation. His age would be difficult to estimate, but he is obviously a long-serving officer who gives the impression that he knows everything about you and is interested only in having it confirmed. He spends a moment looking at the papers in front of him. You are not deceived by the humorous sparkle in his brown eyes. You sense that it may shortly turn into an accusing gleam. But at the beginning he doesn't threaten. He starts on a quiet, disarming monotone, his eyes on his notes.

"Have you any idea why you are here?"

"Well," you say, "I was reading this crime story—"

He looks up with more interest. "So you read crime stories?"

"Sometimes, yes."

"Do you ever get ideas from what you read?"

This sounds like a question to duck. "I'm not sure what you mean."

"It's obvious what I mean," he tells you sharply. "So-called ingenious methods of murder. Anyone who reads crime stories knows how devious they are. Writers have been concocting murder mysteries for at least a hundred and fifty years, ever since Edgar Allan Poe. What was that one of his in which an orang-utan turned out to be the killer?"

"*The Murder in the Rue Morgue?*"

"Right. I don't get much time for reading in this job, but I know the plots. Years ago in those country house murders it was sufficient surprise for the butler to have done it. Most of them are a sight more ingenious than that, of course. There was the mad wife in the attic. There was the postman nobody noticed, who actually carried the corpse away in his sack. Did you read that one?"

"I may have done."

"Chesterton. I met him once, many years ago. I've met them all. It dates me, doesn't it? Dorothy L. Sayers. Agatha Christie. She was a fiendish plotter. Sweet lady, though. Rather shy, in fact."

Not only does it date him, you think to yourself; it takes some believing. G.K. Chesterton must have died fifty years ago, at least. Theoretically it's possible that they met, but it seems more likely that he is making it up.

"You sound like a real enthusiast," you venture, still unsure where all this is leading. Is he doing this to make you feel inferior?

"The Agatha Christie story that impressed me most," he says, "was the murder that turned out to have been committed by the narrator of the story."

"Yes, clever."

"I came across one in which the detective did it. There's no end to the twists in these stories. One of these days I fully expect to find out that the reader did it. Not so much a whodunnit as a youdunnit."

You smile nervously. "That would be stretching it."

"Oh, I don't know." He eyes you speculatively. "You didn't answer my question just now. Do you get ideas from crimes stories?"

"Not that I'm aware of," you say. "I don't know what use I could make of them."

He fingers his beard. "That remains to be discovered. Let's talk about you. Shall I lay out the essential facts? I want to ask you about a Saturday evening towards the end of last summer."

"Last summer?" Your hand finds the edge of your chair and grips it. This isn't going to be easy. Last summer was a long time ago. You have sometimes wondered how reliable a witness you would be if you were ever called to testify to something you saw the same day. But last summer . . .

"To be precise, the last Saturday in August. You were expecting a visitor, a rather special visitor, so special that you'd put a bottle of champagne on ice and . . ." He looks up and arches his eyebrows, plainly inviting you to continue.

You frown and say, "There's obviously some mistake."

He stares back. "What's your difficulty?"

"What you just said. It has nothing to do with me."

"Are you certain?"

"Absolutely."

He folds his arms. "What exactly is your difficulty? Remembering the day? It was an unusually warm, still evening. Still as the grave. Days like that deserve to be remembered. You *do* remember it?"

"The day?"

"The last Saturday in August."

"It isn't not simple. I suppose I could if something were to jog my memory."

He says with faintly sinister sarcasm, "If necessary I can arrange that. Let's get to the bubbly, then—the champagne. More up your street than trying to remember which day it was, I dare say."

"What do you mean? I'm not in the habit—"

"I didn't say you were. But you wouldn't object to a glass of fizz on a sweltering Saturday evening in summer?"

"I don't know what you're talking about."

He presses on, unperturbed. "We're simply establishing the possibility of the scenario I gave you. It could have happened to anyone."

"Not to me."

"Let's put it to the test. You *have* drunk champagne at some time in your life? You don't deny that?"

You give a shrug that doesn't commit you to anything.

"Presumably you prefer it cooled?"

"Most people do."

"So if you *did* have a bottle of champagne—a good champagne, a Perrier Jouet '79, shall we say—you'd have sufficient respect to put it on ice?" He spreads his hands to show how reasonable the proposition is.

You refuse to be lured into some admission that will incriminate you. "Listen, it's becoming more and more obvious that you are talking to the wrong person. I'm not in the habit of drinking champagne on Saturday evenings."

"Pity. It would make you more co-operative. However, the point is immaterial. As it turned out, nobody drank the champagne."

A pause.

"As *what* turned out?" you ask.

He gives you a long, level look. "We're coming to that. Let's stay with the champagne a moment. You wouldn't drink it alone, would you? It isn't the sort of drink you have alone. Champagne is for lovers."

You stare at him and say, "This is getting more and more ridiculous."

"Is there someone in your life?"

"If there is, it's no concern of yours."

"Correction," he says before you have got out the words. "It *is* my concern. It assuredly is."

You press your lips together and shake your head.

He continues to probe. "Don't tell me you haven't a lover. Look, I may seem old-fashioned to you, but I know what goes on."

"Not in my life, you don't," you tell him firmly. "That's becoming clearer by the minute."

"All right, if it's the term 'lover' you object to let's settle for friend, then. Intimate friend. Someone who makes your heart beat faster. This is a crime of passion—I'll stake my reputation on that."

"A *crime*?" Now is the moment to make a stand. "You're talking about a crime?"

"That's what I said."

"Involving someone I know?"

"Involving you."

You are silent for a moment. Then, with an effort to stay in control, you say, "If you are serious, I think I'd better ask for a solicitor."

His face creases into a pained expression. "Don't spoil it," he tells you. "We were getting on so well. Let's leave the love angle for the present. We'll go back to Saturday evening. No more beating about the bush. It was about nine. You were at home, alone. But your, em, visitor was expected any minute, so you had the champagne ready in a bucket of ice."

"All of this is rubbish."

He lifts a warning finger. "Have the goodness to hear me out, will you? You're getting the kid-glove treatment, but there are limits. You had the house to yourself because your spouse, is it?—or partner, is that more accurate?—was away for the week-end."

You sigh loudly and say nothing. Might as well let him continue. He's making a total idiot of himself.

"A romantic evening was in prospect. Soft music in the back-ground. The Richard Clayderman album."

"I can't stand Richard Clayderman."

"Your lover can. The candles were lit. After your bath you'd put on something cool and sexy, a white silk caftan."

You roll your eyes upwards. "Me in a caftan?"

"Some kind of robe, then. We won't argue over that. Suddenly the doorbell chimed. You went to the front door and flung it open and said, 'Darling . . .' Then the smile froze on your lips, because it wasn't your lover on the doorstep. It was You Know Who, back unexpectedly from that weekend away."

"You're way off beam," you say. "This didn't happen to me. This is someone else you're talking about."

"You don't remember?"

"I haven't the faintest recollection of anything you've said. What's supposed to have happened next?"

"A blazing row. There was hell to pay with all that evidence of infidelity around you. Champagne and soft music wasn't the norm in your house. You just admitted that."

"Did I?" You feel your mouth go dry. You thought you'd admit-ted nothing, yet there's a disturbing logic in some of what he is saying.

"You protested your innocence vigorously. You're pretty good at that. And all the time that this row was going on, you dreaded hearing the doorbell again, because you knew this time it would be your lover. Zap! You'd be finished, the pair of you. So what did you do?"

"Don't ask me," you say acidly. "I wasn't there."

"You panicked. You snatched up the full bottle of champagne and swung it with all your strength. Crashed it into You Know Who's skull. Murder."

"Untrue."

His eyes open wider. "How can you say it's untrue if you don't remember anything?" He leans towards you again. "You dragged the body across the room and shoved it into the cupboard under the stairs."

You're sweating now. It's apparent that he's speaking of some-thing that really happened. A murder was committed and you're in grave danger of being framed, or stitched up, or whatever the expression is. But why? What has he got against you? Is there some piece of evidence he hasn't brought up yet? So far it's all been circumstantial. They need more than that to secure a conviction, don't they?

You decide to change tack. "Listen, it's clear to me that I need some help. How can I convince you that all this absolutely did not happen? Not to me."

He leans forward and fixes you with his dark eyes. "You really know nothing about it? You'd swear to that?"

You nod and look earnest.

At last he seems willing to reconsider. "In that case," he speculates, "perhaps I got it wrong. *You* were struck with the bottle. You were concussed, so you remember nothing."

"Would that explain it?" you blurt out thankfully.

"So it appears."

"I'm innocent, then?"

He hesitates. "How's your head? Does it feel sore?"

You rub it, pressing hard with your fingers. "That part is tender, certainly."

"At the back?"

"Yes."

He starts writing in his book, speaking the words aloud. "A blow on the back of the head, causing concussion and loss of memory."

You start turning mental cartwheels. "May I go, then?"

He looks up, grinning faintly. "No, I can't allow that."

"Why not?"

"Because there *was* a corpse found in that cupboard and it wasn't yours."

"A corpse in my house? That isn't possible. Whose corpse, for heaven's sake?"

His tone alters. "Watch it. You're in no position to talk like that. You asked whose corpse it was. I told you. It was the corpse of the person I referred to as You Know Who."

"And you hold me responsible? I thought we just agreed that if I was there at all I was out cold."

He shakes his head. "You regained consciousness after a minute or two and picked up the bottle and struck the fatal blow—a much harder one. Your victim's skull was heavily impacted. There's no doubt that the bottle was the murder weapon."

"I deny it."

"I wouldn't, if I were you." He closes his book. "It's my duty to caution you now." He presses his hands together and stares at you solemnly. "Speak that which thou knowest and no more, for by thy words shalt thou be judged."

You gape at him. "That isn't the proper caution. Those aren't the words."

"They are in this place."

You stare around you at the walls blank except for the stuffed fish above his head. "Where am I then?"

He gives you a look with genuine pity in it. "This will come as a shock. You were found unconscious in your house. There was a box of pills beside you. That is to say, a box that had contained pills. Sleeping pills. You swallowed the lot after committing the murder. You've been in intensive care for months, in a coma."

"A coma?"

"I'm afraid you never recovered consciousness. You died in hospital twenty minutes ago."

With heavy irony you say, "Oh, yes, and I suppose you're St Peter."

But your words are lost in a vaporous mist that swirls over you. The floor sinks away, and you find that you are almost weightless. As you drift lower you glimpse the sandalled feet of your inquisitor. You recall his strange claim to have met Chesterton and the others, all dead writers. Then a man in a red uniform takes a grip on your arm and starts to draw you firmly downwards.

Yes, youdunnit.

FUNERAL DAY
by Bill Pronzini

I t was a nice funeral. And easier to get through than he'd
imagined it would be, thanks to Margo and Reverend Baxter.
They had kept it small, just a few friends; Katy had had no
siblings others than Margo, no other living relatives. And the casket
had been closed, of course. A fall from a two-hundred-foot cliff. . .
it made him shudder to think what poor Katy must have looked
like when they found her. He hadn't had to view the body, thank
God. Margo had attended to the formal identification.

The flowers were the worst part of the service. Gardenias, Katy's
favorite. Dozens and dozens of gardenias, their petals like dead
white flesh, their cloyingly sweet perfume filling the chapel and
making him a little dizzy after awhile, so that he couldn't concentrate on Reverend Baxter's mercifully brief eulogy.

At least *he* hadn't been pressed to stand up next to the bier and
speak. He couldn't have done it. And besides, what could he have
said about a woman he had been married to for six years and
stopped loving—if he had ever really loved her—after two? It
wasn't that he'd grown to hate or even dislike her. No, it was
just that he had stopped caring, that she had become a stranger.
Because she was so weak. . . that was the crux of it. A weak, helpless
stranger.

Afterward, he couldn't remember much of the ride to the cemetery. Tearful words of comfort from Jane Riley, who had been
Katy's closest friend; someone patting his hand—Margo?—and

urging him to bear up. And later, at the gravesite. . ."We therefore commit her body to the ground, earth to earth, ashes to ashes, dust to dust. . ." and Reverend Baxter sprinkling a handful of dirt onto the coffin while intoning something about subduing all things unto Himself, amen. He had cried then, not for the first, surely not for the last.

The ride home, to the small two-story house he had shared with Katy a half-mile from the college, was a complete blank to him. One moment he was at the gravesite, crying; the next, it seemed, he was in his living room, surrounded by his books and the specimen cases full of the insects he had collected during his entomological researches. Odd, he realized then, how little of Katy had gone into this room, into any of the rooms in the house. Even the furniture was to his taste. The only contributions of hers that he could remember were frilly bits of lace and a bright seascape she had bought at a crafts fair. And those were gone now, along with her clothing and personal effects; Margo had already boxed them up so that he wouldn't have to suffer the task, and had had them taken away for charity.

Nine or ten people were there, Katy's and his friends, mostly from the college. Mourners who had attended the funeral and also been to the cemetery. Jane Riley and Evelyn Something. . . Dawson? Rawson? a woman he didn't know well that Katy had met at some benefit or other. . . had provided food, and there were liquor and wine and hot beverages. Margo and the Reverend had referred to the gathering as a "final tribute"; he called it a wake. But Katy wouldn't have minded. Knowing that, he hadn't objected.

Katy. Poor, weak, sentimental Katy. . .

The mourners ate and drank, they talked, they comforted and consoled. He ate and drank nothing; his stomach would have disgorged it immediately. And he talked little, and listened only when it semed an answer was required.

"You *are* taking a few more days off, aren't you, George?" Alvin Corliss, another professor at the college. English Lit.

"Yes."

"Take a couple of weeks. Longer, if you need it. Go on a trip, some place you've always wanted to visit. It'll do you a world of good."

"Yes. I think I might. . ."

"Is Margo staying on a while longer, George?" Helen Vernon, another of Katy's friends. They had gone walking together often, along the cliffs and elsewhere. But she hadn't been with Katy on the day of her fall. No, not on that day.

"Yes, Helen, she is."

"Good. You shouldn't be alone at a time like this."

"I don't mind being alone."

"A man needs a woman to do for him in his time of grief. Believe me, I know. . ."

On and on, on and on. Why didn't they leave? Couldn't they see how much he wanted them to go? He felt that if they stayed much longer he would break down—but of course he didn't break down. He endured. When his legs grew weak and his head began to throb, he sank into a chair and stared out through a window at his garden. And waited. And endured.

Dusk came, then full dark. And finally—but slowly, so damned slowly—they began to leave by ones and twos. It was necessary that he stand by the door and see them out. Somehow, he managed it.

"You've held up so well, George. . ."

"You're so brave, George. . ."

"If you need anything, George, don't hesitate to call. . ."

An interminable time later, the door closed behind the last of them. Not a moment too soon; he was quite literally on the verge of collapse.

Margo sensed it. She said, "Why don't you go upstairs and get into bed? I'll clean up here."

"Are you sure? I can help—"

"No, I don't need any help. Go on upstairs."

He obeyed, holding into the bannister for support. He and Katy had not shared a bedroom for the past three years; there had been no physical side to their marriage in almost four, and he had liked to read at night, and she had liked to listen to her radio. He was grateful, now that she was gone, that he did not have to occupy a bed he had shared with her. That would have been intolerable.

He undressed, avoided looking at himself in the mirror while he brushed his teeth, and crawled into bed in the dark. His heart was pounding. Downstairs in the kitchen, Margo made small sounds as she cleaned up after the mourners.

You're so brave, George. . .

No, he thought, I'm not. I'm weak—much weaker than poor Katy. Much, much weaker.

He forced himself to stop thinking, willed his mind blank.

Time passed; he had no idea how many minutes. The house was still now. Margo had finished her chores.

He lay rigidly, listening. Waiting.

A long while later, he heard Margo's steps in the hall. They approached, grew louder. . . and went on past. The door of her room opened, shut again with a soft click.

He released the breath he had been holding in a ragged sigh. Not tonight, then. He hadn't expected it to be tonight, not this night.

Tomorrow? The need in him was so strong it was an exquisite torture. How he yearned to feel her arms around him, to be drawn fiercely, possessively against the hard nakedness of her body, to succumb to the strength of her, the overpowering dominant *strength* of her! She had killed Katy for him; he knew she had, he had no doubt of it. When would she come to claim her prize?

Tomorrow?

Please, he thought, oh please let it be tomorrow. . .

THE BODY OF THE BEER

by Mike Ripley

"I n those days," said the official guide, "it was not unusual to have two breweries next door to each other."

Well, at least he was right about that.

"The museum we are about to enter was the brewhouse of the old Wellbeloved & Barnard brewery, established in 1867 and registered as a company in 1896. Over there"—he pointed to the wet tarmac of a National Car Park—"was the brewery of P. & A. Appledore. That was originally a vinegar brewery which switched to beer production in 1892 under the brothers Peter and Arthur Appledore. Of course the locals joked that they hadn't really changed trades."

Polite laughter from the shivering visitors.

"But they were proved wrong, for in the decade before the First World War, Appledore's ales took major prizes at every national beer competition, winning the *Brewers' Guardian* trophy for draught beer three times, something no brewer has done since. Now we'll go inside. No high heels, ladies? Good. We've got a lot of steps to climb. Brewing begins at the top."

Never a truer word. Arthur Appledore recognised in 1901 that if he wanted to improve the name of his beer, a top brewer was what was needed. And while other managing directors visited the Brewers' Exhibition in Islington looking for new plant and equipment, Appledore went hunting for a brewer.

"Right at the top of the brewery would be the malt store. When we get there, you'll see that brewing in those days was literally an up-and-down process," said the guide. "Please be careful—these steps can be rather dangerous."

Othniel Saggers knew his trade.

Pupilaged at the last of the big London porter breweries, he learned the craft of brown beers and stouts before moving to Burton to unlock the secrets of pale ales. An early member of The Laboratory Club, he spanned both the art and science of brewing and at the 1901 Exhibition, three of his beers took major prizes. Arthur Appledore offered him total control of his brewhouse and he jumped at the chance.

"This is the milling machine," said the guide. "Malt, which has been hauled up a pulley, is finely crushed to form a grist for mashing. It's where we get the expression 'grist to the mill'".

Success was the incentive for Othniel Saggers; the grist to his mill: to be the best. Within a year he had launched a new portfolio of Appledore Ales. Sales rose, prizes were won. *Ale to Adore* read the posters on the sides of trams. *I Adore Appledore* said the advertisements in the local *Gazette*.

"In this vessel, the malt grist in mashed with hot water. It's a bit like mashing tea—people still say that, don't they? This is the first stage of any good brew."

By the time Sir Robert Barnard became chairman of Wellbeloved & Barnard in 1912, the company was undoubtedly the second brewer in the town.

Sir Robert recruited new brewers, invested in the most modern equipment, insisted on a spotlessly clean brewhouse. Still Appledore Ales won the prizes and sold the most. Even though no Wellbeloved had actually entered the brewery for 20 years (except for annual general meetings or to draw their directors' allocation of spent hops for their rose gardens), their name was used mercilessly. *I'd Love A Wellbeloved* read the signs on the horse-drawn buses; *Wellbeloved. . .For Taste* said the hoarding at the railway station.

But try as he might, Sir Robert could not dent Appledore's growing reputation. Then the Kaiser came to his aid.

"This is one of the two coppers—think of them as large kettles, ladies—where hops were added to the wort. No, we don't call it beer yet. These were installed in 1915, no mean feat with a war on, after the brewery was hit during a Zeppelin raid. The locals reckoned that Mr Appledore next door must have had the Germans on his side!"

It was a fluke of course. A homeward-bound Zeppelin lightening its load of bombs. One landed in Wellbeloved's main yard killing two under-brewers and a cooper and taking out the wall of the brewhouse.

Sir Robert responded with furious activity. Beer from stock was blended and reblended to keep the pubs supplied. More beer was bought in from a friendly brewer in the next town (even though Appledore was just down the street) and a new slogan appeared everywhere: *Wellbeloved by King, Not Kaiser*. Public sympathy turned into increased sales, but Sir Robert's masterstroke was to appeal to the patriotism of Appledore's quiet genius, Othniel Saggers.

In a move which made the front page of the *Gazette*, Mr O.A. Saggers was appointed head brewer *and* director of Wellbeloved & Barnard with carte blanche to rebuild the brewery. What was not reported was the private arrangement with Sir Robert that Saggers would become full partner and the name of the company changed to Wellbeloved, Barnard & Saggers, on the winning of a major brewing prize as soon as national competitions resumed in peacetime.

Patriotism is all very well but sometimes needs a hand.

"Down these steps and then up those over there and we go into the fermentation room. That's where the serious business starts and we get al-co-hol." The guide rolled his eyes and paused for audience reaction.

"Hopped wort from the coppers would be cooled and run into these fermentation tanks and then the yeast, a living organism, is pitched in. Yes, this is where things really happen."

In anticipation of the 1920 Brewers' Exhibition, Saggers had put aside the smallest of his fermentation vessels for what was to be his first Wellbeloved competition brew. He had the 10-barrel circular vessel, made of best pine from New Zealand scrubbed spotless and a wrought iron catwalk and stairs erected over it so he could examine the yeast head and crust from above and aerate the brew from the centre by hand. (All brewers have their idiosyncrasies!)

The only thing known about the brew was that it would have a 10-day fermentation followed by two weeks' conditioning in cask in a roped-off area in the brewery cellar. The original gravity was known only to Saggers and the local Excise, but it was rumoured to be high. The raw materials were drawn from store and handled by Saggers alone.

It was to be his finest brew. It was to be his last.

"Fermentation produces alcohol and carbon dioxide," said the guide, "and that can be dangerous. Why, the head brewer at Wellbeloved's was overcome by CO_2 fumes and died right here, in 1920. And he should have known better."

The early shift boilermen found Othniel Saggers at 5am, on the floor of the fermentation room.

The local doctor said he had been overcome by carbon dioxide, missed his footing, toppled off the catwalk and smashed his head in on the stone floor. Quite likely he had been drinking. A succinct if not terribly scientific diagnosis from a Temperance member of the medical profession.

Sir Robert ransacked the brewery until he unearthed Saggers' Brewing Room Book, then gave orders that Saggers' instructions were to be followed to the letter. The brew was racked into cask, nurtured and nursed and packed off to the Brewers' Exhibition.

The result was humiliation. "Mawkish thin and sour" were some of the kinder comments of the judges in private. In public, the beer was labelled "Unfit for Competition" and returned to Wellbeloved & Barnard.

"But of course," said the guide, beaming, "this fermentation room is famous not for its beer but for the murder which took place in 1936".

Every four years Sir Robert tried to recreate a competition brew from Saggers' notes. Good management and sound investment helped Wellbeloved & Barnard through the recession years, in fact they prospered while Appledore's fortunes declined. But this brought him no cheer. Between the companies was a wall of silence and nothing would persuade Sir Robert to ask the ageing and increasingly embittered Arthur Appledore what the secret of the "lost" brew could have been.

In three successive competitions, Wellbeloved's beer was rebuffed and (politely) ridiculed, but Sir Robert persisted.

In one last attempt in 1936 (the year of his retirement at a lively 75), Sir Robert determined to supervise the brew personally. He even went to the extent of a personal examination of the first setting of a "rocky" yeast head as Saggers had done on the day of his death. That was how, at 4am, he found Arthur Appledore mounting the catwalk above the competition brew.

Appledore, himself 85 at this time, climbed slowly and carefully and did not even falter when Sir Robert spoke to him for the first time in over 20 years.

"What in God's name are you doing in my brewery, Appledore?"

The older man mounted the last step on the catwalk before he turned and looked down.

"Your brewery, Barnard, but *my* beer! Saggers created this for *me*!"

Appledore's left hand pointed accusingly at the open fermenter below him. His right hand remained deep in his overcoat pocket.

"We'll see about that!" shouted Sir Robert as he started up the iron steps.

"If you don't mind the crush," said the guide, "we can all fit on the catwalk, which is where the bodies were found. Be careful, though, it can be very slippery."

Appledore was struggling to free his right hand from his pocket as Sir Robert reached him—struggling to pull something free.

Sir Robert assumed it was a weapon and hesitated a yard from his quarry. Below them, through the slatted iron catwalk, the competition brew foamed quietly.

"Get back!" shouted Appledore, freeing his hand at last.

He held not a gun but a conical flask with a cork stopper which he reached for with his left hand. Sir Robert lunged for his arms. As they stuggled, the cork came out and straw-coloured liquid splashed over their clothes. Sir Robert inhaled the fumes it gave off.

"Vinegar! You swine!"

"Acetic acid culture, you ignorant upstart," gasped Appledore as they struggled. "You never even suspected, but my culture is what has turned your thieving brew bad."

They were swaying wildly now, locked together. The liquid from the flask was spilling on to the cat walk but missing the yawning fermentation vessel.

"You've poisoned my brews," wheezed Sir Robert.

"Saggers created them for me!" shrieked Appledore. "The culture works when the beer goes into condition in the cask. The stronger the brew, the more alcohol gets turned to acid. Your so-called tasters don't notice a thing but by the time it gets to the competition, your beer is rank and foul and I'm damn glad of it."

"Well not this one!"

With a huge effort, Sir Robert pulled Appledore off his feet and to one side. The flask spun away, shattering on the catwalk but missing the precious brew.

Appledore's eyes ignited.

"If I can't kill you beer, I'll kill you." He lunged for Sir Robert's throat. "Just like I had to get rid of that turncoat Saggers."

Frightened now, Sir Robert backed away looking to escape. But the exertion of the tussle had been too much.

Perhaps he felt a stunning pain down his left arm, perhaps he heard the pressure explode in his brain. He could say nothing for his jaw had gone slack.

Sir Robert crumpled into a sitting position on the catwalk and expired.

Appledore swayed back on his heels stunned—then jubilant.

"I'll show you what an old vinegar brewer can do," he muttered as he bent over to scoop up the remains of the flask, determined to sweep the culture into the beer with his bare hands if necessary.

His fingers closed around the broken neck of the flask. A few drops had remained clinging viscously to the glass, but in his haste to shake them into the fermenting vessel he slipped.

A younger man would not have noticed, but Arthur Appledore was not young. He pitched forward, sprawling over the edge of the catwalk.

Still clutching the broken neck of the flask, Arthur Appledore's arm and hand had been bent under him, jammed by the edge of the ironwork. The jagged glass entered his throat as he fell, slicing the jugular. He rolled over on to his back and bled to death, his blood making quiet plopping sounds as it dripped into the yeasty crust below.

"The local *Gazette* called it a Tragic Occurrence," said the guide. "Sir Robert had obviously killed Arthur Appledore and then has a heart attack when he realised what he had done. Insane jealousy, they put it down to. What may surprise you is that the special brew was racked and sent to the Brewers' Exhibition as if nothing had happened. A lot of people thought that was in bad taste—and it certainly did not win any prizes that year!"

But there again the guide was wrong.

Tasted "blind", Wellbeloved & Barnard's competition brew was unanimously voted Champion beer by the judges without recourse to a second-round "taste-off". It was the only time, before or since, a beer achieved such an outright win. It was only when its identity was revealed that the Exhibition organisers awarded premier place to the runner-up, out of deference to the memory of Arthur Appledore.

In conclave, the judges all remarked on the distinctive flavour of the beer and all agreed that it was "an exceptionally full bodied brew".

AT HOME

by Michael Z. Lewin

"This looks good," F. Q. Smith said. He sat down at the table.

His wife served main course portions to F. Q. and to each of the children before taking a smaller portion herself. This was the norm, when he was there.

"Nice to have you here," Mrs. Smith said.

"Strictly nine to five today," F. Q. said easily. "Even when you're a private detective placed *in situ* on a long term undercover job, you have to arrange some time off to see your family. I'm not sure. It may be part of the agency contract these days. I'll have to look into that. But I'll tell you, Sally, some of the things I've seen in there, the corners cut, the things they do... It's going to make a hell of a report, it really is."

"That's nice."

"So," F. Q. said, "what did you do today?"

"Who are you asking?" Jeremy asked his father.

"Your mother. You'll have your turn."

Jeremy turned to his plate.

"Sally? Since the children left for school."

"08.35 I washed the dishes. 08.45 cup of coffee. 08.55 I got the vacuum cleaner out."

With a slight laugh F. Q. interrupted, "Everything happened

exactly on a fifth minute today?"

No one echoed his laugh.

"Not all day. That's just the way it started. 9.15 took vacuum upstairs. 9.18 began on Lizzy's room."

"I don't like you in there," Lizzy, who was seventeen, said. "You know I don't like you in there. I can vacuum my room myself." Jeremy looked at her and sighed, but she couldn't control herself.

"Got something to hide, huh?" F. Q. said.

"No."

"What secrets are there in your room that cleaners might disturb?"

"None."

"With a vacuum cleaner one only deals with floor, skirting board, maybe with an attachment over the curtains, a chair." F. Q. leaned back and tried to visualize the situation.

"Haven't you ever heard of privacy?" Lizzy Smith said with feeling. "Haven't you ever heard of that?"

"Of course, but we're in a family here. What sort of secrets have you got from your mother?" Smith turned to his wife. "What do you think, Sally?"

"It's not a big deal."

"Little deals become big deals. I think maybe I'll have a look around your room tonight, Lizzy. If I have the time." He looked at her. "If you don't object."

"Have I got a choice?"

"I don't have a warrant," he said.

With patience born of practice Sally said, "I'm sure she doesn't mind."

Lizzy ate a mouthful of food chewing with more force than usual.

"I can hardly count the number of times I've told people, 'I haven't got a warrant,'" F. Q. said. He ate. "Mmmm, this tastes good. It's nice to have real food."

He looked up at his wife.

"I finished the housework at 11.15," she said. She looked at him. He nodded. She had just asked if he wanted an activity-by-activity breakdown and had just said not now. "Then I washed my hands and put on some make-up and went to town."

"Make-up, eh?"

"Eyeliner, lipstick, a touch of blusher."

He nodded. He turned to his son. "Good day at school, Jeremy?"

"It was all right. There were no deviations from the normal Friday time-table."

F. Q. looked expectantly.

"Dad?"

"Yes?"

"Are you, uh, working this weekend?"

"You can never tell when you'll be called out in my business," F. Q. said.

"I know all that," Jeremy said.

"Don't be cheeky, young man." Smith stared at his son.

After a few seconds of staring back, Jeremy said, "Sorry."

"You're not usually cheeky," Smith said. He looked at the boy, thinking.

"I said 'Sorry.'"

"I hear the word but I don't hear the sincerity," F. Q. said. "That tends to suggest what we call in the business a hidden agenda."

"My school bag is in the hall. My coat is on the hook."

"Where is your bike?"

"In. . . It's not in the garage."

"Why not?"

"I loaned it to Roger."

"What's wrong with Roger's bike?"

"His was stolen. He wants to go over to see his cousin. They're going fishing."

"Do they usually go fishing on a Saturday?"

"Quite often, yes."

"Where?"

"The bit of the river down by Wallbridge. The fishing club has rights there and the cousin is a member."

"Is Roger a member?"

"I. . . I don't know."

"I think you do know. He isn't, is he? Is he?"

"He uses his cousin's father's licence."

"Ah ha," F. Q. Smith said. He took a mouthful of food and enjoyed it. "And don't you plan to use your bike this weekend?"

"I have a lot of homework," Jeremy said, and then regretted it.

"We'll see about that later," Smith said. He looked over at his wife. "And now, Sally. I believe we were about to go to town. Food shopping, was that? For this delicious meal?"

On Monday morning at 09.18 Sally Smith began to apply her make-up. By 09.53 she was in the car for the hour's drive to Bristol. At 11.02 she was called from the waiting room and at 11.03 she was settling into an upholstered chair on the third floor of the Bristol Psychiatric Clinic, across the desk from Dr. Angus Royce.

By 11.05 she made it clear that as far as she and the children were concerned, her husband's home visits were hell.

"Progress in a case like this is slow, Mrs. Smith," Dr. Royce said. "We knew that from the outset. Just try to stick with it and hope for the best."

DEAD MAN'S BLOOD

by Mike Phillips

As soon as I saw her I felt guilty, mainly because I hadn't seen her since the funeral and although she'd phoned me a number of times and left messages, I hadn't replied. Now here she was, waiting outside my door, and there was no escape.

I went up to her, bouncing a little in my Nikes, giving it the youthful joviality, and working out excuses in my head. She looked worried, and when she turned and saw me, her expression only lightened a little.

I gave her a big hug, trying to get my arms right round her and not succeeding because she was fatter than ever.

"Sammy you dog," she said.

"Nina," I said sincerely, "I've been meaning to get in touch with you. But you know how it is."

"I know how it is," she said. "So you can skip the excuses you dog."

"Let's go inside," I told her, changing the subject.

She nodded and I unlocked the door and went up the stairs first. I knew it would be embarrassing if I was behind her, watching while she hauled herself up the three flights, and things were bad enough.

I gave her the sofa and went to put the kettle on, so that I could have a moment to think about her and adjust.

There was actually something overwhelming about her size, and thinking back I couldn't remember her being quite so big.

I'd met her husband, Charlie, at my first job on a local paper in South London. That was twenty years ago, and, apart from the editor who'd hired me, he was the only one of my white colleagues who didn't treat me with indifference or suspicion. I was at a loss to explain his ease and friendliness, until, one day, a pretty mixed race girl had turned up to meet him after work. She'd been slim then, and looking back it was hard to identify her with the woman she was now. Perhaps it was to do with living in Australia where she and Charlie had gone about seven years back. He'd done well and they'd come over about a year ago for a holiday and to look up old friends, which is what Charlie was doing as he drove up the M1 and ran into a jack-knifing lorry. At the funeral I hadn't known her till she came up to me.

Whatever it was she wanted, it must have been something serious to make a woman whose flesh was so far out of control come looking for me, knowing that three flights of stairs were waiting at the end of the trip.

"What's the problem?" I asked her.

"Claudette," she said immediately. "You remember her. My foster daughter."

Now that she mentioned it, the girl had been at the back of my mind. Nina and Charlie had been unable to have children and they'd adopted a boy who, at the age of thirteen, had been stabbed to death in a pointless incident while walking home from school. After that they'd fostered a series of mixed race children. Claudette had been the latest and she'd been with them when Charlie died. They were going to be happy at last. As it happened, young Claudette's mother had died and her father whereabouts were uncertain, so she had become theirs. She used to go and visit them Down Under, and when they came back she'd been waiting at the airport. Somehow the saddest thing at the funeral had been to see those two fat women crying in each other's arms. That same day I had told Nina how well I remembered how kind Charlie had been when things were tough, and promised that if she was staying in England, I'd help her as much as I could, for his sake.

"She's getting married tomorrow," Nina said, "I've been trying to get you for a fortnight now."

A wedding invitation. For a moment I wondered why they hadn't just sent it to me, then I began thinking about what I'd wear.

"Oh, great," I said, then I stopped when the expression on her face told me that it wasn't.

"I'm really worried Sammy. I can't stop her, but something tells me that it's a disaster."

"People get married every day," I told her, "and she's a big girl now,
What is she? Twenty five? Twenty four?"

She frowned angrily.

"Come off it. I'm not stupid. It's not that."

She stared at me, deep in thought, and I waited. Then she twisted
round and dug into her bag.

"Look at this picture."

It was a photo of a girl who had to be the daughter. She was fat,
not quite as fat as Nina, but definitely fat, and she hadn't started out
with Nina's prettiness. She had a dull, square face with a blotchy skin
in which splahes of dark pigment alternated with a lighter brown.
When I saw her last she had been a plump, unattractive teenager.
Now she looked a said unappetising woman.

"Okay," I said. "What's the point?"

Instead of replying she handed me another photo, and in the
moment I looked at it I had a flash that told me exactly what she
was worried about and why.

The man in the picture was black, young, in his early twenties,
and good looking. But that wasn't all. He had a style and presence
which must have been the result of careful grooming and which
gave him the look of a second-hand movie idol. His hair had been
straightened and teased into shiny waves, he was wearing a grey
check suit which looked like Valentino, and his arms were folded
in front of him to display three gold rings and a large Rolex.

I blinked.

"Wow," I said. "He looks like a hell of a son in law."

As it happened the first question that occurred to me was why a
boy who looked and dressed like that would go out with Claudette,
never mind marry her. But I didn't want to be the first to say it.

"He drives one of those sporty little white cars, a Golf or something. Everything about him is flash. I was happy when I heard she
had a boyfriend. But one minute she met him. Next minute they are
getting married and when I met him I couldn't work it out. I love
Claudette, and I want to see her happy, but try as hard as you can,
you can't put these two together. She's not his sort."

I saw.

"Well," I said. "The thing is that if they like each other, it doesn't
matter. That's the great thing about love. It alters every perspective.
People in love don't care about differences."

Sometimes I surprised myself. I didn't believe a word of the plati-
tudes I'd just uttered. But even so, when I said it, not believing it, I
still meant it.

"Jeeze," Nina bellowed scornfully. "I don't have to take that
nonsense from a man who puts on his running shoes every time

somebody says marriage. Besides, that is not it. Listen Sammy, I'm
not some hysterical old bag coming to you for a cup of tea and some
reassuring bullshit. There's more to it than that."

I should have known. She wasn't the sort to waste her time.

"All right," I said. "Have another cup of tea and tell me."

It wasn't an extraordinary story, but she told it with all the drama
it has acquired in her imagination. I had composed myself to listen
patiently, but it was only a few seconds before I was gripped; and
I began to feel, somewhere in between my gut and the back of my
mind, an odd sparkle of heat that told me I would have to go out
and chase this one down.

Claudette worked in a Citizens Advice Bureau, and the young
man, whose name turned out to be Vernon King, had come in one
day asking for advice about an insurance matter. They had got to
talking, and he had returned the next day to thank her. This was
unusual and when he asked her out that night she had jumped at
the offer. She was a little suspicious, of course, because this was a
rare event, but going out with Vernon was too good to miss.

They'd slept together right away, and by the end of the week they
were planning to get married soon. This was the first that her foster
mother had heard of the matter, and at the time she'd actually been
delighted, because her secret fear had been that Claudette would
become, as she grew older, more and more isolated and alone.

Her attitude changed when she met Vernon. She'd been expecting someone different. Perhaps a hard working, ambitious young
man who needed a quiet and industrious partner – someone who
wouldn't be extravagant or demanding. Or perhaps a man who was
a little older in search of someone steady.

Instead, she found Vernon, with his showy clothes and car and his
showbiz patter, more or less alarming. He came from Birmingham,
or at least, he talked like a Brummie.

"He said he was a law student."

She rolled her eyes at me and I laughed. Being a law student used
to be the favourite occupation of many of the black hustlers of our
youth. The real joke, though, was that some of them had made it,
and were now conning people legally. Even so, it was a bad sign.

"I rang the college," she said, "and they said he had left the course.
When I told her she said that she knew all about it. He dropped out
for a year to make some money, and he was working as assistant
manager at a wine bar in the City."

Nina persevered. She rang the wine bar and was told that Vernon
had worked briefly behind the bar but wasn't there any more. When
she told Claudette this bit of news the girl reacted angrily, accused
her of spying and interfering, and threatened never to speak to her

again if she kept on trying to sabotage their happiness.

"She was brainwashed. I could hear him talking."

I shrugged. In any case Vernon looked the type who might inflate his prospects and none of this seemed sinister. But Nina had saved the best for last.

After the row with Claudette she had resolved to accept Vernon at face value. The very next day, while waiting at a bus stop on the way to work, she had seen his car pull up to drop off an attractive young woman out. The couple had given each other a farewell kiss, so passionate and at the same time so familiar that she just knew that they were established lovers.

Vernon had been so absorbed in gazing adoringly at the young woman, that he hadn't noticed Nina staring at him from a few yards away.

"So what did Claudette say about this?"

She sighed heavily.

"I didn't tell her. I didn't think she'd believe me, and anyway he'd probably say I was mistaken or lying. I don't know. I thought maybe it was better keeping quiet and trying to find out what's really going on. I want to know where he gets his money for a start."

She stopped and looked intensely at me, her big brown eyes moist.

"You'll help me won't you Sammy? I couldn't think of anybody else to turn to."

I agreed quickly, because I knew that I would sooner or later and I didn't want to draw the process out longer than necessary. The problem was that, coming from the Caribbean, I'd been brought up in a culture where middle-aged women ruled the roost and it was hard to say no.

Besides all she wanted was to find out about the boy's background and how he earned his living. If anything bad was going to happen she wanted to know where it was coming from, so that she could protect Claudette. That's what she said, anyway, and I could sympathise with all that.

The next day was the wedding.

They did it at the registry in the old Town Hall at Marylebone. It wasn't particularly romantic. It wasn't particularly unromantic. It wasn't anything. Claudette was supported by half a dozen of her chums from the CAB, all of them white and female. Most of them around forty or older, dressed in tarted up versions of their work clothes – three quarter length skirts, shirts and sweaters – with only one hat and one suit between them. You could tell just by looking that they were workmates rather than close friends, but they were behaving with the sprightliness appropriate to the occasion, one or two furtively clutching little bags of rice. All of which made an interesting contrast to Nina, massively gloomy and dignified in a pumpkin coloured dress and a white hat with flowers round the brim.

The girl in the suit was young, about thirty, pretty, with smooth close cropped black hair, deep green eyes, a mobile mouth, and I found myself drawn to her right away.

That's how it is at weddings. You can live like a monk for weeks. Then you drop in at a wedding, anybody's, and in five minutes you're chatting up anyone who looks possible.

In any case, it was a good cover behind which to study the bridegroom. None of his friends, if he had any, seemed to have turned up. But he looked like up prince next to Claudette. They were both wearing white and while she looked more frumpish than ever, his clothes accentuated his graceful athletic figure and his smooth handsome features.

There had been something nagging away at the back of my mind, and studying Vernon, I suddenly got it. Twenty years ago when young black people like this got married, there would have been a gaggle of relations, toddlers, distant uncles, family quarrels, the lot, all presided over by an old granny. Since then we'd become English, and these kids were isolated in a way we used to think of as belonging to the whites.

"Are you a friend of his?" the girl in the suit asked me, her eyes on Vernon.

"In a way," I said.

That settled my identity, and it wasn't too long before she told me how surprised, and she pleased, she added hastily, they all were at the CAB that all this was happening for Claudette.

"She's such a nice girl," she said, gazing soulfully at Vernon.

I managed a few words with Nina on the pavement before we all went our separate ways. She didn't say much, except that she still wanted me to do what I'd promised. I said I would and told her that I had no hurry because I was taking the lady in the suit out to lunch. She looked disapproving and heaved herself into the taxi she had waiting without another word.

My new friend had the day off and we spent the afternoon celebrating one way and another, so that it wasn't till late on the evening that I thought about Nina's troubles again.

It was half past ten and I'd just woken up, passing from one kind of stupor to another. The difference being that in the second stage I was no longer at the mercy of my spinning dreams and I could begin to control the roaring darkness in my head.

I was downing a couple of aspirins when it struck me that I was thinking about the wedding. I had been dreaming about it but I had that infuriating sense of not being able to remember. In between getting up and fetching the aspirins the whole thing had faded, leaving me only with an odd feeling of apprehension.

At that point I determined to make one phone call, so that I could tell Nina I'd done something and then forget about it.

I rang Wolverhampton, almost hoping that Wally wouldn't be in so that I could lie back on the sofa and fade to black.

He answered on the first ring.

"Wally," I said, "my old spa. How's business?"

He sussed me immediately.

"Sam? Sam Dean?"

"That's right. I just rang you for a little favour. There's a few bob in it for you."

An essential precondition.

Wally described himself as a freelance photographer, and it was true that he spent half of his time, camera in hand, roaming the Midlands looking for setups he could sell to the local papers and agencies.

Once upon a time, during the riots, he'd even got a couple of police brutality pics on the front page of three of the tabloids. But his real occupation was snapping girls – from expensive portfolios for naive and pretty black kids who wanted to get into the model business to soft porn for the lower end of the dirty magazine trade. On the side he organised a gospel choir and preached occasionally on the local fundamentalist circuit.

When I did stories in the Midlands I'd always hire him for the photos, because he was a hustler with a beautiful voice, a smarmily persuasive presence, and he seemed to know everyone and everything in the black communities there. Tell Wally what you wanted and he'd get it done.

I told him about Vernon King and he interrupted me as soon as he heard the name.

"I know the guy," he said.

"What about him?"

"I did some nice pics for him. He's into martial arts, and I've got good bare chest photos. He was going to send them to radio stations for a DJ job. He made it? You're doing a story? I've got the negatives."

I should have known. Radio was the magic magnet for hustlers with an ego, a line of chat and no talent.

"I don't think so," I said. "He's in London now."

"I thought I hadn't seen him around."

"Do you know anything about him? How he makes his living? Stuff like that?"

"I don't know. He used to live with a girl. A nurse. Something like that."

"Know anything about her."

"No. But look. I'll find out. Okay? Gimme a couple of days."

I put the phone down with a feeling of relief, Wally would cost me money, but I could probably get it back from Nina, if I could get it up to ask her, and in any case whatever he came up with would get her off my back.

I lay back on the sofa and went back to sleep. Round about one o'clock I woke up and ran *The Searchers*, a movie my son had lent me on his last visit. I'd first seen it at the Dalston Plaza over twenty years ago, but he was becoming a cinema freak, and I knew it would please him if I watched it again and talked about my reactions.

I fell asleep again before the end. It was a normal night.

The phone range just after nine in the morning and Nina's voice emerged, sounding breathless and agitated.

"He's gone," she said. "Disappeared."

"Hold on a minute," I said.

I put the phone down, went into the kitchen and looked out the window. This was it. Something told me I'd have to shut the door firmly in Nina's face right now, to avoid being sucked into some kind of trouble that was nothing to do with me. The two people closest to me, my son, and Sophie, my photographer friend, would disapprove.

Sophie was in Canada with a feature writer on a travel assignment, and I hadn't heard from her for a fortnight. I didn't want to think about that, but the last time we'd argued about the things I did, she'd said that she could understand about devoting your life to a cause, even dying for something important. After all she was Argentinian, she knew about such things.

As this point her bosom heaved and she gave me her angry Hispanic look, reducing me to total submission. She couldn't understand she went on, her tone softening, what made a man like me persist in getting mixed up in the sordid and petty affairs of people I didn't even care about.

"What percentage?" she shouted, her English deserting her a little. "What percentage?"

My son, barely a teenager, was more cautious in what he said, but I think he would have agreed. Sometimes, I thought, when he forgot about not liking her, they seemed to be joined in a conspiracy to change most things about me.

I backed away from the window and picked up the phone.

"Nina?"

Now was the time to tell her.

"Sammy. Are you there? Sammy I don't know what to do. I'm so worried."

"Don't worry," I said. "Tell me what's happened."

There wasn't much to tell. They'd gone back to Claudette's flat, because they weren't going on honeymoon for another month. This was what they said, although Nina reckoned he was broke and they couldn't afford it anyway. They'd consummated the marriage. This was a coy bit.

"Yes, I can imagine," I said. "Tell me why you're so worried."

A few hours later I was on my way to the City. I was wearing my grey YSL suit, a shirt with wide grey stripes, a blue on blue Balmain tie with matching hankie and white shoes. I figured I would fit right in.

The wine bar was a cellar near Ludgate Circus in a little maze of narrow twisting streets in front of St Paul's. Not quite the centre of the City, but close enough.

Near the entrance a young fair haired man was standing, talking rapidly into a portable telephone. Opposite was a young woman with the same colouring occupied in the same way. They were both wearing double breasted sharp navy blue suits, the only difference being that her's came with a skirt that ended just above the knees. I wondered if they were talking to each other. It wouldn't have surprised me.

I pushed past them and went in. The place was full of customers, nearly all of them wearing suits, and the din of their quiet lunchtime conversation was almost enough to drown out the muzak. But not quite.

I took my place in the queue at the bar and when the barman raised his eyebrows at me I leaned over and shouted that I was looking for Vernon King.

He looked puzzled.

"He works here sometimes."

He shrugged his shoulders, then lifted a finger and hurried over to a man loitering at the end of the bar, who motioned to me. I followed him over to a corner of the room, near the door, where it was quieter, but not much. Once I was up close to him I realised that I'd been decieved by his mop of iron grey curls. He was actually quite young, probably in his late twenties, but he had a thin white face that lived underground.

"Vernon worked here occasionally, but not any more. Who are you?"

"I'm his uncle, I'm only here for a couple of days and I wanted to see the boy. See that he's okay."

He looked sympathetic, as if he wouldn't have liked to be Vernon's uncle. I put on an air I imagined to be credibly harmless. He studied my tie, my suit, my shoes, his eyes shifting up and down.

"Look," I said. "I'll be honest with you. His mother's not well. I guess if you know him you know there's a few problems in his background."

I cocked my head and smiled ruefully at him, a man of the world plagued by family duties. He didn't smile back, but his mouth twitched a little as if he'd have liked to.

"Right," I said. "She threw him out of the house. Now she's not well. She's confined to bed you know or she'd have been here herself. I mean can you imagine? Anyway she wants me to give him a letter. I can understand if you don't want to give out your employees' addresses. Right. But can you forward the letter?"

He was falling for it. He nodded.

"Yes. I'll do that."

I put my hand in my pocket, felt around a little, then swore angrily.

"Bugger it, I left the letter back at my friend's flat. I'll have to go back there then bring it to you later. How do I get to Balham from here? What time do you close?"

I pronounced it BAL–HAM, I was really working my self into the part. He looked more tired than ever.

"Wait a minute," he said. "I'll give you the forwarding address. You can send it yourself."

He disappeared behind the bar, and I felt a surge of exhilaration, which lifted the depression I'd been feeling ever since Nina had told me that Vernon had walked out of Claudette's flat at nine o'clock the night before, to do some late night shopping, and hadn't come back. That morning they'd tried the hospitals and the police. But no luck. She'd known it all along.

When the manager brought me the address scribbled on a scrap of paper I didn't need any acting to show that I was chuffed. This time he really did smile.

On the way out the blonde man was just coming down the steps, putting his phone away, but outside his partner was still going strong. Her eyes rested on me for a moment and I gave her a big smile, but instead of responding she frowned, raised the phone higher in front of her face, and turned her back on me. You can't win them all.

Back in the flat I rang Nina at the Building Society where she worked. I told her I had something to follow up.

"The thing is," I said, "I'm not sure exactly what you want to do about him. You can't drag the man back to Claudette if he's left."

"No. I don't want to do that. But I want the situation settled. We have to know what his intentions are. If he's coming back. Or what the hell he really wants. He can't mess her about like this."

I asked her what Claudette thought about it.

"What do you think? She's a bit disillusioned."

The rest was business. I told her that locating Vernon might take time and money. I would have to get some help.

"Go ahead," she said immediately. "Spend what you have to and let me know."

I cut her off and rang Maman Nightingale.

"Sammy," she said accusingly, "Where you been?"

She still spoke with the accent of her French dialect she'd brought from St Lucia.

I'd known her ever since I was about nineteen, when I was courting her sixteen year old daughter, Francine, along with half a dozen other boys. None of us captured Francine, because she got pregnant by a reggae drummer who played with a group that had once topped the black music charts, and now she lived round the corner from her mum with a gaggle of kids. But, in any case, most of us used to hang around Maman Nightingale as much for the food and the company as for the chance of squeezing up Francine.

Maman cooked the home food our own mothers had either given up or couldn't go to the trouble to go down the market and get. Black puddings and pigs' feet, long sweet fruit drinks and she kept a pepperpot stew going on the stove for weeks. The moment she saw one of her boys as she called us she'd go to the kitchen and get a plate.

She was one of the fattest women I knew, but she had no shortage of suitors. Her sex and vigour was legendary, and she had her last baby after Francine left. This was Aubrey, the youngest and the biggest of her four sons.

"Where's Aubrey, Maman?" I asked her when the greetings were over.

"Upstairs, watching TV. You want him?"

I did. Aubrey had grown up like his brothers, in and out of a series of residential homes, and had a reputation for violence. On the other hand, although he was built like Arnold Schwarzenegger, one of his heroes, he was a nice polite boy with a courteous, gentle air. He spent his mornings at the gym, his afternoons watching videos, and his evenings round a variety of clubs. Occasionally he was arrested. Not a bad life. I'd watched over Aubrey when his mum was out shopping, I'd taken him to the park to stumble over his first football, and he did errands for me with an uncomplaining tolerance. At a price.

When he came on the line I told him what I wanted and he agreed, in his pleasant way, to meet me later on outside Finsbury Park station.

I rang Wally in Wolverhampton next, but this time there was no reply.

That didn't surprise me, and I lay back on the sofa, feeling like a general at rest, running over the setup in my mind. My strategy was simple. I would take shifts with Aubrey watching the forwarding address where Vernon was bound to show up sooner or later. I hoped. If we could be sure he lived there, the women could come along and do the business – tell him off or whatever it was they had in mind. If he didn't, we could follow him until we knew where he was staying. Risky, but I couldn't think of anything else.

I spent the afternoon dozing, in preparation for what I thought would be a wakeful night. It would be lunchtime in North America, and I wondered what Sophie was doing.

Suddenly the day had gone and the evening was following it, moving fast. I got down to Finsbury Park with a few minutes to spare before ten, and parked outside the hall near the station.

I knew the spot well because my family had lived not far away, back down towards Highbury and I'd gone to school there. I'd never liked it very much and I'd promised my self long ago to shake the dust of these ugly streets from my feet without regret, but even so, the memories kept flooding in.

Those days the pavement I was looking at would be swarming with kids waiting to go into the hall. A cinema at first, it had become a rock club during the heyday of the music, then when the teds faded, it had turned into an Irish dance hall. As the area changed again it reopened as a bingo palace. Now it was boarded up and dark, waiting for its next transformation.

The door of the car squeaked and Aubrey got in smoothly, considering his size. The old banger sighed and squatted lower on its tyres.

"Hi," Aubrey said, "Looks like you're dreaming."

He was wearing a sleeveless pullover and 501s, and carrying a denim jacket and a sports bag. He looked like the bad boy that he was.

I described Vernon and told him about the setup while we drove east towards the street where we were going to watch for Vernon. A little way up we stopped at a fast food joint run by a Trinidadian Indian and bought some fried fish to supplement the patties that Aubrey's mum had given him for the night. I left him sitting in the car, with strict instructions to ring me from the phone booth on the corner if Vernon showed up, and to drive carefully if he had to follow him anywhere. He nodded calmly, humouring me, while he plugged in his Walkman and fitted the headphones over his ears, and as I walked away he was munching contentedly, his head nodding in time to the music.

I wasn't worried about him, though. Aubrey started getting into trouble as a ten year old lookout for a gang of steamers, and he'd worked his way up since then, through TDA and B&E. If Vernon showed up Aubrey wouldn't miss him, and he'd stick to his quarry wherever he went.

Back home I rang Wally again.

"It's late man," he grumbled. "I was in bed."

That meant he had company.

"Okay," I said. "Make it quick."

"There's nothing much. Seems like he split up with the nurse girl months ago, and went to London."

"Anything else?"

"No. I didn't know what you wanted. He wasn't in no trouble."

"What about the girl? You saw her?"

"No. She's in London too, I think."

"What about her? Any trouble?"

"Well. Not exactly. Except that she got sacked from her job a while back. It was a big thing. Some old guy she was looking after fell out a window. They were going to charge her with neglect or something, but she got off. She lost the job, though."

He gave me her name, Norma Chambers, and described her. I couldn't see what it all had to do with Claudette, but I was clutching at straws. Maybe the girl friend had bumped into Vernon and spirited him away. These things happen, I told myself.

After that I waited and I must have gone to sleep because when the phone rang it was about two in the morning, and I came up fighting the blackness and an agonising pain in my arm where I'd been lying on it. I stood up and fell over because my leg had gone to sleep too. When I reached the phone crawling on my hands and knees I was also groaning and cursing.

"He's here, a white Golf. Right?" Aubrey said, "What do you want me to do?"

"Just watch and see if he stays there. If he doesn't, follow him till he goes home and then ring me. If not just wait till I come."

"Okay."

He sounded cool and unconcerned, as if all this was in a night's work, and maybe it was.

I decided to give it till the morning before going down. He might be just visiting. Besides it would have to be Claudette who went barging in. All I had to do was establish where he was.

I settled down to sleep again but I was too charged up, so I put *The Searchers* on again to catch the bit I'd slept through the night before. After an hour or so it was just coming to an end when the phone rang again. I picked it up, expecting Aubrey to tell me he was on the move, but this time it was Nina.

"Sammy." She sounded breathless, with a note I hadn't so far hear to her voice. "Can you come over? Please. Something's happened."

"What?"

"Just come. I'll tell you."

Less than half an hour later the taxi was pulling up outside her house in Tottenham, one of those dinky little redbrick two stories off Black Boy Lane which they'd built after the war to accomodate working class people with an itch for ownership, complete with a garden and access to the allotments. Back then, before they'd run the Victoria Line out there, this had been cheapo housing. Now Nina was mortgaged to the throat to pay for it.

She was up and waiting, because the door opened before I could ring.

"She's in there," she whispered. Her eyes rolled. "They tried to kill her tonight."

"What? Who tried to kill her?"

She shushed me, putting her finger to her lips.

"We don't know. Someone got in tonight and they turned the gas on. It was only luck she's alive."

"Ma," Claudette's voice called from the living room.

Nina inclined her head and we went in. Claudette was sitting huddled up on the big sofa. She was wearing a dressing gown with a nightdress under it, but she had the French windows open, and I could hear the early birds beginning to sing out in the back gardens.

"Uncle Sammy," she said tearfully and I went and embraced as much of her as I could.

"What happened?" I asked her.

"I don't really know," she said. "I might have left the gas on, Ma."

She looked at Nina hopefully, as if she wanted her to say that she'd been mistaken.

"Hold on," I said, "Tell me what happened."

"I'll tell you," Nina said fiercely. "I couldn't sleep thinking about the whole situation, and round about two o'clock I rang her to see how she was."

"Wait a minute Ma." Claudette said. She wasn't going to be deprived of her bit of drama, I could tell.

"I was waiting up, in case."

She paused, she didn't say in case of what, but I guessed it must have been in case Vernon came back or a hospital rang to say he was a patient or the police to say they were holding him.

"I didn't get to sleep till gone half past one, and I don't know how long I was asleep, but something must have woken me. I was sort of half asleep and I felt like there was someone moving about. At first I thought I was imagining it, like a dream. Then after I thought it had to be Vernon, so I didn't say anything. I thought any minute he would come in and tell me what was going on. Then it went quiet, and I started calling out, but there wasn't any answer. So you know how it is when you're half asleep already, I just kind of dropped off. I don't know how long, then the phone rang. I got up. I felt kind of funny, and when I realised it was Ma, I was just going to tell her to ring in the morning, then I smelled this gas."

"That's what she said," Nina piped up. "Oh my God Ma, the gas. I told her to go and turn it off without switching on the lights. By luck she hadn't touched the electricity because sometimes these things blow up. So she turned it off and opened the windows, and I went straight round there and fetched her."

"Could she have left it on?"

"No. She had dinner here with me. She didn't cook at all tonight."

Claudette nodded in confirmation. I thought about it. Claudette might have been screwed up and overweight but she wasn't stupid. If things had happened as she described then it was possible someone was trying to kill her. But it was about two when Aubrey had rung me. It couldn't be Vernon.

"Are you sure about the time? When the person came in."

"About two, I know because I was going to ring Ma before I went to sleep, and I looked at my watch about half past one and decided it was too late.

"It's Vernon," Nina said, "Isn't it?"

I said I didn't think so. Then I told them where he was and what time he'd got there.

Claudette began heaving herself to her feet.

"I'm going there Ma."

"No." I said quickly. I raised my eyebrows at Nina, enlisting her support. "It's too late and I don't even know if he's still there. Leave it till the morning. That's best."

"He might be in trouble."

She was close to tears, and I felt a sort of admiration. Her husband had walked out of her, someone was trying to kill her and her first concern was for him. Nina stepped in then, and together we talked her out of it and coaxed her up the short stairs to bed. She'd stopped crying though. She knew now that her beloved Vernon was safe and that she'd probably see him the next day. All was right with the world.

Afterwards Nina insisted on cooking breakfast and talking over the situation. If Vernon was still there in a few hours, she thought, she would take Claudette to see him. I sat listening to her, relaxing into the coming day. Occasionally Aubrey crossed my mind, but there was no point, I thought, in both of us being out there. That was my excuse anyway.

It was gone seven and the sun was coming up over the allotments before I brought myself to make a move. I walked down to the Hight Street and caught a bus down to Finsbury Park. Going in this direction, towards Camden Town and the West End the bus was already almost full, and I began to worry that I'd left it too late.

I was right, when I walked down the street where I'd left Aubrey, my car was gone, and so was the white Golf. I swore aloud, and when that didn't help I stood staring at the front at the house. The blank curtained windows didn't give me for any inspiration. A ginger haired woman came hurrying out and stared at me for a moment as if she wanted to ask me why I was standing there gazing, but then she changed her mind and hurried off. I gave up and went home.

He was there waiting for me. He had a rueful air which told me what had happened.

"I lost him," he said immediately. "A taxi came. He got in and they went to Camden Town. He got out and by the time I parked he'd gone. Sorry."

"Don't worry Aubrey, nothing you could do. Go home and get some sleep. Tell your mum hello, and I'll see you tonight again. Same time, same station."

He gave me the clenched fist and went. I rang Nina and told her. We agreed that it was time to stop pussyfooting around. If Vernon showed up again that night she had to go in and confront him, no matter what it was. Get it over with. Tonight would be the night. As for the strange affair of the gas being being turned on, unless Vernon could shed light on it, there was nothing to be done except keep an eye on Claudette and hope for the best. I made it cut and dried because I wanted to be done with the whole affair, and later on, thinking about it, I never could get rid of the feeling of regret and guilt that our last conversation had been like this.

I spent the day mooching around. I started work on a feature I'd been putting off till the deadline, gave it up and went to the shops, came back and read a couple of chapters of a book about the Crusades, watched a soap opera on telly, fell asleep, worked on the article, gave it up again. I didn't get going until well into the evening. They say you can have premonitions. When my Granny died my mother saw her coming down the stairs, thousands of miles away. My sister woke up in the night crying. In the Caribbean stuff like that is normal, and sometimes I felt as if I was missing a sense. When the phone rang I picked it up without suspicion.

"Uncle Sammy?"

Claudette. Who else?

"Is she with you?"

"Nina? With me? No."

She was tearful. Ma had insisted that she stayed at the house in Tottenham for a while and she'd gone over to the flat a few hours ago to fetch some of Claudette's things. She hadn't come back and the telephone wasn't anwering.

I looked at the typewriter and groaned inwardly.

"Okay," I said. "Don't worry. I'll go and see. She's probably stopped off somewhere."

But I was alarmed.

Claudette's flat was near the top of a block in Paddington, six stories up, and not too far from where Maman Nightingale lived. It had been built as council flats and then taken over for use by a couple of housing associations. Since then the amenities had improved and the graffiti had gone.

I parked in the courtyard and went up in the lift. Claudette's flat showed dark through the glass at the top of the door and when I rang there was no answer. I kept ringing. Suddenly the door behind me opened.

"You from the police?"

A skinny white woman with greying hair and haggard features was looking at me from the doorway of the flat opposite.

"No. I'm a friend of hers".

A tortoiseshell cat sprang out from behind her legs and streaked down the corridor.

"Come back Sheba," she shouted. She walked down the corridor and turned to look back at me. "She fell down the stairs. They took her to St Mary's. They came round earlier asking about her next of kin but I didn't really know her."

I stood there stupidly. I'd just talked to her. The woman came back down the corridor closer to me.

"I've said all along them stairs was dangerous. It'll take this for them to do something about it."

"You mean she's. . . ."

I'd sneered at actors in the movies a thousand times for doing the same thing, but I could not at the moment bring myself to say the word. Dead.

The woman looked at me sympathetically.

"Yes dear. I'm sorry. It was an accident. I'd get round the hospital if I was you."

Till then I hadn't noticed that the area round the head of the stairs was cordoned off with a rope. Or maybe I had, without realising the significance.

I got back into the lift and I was halfway down before it struck me that if Claudette was alive and well in Tottenham the person who fallen down the stairs must be Nina.

There were a couple of police at the hospital, a man and a woman, and when I told them what I thought, they called a nurse, and took me into a room where Nina was lying. Her face was grey and her features were set firm as if she was about to do something difficult. She had broken her neck and her skull, they said, and her heart had stopped.

I rang Claudette and told her, and asked her not to come, but she insisted. That was how it was that night. Sitting in the corridor cuddling Claudette I kept thinking about myself and what my son would feel in the same circumstances and whether Sophie would come back soon, and somehow my mind kept chasing round the fact that with her size Nina wouldn't go anywhere near those steep concrete stairs. She'd told me that more than once about tall buildings. It was a joke. "If there's no lift, baby, I ain't going," she'd say.

A young doctor gave me some tablets for Claudette. She was in shock, he said, and had to rest. I took her home then. On the way, the weeping sounds she made tore at my nerves like a rusty rasp. I felt myself getting angrier and angrier, as if the next move, the next sound from the seat beside me would drive me over some sort of edge.

Somehow we got down to Tottenham. Claudette didn't stop crying. The funny thing was that I half expected her to lay into some food the moment we got it, but she didn't, and thinking about it, I couldn't remember having seen her eating.

The other funny thing was that when she called me Uncle Sammy, I realised that I was now the nearest thing to a relative she had, and in the short term anyway, I was going to be partly responsible for her life. It wasn't a responsibility I wanted.

It was early in the morning before Claudette nodded off, and then I stretched myself out on the sofa downstairs and went to sleep. It had been a bad night and my sleep was full of nightmares, but I didn't wake till halfway through the morning. I climbed the stairs and listened. No sound from Claudette, so I went back down and started the phone calls.

Aubrey first. He had gone to Finsbury Park the night before and watched long enough to see Vernon arrive with a woman. When

I didn't turn up, he'd figured something else was going on, or I'd changed my mind, and he went home.

I thanked him and asked him to come over to Nina's. Sometime during the night it had struck me that Nina might have been killed in place of Claudette. If that was so, a little protection would be a good idea, and Aubrey could crunch anyone who near her. No worries. Besides I needed to get out of there, and his company would probably do her good.

Next I rang Inspector Borelli, the only policeman I knew. It was Saturday, but he was on duty.

"Franco," I said. "I need a favour."

"No," he grunted immediately.

Borelli was an old classmate at my school in Islington. We weren't friends. Far from it. I'd thought he was a racist lout who I was glad to see the back of. But by the time we'd met again, he was wearing suits and struggling to master the sociological jargon which would give him the protective colouring needed for the senior jobs. I still didn't like him but he was a good contact I couldn't afford to throw away.

Today he was going to be awkward. I guessed that he would eventually do what I asked but I'd have to beg. At school I'd been quick and clever enough with words to beat him up in the classroom the way he'd done to me with his fists in the playground. My suspicion was that now we were grown up, he'd have done quite a lot to keep me coming back, my sarky tongue smoothed into gracious forms of flattery. It wasn't just that it made me him feel clever and superior. He knew it hurt a little.

"Franco. This is nothing, man."

I told him about Nina's accident and asked him to find out whether the police suspected foul play. That was easy and it wasn't really inside information, but I was only softening him up.

"If I've got time," he said.

"Just one more thing."

I gave him the names. Vernon King and Norma Chambers and told him I wanted to know if they were known in Brum.

"You must be joking."

"Nothing confidential," I said hurriedly. "No details. All I want to know is if there's anything out of order. Generally."

He sniggered.

"What's in it for me?"

I was on firm ground here.

"If it works out a couple of serious arrests. Listen. You'll be a hero."

"Bullshit."

But he was interested.

"What's the connection?"

Blowed if I'd tell him that.

"I don't know yet."

"I'll think about it." he said.

I told him that I needed to know right away and I'd ring him back, and he grumbled a little before agreeing. So far so good.

I went up to see if Claudette was stirring and found her wide awake gazing tearfully into space. I told her about Aubrey and why I had asked him to come over and she nodded vacantly. I had the feeling she'd forgotten about Vernon and all that.

"It's funny," she said, sniffling. "I always used to want my real parents. Even when I knew they really loved me. Now I couldn't care less, if I could just have them back."

She wailed aloud then and burst into tears. I made soothing noises, but it didn't do any good, so I made her some tea, and sat with her while she wept, till the doorbell rang.

Aubrey was standing there grinning. Behind him a taxi stood with its engine running.

"Pay the man," Aubrey said.

I paid, while he went into the house, and when I went back in he'd already made himself comfortable in an armchair, his headphones in place, nodding and tapping his feet.

I told him what to do and left without going back upstairs.

Finsbury Park was crowded with weekend shoppers, but when I got on to Vernon's street it was quiet, almost deserted. I marched straight up to the house and rang the first bell I saw. The ginger haired woman answered, and I think she recognised me, because she shuffled backwards a little and her expression was suspicious and unfriendly. I didn't ham it up.

"I'm looking for Vernon King," I said.

"There's no one by that name living here," she said. At the same time she made a motion as if to shut the door.

"Norma Chambers?"

"She's upstairs," she said unwillingly. "Third floor. Ring the bell".

This time she did slam the door before I could shove my way in, and I rang the third floor bell, and rang it again when no one answered. Eventually, just as I was about to give up the door swung open.

The black woman who stood there was tall, her hair cut short in a style that gave her thin strong features a haughty Amazonian look. She was wearing a loose white blouse and a short leather skirt from which emerged a pair of shapely legs which seemed to go on forever. There didn't seem to be anything whatsoever wrong with her.

"Yes?"

I nearly stammered before I caught myself.

"I'm looking for Vernon. Vernon King."

"Why have you come here? He doesn't live here."

Her eyes looked as if it wouldn't take a lot to make them angry.

"You know him. He's been here two nights."

"So what? Who are you?"

I told her who I was and why I was looking for Vernon. When she heard about the marriage she frowned, and when I'd finished she stood aside.

"Come in."

It was an elegant flat, with a spareness that suited her. We sat opposite each other round a small dining table.

"We went together in Birmingham," she said. "But I packed all that in when I left. I'll be honest with you. I've had enough of Vernon and men like him."

She gave me a sudden smile that was frank and open and charming. I'd thought she was in her late twenties, but now she looked younger.

"I don't know how he found me," she continued, "but he turned up the other night, drunk, demanding to speak to me. I had to let him in. I know him. He wouldn't have gone away before everyone around here had woken up and fetched the police."

"So you let him in."

She looked rueful.

"I shouldn't have, but I did. Then I realised he was too drunk to drive, so I let him stay till the morning. He went early."

"You haven't seen him again?"

I was offering her the chance to lie, but she didn't take it.

"He came back last night. He wouldn't go the other morning till I'd promised to talk to him. About us."

Her mouth twisted scornfully on the words.

"There was no us, but I saw him. We came back and talked. He wasn't too sober, and he brought a bottle of champagne. Any excuse. This time he tried to rape me."

She shifted her eyes to the table top.

"That was it. He never told me he was married or anything like that. The bastard."

"Any idea where he is?"

"No. I didn't want to know. I told you I don't want anything to do with him. I don't suppose a man like you would understand but he's just a boy without a future,"

She smiled at me again, with a lot of warmth, and I began wondering what life would be like with a woman like this.

As if she could read my mind, she smiled at me again.

"Want some coffee?"

I did, and we sat talking for a while. She told me about herself. She'd been a nurse, then dropped that when she left Birmingham, and now she was a receptionist at an advertising agency. She was excited to meet a reporter like me, she said, because she was interested in public relations. Maybe I could give her some advice. She hadn't many friends in London, and sometimes she got confused and lonely.

"Not lonely enough, though," she said laughing, "to start up again with bastard Vernon."

The morning wore on, while I worked on tearing myself away. At first I'd thought she was aloof, beautiful and sexy. Now she reminded me of my younger sister. It was like talking to a different woman. I could see exactly why Vernon would come back, but that didn't solve any of the puzzles I was wrestling with.

In the end I arranged to come back and let her know what was going on. We exchanged phone numbers.

"Don't forget," she said at the door. Her eyes shone, then she leaned forward impulsively and kissed me, a soft dry pressure that was like a promise.

By the time I got home I'd calmed down sufficiently to ring Borelli.

"Where've you been, you prat? I've rung you twice already."

"Legwork," I told him. I only wished.

"Well the bloke's a wanker. Nothing on him. Parking tickets. Bollocks. This Norma, though. She's a bit tasty. You know what I mean?"

"What's she done?"

He told me the story briefly, using general terms and euphemisms but I got the gist of it.

Norma had been working in a nursing home near Coventry, and one of her patients, a geriatric white man named George Armstrong, had taken a great liking to her. That was normal. His family had been wiped out in a plane crash years before and, like a lot of old people in those circumstances, he needed someone on whom to fix his affections. So there were no problems until the old man fell out of a top floor window one dark evening. He shouldn't have been in that spot and Norma had been on duty. The nursing home, worried about taking the rap, blamed Norma and sacked her.

"What made it worse," Borelli said. "was that he turned out to have loads of money, loads. Just before his little accident he changed his will and left Norma a sizeable coming of it, nearly a couple of hundred grand. Most of that had been coming to the nursing home under the old will, so they challenged it and got it set aside."

"What about the bulk of it?"

"He left it to a daughter. But he'd lost touch with her long ago and they couldn't find her. That was what Norma said, that she reminded him of his long lost daughter, which was a joke really. They said he was more or less senile and totally dependent on her. Like she bossed him around. They said she even did his naughties for him. You know, the old hand jobs. Don't know how he lasted as long as he did."

"So all she got was the sack?"

"That's right. I wouldn't repeat this, but some of my colleagues feel she was lucky not to be charged."

Something he'd said was careering through my head like a stream of bubbles.

"Franco. Who would know the details of all this stuff? The will and everything."

"Can't help you there. Try the lawyers."

"Thanks".

His tone changed.

"I hope I haven't been wasting my time."

"You haven't. You'll hear from me soon."

"See that I do."

I rang Wally.

"Wally. Norma Chambers, Vernon's girl friend. The case she was involved in when she got the sack. The old bloke. I want to know the solicitor that represented the old man. Drew up his will. That kind of thing."

"Bloody hell," Wally said. "I've got a job on."

"Come on Wally. It's no big thing. Just ring the local paper. You know guys there."

"Okay."

I put the phone down and thought over what Borelli had said about Norma. The woman I'd met had been nothing like that. Except that, thinking back, she'd fallen for my charms a little too readily. I was as ready as the next man to believe I was irresistible, but a lady like Norma could choose from half the men in London.

The phone rang. It was Wally with the name of Armstrong's solicitor and his home number.

"Wally, you're a prince."

"Don't worry with prince. Send some duns."

I called the number. A woman answered and told me that Mr Hibbert was away.

"Am I speaking to Mrs Hibbert? Where can I contact him? It's urgent."

"Yes. I'm Mrs Hibbert. Who are you?"

Her voice was cool, but I was ready.

"I'm ringing from Birmingham radio," I gave my voice a self important tone. "We're doing a phone-in on the changes in legal representation and what it will mean both to the public and to the profession. We wondered whether he'd like to be on the panel."

She didn't hesitate.

"He's at a conference in London. I'll give you the number of his hotel."

After she'd done that there was a tiny pause.

"Birmingham Radio. Which one is that? BBC or independent?"

"Both, actually," I said firmly.

I rang Claudette. Aubrey answered. He was fine. Claudette was fine. Everything was like cool you know Sammy. I told him I would want him later if things worked out and he said yes. He had a calm I envied.

The hotel was one of those respectable old-fashioned ones in Marylebone. The desk clerk eyed me coldly when I asked for Hibbert.

"They're both out."

"Both?"

"Mr and Mrs Hibbert."

"I'll wait. Can you tell me when he arrives?"

He nodded and waved to one of the padded seats in the lobby.

I found a three months old *Vogue* and read it carefully. I could hear the clattering of cutlery when the door to the dining-room opened. Tea time, so I guessed he might back soon. But he left it late, and round about five I was beginning to worry that Hibbert wasn't coming back for his tea when I saw the desk clerk pointing me out to a couple who had just walked in.

They looked at me. I smiled and nodded, then the couple exchanged a few words and Hibbert handed the woman a room key. She walked into the back of the lobby towards the lifts, while he approached me. He had reddish blond hair and short moustache, and he was wearing a smart light grey suit. He looked like a man who liked a bit of a laugh and a glass of whisky.

I shook his hand and told him who I was. When I told him what I wanted to know about George Armstrong, he frowned.

"I was under the impression you had a message for me. If you want to talk about this, make an appointment with my secretary and see me at the office. But I warn you, I don't discuss the confidential affairs of my clients."

"This isn't confidential, Mr Hibbert. I can find out in other ways, but I need to know quickly."

He raised his eyebrows.

"Good afternoon to you," he said.

He turned and made to walk away, but I moved in front of him.

"Mr Hibbert. This is dead serious. Life and death. I think you should know that I spoke to Mrs Hibbert on the telephone a short time ago, and she was in Birmingham."

His gaze flicked towards the lifts and then he looked around rapidly as if checking to see if anyone was listening. Then he stared at me again, his eyes angry and intent.

"I don't want to know anything confidential. I really don't. But you can save us both some trouble by giving me just a few minutes. Do you want to tell Mrs Hibbert you'll be a couple of minutes?"

He would have dearly loved to kick me in the pants. But I was betting on the respectability I'd read from his profession and from the tone of the hotel. He'd bring his small town stuffiness with him and he didn't want it disturbed, even at the price of a few minutes conversation with an untouchable. A couple of clergymen walked past and looked at us curiously, as if they were wondering what we were doing together. I smiled at them. But it rattled Hibbert.

"Come into the bar," he said.

Our little chat took less than fifteen minutes.

"I want you to understand," Mr Hibbert said when he'd finished, "that none of this is privileged information. But neither is it for publication, and if you mention my name in connection with any of this I shall sue you back to the gutter."

"I understand," I said, smiling warmly at him. "Thank you very much, and give my love to Mrs H. Okay? You know what I mean?"

He breathed out sharply. If looks could kill.

People were on their way out for the night and the pubs were filling up by the time I got back home. I climbed the stairs tiredly, thinking about being out with a woman, at a party or a restaurant, but I had too much to do tonight, and even if I hadn't, I wouldn't know who to ask, now Sophie was away.

On the phone Claudette sounded as dispirited as I felt. I asked her whether she and Vernon had made their wills before they got married.

"Yes. In case anything happened to either of us."

There was a long pause while this sunk in. I asked her to get Aubrey. It had taken me a long time to get there, but now I knew what was going on and what I wanted to do.

I drove fast to Finsbury Park, but as I had half expected, there was no one there and Norma didn't answer her bell. I got back in and drove up to Tottenham. By now I felt like the Ancient Mariner.

Aubrey answered the doorbell. Claudette was upstairs lying down, he said. I waited till he was sitting opposite me and came straight to the point.

"I think I know what these people are doing and why they're doing it. But they can't really be stopped, cause I don't have any evidence, I mean I think they did her mum, but it's impossible to prove, I have to try and get them to give themselves away somehow, to panic them into giving me some kind of edge on them."

He grinned sceptically.

"You think they'll do that?"

"I don't know, but maybe I can get them to lay off her, Claudette, before anything else happens. The thing is they're not at Finsbury Park anymore. I might have blown it by going to see her today and they'll make themselves scarce for a while. Just in case. If they do that it's the end. No one's going to chase after them because I'm suspicious. So I have to find them."

He was sitting up straight nodding intelligently, like a little kid.

"Okay, The only thing I can think of is having a look in her flat to see if we can find anything to tell us where they've gone. That's where you come in."

His face went through some interesting changes when he realised what I was asking him. First he looked puzzled, then amused and finally he frowned. Embarrassed.

"No," he said, "I don't do that any more. After the last time I promised Maman."

"I'm not asking you to steal," I said, "Just go in and take a look."

But nothing I could say would shift him. Finally I had an inspiration.

"Suppose Maman says it's okay?"

His face cleared up.

"Oh. If she does. No problem."

"Let's go talk to Maman."

He hesitated.

"What's the matter now?"

He pointed to the ceiling.

"You leaving her on her own?"

I hadn't thought of that, and eventually we decided to take her with us to Maman's.

It turned out easier than I thought it would. I took Maman into the kitchen and explained the problem. I swore Aubrey would come to no harm, and after a little thought, she told me that her heart had gone out to Claudette and she would like to help.

"But if anything happen to that boy," she waved a spoon. "Is you I come looking for Mister Sammy,"

I swore again to look after him, and we left. Claudette was sitting in Maman's favourite chair being fussed over, and she looked in spite of everything as if she was enjoying it.

Norma's flat was dark and there was no sight of Vernon's car. Aubrey slipped out and walked across the pavement. He walked confidently with a soft springy tread, and although I was watching him he seemed to disappear into the hedge. The next quarter of an hour was bad. I sweated and trembled and every couple of minutes I wished I hadn't thought of such a stupid idea. Then suddenly he was there again, crossing the road, as if he'd just been for a quiet stroll.

He got in the bar and handed me a sheet of paper.

"This was all I could find," he said. "It was next to the phone and it looked new."

It was an address near Hyde Park. I knew the place too. It was a huge block of luxury flats which were owned by the Church of England and let to transients, usually from the Middle East, at massive and inflated rents. I could see Vernon in such a place.

"This could be it," I said, my excitement rising. "Let's go."

On the way I talked about the options with Aubrey. I talked. He listened. If I could kid them into thinking I knew more than I did, maybe they'd tell me enough to get up a case against them, or maybe they'd do something stupid. It didn't occur to me that they might do anything dangerous, which just shows how stupid I was being.

The block was off a quiet square. At this time, about ten, it was still choked with cars and we only found a parking place after a few circuits. I felt Aubrey in the car and went up in the lift, which whirred softly. When I got out, my feet seemed to sink into the carpet. There were soft and discreet lights up and down the length of the corridor. It was that sort of place.

Flat 31 had a white door and a gleaming brass knocker. I knocked, and a man's voice called out.

"Who is it?"

I tried a high and affected delivery.

"Room service."

I don't know why I said that, I had no idea whether there was such a thing in the place. But I was almost sure that Vernon wouldn't either.

I must have been right, because the door opened almost immediately, and he was standing there. He was wearing a white short sleeved silk shirt and baggy blue trousers, cinched in tight round his narrow waist. Up close I noticed his big brown eyes and long eyelashes.

"Evening," I said, just the way I'd rehearsed it on the way up. "Can

I come in? I'm from downstairs."

He'd only seen me briefly at the wedding, and I was banking on him not remembering for a bit. Something flickered around his eyes, though, but he gave way. I went in quickly, guessing that he realised that he'd seen me before, without being quite able to place the occasion.

The room was bigger than I'd have expected from outside, stretching away to end in windows which gave a view of the square, its lights gleaming through the trees in luminescent green haloes. At the far end was an archway which led to a large kitchen, and nearest me was a closed door which I guessed concealed the bedroom. The furniture was cream-coloured leather grouped around a big round coffee table.

He was behind me, but somehow I felt the moment when it struck him who I was.

"You. Out," he shouted suddenly. "Out."

So he'd recognised me. Big deal.

"Claudette, your wife, sent me," I said facing him. "I've got to talk to you."

"What goes on between me and her is our business," he said. "Get out. Now."

He gestured with his thumb, but I backed away from him further into the room. Like Norma he had the rising inflection and the tight vowels of a Brummie, and that reminded me. There were two glasses beside the bottle on the coffee table.

"It was your business when you got married. That's right," I said, "even though you didn't tell her about all that money."

I rubbed my thumb and fingers together in his face. Talking about it to him, I didn't have to pretend anger.

"Yeah. That's your business. But someone pushed her mum down the stairs and that's a different ballgame. I'm going to get you for that."

He was worried. I could see that from the way his forehead creased up, but then the rest of his face screwed up angrily and he growled at me.

"Piss off".

I didn't hear the rest of what he said, because I took a couple of quick steps to the bedroom door and banged on it.

"Norma," I shouted. "Come out here, Norma."

Out of the corner of my eye I saw the kick he aimed at me and moved fast enough to deflect it. Even so his foot grazed my thigh and I stumbled half on to the carpet.

"Yeeagh," he screamed, and came at me in a sort of springing dance that I recognised from the martial arts movies. I scrambled to get behind the sofa, but I wouldn't have made it if Norma hadn't opened the bedroom door and come out just then.

"Vernon," she said sharply, and he stopped.

"Hello Norma," I said. "Fancy seeing you here."

She smiled at me, the smile that I guessed she used when she wanted people to roll over with their paws in the air. She was wearing the same leather skirt with a shirt that was open almost to the waist. The way she looked made me want, even in the circumstances, to lie at her feet with a silly smile.

"Piss off," Vernon said. He pointed at the door again.

"No," Norma said. "Let him talk. I want to hear this."

She crossed the sofa, sat down and patted the spot next to her. She leaned forward and I could see her big brown breasts moving inside the shirt.

"Come on," she said.

"Leave it out, Norma," I said, sitting down. "I'm not a randy old age pensioner yet. I just came to talk to you and get a few things sorted out."

Her expression changed, a pair of hot and angry eyes bored into mine.

After everything that had happened, I didn't have what it took to be subtle.

"I want Claudette left alone, and I want to know who killed her mother."

She smiled again, almost lazily. The rapidity of her mood swings had me almost confused.

"Vernon's left her alone. I thought that was the problem. He didn't realise what a pig she was until after the wedding, then he left. There's no crime in that, and we don't know anything at all about the other thing you mentioned."

She paused, watching me with a feline calculation. I had the feeling that she knew her words were cruel and that the cruelty gave her pleasure.

"Besides, whatever happened. Nobody can prove that Vernon had anything to do with it."

"For a clever person," I said. "You're dead stupid, I saw the old man's solicitor today. Mr Hibbert. You remember him."

I saw that she did.

"Well, he told me a story about this businessman in Wolverhampton. It seems that he gave this black girl a job back in the sixties. That was in the days when old Enoch was stirring things up around there, and he got himself a hell of a reputation as a decent liberal. But when she got pregnant, he threw her out without thinking about it. This should interest you, Vernon."

It must have done because he didn't even snarl at me. Norma was still watching with her cat's eyes, and I hurried on in case anyone was encouraged by the pause to interrupt.

"He didn't show any signs of worrying about it when she moved out of the area and disappeared, but years later his wife and two daughters flew into a mountain in Spain, and his conscience began to bug him. But he still didn't do anything until he began to twitch, and dribble and forget who he was and he bought himself into the nursing home where he met you. You know the rest."

"Don't stop," she said. "Make it up as you go along."

She couldn't have been happy. But I couldn't read her expression.

"You were really good to him, like a daughter, he thought and he empowered you to do some business for him, like hiring somebody to find his daughter. But, surprise, surprise, the agency couldn't trace her. Not with you giving them their instructions. I am right? I mean the old man must have thought it was just like old times with you doing his errands in the day and giving him his little comforts after hours."

She tried to hit me. Her hands were quick, but something in her eyes told me it was coming and I had enough speed left to catch her wrist as she I swung at my face. I'd have held her, although she was strong, but while were were wrestling on the sofa, Vernon grabbed me from behind and began squeezing my throat. He must have got hold of a nerve, because the pain was excruciating. My eyes began to mist over and I heard a roaring in my ears. Norma said something and the pain subsided a little. Vernon had let go of my throat, but he still held my chin delicately in one hand, with the other poised on the back of my neck.

"Don't move," Norma said. "He can break your neck before you can wink."

I grunted. I had no intention of moving. My heart was thumping in my chest like a sledge hammer and the pain in my neck had spread.

She got up and moved to the armchair opposite. She leaned back and crossed her legs. Now she was at ease I could see that she was wearing nothing under the leather skirt, but by now the fact meant nothing at all to me.

"What else?"

She was smiling again.

"I can't talk like this," I said in a thin strangled voice.

Her smile broadened and she nodded at Vernon. He took his hands away, but they stayed resting, either side of my head, on the back of the sofa.

Suddenly she burst out with it.

"I did everything for that old git. He wanted me to have that money. Me. It was mine till those greedy bastards robbed me. You know what that feels like? You know how it feels?"

"What about Claudette? How do you think she would feel about being robbed." I said.

"What about her? She was getting value for money. Besides," the smile came back. "She'd never know, would she?"

Suddenly I understood I'd been barking up the wrong tree. Vernon hadn't pushed Nina. It was Norma. The pattern fitted. Old Armstrong had fallen out of the window, and it had worked, so she'd done it again.

She must have seen some change in my expression.

"You've got no proof of anything, anyway," she said.

"You're right," I said. "I shouldn't have accused you."

I made to get up and Vernon's hands were back on my throat.

"I'm not that stupid," Norma said. "Once you start talking to whoever you feel like, people will start making connections the way you did. No one's going to bother with us right now, but I don't think I fancy you going round telling lies about us."

"The police know that I'm here," I said. "Detective Inspector Borelli. Paddington. I'm supposed to tell him what happened."

She laughed merrily.

"Pull the other one," she said.

She got up and went into the other room. Vernon's grip didn't relax. When she came back, she was holding a syringe.

She held it up.

"Smack," she said.

I kicked my legs feebly and she laughed.

"Relax, you'll enjoy it."

"There's a bloke downstairs. Waiting in my car."

I described the car, and she went to the window and looked out, then she came back.

"I can see the car," she said. "But there's nobody in it."

"He must have gone to phone for a drink of something. He'll be back."

"Sure," she said.

She didn't believe a word of it. In my head I cursed Aubrey for not being on the job. She came towards me with the needle, and I braced myself to try and pull Vernon over my head, broken neck and all.

Just then there was an almighty crash. In my desperate state it sounded like a thunderclap. The wrath of God. The door swung halfway off its hinges and Aubrey was coming in, a marvellous, beautiful sight.

I'll give Vernon credit. He went for Aubrey like a dog off the leash, and I didn't bother to sit around rubbing my neck. As he let me go I lashed out at Norma, who was still staring as if transfixed, at the door. I caught her on the jaw and she went down, so I took the needle out of her hand and threw it across the room. By the time I looked up to see if Aubrey needed my help, he had Vernon down on the ground and was kicking him methodically. Fortunately, he was wearing sneakers, but I shouted at him to stop. Just in case. Then I went over and embraced him. He took it stoically, with a little bashful grin.

"That was great," I said. "I was never so grateful to see anyone in my life."

"I thought I'd better come up," he said, "and take a look through the letter box."

No one had noticed.

"And how did you do that man?"

I pointed at Vernon lying in a heap on the floor, and Aubrey's expression turned scornful.

"Tae Kwan Do," he said. "He's a wally."

I rang Borelli then, and while I was talking Norma got up and stretched out on the sofa. I put the phone down and looked at her when I was finished.

"I'm sorry Norma," I said, and I was.

GEORGE SMILEY GOES HOME

John le Carré

INTERIOR a laundry and drycleaning business in the King's Road, Chelsea, DAY.

A fogged picture slowly hardens, as the steady, near-expressionless monologue of a cockney working woman grinds on. It is the voice of LILLEY, the shop manageress, a dumpy, crippled little woman in a rabbit jacket. She is talking, near enough to herself, supplying background music to her own actions as she accepts the customer's tickets, limps to one rack or the other, stands on a stool or uses a steel grappler in order to fetch down a brown paper parcel or a peg-full of dry cleaning.

Still talking, she takes the money, rings up the change, turns to the next customer, receives a fresh supply of dirty clothes. The shop is busy and she deals with the shifting knot of customers expertly. Among them is George SMILEY, and though he is already near the counter, there is unobtrusive comedy in the way he constantly allows himself to be bypassed by less diffident customers. He holds out his ticket, almost gets LILLEY to take it—only at the last moment to see himself supplanted.

SMILEY is late fifties, bespectacled, fat, shy-looking. He wears a dark suit.

LILLEY
(busy all the time)

... I don't like youth. I'm not saying anything about young people—(fetches down a parcel)—we were all young once—laundry or dry, dear?—We all missed our chances, I dare say, or took them and lived to regret it—(to another customer)—Done your list, have you? In the basket then, that's the way—They don't *do* anything, they don't want to work, they're half dead, same as my nephew. I said to his mother—(taking a ticket)—name, dear?

YOUNG MALE CUSTOMER

Eldridge.

LILLEY
(pulling down a parcel)

—"give him everything he wants", I said, "but don't *spoil* him. If you spoil him he'll turn to crime, *then* where will he be?" Gives him an electric guitar for his Christmas, all her savings and half next year's. Still it's what she wants, you can't stop them. Name, dear?

SMILEY
(as LILLEY takes his ticket)

Smiley. George Smiley.

LILLEY
(studying ticket)

You want to learn to stand up for yourself, darling, don't you. I like "George". I always said I'd *have* had a George, if I'd had one. Which is it, dear?

SMILEY

I'm sorry?

LILLEY

Laundry or dry, dear?

SMILEY

Oh laundry. Yes, laundry.

Turning her back on him, LILLEY peers up into the shelves, as she continues her flat monologue.

Hey-diddle-dee, where can you *be*? (Starts climbing a ladder, grapple in hand) How long ago, darling, remember?

SMILEY

Last October. The twenty-ninth. A Thursday.
Reaching, LILLEY turns and peers down at him. Beat.

LILLEY

What are you, brain of Britain?

SMILEY

No, no, it was just the day she left . . . for the country . . .
(repeats) Smiley . . .

LILLEY
(still searching)
. . . That's the most important thing in life. Smile. They ask me at the training course. Lilley, they say, what's the most important thing?—(as she takes down parcels, examines labels, returns them)—Give them a smile, I say. I had a bloke walk in yesterday, no class but chivalrous. He said to me "that's the first smile I've seen all week". (She takes down another parcel and stares at the label, then at Smiley, seeming somehow to compare them. Finally:) What's your address, then, dear?

SMILEY

Bywater Street.

LILLEY
(still unsatisfied)
What number, darling.

SMILEY

Nine. Nine, Bywater Street.
With a shrug, LILLEY starts down the ladder.

LILLEY

It says "*Lady Ann* Smiley."

SMILEY

That's my wife. She's away.

LILLEY
(approaching till)
You a lord then?

SMILEY
No, no. She is. I mean she's the daughter of one.

LILLEY
What does that make you, then? (Rings up two pounds eighty, takes his money, turns to the next customer) Laundry or dry, dear? In the basket then, that's the way . . .

SMILEY
(as he takes his change and escapes)
Excuse me . . . good day . . . thank you . . .
As he exists, we hear LILLEY's voice, to the other customers, droning on.

LILLEY
(as we dissolve)
I remember her, see? That's why I was suspicious. Beauty and brains, they're like oil and water, that's what I say.
We have long DISSOLVED over LILLEY voice to: EXT. KING'S ROAD DAY, and are following SMILEY as he walks, laundry parcel under his arm, along the pavement, past swinging shoppers to the turning marked "Bywater Street". He enters it.
NEW ANGLE, SMILEY'S POV.
Bywater Street is a cul-de-sac. We follow SMILEY past the parked cars.
NEW ANGLE, showing the door of Number Nine, Bywater Street. One full milk bottle on the doorsteps. SMILEY still has the parcel under his arm as he moves up the steps to his own front door. He is at the top step when:
CLOSE on SMILEY. Nothing dramatic, almost nothing at all. But a momentary hardening of his expression.
CLOSE on the lower window. Did we see a shadow? Did SMILEY? Is the net curtain very slightly moving?
CLOSE on SMILEY. He holds his own front door key in his hand. Transferring his gaze from the window, he looks downward, at his feet.
NEW ANGLE, SMILEY'S POV. At Smiley's feet, a tiny wedge of wood lies on the doorstep, where it has fallen from its place in the lintel.
NEW ANGLE. The door in CLOSE-UP, showing the two sturdy Banham deadlocks. Reaching up, Smiley very quickly runs his hand

along the lintel, confirming his suspicion that the wedge is no longer
in place.
CLOSE on SMILEY as he discreetly drops the door key back into his
pocket. Then, without further hesitation, he presses his own front
door bell.
HOLD Smiley as he waits impassively, the parcel under his arm.
From inside the house, footsteps approach.
We HEAR the sound of a chain being unlatched.
ANOTHER ANGLE, over SMILEY'S shoulder, to show life continu-
ing perfectly normally in the street. A mother pushes her pram, a
lonely queer exercises his dog, the milkman continues his round.
ANOTHER ANGLE as the door brightly opens, showing:
>A tall, fair, handsome thirty-five-year-old man, dressed in
>a light grey suit and silver tie. Scandinavian or German.
>Could be a diplomat. His left hand nonchalantly in his jacket
>pocket.

STRANGER
(German accent)
Good morning.

SMILEY
Oh. Good morning. I'm sorry to bother you.

STRANGER
Not at all. How can I help you?

SMILEY
Is Mr. Smiley in, please? Mr George Smiley? My name is
Mackie, I live round the corner. He does know me.

STRANGER
George is upstairs just at the moment. I am a friend of his, just
visiting. Won't you come in?

SMILEY
No, no, it's not necessary. If you'd give him this. (He takes the
parcel, hands it to him.) Mackie, Bill Mackie, it's his laundry.
He asked me to pick it up for him.
Ignoring the parcel, the STRANGER opens the door still wider.

STRANGER
But I'm sure he would like to see you for a moment!
(He calls into the house)

George! Bill Mackie is here. Come down! He has not been
well, you see. He loves to be visited. But today he is up at last,
such a joy.
(Back to SMILEY)
There, I can hear him coming now. Please come in; you know
how he is about the cold.

SMILEY

(dumping the parcel into the STRANGER'S one free arm)
Thanks, but I must be getting along.
EXT. BYWATER STREET. SMILEY making briskly along the pave-
ment, away from his house, towards the King's Road. As he walks,
CLOSE fast on successive car numbers, aerials, wing mirrors, etc.
Smiley's expression impassive, functional, not a backward glance.
Track him round the corner, into the King's Road, along the pave-
ment towards a line of phones, most of them smashed.
INT. A filthy phone box. SMILEY talking into the phone.

SMILEY

. . . height five eleven, colour of eyes blue, colour of hair
light brown, youthful hairline, powerful build, clean shaven,
German accent, northern at a guess, possibly left handed. Two
unfamiliar cars parked in the street, GRK 117F, black Ford
van, no rear windows, two aerials, two wing mirrors, looks
like an old surveillance horse. OAR 289G, green Datsun
saloon with scratch marks on the offside rear wing, could
be hired. Both empty, but the Datsun had today's *Evening
Standard* on the driving seat, late edition. They're to wait till
he leaves, then house him, that's all. Two teams and ring the
changes all the time. A lace-curtain job. No branch lines, no
frightening the game. Tell Toby.
(So far, he has a deadpan expression. Now his manner is torn between fear for his wife, love for her, and plain anger.)
And then, Peter . . . ring Ann for me, will you. Tell her that if
by any chance she was thinking of coming back to the house
in the next few days—*don't*.

"IT'S CLEVER, BUT IS IT ART?"*

By M.J. Trow

The throng had thinned out a little after lunch and the pair were able to be more selective. Before, it had been a matter of edging past, touching titfers, smiling politely and gulping at the champagne before a careless elbow took its toll.

"What about that one, Mr Livingstone?" the younger man asked, slurring the words from the left corner of his mouth.

Mr Livingstone raised his pince-nez that dangled, after the style of Alma-Tadema, on a chain around his neck. He looked at the old lady his companion had pointed out. There was something about her bearing, something in what she was wearing . . . No. He shook his head.

"Let's peruse the Rubens, Daniel," he said loudly and whisked the young man away. He caught him sharply in the shin as they turned into the Upper Gallery.

"You're reading that programme upside down, man," he hissed, twisting his lips into a smile for the benefit of the passers by, alarmed by the terseness of his remark. After all this *was* the National Gallery. And it *was* celebrating its sixtieth birthday. It was a shrine. A dedication to God and the Nation. Even whispers had to be delivered in hushed tones.

* From "The Conundrum of the Workshops" by Rudyard Kipling 1890

"How about that one then?" Daniel had caught sight of another elderly female, crouching beneath a vast canvas of cherubim and seraphim.

Mr Livingstone raised the pince-nez again. "Hmm," he nodded, "This one has distinct possibilities. Are you ready?"

Daniel nodded, a little too enthusiastically perhaps for Livingstone's taste. He squeezed him into a corner, covering his mouth with the programme, "Now, one last time; tell me again."

"I am Lord de Lancey, looking for a painting to buy. Money is no object. You are . . . who is it today, governor?"

"Stop that governor nonsense, Solomon. You're not in your ghastly East End tenement now. I've spent a fortune putting you through Miss MacNeill's School for Speech and Haute Couture. Any more of it and I'll be asking her for my ten shillings back. Today I am Hercules Brabazon Brabazon. I specialise in still life. Which is precisely what you'll be if you muck this up. Got it?"

"Indubitably," Solomon's shady Cockney vanished into the velvet tones of Eton and Trinity. For ten shillings, Miss MacNeill had really done a magnificent job.

"Right," hissed Livingstone, "Here goes," and he broke away from the young man, "No, no, sir, I cannot prostitute myself . . ." and he collided with the old lady. "Madam, forgive me. I must apologise."

"Come, come, sir." Solomon was with him, gripping his elbow, "You may be Hercules Hercules Brabazon, a struggling artist. You may be starving in a garret in . . ." his eyes glazed over as his words failed him. Livingstone pulled an excruciated face, sucking in his lips as though he had just swallowed a lemon—

"Tite Street. But I, Lord de Lancey, cannot possibly . . ."

Livingstone hit him with the chain of his pince nez. The old lady had moved away from the bizarre pair.

"Pathetic!" snarled Livingstone, "All the finesse of a dray horse. Take it slower, man. You may as well carry a placard on your head with the legend "I am a confidence trickster." Now, look as if you're vaguely interested in art and leave the choice of target entirely to me."

"Very good, Mr Livingstone," and Lord de Lancey retired once more behind the unprepossessing facade of Daniel Solomon, part-time sharper's assistant and sometime glimmer of Shadwell parish. And behind the upside down programme.

But he didn't stay quiet for long.

"Oh my stars!" he flattened himself against a particularly nasty sunset of Alfred Clint's and clutched his top hat nervously.

"What the Devil's the matter?" Livingstone asked him.

"Esclap," Solomon croaked.

"What? None of your gutter cant here. Speak English."

"The law." He'd turned quite pale.

"Solomon, you've turned quite pale. Get a grip on yourself, man," Livingstone's eyes flashed around the murmuring ensemble, drifting like cattle on the cud, lowing contentedly before the canvasses.

"There," Solomon said, "The bloke in the bowler and the Donegal."

"Ah, of course," Livingstone viewed his quarry through the pince-nez, "I should have known. No dress sense at all. Who is he?"

"Name of Lestrade," Solomon whispered, "A miltonian from the yard."

"A detective from Scotland yard, eh?" Livingstone was quietly chewing the chain of the pince-nez, "What rank?"

"Er . . . Inspector. Look at those eyes. Shifty. That rat-like face. Ferretty. That nose . . ."

"Yes," Livingstone frowned, "Where's the end of it?"

"Bitten off, they say," hissed Solomon, "What's he doing here? He's on to us."

Livingstone twirled gracefully on one heel so that he stood between his man and Lestrade, "Not possible, Daniel," he said calmly, "Look at me. In the face, man. Now watch my lips 'Not possible'".

He had his back to the Yard man, staring icily at Solomon the whole time. "Now, there are two men with him. Right?"

Solomon's left eye crept cautiously upward over Livingstone's right shoulder. He nodded.

"Do you know them?"

Solomon shook his head.

"The secret of a truly great artist like myself is observation. The tall one. The one with the curly blonde hair and blue eyes. You've known more of the boys-out-of-blue than I have. Does he look like a policeman?"

"Well, I . . ."

"Of course he doesn't. Look at his clothes, man. His bearing. Eton, I'd say. And probably the Guards."

"Which Guards?" Solomon asked mindlessly, waves of panic running through him.

"*The* Guards," a horrified Livingstone told him.

"What about the other one?" Solomon quivered, "The little one. Was he in the Ghurkas?"

"Please," Livingstone was brittle, "Spare me your working class wit. That is Mr Edward Lutyens. Second to Ruskin he is the most revered art critic in the country. But unlike Ruskin, he probably knows that even married ladies have pubic hair."

"Aaargh!" a strangled cry from a married lady nearby told them that they had lost another quarry.

"Damn!" Livingstone snarled.

"What say we get out of here, Mr Livingstone?" Solomon hoped.

"What say you stop your knees knocking and act like a man? You say this Lestrade knows you?"

Solomon nodded, swallowing, "Felt my collar a couple of years back."

"What for?"

"Because the bastard enjoys it," Solomon's whisper had become falsetto.

Livingstone patted his arm, "There, there, my dear fellow. Down, down, thou climbing sorrow. We've got to face him."

"What?"

"What did he arrest you for?"

"Well, I wasn't exactly arrested . . ."

"Questioned, then?"

"Knobbing," Solomon looked a little sheepish.

Livingstone instinctively took a pace backward, careful to keep his back tightly against Huskisson's "Fairies".

"It's a fairground game," assured him, "Under and Over."

Livingstone looked relieved, "All right," he said, "Now, remember. You are Lord de Lancey. Third son of the Marquess of Uffington. Educated at Eton and Trinity. Ask this Lestrade if you've met before. Give him one of your cards."

Solomon's jaw and programme dropped simultaneously, "Are you mad?" he hissed.

"Do it, Daniel," Livingstone said through clenched teeth, "The art world has turned its back on me once too often. Today, it starts paying up in earnest."

"No, look, couldn't we stick with the women? What about her over there? That one with the horse face and the awful frock?"

"That is Kate Greenaway, Daniel," Livingstone told him, "She doesn't sponsor poor artists. She *is* one. Now leave the subject to me please. Go on, man. The place will be shutting soon."

And Solomon drew himself up to his full height and with his knees knocking and his heart thumping crossed the floor of the gallery to the trio of spectators who were admiring the Tissot.

"Bless you," said Lestrade as he arrived.

"Ain't we met, sir? By Jove, I know that face!"

Livingstone curled up in a corner. Solomon sounded like a Regency Buck only eighty years too late.

"Er . . ." the Inspector's eyes narrowed.

"Eton, was it?" Solomon suggested.

"No," said Lestrade.

"Trinity, then," Solomon persisted.

"No, I don't believe."

"This is Inspector Sholto Lestrade," said the tall, blonde curly man, "I am Harry Bandicoot. This is Mr Edward Lutyens. You have the advantage of us, sir."

Lestrade looked at his big companion. It was a common situation. Most people had the advantage of Harry Bandicoot.

"My card," Solomon flipped it adeptly from his waistcoat pocket, "de Lancey. Lord. Son of the Marquess of Effingham, don't you know."

"Really?" said Lestrade.

"Inspector?" Solomon was in full flight, "On the buses, are you?"

"No, the police," Bandicoot leapt in with his usual subtlety.

"Really? Peeler, eh?"

Livingstone was about to crawl away, his partner rumbled, when he heard sounds of merriment from the floor. He saw Lestrade tip his bowler, Bandicoot shake Solomon's hand. Even the acerbic Lutyens was smiling. Good God, had Solomon actually pulled it off? And as he turned, Livingstone's joy was complete. There stood a large old lady, arguably the wrong side of sixty, awash with makeup that gave her a deathly pallor. Her jewels would have shamed any Maharajah and she was alone and she was patently a suitable case for treatment.

She craned forward with her lorgnette to examine one of Richard Dadd's later works and sighed, "I'm very much in two minds about this painting!"

He was interrupted in his approach to the dowager by a beaming, triumphant Daniel Solomon, whose Lord de Lancey had clearly, bearing in mind Lutyens's presence, been a critical success.

"Well?" Livingstone sidled behind one of Landseer's bronze mastiffs.

"Very," grinned Solomon.

"I mean, how did they take it?"

"Lestrade didn't know me from Adam," he said.

"You see. I told you. All you need is nerve, Danny boy. What of the others?"

"The blond one is obviously an idiot. Lutyens was too absorbed in his paintings."

Livingstone noticed that Solomon's vowels were better, his consonants sharper than erstwhile. The de Lancey persona had stayed. Well, that was to the good. Chance to deflate the cocky young puppy after the dowager was safely bagged.

"The blond one's here taking advantage of the Gallery's celebrations to buy a painting for his wife. It's her birthday and he wants to surprise her."

"Why does he need a Scotland Yard Inspector?" Livingstone was prepared to play Devil's Advocate for a while. He didn't want to rattle his young protegé, but at the same time, he couldn't risk walking into a trap.

"They're friends," Solomon told him, "Lestrade's off duty."

"Do they ever sleep?" Livingstone wondered aloud.

"Trust me," it was the young man's turn to pat shoulders, "The arm of the law isn't as long as all that. You were right, Livingstone . . . er . . . Mr Livingstone. You persuaded me there was nothing to worry about. And there isn't. Now, what about that one over there?"

Livingstone raised his eyes heavenwards, "That's Lady Butler, Daniel. She's painted more soldiers than Catherine the Great got through. Fear not, I've made my choice."

In another part of the gallery, Inspector Sholto Lestrade pressed what was left of his nose against a particularly turgid canvas. He craned first this way, then that.

"Is this the right way up, Mr Lutyens?" he asked.

"Of, course," the expert replied, "It's by J.M.W. Turner."

"Ah," Lestrade nodded sagely. That seemed to say it all.

"You know, Sholto," Harry Bandicoot was doing his best to look knowledgeable, "That de Lancey fellow. He's only a few years my junior, wouldn't you say?"

"Hum? What of it, Harry?" Lestrade turned away a little unnerved by one of Baron Leighton's twenty foot nudes.

"Well, he told us he was at Eton. I don't remember anyone by that name."

"There, there, Harry" Lestrade patted his friend's arm. "You were probably too busy with all that Cocklid and Sissero to notice. Good Lord, is this *the* Thomas Hardy, Mr Lutyens?"

Lutyens raised a tolerant eyebrow, "Well, it's *a* Thomas Hardy, certainly, Mr Lestrade."

"What do you think Letitia would like, Harry?" Lestrade asked.

"Well, I must confess, Sholto, I'm no great shakes when it comes to art. That's why I asked Mr Lutyens along. He knows what I like."

"Perhaps this Conder?" Lutyens suggested as they reached the next canvas.

"Yes, yes, very nice," Bandicoot mused, "I do believe I've met his wife, you know. Anna."

"Whatever you choose, Mr Bandicoot," Lutyens said, "Please not a Millais. I always found him fundamentally Philistine."

"Of course," Bandicoot nodded sagely, "Er . . . what about this?" he consulted his programme.

"Holman Hunt? Better, but still a crude and rudimentary colourist without taste or sensibility."

Lestrade had wondered into the far corner. A canvas of mournful tombstones caught his eye. It was his own fault. He had pressed too closely to see the title, not quite believing it and the ornate plaster frame had fetched him a nasty one as he stooped. And after all that, he *had* read it correctly—"The Churchyard" by Thomas Churchyard.

"There are an awful lot of von Hurkomers," he heard Bandicoot say and felt very much inclined to agree.

Livingstone was ready now, the subject framed by his pince-nez. Solomon, buoyed by his wool-putting over the dark eyes of Lestrade, was ready too. He nodded and the gambit began.

"Call yourself an artist?" Solomon asked imperiously. "You are a rank amateur, sir. Be off with you."

"Please, sir," Livingstone cringed, showing just enough frayed cuff for effect, "If you would but look at my work . . ."

"Gross ineptitude. Utter rubbish, patent balderdash. You can't hoodwink a de Lancey, sir. Not a son of the Marquess of Uppingham, anyway," and Solomon spun on his hired heel and strode away. Then, suddenly remembering his lines, "What did you say your name was, by the way?"

"Brabazon. Hercules Brabazon."

"Yes, well . . . be off with you, Brabazon. I've no time for starving artists, no matter how brilliant they may be. I've only your word for it that you're a genius." And this time he felt for good.

Livingstone hung his head and pulled the tatty crumpled sketch dejectedly from his waistcoat pocket.

"My poor man," a voice made him turn. The bait had been cast on the waters and the hook was being nibbled, "Forgive me, I couldn't help overhearing . . . Did that . . . er . . . gentlemen call you Hercules Brabazon?"

"He did, Madam," Livingstone inclined his head.

"Not Hercules *Brabazon* Brabazon?"

"The same."

"The famous artist!" The dowager clapped her gloved hands together in delight.

"Famous, madam?" Livingstone laughed bitterly, "You are too kind, though, I fear, incorrect."

"But surely, you are well hung in all the major galleries?"

"I do have one small still life in Gallery Three, dear lady. But, alas, it does not pay the rent."

"The rent? Have you fallen on hard times, Mr Brabazon?"

"Rather, madam, I have never left them, Mrs . . . er . . . ?"

"Oh, forgive me. How unutterably rude," she held out her hand for Livingstone to kiss, "I am Lady Throckmorton."

She paused for effect.

"Of the Northamptonshire Throckmortons."

Livingstone kissed the hand elegantly and all but raked the gems from their gold housings with his teeth.

"Why, Mr Brabazon, what have you got there?"

"Oh, a sketch. Nothing, I assure you."

"May I see?"

For a while he feigned coyness, but eventually capitulated.

"Oh, very well, if you must."

She unfolded it carefully and caught her breath, "This is exquisite," she said, "Those grapes, that dead . . . thing. So lifelike."

"A mere trifle," he told her.

She looked more closely with the lorgnette. "So it is." Then she saw the worn cuffs, the inferior gloves, the grubby collar.

"Mr Brabazon, I must buy this instantly."

"But . . .? Oh, no, dear lady. It is not for sale."

"Surely. Shall we say five pounds?" She rummaged in her handbag, then checked herself, "What am I thinking of? Shall we say twenty?"

"No, no, that is far too generous. Oh well, if you press it upon me," and he snatched the notes from her hand, "This will help towards the rent. And indeed, it will go some way towards the doctor's bills. As for the pawnbroker . . ." he sighed and turned away.

"Doctor? Are you unwell, Mr Brabazon?"

"I? No, I am fine, lady Throckmorton. Apart from the astigmatism," he squeezed his eyes delicately and hobbled away from her, "And the assegai at Majuba Hill."

"Majuba Hill?" Lady Throckmorton quizzed him, "But I thought we were fighting the Boers there?"

"Indeed, madam, we were," Livingstone's mind was racing. Had he overplayed his hand? "But the sneaky curs had a contingent of native levies with them. Some cowardly black skewered me as I was sketching the contours of the hill for General Colley."

"Tsk, tsk," Livingstone sensed he had renewed his grip, "The doctor's bills are for dear little Effie. She is three today and has the fever. If only I could retrieve my brushes and my palette . . ."

"Mr Brabazon," Lady Throckmorton held up her hand, "You must say no more. I had no idea that our artists were struggling in this way. I am myself a Patroness of the Arts—oh, in a small way, of course. You must allow me to visit your studio and purchase a vast quantity of your works."

"Madam, I cannot allow it."

"Not?" she looked heartbroken under her rouge, "Tell me it isn't so."

"I have no studio, madam. Oh, I had one for a while of course. But I had to abandon it—the rent was so extortionate. I am currently living under . . ." his voice tailed away.

"Under . . ." she pressed him.

"Under the arches at Charing Cross."

She caught her breath, "But that place is notorious, Mr Brabazon, as a thieves' kitchen. Only the other day, His Grace the Bishop was condemning it in his sermon."

"Indeed, indeed," Livingstone crushed his testicles surreptitiously until his eyes welled with tears, "I fear it is so. At least we know the hour of the day—and the night—I and my thirteen children—by the arrival and departure of the trains."

"And Mrs Brabazon?" Lady Throckmorton's eyes were equally wet, though not for the same reason.

"Alas," he turned to face the nearest Landseer, "The cholera took her two years ago."

"You poor, poor man," she clutched his arm with a power rare in a woman her age, "Here," she ferreted again in her bag, "This is my town address. Please call this evening. Shall we say seven?"

"But I fear, lady Throckmorton, that I have had to sell all my canvasses. I have nothing to offer."

"Talent, Mr Brabazon. You have years of creation ahead of you. If I can play my humble part in ensuring that that talent is not lost to the world."

"Er . . . how humble?" Livingstone ventured, hoping the leer of gold would not pierce the pince-nez façade of abjection.

"Ah," Lady Throckmorton's face fell. "I regret I can only let you have a cheque for £100 at the moment."

"One hundred?" Livingstone stepped back, clutching his heart, "I have no words, dear lady . . ."

"But should you call at seven, I will by arrangement with my bank, be able to furnish you with . . . shall we say £5000?"

"£5000," Livingstone repeated dumbly.

"All right, then," smiled Lady Throckmorton, "We shall say it. A bientôt, Mr Brabazon."

"Indeed dear lady," and Livingstone was still staring at his knees in the lowness of his bow as the dowager swept from the Gallery.

"Rather a change all this, eh, Sholto?" Bandicoot said.

"What is, Harry?" Lestrade asked.

"Soaking up the culture, I mean. Rather a far cry from skull-duggery at the Yard?"

"Ah, yes. It's hard to imagine any crime being committed within these walls. Except for that Turner fellow of course."

"What do you make of this Archer Shee, Mr Bandicoot?" Lutyens asked.

"Bless you," Lestrade and Bandicoot chorussed.

"Three thousand pounds?" Solomon was beside himself.

"As I live and breathe," Livingstone settled back in the snug of the Coal Hole, "At seven tonight."

"This is the last time we drink here, then, governor," the younger man swigged his ale, "I've got to hand it to you. Half inching that bit of scribble from that Brabazon bloke was inspired. Can you draw, by the way?"

"How dare you?" Livingstone bridled. He was glad now he had short changed his underling.

Solomon glossed over the affront in his complacency. "This is retirement then, Mr Livingstone?" he asked, puffing on his cigar contentedly.

"It may very well be, Daniel," Livingstone quaffed his pint.

"And the best part of it was fooling that idiot Lestrade. He didn't have a clue who I was."

Livingstone gathered up his hat and coat. "I have a tryst to keep. At Lady Throckmorton's. See you tomorrow at the usual, place?"

"Tomorrow at the Dock and Doris," Solomon raised his glass, "It's been a pleasure working with you, Mr Brabazon."

"And with you, Lord de Lancey."

Livingstone was shown into an oak-panelled library by a flunkey with greying hair and an ill fitting waxed moustache. The man looked vaguely familiar.

"I will tell Lady Throckmorton that you are here, sir," he said and left.

When the doors opened again, the dowager entered. Livingstone rushed to kiss her hand. This time she wore no gloves and he was surprised at the smoothness of her fingers.

"Madame," he said.

"Mr Brabazon," she gestured to him to sit, "I think we said £4000, did we not?"

"Er . . . I think we said £5000," he corrected her and chuckled, squirming a little on the cushions.

She smiled at him sweetly, "Of course," she said, "how remiss." She crossed to a table and drew out a cheque, signing it with a flourish. Livingstone crossed to her, his fingers wriggling at his sides.

"Dear lady," he signed, as the paper reached his grasp. "Dear lady."

"Dearer than you know, Mr Brabazon," a voice broke the magic of the moment.

Livingstone shot from the lady's side to confront a rather rat-faced man with a Donegal and bowler. He appeared to have mislaid the tip of his nose.

"Have you met Inspector Lestrade, Mr Brabazon?" Lady Throckmorton asked. Her voice sounded suddenly younger, her step was lighter. She smiled sweetly at Livingstone and took off her grey wig, shaking free the long, golden curls.

"How is dear Effie this evening?" Lestrade asked him.

"Er . . ."

"And the arches. Comfortable enough for you? Oh, and the thirteen children?"

"I . . ."

"You know, for a man with an assegai wound, Mr Brabazon, you crossed the floor a moment ago with astonishing speed."

"Ah . . ."

"Letitia," Lestrade crossed to the ex-dowager, "By the way, have you met Mrs Bandicoot? I think we'd better return this sketch to Hercules Brabazon. Carefully wearing gloves, of curse. Unlike you were when you helped yourself from the man's studio the other day, Mr Livingstone. I think Sergeant Collins at the Yard will have a field day with your dabs all over it."

"How did you know?" Livingstone sneered.

"As someone I once knew apparently never said, it was elementary. You see, Mr Lutyens, who was with us at the National happens to know the *real* Hercules Brabazon by sight. Which wouldn't have mattered at all, of course, had Lady Throckmorton been the *real* Lady Throckmorton. We've been watching you for some time. merely waiting for confirmation so to speak. I'm afraid you've fleeced your last old lady, Mr Livingstone."

"Lady . . . whoever you are. I appeal to you . . ."

"Not in the slightest, I'm afraid, Mr Livingstone," Letitia countered.

"You see, it's all over, Mr Livingstone," Lestrade poured himself a brandy, "The gentleman who showed you in, did he look familiar to you?"

"Why, yes. He did," Livingstone admitted, "I couldn't place him."

Lestrade clicked his tongue, "I really must see him about that. But he is getting better. Slowly. Walter!"

"The door opened and the flunkey entered.

"This is Sergeant Dew," he said, "He's been following you since you left the National—a little too obviously, I fear." Dew scowled. It was back to the drawing board for him. "You live rather well for a man with thirteen children. You've never been married in your life. And the closest you've come to the arches are some you tried to draw before you were thrown out of Mr Prinsep's Art School at the age of twenty two."

"That's a damnable lie!" roared Livingstone, "I could have been a great artist. A legend!"

"Of course," Lestrade quaffed his glass, "If you'd had any talent at all."

The door crashed back to reveal a tall blond man carrying an unconscious dark one over his shoulder.

"Ah, Harry," Lestrade said, pouring them all a drink, "I see you've run into Lord de Lancey."

"Indeed," Bandicoot grinned, "And the way he went down after a single right hook, Sholto. I told you he wasn't at Eton."

"Sergeant Dew informed us of your whereabouts. In case you split up—as you did after the Coal Hole, I wanted Harry to be there, just in case. Walter, be so good as to take charge of Mr Livingstone and get some lads to fetch his assistant, will you? I'll see you at Bow Street later. Let's see," he counted silently on his fingers, "That's er . . . fourteen counts of false pretences, ditto of obtaining money under same, eighteen of theft, etcetera, etcetera. I'll leave the paperwork to you, Walter,"

"Thankyou, sir."

"Mr Livingstone," Letitia raised her glass, "A toast before you go. 'Ars gratia artis'."

"'Ars gratia artis'," Bandicoot took up the cry.

Lestrade demurred. His Latin wasn't what it was. But he was a little shocked by Letitia. Surely that meant something rather rude?

THE UNIFORM

Liza Cody

There was a cutting wind that drove the sleet up under your collar. It was dark. I was tired, having been out all day, and all I wanted was home and a hot bath. But I hadn't seen Vinny for a week and he wanted a meal and a drink. We settled for a pie and chips in the Fir Tree.

I won't say it's exactly spit and sawdust at the Fir Tree but I do prefer somewhere more comfortable when I'm off duty. On the other hand, no one knows me in there, and that's always an advantage.

There was a darts match so it was crowded and we ate with our plates on our knees. Vinny, as he always does when he hasn't seen me for a while, wasted a lot of time complaining about how difficult it was to get together, and it was nearly chucking out time before there was any feeling of comfort between us.

He said, "Well then," and squeezed my knee. "Well then, back to yours for a cup of cocoa, eh?" But I was looking at the bar. There was something brewing. A big feller had knocked into a little feller and spilt some beer on his jacket. The litter feller was spoiling for it.

"Mmm?" I said to Vinny.

"Oh Shit!" Vinny said. "Do give it a rest."

The little feller grabbed a bottle off the bar and flicked the dregs onto the big guy's suit. I got up.

Vinny said, "It's not your business. Let's go quick."

"It's always my business," I said, and went over.

The big guy's friends were jeering. "Short arse," They called the little'un. "Get him a chair to stand on," they said. "He wants a crack at Kevin, he needs a stepladder."

Kevin himself didn't really want to know. It's like that sometimes with a feller that tall. So I concentrated on the little one. Someone had him by the sleeve, but he was flailing around like a windmill. "Great farkin' ape," he said. "No farkin' respect," he shouted. "Wants a lesson he does."

"Please don't," I said, letting him clout me one on the arm. Not that it hurt, mind. Just so's he knew he'd hit a woman.

"Out of me bleeding way," he said. He was really wound up.

"No." I said, very quiet. "You'll kill him." Which was a bit of a giggle when you saw the size of him.

"Too farkin' right," he said.

"No, I mean really," I said, getting up close to him so no one could hear. It might've looked stupid because he had broken the bottle and was lunging around with jagged glass. But I was keeping an eye on it all the time.

I said, "No, really. He's a haemophiliac. Just one little cut, he could bleed to death."

"You're kidding," he said, looking at me for the first time.

"Honest," I said. "I know his mum. She's ever so worried about him 'cos he won't take care."

"Silly twat," he said.

"Yeah."

"Might of really hurt him," he said.

"Yeah."

"Still, some of these big apes is really asking for it. Got no respect."

"No," I said. "But there's big and then there's big. You know that."

"I know that," he said. He absent-mindedly put the broken bottle in his pocket. "But does he know that?"

"He will if you walk out that door, won't he?"

"Right," he said. "Thanks, girlie. Could of really hurt him." He staggered away and the crowd closed in round the bar again.

"What did you say?" Big Kevin looked relieved but a bit resentful. His mates just looked resentful.

"I said you'd've killed him."

"Yeah?"

"Well, you could have," I said. "Big feller like you."

"Right," he said. "Always throwing themselves around, these little runts."

"Yeah."

"Always wanting to start something."

"Right," I said. "It must be really boring for you."

"Right."

"Have one on me," the publican said. "That's a lot of broken glasses you saved me."

"I won't," I said. "Thanks all the same." Vinny was standing by the door. He was furious. "I got to get back to the kids," I said, looking over at Vinny.

"Another time, right?"

"Thanks," I said, and pushed through the crowd to Vinny.

Outside it was still tipping down and some of the sleet had turned to snow. The pavement was slippery. I tucked my hand in Vinny's arm but he shrugged me off.

"I suppose you're well chuffed," he said. "Taking charge like that."

"No." I said.

"Can't we have one night out without you stick your nose in?"

"If there'd been a full-blown ruck," I said, "I'd've really been in lumber. Think of the paperwork."

"You could've just walked away like I wanted."

"Sorry, Vinny."

"But no. Got to get stuck in, you. Can't forget for a single minute you're keeping the Queen's bleeding peace, can you?"

I said nothing. He likes a good moan, does Vinny. It's no use trying to pacify him.

"One of these days, my girl, someone's going to give you a right walloping, and then maybe you'll listen when you're told."

We walked on. One of my shoes was leaking and my feet were cold.

"You think you're immune," he said. "You think that uniform makes you immune."

"I'm not in uniform now," I said.

"Right," he said. "But you know what I mean. You make me feel like a right prat steaming in like you did."

"Didn't mean to." I put my hand on his arm again and this time he let it stay there. But he wasn't happy, not happy at all, which was a pity really because I thought I'd done all right and we might have had a nice cosy sort of night.

I could have done with a cosy night because the next day was even colder. There had been a lot of complaints and we had to spend most of the day patrolling the market and the estate behind it. Everyone was out of sorts. There are so many precincts in the area we couldn't even skive off to our cars for a warm-up.

All day long we walked up and down in that mind making our presence felt. Because that is the point. The residents see a lot of uniforms and they know we're doing our job.

It was going on five o'clock and I was about ready to pack it in when I had a shout on the radio about a disturbance outside one of the Asian shops in Canal Street. A couple of us answered but I was nearest so I got there first.

I didn't have a lot time to assess the situation because I came round the corner at a run and practically stumbled over them. There were two men in donkey jackets and a third one on the ground.

"Farkin' tart-raker," they said. Thump. "Keep your farkin' hands off decent women!" Thump. You could smell the drink a mile off, and the one on the ground had spewed up.

"Hold it," I said. "Calm down." But they were too busy thumping and swearing.

"Lay off," I said. "You'll kill him."

One of the fellers doing the thumping turned round then. He said, "It's the poxy farkin' law!" And let fly with his right hand.

I ducked. "Don't do it," I said. "You don't want to hurt me. You'll just make it worse for yourself."

"Poxy law," he said. "Always telling a bloke what to do." And he let fly again. This time he caught me and I went over.

"Pigs!" his mate said. I saw the boot coming but I couldn't do more than roll away.

"Farkin' pigs!" he said.

At least it was warm in St Stephen's, but I can't say it was very comfortable what with the pin they put in my arm. And all those stiches in my lip made it hard to smile.

"You take it easy," my sergeant said. "We'll sort them out for you, never fear. They can't assault one of my squad and get away with it." He's a good sort, our sergeant, but he does see himself as a bit of an avenger.

"We'll round them up for you," he said. "Don't think we won't. The lads are that riled up."

"It's okay," I said, though my teeth felt all wobbly. "They were pissed. They just saw the uniform and went berserk."

He wasn't listening. "Just you rest," he said. "I got to go now, but don't you worry about a thing, right? We'll get it all sorted. Besides your boyfriend's waiting outside."

Vinny held my good hand. "I feel like a bleeding prophet," he said. "I knew you was riding for a fall. You was too bleeding confident."

I wanted to tell him that I was never that confident, but it hurt to talk so I just shut up.

He looked at my face which couldn't have been too pretty just then. "Never mind, love," he said. "I won't say I told you so." He stroked my hand. Vinny can be quite soft then he wants to. He'd even brought me a bunch of daffodils. I tried to smile at him.

"Don't cry," he said. "Your face'll soon heal. And don't you fret about me, I'll stand by you."

Vinny's a funny bloke really. I'd expected him to go crazy, but he looked quite calm and contented.

I opened my mouth to tell him I wasn't crying, but he squeezed my hand tight.

"You know me," he said. "I'm not the kind who cares about your looks. Don't worry about your face."

I hadn't even thought about my face. What I couldn't get out of my minds was the way that feller just turned round and hit me.

"It's the poxy farkin' law," he'd said, and then he hit me. Well, not me really, I thought, not my face—just the uniform.

BOBBY'S BAD DAY

by Barry Gifford

Sailor was changing the oil in the Bonneville when Bobby Peru pulled up in the maroon Eldo.

"Need a hand?"

"Thanks, Bobby, about done."

Sailor slid the pan of dirty oil out from underneath the Bonneville.

"Where's the best place to dump this?"

"Around back. Come on, I'll show ya."

Sailor picked up the pan and followed Bobby down the side of the Iguana Hotel.

"Empty it right in them weeds. Ain't nobody comes back here, anyway. You about ready for a beer?"

"Sure, Bobby, that'd be fine."

"Let's go by Rosarita's. You been there yet?"

"No, haven't heard of it."

"Thought maybe Sparky and Buddy'd taken ya. Come on, I'll drive."

They got into the Cadillac and Bobby guided it slowly along Travis Street, Big Tuna's main drag.

"This your car?" Sailor asked.

Bobby laughed. "Hell no, belongs to Tony Durango. I been datin' his sister, Perdita, lately. Tony's up in Fort Worth with his wife's family for a couple weeks, so he's lettin' me use it. Where's that pretty little lady of yours today?"

"Restin' in our room. She ain't been feelin' well."

"Sorry to hear it. Women are always havin' some kinda physical problem. Been my experience with 'em."

Bobby turned off Travis onto Ruidoso Road and gunned the Eldo up to seventy. He rodded it for five minutes until they came to a closed down filling station, where Bobby slowed down and circled behind the building. A half dozen pickup trucks and three or four cars parked in a row and Bobby wedged the Cad in between a tan Ford Ranger and a white Ranchero.

"Used to be this was a Mobil," said Bobby, as they got out of the car. "Man converted it into a private club and named it after his wife. She left him and he shot himself. The wife owns it now."

They entered a long, dark room where a dozen men, most of them wearing cowboy hats, sat on stools at a bar drinking beer out of frosted mugs.

"No hard liquor here," Bobby told Sailor. "Just beer."

They claimed two stools and Bobby said, "Couple Stars, Jimmy."

The bartender, who was no taller than five feet five or six and weighed at least two hundred and forty pounds, brought over two bottles and two mugs.

"How ya be, Bobby?" he said. "Who's your amigo?"

"Sailor, meet Jimmy, otherwise known as Mr. Four-by-Four. He's always lookin' out for the patron's welfare. Won't let ya drink no more'n forty, fifty beers, 'less you ain't drivin'."

"Howdy, Sailor," said Jimmy. "Enjoy yourself."

He walked back toward the other end of the bar.

"Thought you said this was a private club," Sailor said to Bobby. "How come I'm allowed in without bein' a member?"

"You black?"

"No."

"You an Indian?"

"No."

"Then you're a member."

"I've Got A Tiger By the Tail" by Buck Owens was playing on the jukebox, and Bobby kept time rapping his knuckles on the bar.

"Three or four millionaires in here right now," he said.

Sailor looked around at the other customers. All of them were modestly dressed.

"They look like a bunch of good ol' boys to me," said Sailor. "I guess it's oil money, huh?"

"Oil, gas, cattle, farmin'. Ain't nobody shows off around here. Iguana County's one of the richest in Texas."

"Wouldn'ta guessed it, that's sure."

"Ready for another?"

"Why not?"

When they were on their fifth round, Bobby went over to the jukebox and dropped in some quarters.

"Q-7," he said, climbing back onto his stool, "three times. Pee Wee King's 'Waltz of Regret,' my favorite tune."

Pee Wee's steel guitar rippled through the cigarette haze and buzzed around Sailor's head. His reflection wobbled in the long mirror behind the bar.

"I been studyin' a situation over in Iraaq," said Bobby. "Take two men to handle it."

"What's that?"

"Feed store keeps up to five K in their safe. Need me a good boy for back up. Even split. You interested?"

Sailor knew he was slightly drunk. He rotated his head on his shoulders and flexed his back muscles. He stared at Bobby and worked hard to focus his eyes.

"Be easy, Sailor. There's two employees. I take one in the back to open the safe, you keep the other'n covered. You ain't plannin' on raisin' a fam'ly in Big Tuna, are ya?"

"Lula tell you she's pregnant?"

Bobby grinned, showing three brown teeth.

"Couple grand or more'd give you two a leg up. Get you to the west coast, Mexico, most anyplace, with a few dollars in your jeans. I got it figured good, Sailor. Simple's best."

"I ain't sure, Bobby. I got to consider this careful."

"I respect you for it, Sailor. Don't do a man no good to go in on a deal with less'n a full tank. You had enough?"

Sailor finished his beer and nodded. "Have now."

"Come on outside, I got somethin' to show ya."

Bobby looked around before he opened the trunk of the Eldorado. He peeled back a brown army blanket and said, "That's a double-barreled, sawed-off Ithaca shotgun with a carved pistol grip stock wrapped with adhesive tape. Next to it's a cold Smith and Wesson .32 handgun with six inch barrel. These'll do 'er."

Bobby covered the weapons with the blanket and closed the trunk. He and Sailor got into the car. The sky was dark pink. Bobby turned on the radio as they drove, fiddling with the dial until it landed on a classical music station out of San Antonio playing Gottschalk's "Night in the Tropics."

"I sometimes listen to this serious stuff," said Bobby. "Kills off the mosquitoes in my brain."

2

Sailor bent over the bed and kissed Lula's hair above her left ear.

"Hi, hon," she said. "You been drinkin', huh?"

"Few beers, is all. Feelin' any better?"

Lula rolled onto her back, stretched her arms in the air and yawned.

"Can't tell yet. Where'd you go?"

"Smell's mostly gone. That vinegar really done the job."

"Buddy and Sparky come by earlier."

"How they doin'?"

"Okay, I guess. Sparky said Red's promised to have 'em out of here by the weekend."

"Oughta make 'em happy."

"So where'd you say you was?"

"Went with Bobby."

Sailor went into the bathroom and washed his face. Lula came in and sat on the toilet to pee.

"Hope you don't mind, Sail, I couldn't wait. What's Mr. Peru Like the Country up to?"

"Not much."

"Don't think he ever been up to much good his whole life."

Sailor laughed. "Maybe not."

"Sail?"

"Uh huh?"

"Let's leave here."

"We're goin' to, Lula, real soon."

"I mean tomorrow."

"We got about forty bucks, sweetheart. That'd get us to El Paso."

"Rather be in El Paso than Big Tuna."

Sailor walked out of the bathroom, took off his clothes and got into bed. Lula flushed the toilet, rinsed her face and hands, then came out and picked up her pack of cigarettes from the dresser.

"You shouldn't be smokin' if you're pregnant," said Sailor. "Ain't smart."

Lula stuck a More between her lips and lit it. She took a deep drag, blew out the smoke, and stared at Sailor.

"Who says I'm smart?" she said. "You up to somethin' with Bobby Peru, Sailor?"

"What could I be up to, Lula?"

"He's a stone fuckin' criminal, honey, and you ain't."

Sailor laughed. "I killed Bob Ray Lemon, didn't I?"

"That was an accident. I bet both our asses Bobby Peru done murdered all kinds of people, and meant it too."

"That was in Vietnam."

"He's the kind liked it."

"Lula, I got to get some sleep."

"Buddy told me about that thing at Cao Ben?"

"What?"

"Was a massacre. Soldiers there murdered old folks, women and babies, and dumped 'em in a trench. Bobby Peru prob'ly killed the most."

"Lula, he mighta did, I don't know. But it don't matter now. Lotta guys go outa control in a war and it ain't their fault."

Lula puffed hard on her cigarette.

"I sure enjoy smokin', Sailor. I hate that it's bad for you."

Sailor turned on his side, away from Lula, and pulled a pillow over his head.

"That Mexican woman, Perdita Durango, who's been goin' around with Bobby Peru? Did you know she drowned her own baby? Katy at the drugstore told me when I was out gettin' the vinegar."

"Anything else people told you today you ain't mentioned yet?"

"That man's a black angel, Sailor. You hook up with him, you'll regret it. If you live to."

"Thanks, darlin', I know you got my best interest in mind, and I 'preciate it sincerely. I love you, but I gotta sleep now."

Lula lit a second More off the first and stubbed out the butt on the dresser top.

"Shit," she said, softly. "Shit, shit, shit."

3

"Nice of you to drop by," said Perdita.

Bobby let the screen door bang shut behind him as he came in.

"Told you I would."

Perdita sat down on the couch, shook a Marlboro from the pack on the coffee table and lit it with a red Bic. Bobby roamed around the living room. The taps on the heels and toes of his boots clacked loudly against the hardwood floor.

"You still riled?" asked Bobby.

Perdita laughed. "You still screwin' sixteen-year-olds in the ass?"

Bobby smiled and kept circling.

"Ain't never had no teenaged girl pull a blade on me."

"Wish I'd cut you up good."

"Heard from Tony?"

"Juana called. They're stayin' another week."

Bobby stopped walking and stared at a family photograph on the wall.

"Stayin' a few extra days in the cowtown, huh? This you?"

Perdita turned her head and looked, then turned back.

"Yes."

"How old were you? Twelve?"

"Almost. Eleven and a half. Ten years ago in Corpus."

"Mm, mm. What a tasty thing you must been."

"Nobody was tastin'."

"Shame."

Bobby turned around and leaned down and put his face next to Perdita's from behind.

"The cobra's waitin' to strike, chica," he said.

Perdita crossed her legs and smoked. Bobby lowered his hands into the front of her blouse and cupped her small breasts. Perdita pretended not to care. He rubbed her nipples with the tips of his fingers, making them become rigid. She burned the back of his left wrist with her cigarette.

Bobby jumped back, then grabbed Perdita's hair and pulled her over the couch onto the floor. Neither of them spoke. She tried to stand up but Bobby kept his right foot on her chest while he blew on the back of his wounded wrist. Perdita shoved his leg to one side and rolled away. She stood up and spit at him.

Bobby grinned. "I knew we could be friends again," he said.

4

"Take one of these" Bobby Peru said, handing a plastic-wrapped package to Sailor.

"What is it?"

"Panty hose. Work better'n stockin's. Pull one of the legs down over your face and let the other leg trail behind your head."

They were in the Eldorado about two blocks away from the Ramos Feet Store in Iraaq. Perdita was at the wheel, Bobby was next to her and Sailor rode in back. The top was up.

"Here's the pistol," said Bobby, taking the Smith and Wesson out of his belt and passing it to Sailor. "Remember, soon as we get inside you keep that bad boy up where those hicks can see it. Once they notice the Ithaca and the Smith, they'll know we ain't foolin' with 'em."

Perdita tossed her cigarette out the window and immediately took out another and lit it with the dashboard lighter.

"Comin' up on it now, Bobby," she said.

Bobby slipped the panty hose over his head and adjusted it. His face looked crooked, distorted and flat, the lips pancaked across the lower half and his hair plastered down over his forehead like broken teen on a comb.

"Come on!" Bobby stage-whispered, his head snapping towards Sailor like a striking asp's, "Get that mask on!"

Sailor ripped open the package and pulled a nylon leg over his head, stretching the calf part to fit.

Perdita pulled up in front of the store. The street was deserted.

"Keep it revved, Chiquita. We won't be long," Bobby said.

It was two o'clock in the afternoon and the sun took up the entire sky. As Sailor got out of the car, he felt the intense heat of the day for the first time. Until that moment, he'd been numb. Sailor had passed the preceding hours in a kind of trance, unaware of the temperature or anything other than the time. Fourteen hours, Bobby had said, that's when they'd go in. They'd be out at fourteen-oh-three and thirty seconds, he promised, with something in the neighborhood of five thousand dollars.

Bobby went in first, carrying a black canvas Sundog shoulder bag in his left hand. He raised the sawed-off shotgun with his right and in a firm voice said to the two men behind the counter, "Move into the back room, both of you. Now!"

They moved. Both in their mid-fifties, portly, with wire-rim glasses and crown-bald heads, the men looked like brothers.

"Stay here," Bobby told Sailor, as he followed them. "Keep an eye on the door. If anyone comes in, herd 'em on back, quick."

Sailor held the Smith up high, where Bobby could see it if he looked. Behind him, Sailor could hear Bobby instructing one of the men to open the safe. Neither of the men, so far as Sailor could tell, had said a word.

An Iguana County deputy sheriff cruised up in a patrol car and parked it on an angle in front of the idling Eldo. The deputy got out of his car and walked over to the driver's side of the Cadillac. He looked at Perdita through his aviator-style reflector Ray-Bans, smiled, and placed both of his hands on the rag top.

"Waitin' for somebody, Miss?" he said.

"Mi esposo," said Perdita. "He's in the feed store picking up some supplies."

"You'd best be careful of that cigarette, Ma'am. It's about to burn down between your fingers."

Perdita stubbed out her Marlboro in the ashtray.

"Gracias, officer."

Bobby came out of the store in a hurry, still wearing the panty hose on his head, carrying the shoulder bag and the shotgun. Perdita jammed the gear shift into reverse and peeled out, knocking the deputy down. She floored the Eldo for fifty yards, braked hard, yanked it into drive and spun a mean yo-yo, fishtailing viciously but managing to keep the car under control. Perdita hit the accelerator again as hard as she could and never looked back.

The deputy came up on one knee with his revolver clasped in both hands. He fired his first shot into Bobby's right thigh and his second into Bobby's left hip. The shock of the initial slug caused Bobby to drop the bag. The impact of the second forced Bobby's right hand to twist sideways so that both barrels of the shotgun wedged under his chin. The Ithaca went off, blowing Bobby backwards through the RAMOS on the plate glass window of the feed store.

Sailor had been right behind Bobby until he saw Perdita hightail it. As soon as he spotted the deputy, Sailor hit the ground, losing the Smith as he fell. He put his hands over his hosiered head and kept his face in the dirt until the deputy ordered him to stand up.

HOPPER AND PINK

by Barry Fantoni

The three words painted in flaking gold leaf on the sign outside my office door read, 'press and wait.' Above them was the dusty black silhouette of a pointing hand which directed clients to a buzzer. Most clients didn't bother with that, though; they just walked right in. Not this client. The buzzer went and that was all. I had just gone back to an article in the *Saturday Evening Post* about how much ice cream Americans ate each year when the buzzer went again. It was another short, tentative buzz, as if whoever it was standing in the corridor outside didn't really want the services of a private detective. Thinking eight million gallons was a lot of cow's milk and frozen sugar, I dropped the magazine on my desk and shouted, "Come on in, the door's open."

I had half expected no one to respond. Fooling around with my buzzer was one of the ways the janitor's kid filled his summer vacation, along with getting his head stuck in railings and giving a hot foot to any of my clients who stood around long enough. Just to see anyone walk through the door would have been enough to raise my eyebrows. The guy who materialized practically took them off my forehead. At a guess, he was well over seventy, short, weighed no more than 140 lbs, and was dressed mainly in a multi-check cotton sports jacket with colours that would make a Hawaiian sunset look forgettable. He was wearing the full drape jacket over an electric blue sports shirt complete with a canary yellow polka-dot bow tie, and stone flannel plus-fours. A pair of two-tone golf shoes extended merrily from pale mauve clock socks. As a precaution against looking drab he had chosen a Panama hat with a band of indigo and scarlet satin and decorated it with a lime green feather tinged with crimson. But in each case, the brightness of his clothes, his jacket, his shirt, his bow tie, had faded slightly, mostly by the same degree. The result left him looking like someone who had stepped out of a coloured photograph exposed too long to the sun. Or a vase of dying flowers.

"Mike Dime?" my visitor asked, standing half in, half out of the room. "I do hope I ain't interrupting nothing." A shaft of light from the window cut across his shoes so the white tips shone like snow on a pair of sunlit peaks.

To give my dazzled eyes a rest I let them drop to the cover pic of the magazine in front of me. No change. It showed Hollywood's latest investment, a tall blonde in a two-piece bathing suit who was trying hard to look like an actress. I shook my head slowly. "Just dreaming," I sighed and looked back at the old man in the technicolour outfit. I hoped he wasn't an interior designer pitching for work. "How can I help?"

"Maybe I should have called first," he said with an apologetic smile. "It's always good manners to call before dropping in on someone."

"Wouldn't have made any difference." I waved an inviting hand at the visitor's chair. "Until twenty minutes ago I was on the other side of Philly. Been in West Philadelphia most of the day. Business."

My visitor crossed the room with short, uncertain steps. "I'm so pleased to hear that," he said and sat down as carefully as if there had been a kitten asleep on the shiny leather upholstery. "I sure wouldn't want to interrupt nothing."

I leaned back clasping my hands behind my head and took a closer look at the polite old man sitting across the desk. The top half of his face was dominated by a pair of circular spectacles the size of the big wheel on a penny farthing bike. It gave his dry old face the look of an owl thinking things over but that was a far as the resemblance went. Unlike an owl, he didn't look in the least bit wise, just sad. He didn't speak at once. New clients often find the first sentence the toughest. And it doesn't help to push. I let the heavy tick of the office clock fill in the silence and waited while the old man sat perfectly still, staring at the water cooler by the door. Then, having arranged his thoughts into something he could get his voice involved with, he turned and faced me. "To acquire your services," he asked in the way he might be ordering champagne in an expensive restaurant, "it requires a lot of capital? I mean, maybe you charge more than ten bucks an hour?"

I laughed and leaned forward. "If I charged ten bucks an hour I wouldn't be paying rental on a used auto. I'd be driving this year's Cadillac."

He smiled again, this time with more confidence. "So a ten spot would buy quite a sizeable piece of your professional experience?" He reached forward and placed the something he'd been fumbling in his breast pocket for squarely on the cover of the magazine in front of me. The blonde's two-piece changed from tiger stripes to green.

"Sizeable," I repeated, and looked at the engraved portrait of Lincoln. But I made no attempt to pick it up. "Of course, it wouldn't cover me shooting anyone or getting hit over the head," I said, "but it would certainly entitle you to bend my ear for a while." There was a packet of cigarettes on my desk. I tapped a couple loose and offered one to the old man who held up a palm.

"Thanking you just the same," he said, the remains of the punch drunk Bronx accent falling easy on the ear. "I never picked up the habit of smoking cigarettes. Sure, I smoke a cigar on stage, but that's just for show. As a matter of fact, I can make a full Corona last a couple of months."

I was getting interested. He looked too old for divorce and the mention of stage work had me guessing. I plugged a cigarette into the corner of my mouth and set light to the end. "You an actor?"

This time the smile was broad enough to show his teeth. "A comedian," he answered, but in spite of the smile there was sadness in the way he said it. "I hoped that maybe you might've recognized the face."

I blew out smoke. "Apart from watching the cops in this town chase crime," I said, "I don't get to see much in the way of comedy acts these days."

The old man nodded sympathetically. "Pity. You would have liked us. Hopper and Pink, 'laughter makes a flat world round'. Milly Pink—that was my wife's name—she thought up the tag line. To tell you the truth, Mr. Dime, Milly thought up most of the stuff we did on stage. Clever gal, a real bright spark and the sweetest woman you ever met. She passed over last December, by the way." He paused to swallow something large. "My name is Harry, Harry Hopper," he resumed, brightening a little. "A pleasure to make your acquaintance."

The surviving half of Hopper and Pink extended a small hand across the desk. I reached forward and gave the smooth skin and bird-brittle bones a gentle shake.

"And what is this ten bucks of yours expected to buy?" I asked amiably. "All my gags are old."

Harry Hopper took off his hat and placed it reverently on his lap. "Yours and mine," he said. "In my case seventy-eight years old, and married to Milly for over sixty of them. Young Milly—I still call her that, even though she's dead and gone—young Milly was my life and inspiration, and I ain't ashamed of saying so. No gag I ever cracked, no matter how worn thin ever sounded so bad when Milly Pink was standing on stage alongside me."

I had been listening carefully for a clue as to what Harry Hopper was doing in my office. There hadn't been one. "From what you have told me so far," I said, "I can't see how a private dick can earn ten bucks."

Harry Hopper put a finger to his lips, as if he had expected me to add more. "There's no mystery," the comedian said flatly. "I don't laugh anymore, Mr. Dime, and I don't make folks laugh any more either. Put plain, I lost the worst thing a funny man can lose. I lost my sense of humour, lost it the day Milly died."

I stubbed out my cigarette. "Don't tell me, Mr. Hopper, you want me to find it." I was gagging, figuring that's what an old timer from Vaudeville would go for. But Harry Hopper was serious.

"Why not?" he asked with large hopeful eyes. "Let me tell you, without laughter I might as well be dead. And there are times when I miss Milly so much I wish I were."

I stood up, walked the two paces to the open window behind my desk and looked down at the noisy street below. A freckle faced kid in a baseball hat was doing tricks on roller skates on the sidewalk. A Negro with short white hair thinning at his temples and a stained apron wrapped around his girth was laying mustard on a hoagie. A businessman with an out of town look on his face was mopping sweat off his brow with a handkerchief, his hat held at the end of an outstretched arm, as if he were catching rain. A nun was waiting to cross the street. A cop was staring at a high window in an apartment a block away. A hundred ordinary men and women were doing a hundred ordinary things. Once in a while I wondered what it was like to be one of them. I went back to my chair and sat down again.

"You don't want a private investigator, Mr. Hopper," I said as soothingly as I knew how. "You want a doctor, and not one who hands pills for lumbago."

The comic took off his spectacles and wiped them absently with the end of his tie. "Harry," he said softly. "Call me Harry. Everyone else does."

I crossed my arms. "Okay, Harry let me give it to you straight. A sense of humour is not one of the things a dick gets hired to find. Jewels, autos, dogs, even people—you'd be surprised just how many people lose themselves – but what you are asking. . ." I let my sentence fade.

"I already seen the kind of doctor you're recommending." Harry Hopper said heavily, replacing his spectacles. "You laughed when I asked what you charge an hour. You'd have died laughingly if I told you what that guy took home."

He sounded genuine, but I was still only half convinced that the comedian wasn't shooting me a line. I decided to play him along a little, but gently and not too fast.

"This ten bucks," I said, and nodded at the bill. "Is that some kind of a down payment for hiring me?"

"I want one hour of your time, that's all, Mr. Dime."

"To do what?" I asked. "No one gets paid for sitting around doing nothing."

Harry Hopper began to rise apologetically from his chair. "Maybe there's something else you have to do, something that won't wait an hour?"

"Sit down, Harry," I said evenly. "I've got plenty of time. But if you're feeling lonesome, ten bucks buys a swell bottle of bonded."

"I already tried hiding in a bottle." There was a hint of pain in the man's voice. "Even an old campaigner like me can find solace in a drink or two." Harry Hopper shifted in his seat and recrossed his bony legs. His pants hung in loose folds, like a slack tent canvas. "But as everyone knows the effect don't last long, and soon you got to start looking deeper. You got to start looking for the answers."

I waited until he got comfortable once more. "Answers to what, Harry?"

He gave me another of his big smiles. "You know something, Mr. Dime," he said. "I was seven years old when I walked out in front of a house full of paying customers and told my first gag. Just think of it—a seven year old kid."

I knew Harry had reached the point they all reach. Every client who gets to stick around for longer than three minutes will tell a dick their story. Automatically, I picked up a pencil and examined the lead. There wasn't a lot showing but I didn't expect to be writing much down. Harry's file wouldn't need no notes, no surveillance, no loaded revolvers. Just laughs. I had finally realized why I'd been hired.

"Remember that first gag?" I asked and gave him plenty of room to answer.

"Right here in this very town. The Walnut Street Theatre. You can forget a lot of things in a life as long as mine, but your first laugh, well, that ain't one of them."

It was a humid afternoon. Even though the window was wide open and the desk fan full on, the air was still thick and clammy. Harry Hopper held his hat by the crown and began fanning his face. "Milly was with me right from the word go," he went on enthusiastically. "Her folks were Italian, a knife-throwing act mainly, with a little tumbling and juggling. Milly was the eldest daughter of five, although Pink wasn't her real name. She was originally called Emillia Pinchonetti, but we changed it to make it fit Hopper better. In those days vaudeville shows were a bit like circuses, on the road together for years sometimes. That's how I met Milly, being from a showbiz family myself. We practically grew up together."

I sucked some smoke into my lungs. "No kidding?"

"Sure. Milly and me used to fool around a lot back stage, practicing all the gags we heard the big names perform and imitating the way they did things. Believe me, Mr. Dime, some of those acts we had in them days were good, and I mean good. So like I was saying, we'd be clowning all hours and I guess it must have sounded pretty professional, young as we were. We'd always have an audience of stage hands who'd be laughing tears with me acting like I'd been married fifty years already, Milly playing the part of a real scatterbrain. Then one night we got a chance to show what we could really do. For some reason the husband and wife act that closed the first half of the show didn't turn up; it later transpired she'd run off with the strong man from a show playing in the theatre across the street. My pa Eddie Hopper, who as well as being a top class song and dance man, was also a pal of the manager, suggested that to save the show, he put us kids on. And that's just what happened." The old comedian chuckled to himself. "A couple of kids dressed as grown ups. Ma's high heels and lipstick for Milly, a cane and gloves and pa's long pants tucked up for me."

Suddenly Harry Hopper leaped smartly off his seat and strode to the middle of the floor. He replaced his Panama and gave the crown a friendly pat on top. "Hi, folks, glad to be here," he announced and gave the ends of his bow tie an exaggerated tug. "I just flew in from Las Vegas, and boy, are my arms tired."

I'd heard it a million times—everyone had—but I laughed just the same. The comedian acknowledged my appreciation by tilting his hat. "We did a lot of those one-liners, Mr. Dime. Say, did I ever tell you about the walls of our apartment? I wouldn't say that they are thin, but last night I asked my wife the time and a guy four blocks away told me to get my watch. Did I say thin? The other day I gave the place a coat of paint and the dame next door complained that the colour clashed with her drapes. And the landlord. He's so tight fisted. One time he paid for a round of drinks and it took major surgery to remove his wallet. It was his birthday last week. I gave him a left calf glove?"

I did as Harry ordered.

"Because he never takes his right hand out of his pocket."

So it went on, one corny gag after another, his self-assurance swelling with every punchline. Then, exactly one hour after beginning his routine, he took a short bow and crossed the room to where I was sitting. "You've been a swell audience," he said. "Small, but appreciative. Let me tell you, Mr. Dime. For the first time since Milly died I feel like a human being. Strange, ain't it?"

"Not really," I said. "Laughter makes a flat world round. Remember?" I got up and walked the comedian to the door, where we shook hands. "Drop by any time you're passing, Harry," I called as the door closed. "You know where the buzzer is."

When the room had finally stopped echoing with the sound of Harry Hopper's vaudeville humour, I tried deciding what to do with his ten dollars. Clearly I had earned it; if anything I should have been paying him for the laughs. For want of something better I slipped the bill into an envelope, marked it with his name and put it in the desk drawer.

During the weeks that followed I kept an ear open for the buzzer, a sign that Harry Hopper wanted to give me another chapter of his life. But he never did show. I figured that either he couldn't find ten bucks, or more probably, once was enough. Even so I often wondered what had become of him. I wasn't left wondering long.

A month after his visit I was glancing through *Variety*, while waiting to see a prospective client in the entertainment business, when my eye caught the headline, "Vaudeville Star Dies". The obituary gave a brief but warm appraisal of Harry's career with Milly, and explained that he had passed away peacefully in his sleep. It closed with details of the funeral service to be held at the Mount Miriah Cemetery the following day. I told the secretary that five minutes was too long to wait, even for a theatrical producer, and drove back to my office.

Within minutes of reading the news I was ordering a wreath over the phone.

"I want flowers," I said. "Big, happy flowers."

"You got a price in mind?"

I hadn't. But still had Harry Hopper's ten dollar bill in my desk drawer. I took it out and turned it over between my fingers. "Ten bucks?" I offered.

"Ten bucks won't buy much," the voice came back. "Half a wreath at the most."

I thought about it for a second. "That's not such a bad idea," I said. "Send half a wreath."

The florist gave a snort. "Half a wreath? What are you, bud, some kind of a comedian?"

"Not me," I said. "I can't just about crack a hard-boiled egg. But you should have heard the guy who's paying."

THE HEAVY

by James Crumley

O *kay, tell me one more time—who's Roy Jenson and what's he done?* That's the question, and it's asked of me at least twenty times on the way to Los Angeles, asked by writers, editors, movie buffs, and even a Hollywood director.

Well, you would think that a good old boy who has been in the movies for thirty years working his way up from extra to stunt man to double to featured player would get more respect than that. Roy Jenson has been done in by every star worth his salt in Hollywood—out-foxed by Paul Newman in "Harper"; insulted to the quick by Jack Nicholson in "Chinatown"; had his chopper ripped off and his ass whipped by Clint Eastwood in "The Gauntlet"; found himself upstaged by a charming orangutan and asphalted by Eastwood in "Any Which Way You Can"; had his head blown off by Steve McQueen in "Tom Horn"; and, insult of insults, been gunned down by Goldie Hawn at the end of "The Duchess and the Dirtwater Fox". And that is only a slight list of his achievements in violence. Even in a low-rent rip-off of the "Walking Tall" sequence, Roy Jenson and Joe Don Baker staged the best, most convincing, most horrifying in its realism, the greatest fight I have ever seen on the screen. Although it seems that not very many people outside the movie business know his name, when he is on camera, Roy Jenson makes looking mean, down-right rock-hard bad, look easy, and he does it without falling back on the stylized mannerisms of, say, Jack Palance, or the studied inarticulate threat of the early Charles

Bronson. On the screen Roy Jenson makes looking *bad* look as easy as James Garner makes looking good.

Without villains worthy of their stature, there are no heros worthy of our respect. To make the favorite Hollywood myth convincing, that good will prevail over evil, the evil, the threat of terrible and bloody violence and death, must be convincing. Without the bad guys, the good guys have nothing to do except look good on horseback and strum their aimless guitars. Without Iago, the Moor is simply another neurotic lost in his own insecurities, but poised against Iago's malicious connivance, Othello achieves that tragic stature meant to break our hearts. Hollywood did not invent the heavy, but without the heavy, movies could only do comedy—which is sometimes fired with the intelligence of a Chaplin or a Buster Keaton, but is too often Chevy Chase playing all three Stooges—or middle-class soap operas like "Kramer vs. Kramer" and "Ordinary People", or imitation plays like "Tribute", or one-note biographies like "Coal Miner's Daughter", or movies about movies—which can sometimes be fine, as in "The Stunt Man", or boring inside jokes like "Alex in Wonderland"—or bad versions of bad French films, and last, and least, the ubiquitous and cowardly sequel ("Jaws 12 Eats 10").

Surely it is no accident that "The Great Train Robbery" was the first popular feature film in America. We love violence, we love gunfire, the wonderful explosive crunch of dynamite. We love heros; we need bad guys for definition.

Roy Jenson does not look like a bad guy as I park in front of his modest house up in the Hollywood Hills. I am half an hour late, and he is waiting in the driveway with a can of Bud in his hand. Although his last experience with a writer doing a magazine piece turned out badly—the writer bought Roy's screen persona, portrayed him in the piece as fat, ugly, gross, drunk, and mean—he ushers me through the kitchen door of his home with the sort of shy, charming hospitality that only born and bred rednecks can master. I am pleased to see that he is as nervous about all this as I am, but we are both large beefy athletic types running swiftly toward beer guts in our middle years. We recognize each other, somehow, working class kids who have done far better in life than we had any right to expect, a couple of big kids grown now and often mistaken for truck drivers or construction laborers or bartenders, both of us uncomfortable in professions our fathers never dreamed possible.

Roy's dog Baja barks madly at me as I come in the door. I try to make friends, but Roy does not discourage Baja barking. All the houses on his street have been knocked over except his, he explains, and he credits the dog. I understand, agree. When he finally gets Baja to go out the back door, I see the small pool in the back, the patio nestled against a steep and brushy California hill. Everybody in Hollywood seems to have a pool, I say, making dumb conversation. But Roy wants to talk about the hill, the flood a few years back when the slope dropped into his pool so furiously that it splashed his youngest son's tennis shoe all the way to the garage roof, wants to talk about the forty thousand dollar restraining wall that gave way under the onslaught of the rain and mud. Roy dug the pool and the patio out by hand, shovel and wheel-barrow, moved five dump truck loads of mud by hand. I am impressed. An old roughneck I worked with down in South Texas, I say, told me once that there ain't no such thing as good shoveling or bad pussy. Roy seems embarrassed, wants to know where we should do this thing, this interview, and after a bunch of hem-and-haw and foot shuffling, we end up in the kitchen like two good rednecks with beer cans in our hands, sitting on stools or propped on the breakfast bar or leaning against the counters. Although I do not know yet where he grew up, I know he grew up in a house where the kitchen was the center of the house, the living room reserved for strangers, preachers, and insurance salesmen.

Although he was born in Canada, after his father died when he was six, Roy's mother—who, as he said, had people there—moved him and his brother to East L.A. during the heart of the depression. He grew up hard, watching his mother work two and three jobs, working jobs himself as far back as he can remember, one of the few white kids in his grade school, getting the shit kicked out of him every afternoon as the Mexican kids dribbled him home from school like an under-inflated basketball. After high school, which was interrupted by a stint of running away and working on the Shasta Dam, he went into the Navy at the end of WWII. Something happened in the service. Whatever it was, he came out and went to college in Santa Barbara to get his grades up so he could play football at a real college. Whatever happened in the Navy, Roy came out, as we used to say in the sixties, radicalized, intending to write a novel about what a piece of shit Navy life could be. Whatever he did at Santa Barbara, he did enough of it so that a few years later when a coach at UCLA, where Roy finally played ball, recommended him to the newly formed CIA, the CIA would not have him. As I understand it, though, Frank Gifford was more than pleased to have him opening holes in the line. Roy made All-Coast three years in a row, then went to Clary to play professional ball.

Ah, but this is supposed to be about Hollywood, about movies. Damn right. After his first year at UCLA, Roy went back up to Oregon to work in a lumber camp where he had worked the summer before. When he came back to L.A., he ran into a hustler buddy of his at UCLA driving a Buick convertible with those three holes in the front fender. He had a blonde in the seat next to him and a check for a week's work, more money than Roy had made all summer felling trees up in Oregon.

I wanted some of that, he said. And he got some of it. Quickly. He did his first job as an extra working on "Samson and Delilah". Then there came acting classes and a contract at Warners, classes with Gifford, then doubling, then stunts and whatnot during the seven years of Canadian ball, back in the old days when a lineman with Calgary made six thousand bucks a season, when he made more in six weeks up at Banff doubling Robert Mitchum in "River of No Return" than he made in four months cracking heads in the Canadian league.

Even if his name did not show on the credits, Roy knew he could walk into a movie, see himself on the silver screen doing stunts and doubling, and that Tinseltown bug of fame and fortune lodged in his chest like a heartworm.

As we sit across the breakfast bar, after we have moved from Bud to Scotch, after three hours of stories, and after Roy looks up and asks, are we doing the interview now? I assume it is all right to look at him in person to see if I can see what I saw on the screen. So often when you see them in real life, actors seem so small. Once, a producer introduced me to John Cassavetes at Ma Maison, and Cassavetes, who looks like such an absolute force on the screen, talent and intelligence sparkling around him, seemed like just another guy, a bright, witty guy you might have known in graduate school, but, hell, I wanted to see that wonderful psychotic grin from "The Dirty Dozen". Another time, I had a beer down in Sun Valley sitting next to Clint Eastwood. He was not the Man With No Name or Dirty Harry or, hell's-fire, even Rowdy Yates, just a nice, polite guy, whose reputation as an intelligent gentleman among all the Hollywood sharks seemed well-deserved. And still another time, I chased my favorite actor in the whole world, Warren Oates, down a hallway just to shake his hand and give him the love and blessings of all the literate rednecks in America. He had Warren Oates' face, his pleasant smile, but he was a slip of a man, slight leaning toward skinny. I know, I know—we ask too much of them, those silvered icons of our movie dreams, and perhaps it would be better never to see them outside of the movie houses, but sometimes we do.

And Roy Jenson, like all of them, looks somewhat different across the breakfast bar than he looks in the movies. For one thing, the camera flattens his Nordic face, makes him look mean and, forgive me, dumb. In real life, his face is mobile, intelligent, and when he tells a story or laughs or talks about his children, his face lights up and softens, like the face of your favorite uncle who has had the sort of wonderful and adventurous life you long for in all your adolescent love and hope. When he smiles, you feel at home, and although he looks like the sort of man you would not want to hassle in a bar, he does not look like a heavy at all.

All those physical years, though, show, those years of football and stunts. His large hands are twisted, flattened knuckles and fingers angling off in directions designed neither by god or evolution. The left shoulder droops with the question mark of too many separations, and when he crosses the kitchen for ice and more whiskey, he limps, and you can hear the left knee snap, crackle, and pop with calcium deposits, bone chips, and degenerative arthritis.

Kill the head, they say, and the body dies. But we know that is not how it happens. Last year, easing into his fifties, Roy ran in the 15 kilometer Fireman's Benefit Run along Mullholland. Finished dead last, he said, but finished. Nearly twenty years ago when he went to meet his wife's family in Yugoslavia, he roared off the plane drunk, picked up Marina, a European actress he had met while doing stunts on "The Great Escape", and carried her all the way through the airport in his arms, then went to her parents' home and drank all the slivovitz they had in the house. Those days, these days, the physical life—but somewhere along the way, it changed, and Roy Jenson decided to become an actor. Not a double, not a stunt man, but an actor. And now, not a heavy, but an actor.

Remember "River of No Return"? Remember those frightening scenes with Robert Mitchum, Marilyn Monroe, and the kid charging down the white water in that piss-ant log raft? Well, it was not them. It was a stuntwoman doing Monroe, a stunt midget doing the kid, and Roy Jenson doubling Mitchum. Looked like a lot of fun, right? Looked like them folks was so scared they were probably sucking cloth washers off their underwear, right? True enough. Try to remember, too, that for every minute of film, those people were surviving three hours of damp terror for two-hundred-fifty bucks a day, and that the worst part, the accidents, the flip over the falls, the simple failure of equipment, never showed up on film.

But if you are the baddest ass in the Canadian Football League, if you have to kick ass because you are a bit too small to play pro ball up there, blocking on dudes with forty pounds on you and tackling running backs who have twenty pounds and four yards momentum on you, you sure as hell cannot be intimidated by some sort of movie crap. Right?

I was cool, Roy says, never backed off for a second, but sometimes I would have these nightmares, I would be so scared that I would jump directly out of my bunk in the cabin, wrapped in all my blankets, so scared that I would leap all the way across the cabin and land on the midget in his bunk. Shit, Roy says, he was scared too. I told him the reason big fish could swim, he says, was because they ate little fish, and the midget ate fish for two months before he found out I was shitting him. But we were all scared.

A couple of years later, Roy was doubling Victor Mature in a dog called "The Sharkfighters", working down in Cuba off the Isla del Piñas. It was hard work, eight hours in the water everyday, but not dangerous because they used dead sharks equipped with motors. Not dangerous until the day that Roy noticed all the Piñearos working as extras and technical help had disappeared up into the boats. One, two, three, Roy said as he counted the motorized sharks, counted all the way up to eleven, ah, then twelve. One too many sharks. Out of the water, he said, running on the water like Jesus in a two-hundred-twenty yard dash. To hell with that shit, he said.

A few days later, the special effects man had a heart attack, and the first assistant director fell off the wagon. Roy tried to hide the cases of rum in the jungle, but the first assistant director found a .22 rifle and opened fire, shot at Roy until he brought the rum back to the hotel. Scared me worse than the extra shark, Roy said.

Over the years he has done so much of that sort of thing that he cannot remember the names of the movies, cannot remember the falls, the fist-fights. I mention a George Montgomery/Yvonne DeCarlo/Tab Hunter oater called "Hostile Guns"—the first time I remember seeing Roy Jenson—but I have to do the whole plot of the movie before Roy remembers it. Seems like I did a thousand of those, he says.

But there are moments. Doubling for Leo Gordon in "Kings of the Sun" Roy Jenson had a moment down in Mazatlan back in 1963. Maybe because he is a striking figure of a man, or maybe because he can carry as much tequila as he can drink, but more likely because he understands in his bones the nature of *machismo*—which is not some smart ass kid trying to face you down as you drive down a street in Durango, and not some drunk Mexican banker showing you his .45 automatic, and not some crazy attitude toward women that sets good, hard-working, independent American women's teeth on edge; *machismo* means we will be gentlemen no matter how twisted by drink and drugs and life we find ourselves, and, as Ezra Pound so gracefully said, there is some shit we will not eat; no more, no less—whatever, a small band of extras attached themselves to Roy with that sort of devotion that usually only family requires.

In the scene, Roy had to convince his half-dozen followers to run through fire, without fire suits, on the beach, then fight their way through another two thousand Indian extras—and fight they did, wooden swords and shields clattering like gunfire, some atavistic memory working—and they fought all the way to the top, where George Chakiris felled Roy Jenson with a killing blow.

Of course, just like in the movies, everything came to a stop while they set up the next scene. Roy put on rubber suit, knee pads, elbow pads, which the make-up people sprayed with their version of that wonderful golden dirt-brown we recognize as Indian. And then Roy looked around from the top of the pyramid, watched an ambulance scream through the crowd of Indian extras, thought perhaps somebody had been hurt by accident during the filming of the fight from the beach, then they set the shot, and he did the fall, the longest stairway fall anybody had ever done, down the long steps of the pyramid.

I thought I was gone, he said, but I have always had fast hands, and somewhere down there when I was bouncing way up in the air, I managed to catch a step for a second and slow it down, and I made it all the way to the bottom with only a craped shin and a little crack on the back of my head, but I was dizzy as hell, could not see shit, but when I stood up, there was this funny silence, these two thousand Indian extras spinning around in my eyes, and I thought maybe I was hurt worse than I thought, then all these Indians started banging their wooden swords against their fucking prop shields, all two thousand of them, and shit man I felt like I was in heaven.

As it is supposed to be, anything you work at for a long time, anything you take pride in doing—eventually, you will be captured by your craft, by the necessary pride of professionalism.

We are down in Studio City now, bellied up at Stevie G's, Roy Jenson's home bar. I can tell it is home because when we wander in out of the smog-misted sunlight, Roy's friends give him a raft of shit. He has made the mistake of one martini too many and told them that some dude is coming down from Montana to do a piece about him for *Rolling Stone.* "You don't look like no guitar player," somebody says to him as we arrive. And another points out loudly that his oldest son still considers Roy just about the meanest man alive, the ugliest man he has ever seen. These are not Hollywood people, but working people, and they clearly love and respect this big, battered old fart who chews the end off his cigar, bunches his shaggy eyebrows beneath his Copenhagen gimme cap, and threatens to rip their heads off and shit down their throats. I have to admit that I am pleased and easy among these people, pleased to see that Roy is more than a touch embarrassed about all this.

But I am supposed to be working, right, so I ask what it feels like to have a squib explode against your flesh. Roy should know; he has been killed enough to know; but he gives me a lecture about professionalism, about the craft.

Steve McQueen, Roy says, we were friends. Oh, shit, not buddies or anything like that, but friends, you know. He had been to dinner at my house, we knew each other a long time, that sort of thing. He called me here, Roy says, pointing toward the telephone back by the johns, he called me here to do that bid in "Tom Horn". You know, I must have been a rustler or something, I don't know, but Steve comes in and gives me a piece of paper, a writ or summons or something, and I'm supposed to do this bit, right, supposed to be eating porridge with my left hand, and I've got my gun, see, in my right hand, and I say something like 'fuck it,' but at the same time I've got to put down the fucking spoon and pick up the squib button off camera—shit, they've spent three hours down in make-up putting this sucker on my forehead and another hour on the back of my head so it'll blow off right—and here I am, I have to do a couple of lines of dialogue, get rid of the spoon, pick up the squib, drop the hammer on my pistol, pop the squib when Steve is supposed to shoot me, make sure that I don't tip over too soon before the special effects people blow the back of my head off, and somehow after all this shit, I'm supposed to end with my boots on the table so Steve can blow me away with his carbine because I missed him and killed his horse.

Shit, Roy says, I'm making a thousand dollars a day for this bit, and if I fuck it up, I get another day, but goddamn I did it right. First take, he says, I'm a professional.

Although I do not know enough about the details of the movie business, when Roy tells me that the transition from stunt man to actor is almost impossible to make, I believe him. When he caught the part of Puddler in "Harper" in the mid-sixties, he made the move. Although he has starred in a couple of Mexican films—and it is wonderful being a star, he says, penthouses and limousines, but they want you to play it broad, mugging toward the camera—and managed to run up against some co-star roles in American movies, some of which are still in the can, it is tough making a living, hard to get respect.

Too often it works out like this: when he came back down from Idaho off "Breakheart Pass", Roy felt like he needed something physical to do, so he went to work with one of the co-stars off the film, Bill McKinney, doing landscape and tree-trimming work for five bucks and hour, tough work for an old man, and no respect; Roy and Bill were doing one of the other co-stars off "Breakheart Pass", doing his yard, making things right for a cost party, a party to which they were not invited. The line, Roy said, was drawn just above their names.

Like all of us at the mercy of other people, Roy Jenson waits for the telephone to ring. Tomorrow, he says, I might be on my way to Africa. It's been a good life, he says—then he tells me this story.

When he was working on "The Getaway" down in El Paso, Roy, one of his sons, and a friend tried to fly a Bamboo Bomber, a WWII training plane, from Chihuahua across the Sierra Madre to Los Mochis through heavy weather. As it became clear that they could not make it—they were making a hundred-thirty knots air speed but not moving an inch; the rocky peaks, as they drifted through the clouds, sat there, still waiting—Roy started thinking about dying. Frightened, he said, but not scared. His only regret, he said, that his son sat in the back of the plane. Fuck it, Roy said to himself, if we crash, we'll be okay, we'll walk out of these mountains. Hero talk.

But after he told the story, he told me what it meant. All these years, he said, I've always been afraid in front of the camera, in front of an audience. A few years ago, he said, when I decided to be an actor, I was doing Shakespeare, a reading, you know, in an actor's workshop, and some asshole out there beyond the lights was giggling, and I went out there and grabbed the little bastard by the neck. If it's so easy, I said, you do it. But after we nearly bought it, he said, up in the Sierra Madre, and then we didn't, I promised myself I'd never be afraid in front of a camera or an audience again. Never.

What must it be like, I wonder, this big, crazy bastard doing Shakespeare, or hell thinking of opening down in Orange County doing "The Gin Game". Surely it will not be the same as doubling for Mitchum down that furious river, and never close to that magic moment when two thousand Indian extra pounded their fake shields in tribute.

And when I ask, behind far too many martinis now, what it does to a man to make his nut by doing nothing but bad guys, Roy has no answer. He is standing at the top of his driveway now, and I am down on the street. He looks up the hill and says, there's coyotes up there, you know, and hawks, hell, I saw a hawk bust a raven a couple of days ago. Shit, he says, maybe I'm becoming some sort of Zen asshole. I found some pissants, he says, eating the soap in the shower the other day, and I said to myself "fuck it—they ain't hurting nothing"—so I let 'em alone. I don't know.

Nice talk for a heavy, I say up the dark and drunken driveway.

Roy Jenson ignores that, then says, hey, this ain't some sort of number is it? We're friends now, right? and you'll love me till I die, right?

All the philosophical, psychological bullshit trappings run through my head in one quick moment—the dumb pain of the original Frankenstein's monster, the creature from the Black Lagoon rising and roaring with hurt, all of that, all that evil and pain—and I know, now, the best of the bad guys break our hearts, and I shout back up that dark driveway toward that large, limping figure who has calls to wait for, family to love, and bad guys to play to the hilt, and I shout: You bet your fucking—I'll love you till I die.

MODUS OPERANDI

by Stephen Gallagher

"This is where they came in," the householder, whose name was Valentine, said. "This is exactly how we found it."

"You've left it like this for two days?"

"Well, to be perfectly honest, we were expecting you sooner."

Bruno sensed bait, but he didn't rise to it. Both of them were looking at him; the man big, perhaps a little too anxious to appear confident with a policeman in the house, while his wife was pursed and pinched and icy. From the moment he'd first seen her, Bruno—full name Ralph Bruneau, working out his last week as a Detective Constable before promotion was due to give him a bite at something better than this dreary follow-up work—had been certain that she'd be a real bitch to live with. *My* carpet, he could imagine her saying. Look at the mess they made on *my* carpet.

They were standing in the dining-room around a spray of broken glass, the result of a forced entry through a set of French windows. Beyond the windows he could see most of the way down the length of a perfect garden. The house itself was only a few years old and had been designed in the bogus Tudor style that always seemed to come with the tag of 'Executive Home'; not that Bruno would have minded it, given that its value was probably more than double that of his own place, but given a choice he preferred somewhere with at least a hint of personality. This house had none; for all their frills and ornaments and country-style curtains, the rooms were about as inhabited as the ones he'd expect to see in a mail-order catalogue.

Bruno said, "Didn't the uniformed men explain the procedure?"

"They just took a look around, said they saw a lot of this, and that it was probably kids."

"And they were probably right. Look, these windows are a weak point of the entire house. They've just knocked out the glass and reached in and opened the catch."

"It had a lock on it," Valentine said.

"Yeah, but look at it. You can buy them anywhere and they all come with the same key. What you want is deadlocks on both doors."

"And they'll stop anything?"

"Well, they'll stop kids."

Valentine frowned at the damage and the mess that it had caused. Neither seemed like much. Bruno couldn't say what was troubling him more, the damage itself or the fact that this burglary had probably been the work of mere teenagers. The truth of it was that where professionals were concerned, the best locks in the world wouldn't keep them out of a building like this for more than thirty seconds or so; if it came to the worst, they'd simply jack a door or a window frame right out of the wall and walk in.

The woman said, "Can I clean up, now?"

Bruno turned to her. "Soon as you like."

"What about fingerprints?" Valentine said.

Fingerprints. Bruno said, "I'll be straight with you. It wouldn't make a blind bit of difference. We've only one print team and they've got it up to here. Even if they found something, I'll almost guarantee you we'll have no match for it. These tearaways, they've all seen *Columbo*."

"Tearaways," the woman said, unimpressed.

"And the professionals would know better."

She said, "You're going to do nothing, then?"

For a moment Bruno was tempted to stick his face into hers and say *Yeah, that's exactly what I'm going to do, so what*? But instead he said, "I'll tell you what I'm going to do, and it's the only thing I *can* do. I'll get as exact a description as I can of everything that's been taken. Do you mark your property at all?"

That one surprised her. She looked blank. Score one for Bruno. Valentine said, "No."

"Every now and again, we'll pull someone in. Nine times out of ten we find that he's in possession of property that we *know* he shouldn't have. The problem is, none of it's traceable so he walks. Now, if we've got your details and we can get a match, then we've a case. I know it's not quite as exciting as turning out with the bloodhounds, but that's the way it works." He looked at Valentine. "Is it the first time you've been burgled?"

"More or less."

"More or less?"

"I had a tyre stolen out of the car, once."

Bruno resisted the temptation to comment on this major heist; far too many times he'd had to deal with victims who'd lost almost everything to a crime or a personal disaster, and who didn't have the safety net of an insurance cheque. The Valentines would, without a doubt. In real terms they'd lose nothing . . .

Except, perhaps, their sense of security.

But don't under-rate that, he had to remind himself. These were just ordinary people who, like most, saw very little of life except for the narrow sample that passed before their eyes every day. Something had intruded, something that didn't fit in with all their certainties, and they were probably disturbed more deeply than they'd care to admit. He ought to be used to making allowances; but in the last week before a rise in rank, perhaps his patience was a little thinner than usual.

So he said, "I know how you feel. The only advice I can give you is to make a claim on your insurance, replace what you can, get some new locks on that window and write the whole thing off to experience. I'm not saying we won't get a result on this. But what I *am* saying is, don't go losing any more sleep over it."

Valentine nodded, his wife looked away.

And then Valentine said, "Do you want to look upstairs?"

The sound of vacuuming followed them as they ascended. Where the stairs turned to go on to an upper landing, Valentine stopped by a tall, narrow window. Beneath the window was a table that looked as if it might just about take a telephone, if the telephone wasn't too bulky. The table was empty.

"There was a vase here," Valentine said. "It was the first thing we noticed missing. I was thinking that maybe the boy had broken it and he wasn't saying anything."

"Can you describe it?"

Valentine gave a glance in the direction of the dining room below, and lowered his voice. "It was bloody ugly, I can tell you that."

"Value?"

"I shouldn't think much. I can't imagine why they took it."

They carried on. As Bruno looked up to the landing, he realised that they were being watched.

This, presumably, was 'the boy'. Bruno would have guessed that he was about seven or eight years old, but he stood no taller than the bannister and was watching them through the bars. He seemed pale, slight, bookish; he had a drawing pad, and held it before him almost like a shield. Bruno gave him a smile and the boy didn't respond, but nor did his attention waver.

They went through into the well-lighted master bedroom. The child didn't follow.

"Most of what's gone went from here," Valentine said, indicating the dresser.

"And was this how you found it?"

"Oh, yes. My wife isn't over-keen on household disorder." Valentine's voice was tinged with the irony of understatement. "I've had my work cut out, keeping her away from it."

The dressing-table chair had been upset, and lay on its side on the floor. On the table's surface, reflected threefold by angled mirrors, stood an open jewellery box. An entire tub of face powder had been dumped onto the table's surface and it had rolled and spread in a flesh-coloured cloud to settle over a radius of about four feet. No marks disturbed where it had fallen.

Nothing else in the room appeared to have been disturbed at all.

Bruno said, "So, what are we talking about?"

"There was my Rolex. There was a string of pearls, old family stuff, really quite valuable. Ah . . . earrings. Real diamonds. A couple of gold rings."

"What about those others?" Bruno said, indicating about half a dozen rings that were still pushed into the velvet slots of the box's lid.

"They're gold, too. I don't know why they weren't taken. I mean they didn't even pick up the small change."

Bruno looked, and saw that this was true; a handful of coins, just parking meter money, lay under the power.

He asked Valentine to describe everything, and in his notebook he wrote down a one-line summary of each item; nothing ambitious, and mostly comprising the key words that would tend to pop up in a data search if the entry should ever be destined to see the light of day again. Bruno thought that this was about as likely as kick-boxing in a Convent, but he followed the procedure anyway.

"I'll need a serial number for the watch, if you've got it," he said when his notes had been more or less completed.

And Valentine, looking a touch sheepish, said, "Sorry."

Bruno fixed an eye on him. "What about on the guarantee? Or the original bill of sale?"

"I picked it up abroad about five years ago. Never thought to keep the paperwork for more than a year."

"And I don't suppose there's any record of the import duty."

Valentine smiled, awkwardly.

Bruno reckoned that he knew exactly what was happening, here, and he was making Valentine squirm so that he'd be aware of it too. The watch had probably been brought in without being declared for duty and now was almost certainly the subject of an exaggerated claim; and Bruno, while he didn't really plan to make anything of it, also didn't plan to leave Valentine with the impression that he'd taken him for a fool.

He glanced toward the doorway. The boy was watching them.

He still hadn't said anything, but he was taking it all in. Bruno could understand why. Kids loved policework. He thought to himself, well, what's it to me? and let the Rolex business go; it wouldn't be the first padded claim that had slipped by and it surely wouldn't be the last.

So he took a final glance around the rest of the bedroom, and then turned to the doorway.

"And what about your room?" he said to the boy.

"Oh, I shouldn't think so," Valentine began, but Bruno ignored him and kept his attention of the boy, who was returning his gaze.

"You missing anything, son?" he asked. "Post office book or a piggy bank, anything like that?"

"I don't have a piggy bank," the boy said.

"What's on the pad?"

The boy glanced down. "I think I've worked out how they probably got in."

Valentine said, "Oh, come on, Ben, the man's too busy for your games."

"No," Bruno said. "I'd like to hear this. What do you reckon, Ben?"

"I've drawn it for you," the boy said, and he showed him the pad.

It was an A3 cartridge drawing block. Bruno squatted down at the boy's level in order to take a look. Half of the book had already been used, the pages carefully removed. On the uncovered sheet, the boy had drawn a crayonned plan of his own garden. A bold dotted line, each section carefully hand-drawn and coloured yellow, showed the supposed progress of the thief.

"Next door's bins had been moved," Ben explained. "They could have used those to climb over. And then they could have gone over here for a stone to break the window."

Bruno nodded. 'Over here' was a section of the garden marked

Rokkery. Ben turned the page to reveal a second, equally pains-taking diagram which showed the interior of the house, the line tracking the thief's progress up to the master bedroom and then back again.

"And then on the way down," he explained, "one of them could have seen the vase and decided he liked the look of it, so he put it in the sack to take it for his own house."

Bruno nodded again, taking care to study the diagram without smiling. The boy was intense and shy, his words tumbling over one another now that they were coming out at all; this was clearly important to him, and whatever he might think of his parents, Bruno didn't want to put him down. "Show me the garden again," he said, and as the boy turned back the page he glanced across the hallway to where the doorway to the boy's room stood. It was almost directly opposite, and the door was half-open. Bruno could see a desktop crowded with assembled and painted kit models, and shelves that were equally crowded with books, comics and annuals; there was no way of telling it from where he stood, but he could almost be certain that they'd be indexed or in some kind or order. The USS Enterprise hung suspended on cotton from the ceiling. The tail of what might have been a Lancaster Bomber showed at a similar height just beyond the edge of the door.

Bruno returned his attention to the diagram. It had probably taken hours of patient work. The boy's room had left him with the strong sense of a self-contained fantasy world lying just beyond the threshold. He couldn't help thinking of how his own two had been, back when they were growing; football mad, they'd had team posters on their walls and unwashed kit under their beds and that had been about it. They'd turned out pretty well, robust and outgo-ing, but even so he'd come to feel that he'd missed something vital and mysterious in their childhood.

Just as Valentine was surely missing something in his own son's, if Bruno was any judge.

Bruno said, "That's not bad. That's not bad at all. You know what you've just described?"

"How they did it?" the boy offered uncertainly.

"Well," Bruno said, "it's more than that. Have you ever heard the phrase, Modus Operandi?"

The boy shook his head.

"Every criminal has his own way of doing things. Some of them have habits. Mostly they tend to specialise in one kind of crime, and when they go about it they do things in a particular way. Half the time they don't even realise what they're doing, but it shows up as a pattern and we start to recognise where they've been even before we know who they are. Sometimes it even gets so obvious that we can set them a trap and they'll walk right in. That's why we keep what's called an MO file, full of observations just like the ones you've made."

"MO for Modus Operandi?" the boy ventured, and Bruno showed his approval.

"Exactly," he said. "So what I'm going to do is, I'm going to take your detective work and put it into the MO file. With your permission, of course."

The boy hurriedly tugged out the sheets and handed them over.

"And I want you to have this." Bruno reached into his pocket, and brought out the ballpoint pen that he'd been using earlier. It was dark blue with silver bands, and had the name of the force and a police crest embossed along the side. It was really nothing special. He had at least a dozen more like it in a bundle in his desk.

He held it up for Ben to see.

"We use these for official policework," he explained. "Members of the public can't usually get hold of them, but for you I'm making an exception. Any notes you want to make in the future, this is what you can use."

Now he held it out. Saucer-eyed with wonder, the boy took it.

"What do you say, Ben?" Valentine prompted.

"Thank you." the boy said.

And that was about it. The boy took the prize into his room, and Bruno rolled up the two crayon drawings. He'd probably toss them into the back of his car, forget about them for a while, and eventually throw them out. Valentine went across the landing and half-closed the door to his son's room.

"Kids," he said. "What can you do with them?"

But he said it with a smirk and a half-shrug, and Bruno thought that no, he didn't like this customer at all; there was only one item of any real value in this overdone, overdecorated house, and it was the only one that Valentine didn't see. The excitement of Bruno's visit—a real policeman, on a real case, and here in his own home—had probably given the boy the best day that he'd had in ages; something exciting, someone listening to him, someone taking his imagination seriously for a change.

At the top of the stairway, Bruno jotted on a slip of paper for a moment, and then handed it over.

"It's an incident report number," he said as they descended. "Send it to your insurance company in support of your claim. If anything turns up at our end, someone will be in touch."

"But don't hold my breath?" Valentine said.

Bruno smiled tightly.

"Don't hold your breath."

Once Bruno was gone, Valentine began to unwind a little. With the front door safely closed he gave one faint, silent whistle.

He could feel that it had all begun to go a little sour toward the end, although he couldn't quite put his finger on why . . . probably something to do with the boy sticking his oar in. Anyone could guess that the police wouldn't appreciate being told their business by an eight-year-old; if he'd thought ahead, he might have told him to stay out of the way.

Still, he reckoned that he'd been pretty adept about that Rolex business; he'd picked it up on a business trip to Hong Kong for fifty pounds, cash, and no questions asked, and he'd known even then that it was probably counterfeit, stolen, or both. And there hadn't even been any question about the so-called pearls, which had been in his wife's family for years but which he was convinced had no more value than a string of dried beans. But now that he had what he needed, virtually a police endorsement of his loss, he could go ahead and make his claim safe in the knowledge that he held the high moral ground.

As he passed the foot of the stairs, he glanced up. Ben was at the halfway window looking out, watching the CID man's departure from alongside the empty occasional table. That cheap ballpoint pen was still in his hand.

"Ben?" he called up to him, and the boy turned his head. "Next time somebody gives you something, don't wait to be told what to say."

"I was going to," the boy said defensively.

"And put that somewhere safe. If you lose it, you won't get another."

The boy's face went blank. But he didn't answer back; never did, and a good thing too. He just turned around and went up to his room. A moment later, Valentine heard the door close softly.

Well, he thought, at least we always know where he is.

And then he put the boy out of his mind.

On the first page of a new exercise book, Ben wrote MODUS OPERANDI in bold, firm capitals. And then, because he didn't yet have anything more to note on the subject, he closed the book and studied his new pen instead. He wondered if the bands were real silver. He clicked it a couple of times.

Then he stopped.

It wouldn't do to wear it out. And he certainly didn't plan to keep it in the pencil-case that he took to school; he'd learned the hard way that the stuff you valued could easily go missing, and not necessarily even by stealth. There were people around who would just take it because they wanted to, and then would dare you to do anything about it. And if you did, then the perverse illogic of their ill-formed minds dictated that you'd slighted them and they owed you one, and you'd never be able to break out of the pattern of injustice and persecution except by walking away.

No, it wasn't worth the risk.

It would be the ruin of his red-letter day.

So instead he went over to the bed and crouched down, and from underneath he drew out the old suitcase that they'd let him hang onto after they'd replaced everything with a set of matching luggage last year. Ben couldn't understand why luggage had to match. He'd asked, but no-one seemed bothered to explain.

He liked this suitcase. The handle was broken but it had been around for a long time, and it buzzed with the places it had been and the stories it could tell. Now it was his private safe and he had the only key; his policework pen would be more secure here than anywhere.

He undid the lock, and opened the lid. The pen was still in his hand.

"Here's your new home," he said.

And there he placed it with the Rolex, the pearls, the rings, the ugly vase, and the rockery stone that he'd used to break the window after he'd collected them all together.

FAMILY TIES

by Robert Barnard

In the darkness the young man couldn't find a bell or a knocker, so he banged with his fist on the front door. Then he leaned his head against the cool brickwork of the strange house, his stomach heaving. Inside all was still, and he stood up and banged again. This time his fuddled brain became aware of a dim light appearing in an upstairs window, then of the window opening. It was just then that his gut began audibly churning.

"What the hell do you want?"

"Mr Jacklin? Fred Jacklin?"

"No, it's not. What do you mean, banging on my door at this time of night?"

"It is number fifty-seven, isn't it?"

"No, it's thirty-seven. Why you filthy young bugger—"

For his stomach had finally risen in revolt, and was emptying itself over the gladioli by the front door. As more lights came on in the house the boy fled down the path, out the front gate, and down the road.

Fifty-seven. It must be on this side of the road. His head seemed clearer now—funny that: that clearing out your stomach like that should affect the brain . . . Nice houses. Bigger than your average semi. A damned sight better than Mam's back-to-back in Gateshead—all the rooms so poky, with damp on the bedroom walls, and the two of them getting under each other's feet and on each other's nerves.

Unemployment, that's what did it. Sitting around all day with no money, no hope. He'd had a friend—a nice, normal kid—who'd gone and strung himself up under the strain. In his own case there'd just been one big, explosive row.

Number fifty-seven. That was in darkness too. Went to bed early round these parts, didn't they? He looked at his cheap wrist-watch. Half past eleven. No time. No time when you didn't have to get up early in the morning. When you didn't have to get up at all. This is a nice house, he thought. A semi, but a big, substantial one. Room to move about, be yourself, keep yourself to yourself if you wanted to. Garden could do with a bit of attention, though. He went up the path, and in the darkness felt around the heavy wood front door till he found the bell.

It played the first notes of Home Sweet Home.

Again there was silence on the other side of the door. Well, he supposed, if you were in bed the natural thing was to hope that whoever it was would go away. He rang again. This time there were stirrings on the other side of the door—a light upstairs in the distance, then the sound of someone shuffling slowly down the stairs. The door did not open.

"Who is it?"

"Mr Jacklin? Dad?"

"What did you say?"

"Dad? It's Steve. Your son Steve."

There was silence on the other side of the door. Well there might be, Steve was sober enough now to realize. Then he heard the sound of bolts being drawn across. The porch light came on, but no lights inside the house. The door was opened, but only to the limits of its chain, which was left on. Dimly he perceived a face appear in the crack.

"What do you want?"

"Dad—it's Steve. I'm your son."

"So you said. Bloody funny time to pay a visit."

"I was in Birmingham. I had a row with me Mam, and hitched a lift down."

"You been drinking?"

"Yes. I was a bit sloshed. I knocked on the door of number thirty-seven ... But I'm all right now ... I just wanted to see you."

The scrutiny continued.

"I can see your mother in you. I suppose it's all right."

The figure on the other side fiddled with the chain, and the door was opened. Now a light was put on in the hall.

"Go through to the kitchen. We'll have a cup of tea."

As Steve went through to the kitchen and found the light switch, the hall light was extinguished. Steve smiled briefly. He knew North Country people, his people—they were "near". He and his mother had to be. His father originated, he knew, in Bradford. So if he was careful with electricity it was only to be expected.

His father came into the kitchen now, and pottered over to the sink, filling up a kettle and setting it down on the gas ring. When he turned it was Steve's first view, first proper view, of him. It was something of a shock. He had known that he'd be older than his mother, but this man was about sixty, an old man. And he looked it too, to Steve's eyes. He was wearing an old-fashioned woolly vest, buttoned at the neck, and grubby flannel trousers with braces, hastily pulled on when the doorbell rang, no doubt. His face was wrinkled, and there was a heavy stubble on chin and cheeks that suggested that his last shave had been the day before. But he was at least wide awake. There was a sharp glint in his eyes.

"So you're Steven." He seemed to have difficulty finding anything to say. Not surprising, in the circumstances. "Last time I saw you, you were—how old?"

"Two. Me Mam says you left when I was just over two."

"That'd be about it. Women remember these things . . . What do you do, then, Steve?"

"Nothing. Unemployed. I've been on schemes—youth employment schemes, and that. But they're all fakes—nothing comes out of them. There's nothing in Gateshead at all. Twenty-five per cent out of work. It's diabolical."

"It's bad here too. Very bad. You need to go South, the South–East. That's where the work is."

"I know."

He hadn't expected a warm invitation to make this his home, though he had wondered whether he mightn't stop here for a week or two, maybe a month—getting to know his father, helping in the garden. But the drift of the old man's remarks thoroughly chilled the impulse. There was silence again.

"How's your mother?"

"All right. We just about manage. She has a couple of cleaning jobs, but they're a bit dicey. She helps out at the corner shop if they're short-staffed now and again. We're both around the house most of the time, so we get on each other's nerves . . . We had a big bust-up last night."

He father screwed up his face.

"Always had a temper, your mother."

"It were me as well."

"Nasty tongue with it."

"Is that why you moved out?"

It came out more baldly than he had intended. He had always had a curiosity about his father and what had happened before and after his birth, but he had not intended to show it by any sort of inquisition. But the old man did not seem disconcerted.

"I never moved in." A cunning smile twisted the gnarled face, and Steve saw blackened stumps of teeth. "I know a trick worth two of that. Living with her would practically have been admitting the brat was mine."

"Me."

"That's right. I never lived with your mother. I just slept with her, and slipped her money now and again. She was all right. She inherited that house when your grandparents died."

"It's not a bloody stately home!"

"She was all right," repeated the old man. He poured the tea into two cups, and came across to hand one to Steve. His body smelt of meanness and neglect. When Steve tasted the tea, he found it had not been sugared. Seeing a packet on the table he went over and spooned some in, then he squatted on the edge of the table, watching the old man, his father, rolling a cigarette.

"You got a dog?" he asked, fingering a dog lead that was lying on the table. "Not much of a watchdog."

"He's in the garage. He's old, and lost control of his bowels. I'm sick of clearing up his bloody messes. He's deaf too. I'd have him put down, but it all costs money."

"Sounds like he'd be happier."

The old man shrugged. The boy felt a sudden turn in his stomach which was not due to drink.

"So when I was two you just took off down here?"

"I didn't take off. I sold the business up there and bought a business down here. What's that fancy word the Yanks use? Relocated. That's what I did—I relocated."

"You never told me Mam, though, did you?"

"Oh, she has fed you a line, hasn't she? Well, there was no cause to tell her. She was the girl at the counter, the girl behind the cash register, that's all *she* bloody was. Did she expect to be treated like she was co-director? It was a nice little business selling plumbers' supplies, but she was about the smallest cog in the outfit."

"You didn't tell her until it was all wrapped up, then you said she needn't bother to come in on Monday."

"Saved a bloody scene, didn't it?"

"And that was the last she saw of you."

"It was. Mind you, I sent her a bit of money from time to time—has she told you that?"

"Peanuts."

"Money doesn't grow on trees."

Steve looked around.

"You seem to have done all right."

"Anyway, if I'd sent her anything big, or sent money regular, that would have been practically acknowledging you were my son. I never did that."

"I am though."

"Oh aye. I can say that now you're grown up."

"Oh yeah—marvellous! Thanks! You acknowledge me now I'm grown up and no one's going to grant a maintenance order against you."

"That's right." The old man smiled a smile of horrible complacency. "Let me give you a bit of advice, free, gratis and for nothing, son. There's always folk out there waiting to take you for a ride. You'll never get anywhere if you sit back and let 'em. In this world there's mugs and there's them that take advantage of the mugs. In my book there's nothing to be said for being one of the mugs."

"I could kill you."

The words came out flatly. They sprang unbidden from disillusion, from the shattering of hopes he did not know he had cherished, from a sudden, overpowering distaste. The old man took no notice. He shrugged and turned to wash up his cup.

"Well, that's my philosophy, like it or leave it. I didn't ask you to turn up here, and if you were expecting a tearful family reunion you were off your rocker."

Possessed by a new desire thoroughly to frighten this miserable, mean-spirited, complacent old man who was his father, Steve spelt it out, speaking low and intensely.

"I could kill you. I could put that dog-lead round your scrawny old throat and I could pull it tight and throttle you and no one in this world would care a damn that you were gone."

Still the old man was more puzzled than frightened. He stubbed out his cigarette in an overfull ashtray.

"What would you do that for? I never done you no harm."

"Fathers are supposed to do their sons good." He reached out and took up the dog lead. "It would almost be a public service, I reckon. You'd have been done away with, like that old dog that you're too mean to put out of its misery. And no one would think of coming after me, because you haven't got a son, have you? You've never been mug enough to acknowledge you've got a son."

"Don't be daft." There was a tiny quaver of fear now in the old man's voice, showing that the intensity of Steve had got through to him. "Your fingerprints'd be all over this kitchen."

"I've never been in trouble with the police. My prints won't be on their files."

"You said yourself you knocked at number thirty-seven. You'll have been seen."

"I was spewing my guts up over their gladdies. They didn't see my face. And what if they had? I'm not known here, and I wouldn't be here by the time the police found you." He tested the leather leash in his strong young hands and slipped off the table he had been sitting on. "I could strangle the life out of you and you'd probably lie on this floor till your body rotted and the stink was so foul that someone outside got a whiff of it. I could snuff you out like a candle—use the life you gave me to put an end to yours."

"Why?"

There was open fear now in his face as the boy took a step towards him.

"Because of the way you treated my mother. You didn't just treat her bad, you treated her mean—and you thought yourself bloody smart while you were doing it. And because of the way you treated me. You can't just bring life into the world and slope off as if it's no concern of yours."

"People are doing it all the time."

"They shouldn't." He was now very close to the man, could smell his body, smell his breath. "And because I've never existed for you, I could kill you and nobody'd be any the wiser, nobody'd come after me, and my name wouldn't even come up."

Now he was standing over him, undeniably threatening.

"You young thug! Keep away from me!"

"You're the thug. Hit and run, fuck and run—it's the same principle."

"You're dirt! That's what your mother has brought up—a lump of shit!"

Possessed by he no longer knew what compulsion, to frighten or to kill, the boy suddenly put the lead over the man's head, got his ducking body firmly under his, and tightened the leather around his neck, pulling, pulling.

"Stop! You can't—"

The voice was thick, choked, almost petering out. The boy kept pulling.

"I've left you everything!"

The words got through what seemed like a blanket of blood around the boy's brain. His hands paused.

"I've left you everything. There was no one else. You're my heir. The police will be coming after you all right!"

Steve's hands slackened, the leather relaxed its throttle-hold on
the old man's windpipe. As he attack faltered, his father lay there
very still. Suddenly the boy stumbled over the pathetic heap, ran
through the kitchen and out to the front door. As he pulled the door
to, he heard from the kitchen a hoarse, scraggly laugh.

Next day, standing on the motorway, thumbing a lift from the cars
streaming north, Steve felt almost lighthearted. From time to time
he did in fact laugh. He would never know whether he had been his
father's heir, but he sure as hell would not be it much longer. That
was right. He had had nothing from him, wanted nothing of him.
He would go back to Gateshead, make it up with his mother, then
head south looking for work. He'd see if one of his mates who'd
gone down to London could put him up. Failing that he'd get a bed
in a hostel. There was work, if you could keep clear of the people
who wanted to get you on drugs, or into prostitution. He'd survive.
He had a life ahead of him.

    And it would be a life unstained by . . . that act. He would never
know whether he would have gone through with it to the end, but
a terrible gut-feeling had told him he would have gone on pulling
tighter. It was that cunning old sod that had stopped him. His father
had saved him. For once in his life he had done someone a good
turn.

THE PIETRO ANDROMACHE

by Sara Paretsky

"You only agreed to hire him because of his art collection. Of that I'm sure." Lotty Herschel bent down to adjust her stockings. "And don't waggle your eyebrows like that—it makes you look like an adolescent Groucho Marx."

Max Loewenthal obediently smoothed his eyebrows, but said, "It's your legs, Lotty; they remind me of my youth. You know, going into the Underground to wait out the air-raids, looking at the ladies as they came down the escalators. The updraft always made their skirts billow."

"You're making this up, Max. I was in those Underground stations, too, and as I remember the ladies were always bundled in coats and children."

Max moved from the doorway to put an arm around Lotty. "That's what keeps us together, *Lottchen:* I am a romantic and you are severely logical. And you know we didn't hire Caudwell because of his collection. Although I admit I am eager to see it. The board wants Beth Israel to develop a transplant program. It's the only way we're going to become competitive—."

"Don't deliver your publicity lecture to me," Lotty snapped. Her thick brows contracted to a solid black line across her forehead. "As far as I am concerned he is a cretin with the hands of a Caliban and the personality of Attila."

Lotty's intense commitment to medicine left no room for the mundane consideration of money. But as the hospital's executive director Max was on the spot with the trustees to see that Beth Israel ran at a profit. Or at least at a smaller loss than they'd achieved in recent years. They'd brought Caudwell in in part to attract more paying patients—and to help screen out some of the indigent who made up 12 percent of Beth Israel's patient load. Max wondered how long the hospital could afford to support personalities as divergent as Lotty and Caudwell with their radically differing approaches to medicine.

He dropped his arm and smiled quizzically at her. "Why do you hate him so much, Lotty?"

"*I* am the person who has to justify the patients I admit to this—this troglodyte. Do you realize he tried to keep Mrs. Mendes from the operating room when he learned she had AIDS? He wasn't even being asked to sully his hands with her blood and he didn't want me performing surgery on her."

Lotty drew back from Max and pointed an accusing finger at him. "You may tell the board that if he keeps questioning my judgment they will find themselves looking for a new perinatologist. I am serious about this. You listen this afternoon, Max, you hear whether or not he calls me 'our little baby doctor.' I am fifty-eight years old, I am a Fellow of the Royal College of Surgeons besides having enough credentials in this country to support a whole hospital, and to him I am a 'little baby doctor.'"

Max sat on the daybed and pulled Lotty down next to him. "No, no, *Lottchen:* don't fight. Listen to me. Why haven't you told me any of this before?"

"Don't be an idiot, Max: you are the director of the hospital. I cannot use our special relationship to deal with problems I have with the staff. I said my piece when Caudwell came for his final interview. A number of the other physicians were not happy with his attitude. If you remember we asked the board to bring him in as a cardiac surgeon first and promote him to chief of staff after a year if everyone was satisfied with his performance."

"We talked about doing it that day," Max admitted. "But he wouldn't take the appointment except as chief of staff. That was the only way we could offer him the kind of money he could get at one of the university hospitals or Humana. And Lotty, even if you don't like his personality you must agree that he is a first-class surgeon."

"I agree to nothing." Red lights danced in her black eyes. "If he patronizes me, a fellow physician, how do you imagine he treats his patients? You cannot practice medicine if—."

"Now it's my turn to ask to be spared a lecture," Max interrupted gently. "But if you feel so strongly about him, maybe you shouldn't go to his party this afternoon."

"And admit that he can beat me? Never."

"Very well then." Max got up and placed a heavily-brocaded wool shawl over Lotty's shoulders. "But you must promise me to behave. This is a social function we are going to, remember, not a gladiator contest. Caudwell is trying to repay some hospitality this afternoon, not to belittle you."

"I don't need lessons in conduct from you: Herschels were attending the emperors of Austria while the Loewenthals were operating vegetables stalls on the Ring," Lotty said haughtily.

Max laughed and kissed her hand. "Then remember these regal Herschels and act like them, *Eure Hoheit,* not like your U.S. namesake Herschel Walker."

Lotty gave a reluctant grin. "I don't know who that is, but he must be a thug of some kind."

"That's why I love you, Lotty. Because you must be the only person in America who's never heard of him. He's a football star."

"Oh, football." Lotty gestured dismissively, but she slipped her hand through Max's arm and made a neutral comment about an upcoming concert as they walked downstairs to his car.

2

Caudwell had bought an apartment sight unseen when he moved to Chicago. A divorced man whose children are in college only has to consult his own taste in these matters. He asked the Beth Israel board to recommend a realtor, sent his requirements to them—Twenties construction, near Lake Michigan, good security, modern plumbing—and dropped $750,000 for an eight-room condo facing the lake at Scott Street.

Since Beth Israel paid handsomely for the privilege of retaining Dr. Charlotte Herschel as their perinatologist, nothing required her to live in a five-room walk-up on the fringes of Uptown, so it was a bit unfair of her to mutter "Parvenu" to Max when they walked into the lobby.

Max relinquished Lotty gratefully when they got off the elevator. Being her lover was like trying to be companion to a Bengal tiger: you never knew when she'd take a lethal swipe at you. Still, if Caudwell were insulting her—and her judgment—maybe he needed to talk to the surgeon, explain how important Lotty was for the reputation of Beth Israel.

Caudwell's two children were making the obligatory Christmas visit. They were a boy and girl, Deborah and Steve, within a year of the same age, both tall, both blond and poised, with a hearty sophistication born of a childhood spent on expensive ski slopes. Max wasn't very big, and as one took his coat and the other performed brisk introductions he felt himself shrinking, losing in self-assurance. He accepted a glass of special *cuvée* from one of them—was it the boy or the girl, he wondered in confusion—and fled into the *mêlée*.

He landed next to one of Beth Israel's trustees, a woman in her sixties wearing a grey textured mini-dress whose black stripes were constructed of feathers. She commented brightly on Caudwell's art collection, but Max sensed an undercurrent of hostility: wealthy trustees don't like the idea that they can't out-buy the staff.

While he was frowning and nodding at appropriate intervals it dawned on Max that Caudwell did know how much the hospital needed Lotty. Heart surgeons do not have the worlds smallest egos: when you ask them to name the world's three leading practitioners they never can remember the names of the other two. Lotty was at the top of her field, and she, too, was used to having things go her way. Since her confrontational style was reminiscent more of the Battle of the Bulge than the Imperial Court of Vienna, he couldn't blame Caudwell for trying to force her out of the hospital.

Max moved away from Martha Gildersleeve to admire some of the paintings and figurines she'd been discussing. A collector himself of Chinese porcelains Max raised his eyebrows and mouthed a soundless whistle at the pieces on display. A small Watteau and a Charles Demuth watercolor were worth as much as Beth Israel paid Caudwell in a year. No wonder Mrs. Gildersleeve had been so annoyed.

"Impressive, isn't it."

Max turned to see Arthur Gioia looming over him. Max was shorter than most of the Beth Israel staff, shorter than everyone but Lotty. But Gioia, a tall muscular immunologist, loomed over everyone. He had gone to the University of Arkansas on a football scholarship and had even spent a season playing tackle for Houston before starting medical school. It had been twenty years since he last lifted weights, but his neck still looked like a redwood stump.

Gioia had led the opposition to Caudwell's appointment. Max had suspected at the time that it was due more to a medicine man not wanting a surgeon as his nominal boss than from any other cause, but after Lotty's outburst he wasn't so sure. He was debating whether to ask the doctor how he felt about Caudwell now that he'd worked with him for six months when their host surged over to him and shook his hand.

"Sorry I didn't see you when you came in, Loewenthal. You like the Watteau? It's one of my favorite pieces. Although a collector shouldn't play favorites any more than a father should, eh, sweetheart?" The last remark was addressed to the daughter, Deborah, who had come up behind Caudwell and slopped an arm around him.

Caudwell looked more like a Victorian sea-dog than a surgeon. He had a round red face under a shock of yellow-white hair, a hearty Santa Claus laugh and a bluff, direct manner. Despite Lotty's vituperations he was immensely popular with his patients. In the short time he'd been at the hospital, referrals to cardiac surgery had already increased fifteen percent.

His daughter squeezed his shoulder playfully. "I know you don't play favorites with us, Dad, but you're lying to Mr. Loewenthal about your collection; come on, you know you are."

She turned to Max. "He's got a piece he's so proud of he doesn't like to show it to people—he doesn't want them to see he's got vulnerable spots. But it's Christmas, Dad, relax, let people see how you feel for a change."

Max looked curiously at the surgeon, but Caudwell seemed pleased with his daughter's familiarity. The son came up and added his own jocular cajoling.

"This really is Dad's pride and joy. He stole it from Uncle Griffen when Grandfather died and kept Mother from getting her mitts on it when they split up."

Caudwell did bark out a mild reproof at that. "You'll be giving my colleagues the wrong impression of me, Steve. I didn't steal it from Grif. Told him he could have the rest of the estate if he'd leave me the Watteau and the Pietro."

"Of course he could've bought ten estates with what those two would fetch," Steve muttered to his sister over Max's head.

Deborah relinquished her father's arm to lean over Max and whisper back, "Mom, too."

Max moved away from the alarming pair to say to Caudwell, "A Pietro? You mean Pietro D'Alessandro? You have a model, or an actual sculpture?"

Caudwell gave his staccato admiral's laugh. "The real McCoy, Loewenthal. The real McCoy. An alabaster."

"An alabaster?" Max raised his eyebrows. "Surely not. I thought Pietro worked only in bronze and marble."

"Yes, yes," chuckled Caudwell, rubbing his hands together. "Everyone thinks so, but there were a few alabasters in private collections.

I've had this one authenticated by experts. Come take a look at it—it'll knock your breath away. You come, too, Gioia," he barked at the immunologist. "You're Italian, you'll be interested in what your ancestors were up to."

"A Pietro alabaster?" Lotty's clipped tones made Max start—he hadn't noticed her joining the little group. "I would very much like to see this piece."

"Then come long, Dr. Herschel, come along." Caudwell led them to a small hallway, exchanging genial greetings with his guests as he passed, pointing out a John William Hill miniature they might not have seen, picking up a few other people who for various reasons would love to see his prize.

"By the way, Gioia, I was in New York last week, you know. Met an old friend of yours from Arkansas. Paul Nierman."

"Nierman?" Gioia seemed to be at a loss. "I'm afraid I don't remember him."

"Well, he remembered you pretty well. Sent you all kinds of messages—you'll have to stop by my office on Monday and get the full strength."

Caudwell opened a door on the right side of the hall and let them into his study. It was an octagonal room carved out of the corner of the building. Windows on two sides looked out on Lake Michigan. Caudwell drew salmon drapes as he talked about the room, why he'd chosen it for his study even though the view kept his mind from his work.

Lotty ignored him and walked over to a small pedestal which stood alone against the panelling on one of the far walls. Max followed her and gazed respectfully at the statue. He had seldom seen so fine a piece outside a museum. About a foot high, it depicted a woman in classical draperies hovering in anguish over the dead body of a soldier lying at her feet. The grief in her beautiful face was so poignant that it reminded you of every sorrow you had ever faced.

"Who is it meant to be?" Max asked curiously.

"Andromache," Lotty said in a strangled voice. "Andromache mourning Hector."

Max stared at Lotty, astonished equally by her emotion and her knowledge of the figure—Lotty was totally uninterested in sculpture.

Caudwell couldn't restrain the smug smile of a collector with a true coup. "Beautiful, isn't it? How do you know the subject?"

"I should know it." Lotty's voice was husky with emotion. "My grandmother had such a Pietro. An alasbaster given her great-grandfather by the Emperor Joseph the Second himself for his help in consolidating imperial ties with Poland."

She swept the statue from its stand, ignoring a gasp from Max, and turned it over. "You can see the traces of the imperial stamp here still. And the chip on Hector's foot which made the Habsburg wish to give the statue away to begin with. How come you have this piece? Where did you find it?"

The small group that had joined Caudwell stood silent near the entrance, shocked at Lotty's outburst. Gioia looked more horrified than any of them, but he found Lotty overwhelming at the best of times—an elephant confronted by a hostile mouse.

"I think you're allowing your emotions to carry you away, Doctor." Caudwell kept his tone light, making Lotty seem more gauche by contrast. "I inherited this piece from my father, who bought it—legitimately—in Europe. Perhaps from your—grandmother, was it? But I suspect you are confused about something you may have seen in a museum as a child."

Deborah gave a high-pitched laugh and called loudly to her brother, "Dad may have stolen it from Uncle Grif but it looks like Grandfather snatched it to begin with anyway."

"Be quiet, Deborah," Caudwell barked sternly.

His daughter paid no attention to him. She laughed again and joined her brother to look at the Imperial Seal on the bottom of the statue.

Lotty brushed them aside. "*I* am confused about the seal of Joseph the Second?" she hissed at Caudwell. "Or about this chip on Hector's foot? You can see the line where some Philistine filled in the missing piece. Some person who thought his touch would add value to Pietro's work. Was that you, *Doctor*? Or your father?"

"Lotty." Max was at her side, gently prising the statue from her shaking hands to restore it to its pedestal. "Lotty, this is not the place or the manner to discuss such things."

Angry tears sparkled in her black eyes. "Are you doubting my word?"

Max shook his head. "I'm not doubting you. But I'm also not supporting you. I'm asking you not to talk about this matter in this way at this gathering."

"But, Max: either this man or his father is a thief!"

Caudwell strolled up to Lotty and pinched her chin. "You're working too hard, Dr. Herschel. You have too many things on your mind these days. I think the board would like to see you take a leave of absence for a few weeks, go some place warm, get yourself relaxed. When you're this tense you're no good to your patients. What do you say, Loewenthal?"

Max didn't say any of the things he wanted to—that Lotty was insufferable and Caudwell intolerable. He believed Lotty, believed that the piece had been her grandmother's. She knew too much about it, for one thing. And for another, a lot of artworks belonging to European Jews were now in museums or private collections around the world. It was only the most god-awful coincidence that the Pietro had ended up with Caudwell's father.

But how dare she raise the matter in the way most likely to alienate everyone present? He couldn't possibly support her in such a situation. And at the same time, Caudwell pinching her chin in that condescending way made him wish he were not chained to a courtesy that would have kept him from knocking the surgeon out—assuming he'd been young enough and tall enough to do it.

"I don't think this is the place or the time to discuss such matters," he reiterated as calmly as he could. "Why don't we all cool down and get back together on Monday, eh?"

Lotty gasped involuntarily, then swept from the room without a backward glance.

Max refused to follow her. He was too angry with her to want to see her again that afternoon. When he got ready to leave the party an hour or so later, after a long conversation with Caudwell that taxed his sophisticated urbanity to the utmost, he heard with relief that Lotty was long gone. The tale of her outburst had of course spread through the gathering at something faster than the speed of sound; he wasn't up to defending her to the buzzing throng, and certainly not to Martha Gildersleeve who demanded an explanation of him in the elevator going down.

He went home for a solitary evening in his house in Evanston. Normally such time brought him pleasure, listening to music in his study, lying on the couch with his shoes off reading history, letting the sounds of the lake wash over him.

Tonight, though, he could get no relief. Fury with Lotty merged into images of horror, the memories of his own disintegrated family, his search through Europe for his mother. He had never found anyone who was quite certain what became of her, although several people told him definitely of his father's suicide. And stamped over these wisps in his brain was the disturbing picture of Caudwell's children, their blond heads leaning backward at identical angles as they gleefully chanted "Grandpa was a thief, Grandpa was a thief" while Caudwell edged his visitors out of the study.

By morning he would somehow have to reconstruct himself enough to face Lotty, to respond to the inevitable flood of calls from outraged trustees. He'd have to figure out a way of soothing Caudwell's vanity, bruised more by his children's behavior than anything Lotty had said. And find a way to keep both important doctors at Beth Israel.

Max rubbed his grey hair. Every week this job brought him less joy and more pain. Maybe it was time to step down, to let the board bring in a young MBA who would turn Beth Israel's finances around. Lotty would resign then and it would be an end to the tension between her and Caudwell.

Max fell asleep on the couch. When he awoke around five, his joints were stiff from cold, his eyes sticky with tears he'd shed unknowingly in his sleep.

But in the morning everything changed. Max found the hospital buzzing when he arrived, not with news of Lotty's outburst, but of Caudwell's not showing up for an early surgery. Work stopped almost completely at noon when his children phoned to say they'd found the surgeon strangled in his own study and the Pietro Andromache missing. And on Tuesday, the police arrested Dr. Charlotte Herschel for Lewis Caudwell's murder.

3

Lotty would not to speak to anyone. She was out on $250,000 bail, the money raised by Max, but she had gone directly to her apartment on Sheffield after two nights in County Jail without stopping to thank him. She would not talk to reporters, she remained silent during all conversations with the police, and she emphatically refused to speak to the private investigator who had been her close friend for many years.

Max, too, stayed behind an impregnable shield of silence. While Lotty went on indefinite leave, turning her practice over to a series of colleagues, Max continued to go to the hospital every day. But he, too, would not speak to reporters: he wouldn't even say "No comment." He talked to the police only after they threatened to lock him up as a material witness, and then every word had to be pried from him as if his mouth were stone and speech Excalibur. For three days V. I. Warshawski left messages which he refused to return.

On Friday when no word came from the detective, when no reporter popped up from a nearby urinal in the men's room to try to trick him into speaking, when no more calls came from the State's Attorney, Max felt a measure of relaxation as he drove home. As soon as the trial was over he would resign, retire to London. If he could only keep going until then, everything would be—not all right, but bearable.

He used the remote release for the garage door and eased his car into the small space. As he got out he realized bitterly he'd been too optimistic in thinking he'd be left in peace. He hadn't seen the woman sitting on the stoop leading from the garage to the kitchen when he drove in, only as she uncoiled herself at his approach.

"I'm glad you're home—I was starting to freeze in here."

"How did you get into the garage, Victoria?"

The detective grinned in a way he usually found engaging. Now it seemed merely predatory. "Trade secret, Max. I know you don't want to see me, but I need to talk to you."

He unlocked the door into the kitchen. "Why not just let yourself into the house if you were cold? If your scruples permit you into the garage why not into the house?"

She bit her lip in momentary discomfort but said lightly, "I couldn't manage my picklocks with my fingers this cold."

The detective followed him into the house. Another tall monster; five-foot-eight, athletic, light on her feet behind him. Maybe American mothers put growth hormones or steroids in their children's cornflakes. He'd have to ask Lotty. His mind winced at the thought.

"I've talked to the police, of course," the light alto continued behind him steadily, oblivious to his studied rudeness as he poured himself a cognac, took his shoes off, found his waiting slippers and padded down the hall to the front door for his mail.

"I understand why they arrested Lotty—Caudwell had been doped with a whole bunch of Xanax and then strangled while he was sleeping it off. And of course she was back at the building Sunday night. She won't say why, but one of the tenants ID'd her as the woman who showed up around ten at the service entrance when he was walking his dog. She won't say if she talked to Caudwell, if he let her in, if he was still alive."

Max tried to ignore her clear voice. When that proved impossible he tried to read a journal which had come in the mail.

"And those kids, they're marvelous, aren't they? Like something out of the *Fabulous Furry Freak Brothers*. They won't talk to me but they gave a long interview to Murray Ryerson over at the *Star*.

"After Caudwell's guests left they went to a flick at the Chestnut Street Station, had a pizza afterwards, then took themselves dancing on Division Street. So they strolled in around two in the morning—confirmed by the doorman—saw the light on in the old man's study. But they were feeling no pain and he kind of over-reacted—their term—if they were buzzed, so they didn't stop in to say good-night. It was only when they got up around noon and went in that they found him."

V. I. had followed Max from the front hallway to the door of his study as she spoke. He stood there irresolutely, not wanting his private place desecrated with her insistent air-hammer speech, and finally went on down the hall to a little-used living room. He sat stiffly on one of the brocade armchairs and looked at her remotely when she perched on the edge of its companion.

"The weak piece in the police story is the statue," V. I. continued. She eyed the Persian rug doubtfully and unzipped her boots, sticking them on the bricks in front of the fireplace.

"Everyone who was at the party agrees that Lotty was beside herself. Even people who weren't in Caudwell's study when she looked at the thing know that she said she would kill him and threatened to have him de-scalpeled or whatever you do to surgeons. But if that's the case, what happened to the statue?"

Max gave a slight shrug to indicate total lack of interest in the topic.

V. I. ploughed on doggedly. "Now some people think she might have given it to a friend or a relation to keep for her until her name is cleared at the trial. And these people think it would be either her Uncle Stefan here in Chicago, her brother Hugo in Montreal, or you. So the Mounties searched Hugo's place and are keeping an eye on his mail. The Chicago cops are doing the same for Stefan. And I presume someone got a warrant and went through here, right?"

Max said nothing, but he felt his heart beating faster. Police in his house, searching his things? But wouldn't they have to get his permission to enter? Or did they. Victoria would know, but he couldn't bring himself to ask. She waited for a few minutes, but when he still wouldn't speak she plunged on. He could see it was becoming an effort for her to talk, but he wouldn't help her.

"But I don't agree with those people. Because I know that Lotty is innocent. And that's why I'm here. Not like a bird of prey, as you think, using your misery for carrion. But to get you to help me. Lotty won't speak to me and if she's that miserable I won't force her to. But surely, Max, you won't sit idly by and let her be railroaded for something she never did."

Max looked away from her. He was surprised to find himself holding the brandy snifter and set it carefully on a table beside him.

"Max!" Her voice was shot with astonishment. "I don't believe this. You actually think she killed Caudwell."

Max flushed a little, but she'd finally stung him into a response. "And you are God who sees all and knows she didn't?"

"I see more than you do," V. I. snapped. "I haven't known Lotty as long as you have but I know when she's telling the truth."

"So you are God." Max bowed in heavy irony. "You see beyond the facts to the innermost souls of men and women."

He expected another outburst from the young woman, but she gazed at him steadily without speaking. It was a look sympathetic enough that Max felt embarrassed by his sarcasm and burst out with what was on his mind.

"What else am I to think? She hasn't said anything, but there's no doubt that she returned to his apartment Sunday night."

It was V. I.'s turn for sarcasm. "With a little vial of Xanax that she somehow induced him to swallow? And then strangled him for good measure? Come on, Max, you know Lotty: honesty follows her around like a cloud. If she'd killed Caudwell she'd say something like, 'Yes, I bashed the little vermin's brains in.' Instead she's not speaking at all?"

Suddenly the detective's eyes widened with incredulity. "Of course. She thinks you killed Caudwell. You're doing the only thing you can to protect her—standing mute. And she's doing the same thing. What an admirable pair of archaic knights."

"No!" Max said sharply. "It's not possible. How could she think such a thing? She carried on so wildly that it was embarrassing to be near her. I didn't want to see her or talk to her. That's why I've felt so terrible. If only I hadn't been so obstinate, if only I'd called her Sunday night. How could she think I would kill someone on her behalf when I was so angry with her?"

"Why else isn't she saying anything to anyone?" Warshawski demanded.

"Shame, maybe," Max offered. "You didn't see her on Sunday. I did. That is why I think she killed him, not because some man saw her return to Caudwell's building."

His brown eyes screwed shut at the memory. "I have seen Lotty in the grip of anger many times, more than is pleasant to remember, really. But never, never have I seen her in this kind of—uncontrolled rage. You could not talk to her. It was impossible."

The detective didn't respond to that. Instead she said, "Tell me about the statue. I heard a couple of garbled versions from people who were at the party, but I haven't found anyone yet who was in the study when Caudwell showed it to you. Was it really her grandmother's, do you think? And how did Caudwell come to have it if it was?"

Max nodded mournfully. "Oh, yes. It was really her family's, I'm convinced of that. She could not have known in advance about the details, the flaw in the foot, the Imperial seal on the bottom. As to how Caudwell got it, I did a little looking into that myself yesterday. His father was with the Army of Occupation in Germany after the war. A surgeon attached to Patton's staff. Men in such positions had endless opportunities to acquire artworks after the war."

V. I. shook her head questioningly.

"You must know something of this, Victoria. Well, maybe not. You know the Nazis helped themselves liberally to artwork belonging to Jews everywhere they occupied Europe. And not just to Jews—they plundered Eastern Europe on a grand scale. The best guess is that they stole sixteen million pieces—statues, paintings, altarpieces, tapestries, rare books. The list is beyond reckoning, really."

The detective gave a little gasp. "Sixteen million! You're joking."

"Not a joke, Victoria. I wish it were so, but it is not. The US Army of Occupation took charge of as many works of art as they found in the occupied territories. In theory they were to find the rightful owners and try to restore them. But in practice few pieces were ever traced and many of them ended up on the black market.

"You only had to say that such-and-such a piece was worth less than $5,000 and you were allowed to buy it. For an officer on Patton's staff the opportunities for fabulous acquisitions would have been endless. Caudwell said he had the statue authenticated, but of course he never bothered to establish its provenance. Anyway, how could he?" Max finished bitterly. "Lotty's family had a deed of gift from the Emperor, but that would have disappeared long since with the dispersal of their possessions."

"And you really think Lotty would have killed a man just to get this statue back? She couldn't have expected to keep it. Not if she'd killed someone to get it, I mean."

"You are so practical, Victoria. You are too analytical, sometimes, to understand why people do what they do. That was not just a statue. True, it is a priceless artwork, but you know Lotty, you know she places no value on such possessions. No, it meant her family to her, her past, her history, everything that the war destroyed forever for her. You must not imagine that because she never discusses such matters that they do not weigh on her."

V. I. flushed at Max's accusation. "You should be glad I'm analytical. It convinces me that Lotty is innocent. And whether you believe it or not I'm going to prove it."

Max lifted his shoulders slightly in a manner wholly European. "We each support Lotty according to our lights. I saw that she met her bail and I will see that she gets expert counsel. I am not convinced that she needs you making her innermost secrets public."

V. I.'s grey eyes turned dark with a sudden flash of temper. "You're dead wrong about Lotty. I'm sure the memory of the war is a pain that can never be cured, but Lotty lives in the present, she works in hope for the future. The past does not obssess and consume her as, perhaps, it does you."

Max said nothing. His wide mouth turned in on itself in a narrow line. The detective laid a contrite hand on his arm.

"I'm sorry, Max. That was below the belt."

He forced the ghost of a smile to his mouth. "Perhaps it's true. Perhaps it's why I love these ancient things so much. I wish I could believe you about Lotty. Ask me what you want to know. If you promise to leave as soon as I've answered and not to bother me again I'll answer your questions."

4

Max put in a dutiful appearance at the Michigan Avenue Presbyterian Church Monday afternoon for Lewis Caudwell's funeral. The surgeon's former wife came, flanked by her children and her husband's brother Griffen. Even after three decades in America Max found himself puzzled sometimes by the natives' behavior: since she and Caudwell were divorced, why had his ex-wife draped herself in black? She was even wearing a veiled hat reminiscent of Queen Victoria.

The children behaved in a moderately subdued fashion, but the girl was wearing a white dress shot with black lightning forks which looked as though it belonged at a disco or a resort. Maybe it was her only dress or her only dress with black in it, Max thought, trying hard to look charitably at the blond Amazon—after all, she had been suddenly and horribly orphaned.

Even though she was a stranger both in the city and the church, Deborah had hired one of the church parlors and managed to find someone to cater coffee and light snacks. Max joined the rest of the congregation there after the service.

He felt absurd as he offered condolences to the divorced widow: did she really miss the dead man so much? She accepted his conventional words with graceful melancholy and leaned slightly against her son and daughter. They hovered near her with what struck Max as a stagey solicitude. Seen next to her daughter, Mrs. Caudwell looked so frail and undernourished that she seemed like a ghost. Or maybe it was just that her children had a hearty vitality that even a funeral couldn't quench.

Caudwell's brother Griffen stayed as close to the widow as the children would permit. The man was totally unlike the hearty sea-dog surgeon. Max thought if he'd met the brothers standing side-by-side he would never have guessed their relationship. He was tall, like his niece and nephew, but without their robustness. Caudwell had had a thick mop of yellow-white hair; Griffen's domed head was covered by thin wisps of grey. He seemed weak and nervous, and lacked Caudwell's outgoing *bonhomie;* no wonder the surgeon had found it easy to decide the disposition of their father's estate in his favor. Max wondered what Griffen had gotten in return.

Mrs. Caudwell's vague disoriented conversation indicated that she was heavily sedated. That, too, seemed strange. A man she hadn't lived with for four years and she was so upset at his death that she could only manage the funeral on drugs? Or maybe it was the shame of coming as the divorced woman, not a true widow? But then why come at all?

To his annoyance, Max found himself wishing he could ask Victoria about it. She would have some cynical explanation—Caudwell's death meant the end of the widow's alimony and she knew she wasn't remembered in the will. Or she was having an affair with Griffen and was afraid she would betray herself without tranquilizers. Although it was hard to imagine the uncertain Griffen as the object of a strong passion.

Since he had told Victoria he didn't want to see her again when she left on Friday it was ridiculous of him to wonder what she was doing, whether she was really uncovering evidence that would clear Lotty. Ever since she had gone he had felt a little flicker of hope in the bottom of his stomach. He kept trying to drown it, but it wouldn't quite go away.

Lotty, of course, had not come to the funeral, but most of the rest of the Beth Israel staff was there, along with the trustees. Arthur Gioia, his giant body filling the small parlor to the bursting point, tried finding a tactful balance between honesty and courtesy with the bereaved family; he made heavy going of it.

A sable-clad Martha Gildersleeve appeared under Gioia's elbow, rather like a furry football he might have tucked away. She made bright, unseemly remarks to the bereaved family about the disposal of Caudwell's artworks.

"Of course, the famous statue is gone now. What a pity. You could have endowed a chair in his honor with the proceeds from that piece alone." She gave a high, meaningless laugh.

Max sneaked a glance at his watch, wondering how long he had to stay before leaving would be rude. His sixth sense, the perfect courtesy which governed his movements, had deserted him, leaving him subject to the gaucheries of ordinary mortals. He never peeked at his watch at functions, and at any prior funeral he would have deftly pried Martha Gildersleeve from her victim. Instead he stood helplessly by while she tortured Mrs. Caudwell and other bystanders alike.

He glanced at his watch again. Only two minutes had passed since his last look. No wonder people kept their eyes on their watches at dull meetings: they couldn't believe the clock could move so slowly.

He inched stealthily toward the door, exchanging empty remarks with the staff members and trustees he passed. Nothing negative was said about Lotty to his face, but the comments cut off at his approach added to his misery.

He was almost at the exit when two newcomers appeared. Most of the group looked at them with indifferent curiosity, but Max suddenly felt an absurd stir of elation. Victoria, looking sane and modern in a navy suit, stood in the doorway, eyebrows raised, scanning the room. At her elbow was a police sergeant Max had met with her a few times. The man was in charge of Caudwell's murder investigation; it was that unpleasant association that kept the name momentarily from his mind.

V. I. finally spotted Max near the door and gave him a discreet sign. He went to her at once.

"I think we may have the goods," she murmured. "Can you get everyone to go? We just want the family, Mrs. Gildersleeve and Gioia."

"*You* may have the goods," the police sergeant growled. "I'm here unofficially and reluctantly."

"But you're here." Warshawski grinned and Max wondered how he ever could have found the look predatory. His own spirits rose enormously at her smile. "You know in your heart of hearts that arresting Lotty was just plain dumb. And now I'm going to make you look real smart. In public, too."

Max felt his suave sophistication return with the rush of elation that an ailing diva must have when she finds her voice again. A touch here, a word there, and the guests disappeared like the host of Senacherib. Meanwhile he solicitously escorted first Martha Gildersleeve, then Mrs. Caudwell to adjacent armchairs, got the brother to fetch coffee for Mrs. Gildersleeve, the daughter and son to look after the widow.

With Gioia he could be a bit more ruthless, telling him to wait because the police had something important to ask him. When the last guest had melted away the immunologist stood nervously at the window rattling his change over and over in his pockets. The jingling suddenly was the only sound in the sound in the room. Gioia reddened and clasped his hands behind his back.

Victoria came into the room beaming like a governess with a delightful treat in store for her charges. She introduced herself to the Caudwells.

"You know Sergeant McGonnigal, I'm sure, after this last week. I'm a private investigator. Since I don't have any legal standing you're not required to answer any questions I have. So I'm not going to ask you any questions. I'm just going to treat you to a travelogue. I wish I had slides but I'll have to imagine the visuals while the audio track moves along."

"A private investigator!" Steve's mouth formed an exaggerated "O;" his eyes widened in amazement. "Just like Bogie."

He was speaking, as usual, to his sister. She gave her high-pitched laugh and said, "We'll win first prize in the 'how I spent my winter vacation' contests. Our daddy was murdered. Zowie. Then his most valuable possession was snatched. Powie. But he'd already stolen it from the Jewish doctor who killed him. Yowie! And then a P I to wrap it all up. Yowie! Zowie! Powie!"

"Deborah, please," Mrs. Caudwell sighed. "I know you're excited, sweetie, but not right now, okay?"

"Your children keep you young, don't they, ma'am?" Victoria said. "How can you ever feel old when your kids stay seven all their lives?"

"Oo, ow, she bites, Debbie, watch out, she bites!" Steve cried.

McGonnigal made an involuntary movement, as though wishing to smack the younger man. "Ms. Warshawski is right: you are under no obligation to answer any of her questions. But you're bright people, all of you: you know I wouldn't be here if the police didn't take her ideas very seriously. So let's have a little quiet and listen to what she's got on her mind."

Victoria seated herself in an armchair near Mrs. Caudwell's. McGonnigal moved to the door and leaned against the jamb. Deborah and Steve whispered and poked each other until one or both of them shrieked. They then made their faces prim and sat with their hands folded on their laps, looking like bright-eyed choirboys.

Griffen hovered near Mrs. Caudwell. "You know you don't have to say anything, Vivian. In fact, I think you should return to your hotel and lie down. The stress of the funeral—then these strangers—."

Mrs. Caudwell's lips curled bravely below the bottom of her veil. "It's all right, Grif; if I managed to survive everything else one more thing isn't going to do me in."

"Great." Victoria accepted a cup of coffee from Max. "Let me just sketch events for you as I saw them last week. Like everyone else in Chicago I read about Dr. Caudwell's murder and saw it on

television. Since I know a number of the people attached to Beth
Israel I may have paid more attention to it than the average viewer,
but I didn't get personally involved until Dr. Herschel's arrest on
Tuesday."

She swallowed some coffee and set the cup on the table next to
her with a small snap. "I have known Dr. Herschel for close to
twenty years. It is inconceivable that she would commit such a
murder, as those who know her well should have realized at once.
I don't fault the police, but others should have known better: she
is hot-tempered. I'm not saying killing is beyond her—I don't think
it's beyond any of us. She might have taken the statue and smashed
Dr. Caudwell's head in in the heat of rage. But it beggars belief to
think she went home, brooded over her injustices, packed a dose of
prescription tranquilizer and headed back to the Gold Coast with
murder in mind."

Max felt his cheeks turn hot at her words. He started to interject
a protest but bit it back.

"Dr. Herschel refused to make a statement all week, but this afternoon, when I got back from my travels, she finally agreed to talk to
me. Sergeant McGonnigal was with me. She doesn't deny that she
returned to Dr. Caudwell's apartment at ten that night—she went
back to apologize for her outburst and to try to plead with him to
return the statue. He didn't answer when the doorman called up
and on impulse she went around to the back of the building, got
in through the service entrance, and waited for some time outside
the apartment door. When he neither answered the doorbell nor
returned home himself she finally went away around eleven o'clock.
The children, of course, were having a night on the town."

"*She* says," Gioia interjected.

"Agreed," V. I. smiled. "I make no bones about being partisan: I
accept her version. The more so because the only reason she didn't
give it a week ago was that she herself was protecting an old friend.
She thought perhaps this friend had bestirred himself on her behalf
and killed Caudwell to avenge deadly insults against her. It was
only when I persuaded her that these suspicions were as unmerited
as—well, as accusations against herself—that she agreed to talk."

Max bit his lip and busied himself with getting more coffee for the
three women. Victoria waited for him to finish before continuing.

"When I finally got a detailed account of what took place at
Caudwell's party, I heard about three people with an axe to grind.
One always has to ask, what axe and how big a grindstone? That's
what I've spent the week-end finding out. You might as well know
that I've been to Little Rock and to Havelock, North Carolina."

Gioia began jingling the coins in his pockets again. Mrs. Caudwell said softly, "Grif, I am feeling a little faint. Perhaps—"

"Home you go, Mom," Steve cried out with alacrity.

"In a few minutes, Mrs. Caudwell," the sergeant said from the doorway. "Get her feet up, Warshawski."

For a moment Max was afraid that Steve or Deborah was going to attack Victoria, but McGonnigal moved over to the widow's chair and the children sat down again. Little drops of sweat dotted Griffen's balding head; Gioia's face had a greenish sheen, foliage on top of his redwood neck.

"The thing that leapt out at me," Victoria continued calmly, as though there had been no interruption, "was Caudwell's remark to Dr. Gioia. The doctor was clearly upset, but people were so focused on Lotty and the statue that they didn't pay any attention to that.

"So I went to Little Rock, Arkansas on Saturday and found the Paul Nierman whose name Caudwell had mentioned to Gioia. Nierman lived in the same fraternity with Gioia when they were undergraduates together twenty-five years ago. And he took Dr. Gioia's anatomy and physiology exams his junior year when Gioia was in danger of academic probation so he could stay on the football team.

"Well, that seemed unpleasant, perhaps disgraceful. But there's no question that Gioia did all his own work in medical school, passed his boards, and so on. So I didn't think the Board would demand a resignation for this youthful indiscretion. The question was whether Gioia thought they would, and if he would have killed to prevent Caudwell making it public."

She paused, and the immunologist blurted out, "No. No. But Caudwell—Caudwell knew I'd opposed his appointment. He and I—our approaches to medicine were very opposite. And as soon as he said Nierman's name to me I knew he'd found out and that he'd torment me with it forever. I—I went back to his place Sunday night to have it out with him. I was more determined that Dr. Herschel and got into his unit through the kitchen entrance; he hadn't locked that.

"I went to his study but he was already dead. I couldn't believe it. It absolutely terrified me. I could see he'd been strangled and—well, it's no secret that I'm strong enough to have done it. I wasn't thinking straight. I just got clean away from there—I think I've been running ever since."

"You!" McGonnigal shouted. "How come we haven't heard about this before?"

"Because you insisted on focusing on Dr. Herschel," V. I. said nastily. "I knew he'd been there because the doorman told me. He would have told you if you'd asked."

"This is terrible," Mrs. Gildersleeve interjected. "I am going to talk to the Board tomorrow and demand the resignations of Dr. Gioia and Dr. Herschel."

"Do," Victoria agreed cordially. "Tell them the reason you got to stay for this was because Murray Ryerson at the *Herald-Star* was doing a little checking for me here in Chicago. He found out that part of the reason you were so jealous of Caudwell's collection is because you're living terribly in debt. I won't humiliate you in public by telling people what your money has gone to, but you've had to sell your husband's art collection and you have a third mortgage on your house. A valuable statue with no documented history would have taken care of everything."

Martha Gildersleeve shrank inside her sable. "You don't know anything about this."

"Well, Murray talked to Pablo and Eduardo. . . . Yes, I won't say anything else. So anyway, Murray checked whether either Gioia or Mrs. Gildersleeve had the statue. They didn't, so—"

"You've been in my house?" Mrs. Gildersleeve shrieked.

V. I. shook her head. "Not me. Murray Ryerson." She looked apologetically at the sergeant. "I knew you'd never get a warrant for me, being as how you'd made an arrest. And you'd never have got it in time, anyway."

She looked at her coffee cup, saw it was empty and put it down again. Max took it from the table and filled it for her a third time. His fingertips were itching with nervous irritation; some of the coffee landed on his trouser leg.

"I talked to Murray Saturday night from Little Rock. When he came up empty here, I headed for North Carolina. To Have-lock, where Griffen and Lewis Caudwell grew up and where Mrs. Caudwell still lives. And I saw the house where Griffen lives, and talked to the doctor who treats Mrs. Caudwell, and—."

"You really are a pooper snooper, aren't you," Steve said.

"Pooper snooper, pooper snooper," Deborah chanted. "Don't get enough thrills of your own so you have to live on other people's shit."

"Yeah, the neighbors talked to me about you two." Victoria looked at them with contemptuous indulgence. "You've been a two-person wolf-pack terrifying most of the people around you since you were three. But the folks in Havelock admired how you always stuck up for your mother. You thought your father got her addicted to tranquilizers and then left her high and dry. So you brought her newest version with you and were all set—you just needed to decide when to give it to him. Dr. Herschel's outburst over the statue played right into your hands. You figured your father had stolen it from your uncle to begin with—why not send it back to him and let Dr. Herschel take the rap?"

"It wasn't like that," Steve said, red spots burning in his cheeks.

"What was it like, son?" McGonnigal had moved next to him.

"Don't talk to them—they're tricking you," Deborah shrieked. "The pooper snooper and her gopher gooper."

"She—Mommy used to love us before Daddy made her take all this shit. Then she went away. We just wanted him to see what it was like. We started putting Xanax in his coffee and stuff, we wanted to see if he'd fuck up during surgery, let his life get ruined. But then he was sleeping there in the study after his stupid-ass party, and we thought we'd just let him sleep through his morning surgery. Sleep forever, you know, it was so easy, we used his own Harvard necktie. I was so fucking sick of hearing 'Early to bed, early to rise' from him. And we sent the statue to Uncle Grif. I suppose the pooper snooper found it there. He can sell it and Mother can be all right again."

"Grandpa stole it from Jews and Daddy stole it from Grif so we thought it worked out perfectly if we stole it from Daddy," Deborah cried. She leaned her blond head next to her brother's and shrieked with laughter.

Max watched the line of Lotty's legs change as she stood on tiptoe to reach a brandy snifter. Short, muscular from years of racing at top speed from one point to the next, maybe they weren't as svelte as the long legs of modern American girls, but he preferred them. He waited until her feet were securely planted before making his announcement.

"The board is bringing in Justin Hardwick for a final interview for chief of staff."

"Max!" She whirled, the Bengal fire sparkling in her eyes. "I know this Hardwick and he is another like Caudwell, looking for cost-cutting and no poverty patients. I won't have it."

"We've got you and Gioia and a dozen others bringing in so many non-paying patients that we're not going to survive another five years at the present rate. I figure it's a balancing act. We need someone who can see that the hospital survives so that you and Art can practice medicine the way you want to. And when he knows what happened to his predecessor he'll be very careful not to stir up our resident tigress."

"Max!" She was hurt and astonished at the same time. "Oh. You're joking, I see. It's not very funny to me, you know."

"My dear, we've got to learn to laugh about it: it's the only way we'll ever be able to forgive ourselves for our terrible misjudgments." He stepped over to put an arm around her. "Now where is this remarkable surprise you promised to show me."

She shot him a look of pure mischief, Lotty on a dare as he first remembered meeting her at fifteen. His hold on her tightened and he followed her to her bedroom. In a glass case in the corner stood the Pietro Andromache.

Max looked at the beautiful, anguished face. I understand your sorrows, she seemed to say to him. I understand your grief for your mother, your family, your history, but it's all right to let go of them, to live in the present and hope for the future. It's not a betrayal.

Tears pricked his eyelids, but he demanded, "How did you get this? I was told the police had it under lock and key until lawyers decided on the disposition of Caudwell's estate."

"Victoria," Lotty said shortly. "I told her the problem and she got it for me. On the condition that I not ask how she did it. And Max, you know—*damned* well that it was not Caudwell's to dispose of."

It was Lotty's. Of course it was. Max wondered briefly how Joseph II had come by it to begin with. For that matter, what had Lotty's great-great grandfather done to earn it from the emperor? Max looked into Lotty's tiger eyes and kept such reflections to himself. Instead he inspected Hector's foot where the filler had been carefully scraped away to reveal the old chip.

THE HUNTED

By Cornell Woolrich

Jack Hollinger, U.S.N., up from Yokohama on a forty-eight, swung his arms wildly and shouted, "Shoo!" He squatted cross-legged on the floor in a little paper-walled compartment of the House of Stolen Hours, situated in one of the more pungent alleys of the Yoshiwara, Tokyo's tenderloin. He glanced down at the array of thimble-sized saki cups before him. All of them were empty, but Hollinger hadn't worked up much of a glow over them. A warm spot that felt no bigger than a dime floated pleasantly but without any particular zest behind the waistband of his white tailormades.

He tipped his cap down over one eye and wigwagged his arms some more.

"Outside," he said. "Party no good. *Joto nai*. Terrible." He made a face.

The geisha ceased her stylized posturing, bowed low and, edging back the paper slide, retreated through it.

The other geisha, who had been kneeling to twang shrill discords on her samisen, let her hands fall from the strings. "Me, too?" she asked. And giggled. Geishas, he had discovered, giggled at nearly everything.

"Yeah, you too. Music very bad. Send the girl back with some more saki. And try to find something bigger I can drink it out of."

The slide eased back into place after her. Hollinger, left alone with his saki cups and the dancer's discarded outer kimono neatly rolled up in the corner—they seemed to wear layers of them—scowled at the paper walls. He lit a cigarette and blew a thick blue smoke-spiral into the air. It hung there heavily as if it were too tired to move against the heavy staleness of the room's atmosphere. Hollinger frowned.

"Twenty-four hours shore leave left, and not a laugh on the horizon," he complained. "What a town! I should've stayed aboard and watched the movie. Damn!"

The racket in the public rooms up front where they had been playing billiards all evening seemed to have grown louder. He could hear excited shouts, jabbering voices that topped the raucous blend of phonograph music, clicking roulette wheels, rattling dice cups, and clinking beer glasses. Somebody had started a fight, he guessed. These Japs lost their heads easy. Still, a good fight might take some of the boredom out of his bones. Maybe he'd just . . . *Knock it off, mate*, he told himself. He'd been warned to stay out of trouble this trip.

They were sure as hell taking a long time with that saki. Annoyed, he picked up a little gong-mallet and began to swing it against the round bronze disc dangling between two cross-pieces. He liked the low, sweet noise. He hit the gong again.

There was the sound of feet hurrying across the wooden flooring now, as though a lot of people were running from one place to another. But it remained a considerable distance away, at the front of the big sprawling establishment.

Something whisked by against the outside of the paper screen walling him in. Like the loose edges of somebody's clothes flirting past. The light was on his side. It was dark out there, so he couldn't see any shadow to go with it. Just that rustling sound and the hasty pat-pat of running feet accompanying it. Whoever it was out there, he was in one hell of a hurry.

The pat-pat went on past until it had nearly died out, then turned, started back again quicker than before. He listened to it the way a man will listen to muffle voices coming from the other side of a thick wall, straining for some snatch of meaning. And then it stopped right opposite where he was. There was an instant's breathless pause.

The slide whirred back suddenly, and a blond girl stumbled in toward him, both arms stretched out in mute appeal for help. He was on his feet by the time she'd covered the short space between them. He got a blurred impression of what she looked like as she threw herself against him, panting and trembling within the circle of his arms.

She was all in. Her blond hair fell over her forehead in a disordered, brilliant splash. Two or three flecks of red spattered the front of her gold evening gown. The gown was cut low, swooping over well-formed breasts, dropping in a wide V. She was barefoot, he noticed, but you always had to leave your shoes at the door when you came in. Her face was attractive, with wide-spaced brown eyes, a full, sensuous mouth. Her breathing was the quick, agonized panting of a hunted thing.

Hollinger looked down into her eyes—and whistled. He could tell by the contraction of the pupils that she'd been drugged. An opium pill, maybe, or a strong dose of morphine. He couldn't be sure whether it hadn't taken effect yet or whether she was just coming out of it.

Sound suddenly broke from her lips, and she sobbed against his shoulder. "Say you're real. Please. Tell me I'm not seeing things." Her fingers pressed hard against his chest. "Hide me. Don't let them get me. I didn't do it, believe me. I *know* I didn't do it."

He had squared off toward the opening in the slide because the tramping of feet was coming this way now and he wanted to be ready.

She pulled at his jumper, wrinkling it with her fingers. "No, don't fight them. Don't you see—that would be the worst thing you could do. It's not just people, it's the police!"

Police? Hollinger swore. He took a quick step over and slammed the slide shut. He kept his hand on it tentatively, as though not sure of his next move. He thought briefly of the warning he'd got before leaving the ship, and the idea of the brig for thirty days didn't exactly appeal to him. But—this girl. An American, and in a jam and . . .

"Why are they after you?" he asked suddenly. "What did you do?"

"They think I . . . I murdered the man I came in with. I found him stabbed to death . . . just now . . . just now in the room with me when . . . when I woke up. I know it sounds silly, I know. They'll never believe it. It's too . . ." She broke off, shaking her head in despair. She opened her hands wide, indicating the crimson flecks on her bodice. "This blood all over me . . . and the dagger in my lap when they came in . . . oh please, please, get me out of this awful place. Please! I know I didn't do it. I *couldn't* have . . ."

He eyed her ruefully.

She seemed to sense what was passing in his mind. She smiled wanly. "No. No, it wasn't anything like that. I'm not . . . the man was my fiancé. We were going to be married tomorrow. We were slumming. We stopped in here . . ."

His indecision didn't last long. There wasn't time. The footsteps were loud in the corridor now. And then they stopped right next door. Hollinger grabbed up the geisha's discarded robe. "Get into this," he said. "Quick. They'll be in here in a second. Maybe we can swing it." He jumped back to where he was sitting originally, collapsed cross-legged on the floor. The girl worked quickly wrapping the robe around her. He pulled her down beside him, snatched off his white cap, poked it inside-out and jammed it down over her telltale golden hair.

He pulled her against him, surprised at the warmth of her, surprised at the way she molded herself to him. "I'm sorry," he said, "but this is our only chance. Keep your face turned away from the door. Don't let that dress show through the kimono."

"Suppose they talk Japanese to me?"

"I'll do all the talking. You just giggle the way all these gals do." His arm tightened around her, and he felt her body tremble involuntarily. "Okay now, this is it. Here they are."

The slide hissed back. Three bandy-legged policemen stood squinting into the lantern light. Behind them was a fourth little man in plainclothes. And in back of him, craning and goggling, was a huddled group of curious customers.

Hollinger put down one of the saki cups, wiped his mouth with his free hand. "Well," he said slowly, "what's the attraction?" He stared at them belligerently. "Go on, beat it! Scram."

"You see gal?" the detective demanded. "You see yellow-hair gal run by here." He smiled deferentially. "'Merican gal, sir. Like you."

"I haven't seen any gal but Mitsu-san here." He stared at the detective. "I don't think I like your barging in here like a damned . . ."

The plain-clothesman smiled at Hollinger and then snapped something in Japanese at the girl. Hollinger's growl turned nasty.

"Listen," he said. "You want to get kicked out of here on your backside?"

The girl, quaking against him, managed to produce a high-pitched giggle. Hollinger warmed inside, pulled her closer to him.

"Fool gal," the detective snapped contemptuously. His mind seemed to grasp the fact that he was facing an American sailor, and he turned quickly, bowing at the waist. "So sorry to disturb, sir. Pliss overlook." The three policemen bowed, too.

"Sayonara," Hollinger said pointedly. "Goodbye."

The screen slammed shut again. Someone barked a curt order, and the trampling feet moved on. He heard them stopping along the corridor, looking into every cubicle.

"Don't move yet," Hollinger said, his mouth close to the girl's ear. Her head nodded, and she kept quiet as they listened to the retreating footsteps. She moved, finally, ready to straighten up. He caught her quickly as the screen began to ease back again.

He brought his lips down against hers fiercely, covering her face with his own, turning her away from the screen.

"I bring saki you order . . ."

The geisha stopped dead in her tracks, glancing in slant-eyed surprise at the pair. "You find another girl?" she asked.

Hollinger lifted his head, his blood racing with the memory of that quick kiss. "Yeah, I found a new girl. I like her better than the other girl. So long." He jabbed his thumb at the screen.

The geisha backed out submissively, still peering curiously at the other girl. The slide closed shut with a final whisper.

"Let's go," Hollinger said. The girl straightened and looked up at him, her fingertips pressed wonderingly to her mouth.

"Come on, we've got to step on it. She looked damned suspicious." He jumped to his feet, took a quick look out, then motioned for the girl to follow. She obeyed, holding herself very stiff and straight.

2

The clamor at the front hadn't abated any. Through a gap in the partitions, he caught a glimpse of two white-garbed interns bringing in a stretcher. There was no out that way.

The girl looked at him in terror. "They've trapped us," she said. "We'll never be able to get through all those people. I'm sorry I ever got you into this."

"We'll try the back way. There must be another exit." He threw his arm around her. "Lean against me, like you were dizzy. We're going out for a breath of air, if they ask us. Take little pigeon-toed steps like you were going to fall flat on your face any minute. Buckle your knees a little, you're too tall. Keep your head down."

They wavered through the maze of paper-walled passageways, sometimes in darkness, sometimes in reflected lantern-light. The place was a labyrinth; all you had to do to make new walls was push a little. The only permanent structure was the four corner-posts and the top-heavy tile roof.

They detoured around one of the slides, sidestepping the police who were returning from the back. A hurrying geisha, carrying refreshments on a tray, brushed against them, apologized.

"We'll make it," he assured her.

The stampeding suddenly started behind them again. Evidently the first geisha had voiced her suspicions. They began to move faster. The wavering gait became a run, the run became tearing headlong flight. He slashed one more of the never-ending screens back into its socket, and they were looking out on a rear garden.

Apple-green and vermillion lanterns bobbed in the breeze, a little humped-back bridge crossing a midget brook; dwarf fir-trees made showy splashes of deeper darkness. It all looked unreal and very pretty—except for the policeman standing there. He turned to face them. They'd come to a dead stop, and they watched him swing a short, wicked-looking little club on a leather strap.

Hollinger whispered, "I'll handle him. Don't wait, just keep going across that bridge. There must be a way of getting through to the next street over."

The cop said something that sounded like, "*Boydao, boydao!*" and motioned them back with his club.

"Take it!" Hollinger snapped at the girl. He gave her a shove that sent her up one side of the sharply-tilted bridge and down the other. She almost tumbled off into the water.

Hollinger threw himself on the policeman, and they struggled on the fine sand that surfaced the garden path. Hollinger held him in an awkward head lock, his left hand clamped across the Jap's mouth to keep him quiet. His right fist pounded against the bristle-hair skull while the policeman's club lashed out with dull, brutal thuds. The cop bit Hollinger's muffling hand. Hollinger threw his head back, opened his mouth as if to scream, but held the cry in his throat until it died.

The girl stood on the other side of the bridge, her hand held to her lips once more, her body bent forward in the darkness. Hollinger had no time to waste. Lanterns were wavering nearer in the interior of the house, filtering through the paper like blurred, interlocked moons.

He sucked in a deep breath and lifted the squirming cop off the ground, tossing him like a sack into the stream. The bulge of his chest and the sudden strain of his back and shoulder muscles split his tight jumper from throat to waist. There was a petal-shaped splash and the little brown man swiveled there in the sanded hollow, half-stunned by the impact, water coursing shallowly across his abdomen.

Hollinger vaulted across to the girl with a single stretch of his long legs, caught at her as he went by, and pulled her after him. "I told you not to wait. I told you . . ." He clamped his jaws shut, glared at her fiercely. "Come on, let's go."

They found the mouth of an alley giving onto the rear of the garden behind a clump of dwarf firs that were streaked single file along its narrow black length between the walls. Hollinger pushed the hobbling girl in front of him. They came out at the other end into the fuzzy like brightness of one of the Yoshiwara streets.

It was strangely deserted; seemed so, at least, until Hollinger remembered that most of the usual crowd must have been drawn around to the front of the building. They ran down the alley to the end of the block, then turned a corner into another that was even more dismal. But this one was more normally crowded. Heads turned after them, kimonoed passers-by stopped to stare. A zigzagging bicycle rider tried to get out of their way, ran into them instead and was toppled over. Hollinger's eyes scanned the crowd, looking for the yellow and black arm bands of the Shore Patrol.

"If the alarm spreads before we can get out of this part of town, we're sunk," he said. "They'll gang up on us. Come on, faster."

"I can't," she whimpered. "It's . . . it's this pavement. The ground's cutting my feet to pieces." He was without shoes, too, but his soles were calloused from deck-scrubbing. He was two arms' length in front of her, hauling her after him. Betraying flashes of gold peeped out from the parachuting kimono, blazing a trail of identification behind them.

She stumbled and bit her lips to keep from crying out. He grabbed her up in both arms, plunging onward with her. The extra weight hardly slowed him at all. He could smell the scent of her hair in his nostrils, deep and musky. His arms tightened around her, and he kept running, faster, faster. A paper streamer hanging downward across the lane got snared in some way by their passage, ripped off its wire and flared out behind his neck like a long loose muffler. The shopkeeper whose stall it had advertised came out sputtering, both arms raised high in denunciation.

"Look," Hollinger muttered, winded. A taxi had just dropped a couple of fares in front of a dance-hall ahead. Hollinger hailed it with a hoarse shout. Its gears grinded and it came slowly backward. Hollinger let the girl fall on the seat, ran along beside the cab for a minute as the driver went forward again, and then hopped in after her.

"Drive like blazes," he snapped. "Ginza . . . anywhere at all . . . only get us out of here. Fast, savvy? Fast!"

"I go like wind," the driver agreed cheerfully. He stepped on the gas, his head bent forward under its bright golf cap.

The girl was all in. The sudden release of all her pent-up tension finished the last of her control. She crumbled against his chest, her head buried in his shoulder, her fingers clutching his arm tightly. He didn't speak to her. He rested his head against the cushions, feeling the slow trembling of her body against his. He pulled in a long shuddering breath, slowly, tasting it like a sip of icy wine. He looked at the teeth-gashes on his hand and felt real pain for the first time.

A sudden diminution of the light around them—a change to the more dignified pearly glow of solitary street lights—marked the end of the Yoshiwara.

At the end of a long five minutes, the girl pulled herself up. "I don't know how to thank you," she said weakly. "I mean . . ." She smiled wearily. ". . . there just aren't any words."

He didn't know what to say, so he kept quiet.

Her face became suddenly earnest. She brought it close to his, her eyes intensely serious. "I didn't do it! Why, I was going to marry Bob. I came here to . . ." She stopped suddenly, confused.

He looked at her sharply, her words somehow leaving an empty vacuum inside him. He started to reach for her hand, then drew back.

They were coming into the long broad reaches of Ginza now, Tokyo's Broadway. The lights brightened again, glaring against the flattened, charred remains of precision bombing. The familiar smell of mixed wood smoke and dried fish seeped into the open cab. And slowly, the ruins gave way to the city. This was downtown, the show-part of town, modern, conventional, safe. Safe for some people.

"I suppose . . . I should give myself up," she said. "The more I run, the more they'll think I did it. I . . . I lost my head back there . . . the knife and the blood, and that horrible manager yelling at me."

"Suppose you tell me all about it," he urged gently. "I guess we're in this together now." He paused. "You say you didn't do it. All right, that's good enough for me. I don't know who you are, but . . ."

"Brainard," she said. "Evelyn Brainard. I'm from San Francisco."

He said, "Please to meet you, Miss Brainard," and after what had gone on in the past half-hour, he expected her to smile. She didn't. He took her hand in his own and said, "I'm due back on shipboard tomorrow noon, and we're shoving off for Pearl right after that. If we're going to do anything, we've got to do it fast."

She nodded, her hair reflecting the bright lights outside the cab. They had already reached the lower end of the Ginza, were heading slowly back again.

"We've got to get you off the streets first. Every good cop in the city is probably looking for you by this time. Know anyone here you can hole up with?"

"Not a soul. Bob Mallory was the only one. I just got off the *Empress* yesterday afternoon. I've a room at the Imperial . . ."

"You can't go back there," he said. "If they're not there already, they'll be there damned soon, you can count on that. What about this Mallory . . . where did he hang out?"

"I don't know, he wouldn't tell me. He gave me an evasive answer when I asked him. Somehow I got the idea he didn't want me to find out."

"I thought you were engaged to him."

"I was, but . . ."

"Well, it wouldn't be much help, even if you did know. They'd probably check there as soon as they finished with your own place." They drove on in silence for a minute. Finally, he said, "Look, don't get offended, but . . . I've had a room since yesterday. It's not much of a place, and my landlord is a crazy bugger, but it would be safe and you could stay there while I . . ."

A small smile tilted the corners of her mouth. "Thanks," she said.

He gave the driver the address. It was a Western-style building in one of the downtown reaches of the city, little better than a shack really—clapboard under a corrugated tin roof. But it had wooden doors and walls. And windows with shades on them.

He said, "Wait in the cab a minute. I'll get the landlord out of the way. Just as well if no one sees you going up."

After he'd gone in, she caught sight of the driver slyly watching her in his rear-view mirror. She quickly lowered her head, but with the terrifying feeling that he'd already seen she was white, even in the dimness of the cab's interior. Hollinger came back and helped her out. "Hurry up. I sent him out to the back on a stall."

Going up the unpainted wooden stairs, she whispered, "The driver. He saw I wasn't Japanese. He may remember later, if he hears . . ."

He made a move to turn and go down again. The sound of the taxi driving off outside reached them, and it was too late to do anything about it.

"We'll have to take a chance," he said.

There was nothing Japanese about the room upstairs. Just a typical cheap lodging house room, universal in appearance. Flaked white-painted iron bedstead, wooden dresser.

She sat on the edge of the bed, wearily pulled off the white cap. Her hair tumbled down to her shoulders in a golden cascade, framing her face. She looked down at her blood-stained gown, and a shiver of revulsion worked over her body.

"Would you like to change. I mean . . ."

She stared at him with wide, frank eyes. "I'd like to. Is there anything? I'd . . . like to."

He yanked a small overnight bag from the top of the dresser, pulled out a clean white jumper and a pair of trousers.

"This is all I've got," he said.

"It'll do fine. I just want to get out of this." She indicated the blood-stained gown again. Then she turned her head, her eyes searching the walls.

"There's just this room," he said softly. "Maybe if I stepped outside."

"No. No," she said quickly. "Don't leave me. Please."

She slipped out of the kimono, turning her back to him. He watched while she lowered one thin strap of her gown. The other strap slid off easily as he watched.

"Tell me all about it," he said. "The whole thing from the beginning. Talk low."

3

"I hadn't seen him in three years. We were engaged before he left the States. He came out here with the Occupation forces in the beginning. Then he stayed on when his hitch was up. I was to come out after him. But he never sent for me."

She sighed deeply, unrolled the jumper and trousers and put them on the bed. She had lowered both straps of the gown, and nothing held it up now but the rich curve of her breasts.

"He kept putting me off. Finally I got tired of waiting. I paid my own fare, came out without letting him know. I was getting worried. All this Korean business, and not hearing from him . . . I was getting worried. I didn't tell him I was arriving until the night before last. I sent him a cable from the ship. He met me yesterday at Yokohama."

She bent over, pulling the long gown up over her thighs, past the swell of her breasts, over her head. Her hair tumbled down over her outstretched arms. He knew he should turn away, but he sat there watching her. She didn't seem embarrassed. She was engrossed in her story, and she moved swiftly, dropping the gown on the floor, dropping the blood-soiled garment like a loathsome thing.

"He'd changed. He wasn't glad to see me, I could tell that right away. He was afraid of something. Even down there on the pier, while he was helping me to pass through the customs inspection, he kept glancing nervously at the crowd around us, as if he were being watched or something."

"When we got here, it was even worse. He didn't seem to want to tell me where he lived. He wouldn't talk about himself at all. I'd been sending my letters to the company office—he'd taken a job here, you see—and . . . I just couldn't make head or tail of it. This morning when I woke up, there was a piece of white goods tied around the knob of my door—like a long streamer or scarf. When I happened to mention it to him later on, he turned the ghastliest white. But I couldn't make him talk about that, either."

Hollinger nodded, watching the girl in her underwear now, watching the sharp cones of her bra, the thin material that covered her wide hips. "White's the color of mourning in this country. It's the same as crepe back home."

"I know that now. I'll spare you all the little details. My love for him curled up, withered. I could feel that happening. Do you know what I mean? You can feel it when something like that happens."

"Yes, I know."

The girl pulled the jumper over her head. It came down to her thighs, leaving her long, curved legs exposed. The jumper was large on her, the V in the neck coming down below the line of the bra. She looked at the fit and suppressed a smile.

"Anyway," she said, "we were sitting in a restaurant tonight and I happened to say, 'Bob, this is dull. Can't you take me to one of the more exciting places?' He didn't seem to want to do that either. As though he were afraid to stray very far off the beaten path."

"Funny," he said.

"We argued about it a little. The girl who was waiting on us must have heard. Because not long after that he was called to the phone and as soon as his back was turned, this waitress came up to me. She said if I wanted to see the real sights, I ought to get him to take me to the Yoshi. The House of the Stolen Hours, she said, was a very nice place. Then Bob came back. And although he'd looked scared when he went to the phone, he was all right now. He said there'd been a mistake . . . no call for him at all.

"It never occurred to me that there could be anything pre-arranged, sinister, about this sequence of events—that it might be a trick to get us in an out-of-the-way place where we couldn't easily get help.

"Like a fool, I didn't tell Bob where I'd found out about the Yoshiwara. I let him think it was my own idea. I had a hard time talking him into taking me there, but finally he gave in."

She pulled on the trousers, held them out from her waist and looked down in disdain. She took the sash from the kimono, then, doubled the extra fold of material, and knotted it around the waist in a belt. "There," she said. "Let's hope no Commodore sees me."

"What happened next?" he asked.

"Well, we were shown into one of the little rooms and told just where to sit, to enjoy the entertainment."

"There's something right there," he interrupted. "What difference would it have been *where* you sat, when you just unroll mats on the floor? Who told you where to sit?"

"The manager, I guess it was. Yes, he spread out one mat for me, pointed, and I sat down. Then he spread the one for Bob *opposite* mine instead of alongside it. They spread the tea things between us. Mine tasted bitter, but I thought maybe that was on account of drinking it without cream or sugar."

"A mickey," he said. "Plain and simple."

"There was a lantern shining in my face, I remember. My eyes felt small, like pinheads, and the lantern light dazzled them. I began to get terribly sleepy. I asked Bob to change places with me, so I'd have my back to the light. He sat where I'd been, and I moved over to his place."

Hollinger took out a cigarette, offered her one, lighting it for her. She drew in the smoke quickly, let it out in a tall, grey plume.

"A few minutes later it happened. Even I saw a gleam of light, shining through the screen from the next compartment behind Bob's back—as though someone had opened a slide and gone in there. A big looming shadow hovered over him and then it vanished, and the screen went blank. I was feeling dizzy, and I couldn't be sure if I'd really seen it or not."

She squeezed out the cigarette, stepped on it nervously.

"Bob never made a sound. I thought he was just bending over to pick up his cup at first, but he didn't straighten up again. He . . . he didn't . . ." She threw herself into his arms, the uniform smelling clean and pressed, the scent of her hair mingling with it. "It was awful. He just kept going lower and lower. Then the cup smashed under his chin and he just stayed that way. Just bent in half like that. And then I could see the ivory knob sticking out between his shoulder blades, like a horrible little handle to lift him by. And red ribbons swirling out all around it, ribbons that *ran!*"

She caught a sob in her throat, held him tighter.

"The last thing I saw was a slit, a two or three-inch gash in the paper screen behind him. My own head got too heavy to hold up and I just fell over sideways on the floor and passed out."

She pushed herself away from him and began pacing the floor.

"But I *know*, I know I was sitting on the opposite side of the room from him. I *know* I didn't touch him!"

"All right," he said. "All right."

"When I opened my eyes, I was still there in that horrible place, in the flickering lantern light, and he was dead there opposite me, so I knew I hadn't dreamed it. The dream was from then on, until I found you. A nightmare. The slide was just closing, as though someone had been in there with me. I struggled up on one elbow. There was a weight on my hands, and I looked down to see what it was, and there was the knife. It was resting flat across the palm of one hand, the fingers of the other hand folded tight around the ivory hilt. There was blood on the front of my dress, as if the knife had been wiped on it."

"That's the symbol of transferring the guilt of the crime to you," he told her.

"Then the slide was shoved back, almost as if they'd been timing me, waiting for me to come to before breaking in and confronting me. The manager came in alone first. He flew into a fury, yelling at me, shrieking at me. I couldn't think of anything to say. He pulled me up by one arm and kept bellowing into my face, You kill! You kill in my house! You make me big disgrace!"

She sat down on the edge of the bed, almost spent, her face showing tired lines.

"I tried to tell him that Bob had been stabbed through the paper screen from the next compartment, but when I pointed to where the gash had been, it was gone. The paper was perfectly whole. He kept yelling, and then he stamped out to call the police. That was when I left. I got up and ran. I ran the other way, toward the back. I couldn't find my way out, but I remembered hearing your voice when you came in. You . . . you said, 'Here's looking at you, kids,' and I knew you were an American, and I knew I had to find you because that was the only thing that . . . that I could think of."

4

She sighed deeply. "That's the story, sailor. All of it. And here I am in your clothes. And here you are."

He stood up abruptly. "Here you are, maybe, but I'm on my way back there."

She put one hand on his arm, and he looked at the way she filled out his jumper, shaking his head in mild surprise. "They know you helped me get away," she said. "They must be looking for you, too, by this time. If I let you go back there again . . ."

"Sure they're looking for me. But that's the one place they *won't* be looking. Something sure as hell happened to that slashed paper, and I want to find out what. You say you saw a slit in the paper. When you came to, it was gone. Well, somebody sure as hell took it. Maybe the manager is in on it. I don't see how they could do that in his house without his knowing it."

He began pacing the room. "I've got to locate the exact compartment you were in, and that may not be easy."

"Wait," she said, "I think I can help you. It's not much to go on
but . . . those lanterns in each cubicle . . . did you notice that they
all have a character heavily inked on them?"

"In Japanese," he said. "Laundry tickets."

"I know, I know. But the one in our booth was finished in a
hurry or something. The artist probably inked his brush too heavily.
Anyway, a single drop of ink came to a head at the bottom of the
character, with the slope of the lantern. It ran down a little way, left
a blurred track ending in a dark blob. It was staring me in the face
in the beginning, before I changed places, that's how I know. Here,
Look . . ."

She took a charred match stick, began drawing on the dresser-top.
"It's very easy to remember. Two seagulls with bent wings, one
above the other. Under them, a simple pot-hook. Then this blot
of dried ink hanging down from that like a pendulum. Look for
that, and you'll have the cubicle we were in. I don't think they
bothered to remove the lantern. They probably wouldn't expect a
foreigner to notice a little thing like that."

"Neither would I," he said approvingly. He picked up a razor
blade from the edge of the washstand, carefully sheathed it in a
fragment of newspaper.

"What's that for?"

"To let myself in with. In some way, paper houses are pretty
handy. Lock yourself in here behind me, just to be on the safe side.
I'll let you know when I get back. Don't open up for anybody else."

She moved after him to the door. "You'll never make it in that
uniform. It's all torn. I shouldn't have taken your clothes. You need
them."

"I've dodged S.P.'s before," he said. "Try to get some sleep, and
get that dope out of your system."

He turned to go, and she caught at his arm.

"Be careful," she said. "Please be careful." She lifted her lips to his,
kissing him gently. "Come back."

"You couldn't keep me away," he said. "Remember what I said
about opening doors."

The House of the Stolen Hours seemed deserted.

Hollinger couldn't be sure whether or not the manager slept here
after hours or not. The geishas and other employees probably didn't.
He took out the razor blade and made a neat hair-line gash down
alongside the frame, then another close to the ground, making an L
around the lower corner. He lifted it up like a tent-flap and ducked

through. It crackled a little, fell stiffly into place again. He could hear bottle cricket chirping and clacking rhythmically somewhere ahead. He knew that crickets were used as watchdogs in Japan, stopping their chirping whenever a stranger enters a house. He winced as they broke off their song after the first tentative steps he took. He'd have to be careful now, damned careful.

He worked his way forward, feeling his way along the cool slippery wooden flooring with a prehensile toe-and-heel grip, shuffling the multiple deck of screen aside with a little upward hitch that kept them from clicking in their grooves. He waited until he was nearly midway through the house, as far as he could judge, before he lighted his first match. He guarded it carefully with the hollow of his hand, reduced the light to a pink glow. The place seemed deserted.

He tried six of the cubicles before he found the right one. There it was. Traces of Mallory's blood still showed black on the floor. The smeared ink-track on the lantern was just a confirmation. He lit the wick and the lantern bloomed out orange at him, like a newly risen sun.

The location of the blood smears told him which of the four sides to examine. The screen in place at the moment was, as the girl had said, intact. He ran his fingers questioningly over the frame, to see if it felt sticky or damp with newly-applied paste. It was dry and gave no signs of having been recently inserted. He could see now that the inserts weren't glued into the frame at all. They were caught between the lips of a long, continuous split in the bamboo and held fast by the pressure of the two wood halves closing over them again, bolstered here and there by a wooden nail or peg. They could not be put in in a hurry.

But they *could* be taken out in a hurry!

He shoved it all the way back flush with the two lateral screens, and squinted into the socket. There were *two* frame edges visible, not just one. He caught at the second one, and it slid out empty, bare of paper. But there were telltale little strips and slivers of white all up and down it where the paper had been hastily slashed away.

He stood then and nodded grimly. Probably the frame itself would be unslung tomorrow and sent out to have a new filler put in. Or destroyed. There hadn't been the opportunity tonight, with police buzzing all over the place. He didn't think, now, that the rest of the staff had been in on it—just the manager and the murderer.

The fact that the girl's last minute change of position hadn't been revealed to them in time showed that. The geishas waiting on the couple would have tipped them off if they had been accessories. They hadn't, and Mallory had been killed by mistake. But she'd only arrived the day before—why did they want her out of the way? And why not him?

Hollinger thought about it.

There was no audible warning. But his shifting of the slide had exposed the compartment beyond. And the lantern light, reaching wanly to the far screen threw up a faint gray blur that overlapped his own shadow. The other shadow owned an upraised arm that ended in a sharp downward-projected point.

The dagger came down abruptly. There was no sound. Only the dagger slicing downward in a glittering arc. He threw himself flat on the floor, rolling as he hit. His torn jumper flapped out under him and the dagger pierced the cloth, pinning it to the floor. The other man threw himself on Hollinger, the full weight of his body crushing Hollinger's chest to the floor.

They both had sense enough not to try for the knife. It was jammed in the floor halfway up to the hilt.

Hollinger was flat on his stomach, and the man felt like the sacred mountain of Fujiyama on top of him. He was pinned down by eight inches of steel through a jumper he couldn't work himself out of. He nearly broke his back trying to rear up high enough to swing his shoulders around and get his arms into play.

Clutching, apelike hands found his throat, closed in, tightened there. He lashed out with the back of his hand, felt the blows glance harmlessly off a satiny jawline. He gave that up as a bad bet, swung his legs up instead. Then he looped them around the big Jap's neck in a tight scissors lock and began to squeeze.

The hands left his throat, and a strangled cry escaped the Jap's lips as he reached for Hollinger's legs. Hollinger let him pry them off—the hold had been a temporary measure anyway, too passive to get any real results. Both men rolled over on the floor, breaking; the Jap scrambled to his feet, blowing like a fish on land.

Hollinger straightened, came up at him swinging. His right went wide, streaked upward into empty air. The Jap cupped a slapping hand to his elbow, gripped the thumb of that hand at the same time. Hollinger felt himself rising from the floor, turning as he vaulted through the empty frame. His back came down with a brutal thud that rattled his teeth. He squirmed on the floor, half-paralyzed. The Jap whirled to face him, stamped both feet in a new position, crouched again.

Jiu-jitsu. Great.

Hollinger watched the Jap circling in like a preying wolf. He stumbled to his feet, weaved around warily, every muscle in his body protesting.

The big hands shot out at him again, open. Dizzily, he lurched to one side, still stunned. The Jap wasn't quick enough in shifting positions. His legs and shoulders swung, exposing his flank for a second. Through a dizzy haze, Hollinger saw the opening and sent a quick short jab to the Jap's ear. The blow rocked him for an instant, held him long enough for Hollinger to wind up a real one. He lashed out with his fist, catching the Jap right between the eyes. He went over like a ninepin, and Hollinger stood swaying, his bleary eyes watchful.

There was a board-like stiffness about the Jap's middle that caught Hollinger's eye. It had cost the Jap the fight, whatever it was. A wedge of white showed in the kimono opening, below the rise and fall of his huge chest. Underclothing maybe. Whatever it was, it had kept the Jap from pivoting out of range of Hollinger's finishing blow.

Hollinger bent over him, pulled the garment open. Paper. Layer after layer of stiff, board-like paper, rolled around him like a plaster cast extending from ribs to thighs. A narrow sash held it in place.

Hollinger rolled the Jap out of his queer cocoon by pushing him across the floor, like a man laying a carpet. The Jap had evidently slashed the whole square out of the screen first, then quickly slit that into two strips, narrow enough to wind around himself. The knife-gash itself showed up in the second section as it peeled free, the edges driven inward by the knife. Any cop worth his salt would be able to figure out what had really happened with this to go by.

He shoved it out of the way. Then he straddled the still stunned Jap and gripped him by the throat. "Who was it?" he asked in a low voice. "Who was in there? Who killed the American?"

"No," was the only answer he could get. "No. No."

He slammed the back of his hand into the Jap's face. "Open up, damnit."

"No see. Man go in, come out again. I no know."

He hit the Jap again, harder this time. The big man's eyes went wide with fright.

"Denguchi do," he blurted. "Denguchi do! I no do, he do. He get money for to do, he hired for to do . . ."

"Who hired him?"

The yellow man's eyes glazed.

"Who hired him? Goddamnit, who hired him?"

The eyes closed. The head rolled over heavily. Hollinger swore, got up quickly and then rolled the paper into a long staff. He tucked it under his arm, took it out with him. Nothing more could be done there tonight.

The landlord was snoring in his lighted wall-niche when Hollinger got downtown again. He chased up the stairs past him, shook the knob of the door triumphantly.

"Evelyn, open up. It's me. Open up and listen to the good news."

There wasn't a sound from within.

5

He figured she was in a pretty deep sleep after what she'd been through earlier. He began to rap on the door gently.

"Evelyn," he called, "it's me. Let me in."

A puzzled frown crossed his brow. He knocked on the door a little louder. He crouched down, then, looked through the keyhole. The light was still on inside, and he could make out the pear-shape of the key on the inside of the door.

Alarmed now, he threw his shoulder against the door. The cheap lock tore off on the fourth onslaught. The landlord appeared but was no help at all.

The girl was gone.

Hollinger's eyes swept the room. A corner of the bedding was trailing off onto the floor. One of the cheap net curtains inside the window was torn partly off its rod, as though somebody had clutched at it despairingly. The window was open all the way. There was a tin extension roof just below it, sloping down to the alley below.

It hadn't been the police. They would have come in by the door and left the same way. He thought about the name the Jap had blurted. Denguchi. That was all he had to go on.

Where would they take her? What could they possibly want with her? Just to hold her as hostage, shut her up about the first murder? He didn't think so. It was *she* they'd meant to get the first time, and not the man. Now they'd come back to correct the mistake. Then why hadn't they killed her right here? Why had they gone to the trouble of taking her with them?

He had a sudden hunch, remembering Evelyn's remark in the taxi: "*He didn't seem to want me to know where he lived.*"

He grabbed the landlord by the shoulder. "How do you find an address in a hurry, an address you don't know?"

"You ask inflammation-lady at telephone exchange . . ."

He grinned. Not so different from home after all. He started shoving the landlord downstairs ahead of him. "Do it for me. I can't speak the lingo. The name's Robert Mallory—and tell her to steer the police over there fast!"

The landlord came out in a moment and threw a "Twenty-five" and a tongue-twisting street name at him.

"Take care of that piece of paper upstairs for me," he shouted. He ran out onto the streets saying the street name over to himself out loud. If he dropped a syllable, Evelyn . . . He left the thought unfinished. He caught a prowling cab and kept repeating the name over and over, even after he was in it.

"I hear," the driver sighed finally. "I catch."

Mallory had done himself well. His place turned out to be a little bungalow on one of the better-class residential streets.

He didn't waste time on the front door. He hooded the tattered remains of his jumper over his head for padding, bucked one of the ground floor window panes head on. It shattered and he climbed in, nicking his hands a little. A scream sounded through the house.

He ran down the hallway toward a light at the back. As the room swung into his vision, he saw Evelyn, writhing, clutching at her throat. She was bent backward, her breasts thrust against the fabric of the jumper he'd loaned her, a pair of strong brown hands tugging at the scarf wrapped around her throat.

Hollinger caught a faint movement behind the stirring bead curtains bunched over to one side of the entryway. The girl's eyes fled to his in panic, indicating the curtain.

He caught up a slim teak wood stand quickly, rammed it head on into the curtain at stomach level. A knife slashed out at him. It sliced the air with a menacing whick. He reached out at the brown fist holding it, yanked it close to him, vising it against his chest. Then he shot a punch out about two feet above it.

There was a cry of agony and the man reeled out into the open, a short little barrel in a candy-striped blazer. Hollinger twisted the knife out of his hand, exerting all the pressure his shoulder muscles could put to bear. He brought his fist back, sent it forward in a short, jabbing motion that knocked the man out cold.

Something white streaked by, and when Hollinger looked over at Evelyn, she was alone, coughing, struggling to unwind the sash around her throat. She staggered forward, fell into his arms with a jerky backward hitch of her elbows, like something working on strings.

A door banged closed somewhere upstairs.

The girl had collapsed into a chair. He found a water tap in a Western-style kitchen adjoining the room, filled the hollows of his hands, came back and wet her throat with it. He did that three or four times until she was breathing normally again.

"That's the girl," he said. "You're a tough one to kill."

She managed a wan smile. "It would have been all over before you got here if she hadn't wanted to . . . to get it out of her system . . . to rub it in that he'd been hers, not mine."

"Who was she?"

Her gaze dropped before his. "His wife," she said slowly. "Legally married to him by the Shinto rites. Poor thing. She . . ."

He shook his head at her. "A nice guy, your boyfriend," he said. He turned. "She's still in here someplace. I heard her go upstairs."

She reached out, caught him by the arm. "No," she said, a peculiar look on her face. "I don't think so. She . . . loved him, you see."

He didn't at all. A whiff of sandal-wood incense crept down the stairs, floated in to them, as if to punctuate her cryptic remark.

There was a loud banging at the front door. They listened while the door gave, and they they heard the clack-clack of wooden shoes against the flooring. The police-watch trooped in, flourishing clubs, hemming them in against the wall.

"*Now* you get here," Hollinger said.

"Hai!" the little detective said, pointing to the professional hatchet man on the floor. Two of the cops began whacking him with their clubs. They turned him over on his face, lashed his hands behind him, and then dragged him out by the feet, Oriental style.

The police had, evidently, been playing steeplechase, picking up the traces Hollinger had been leaving all night long. They had battered the Stolen Hours proprietor, the furled wallpaper, the landlord, and the first taxi driver, the one who must have gone back and betrayed Evelyn's hiding place to Denguchi.

The detective, puffing out his chest like a pouter pigeon, said to Evelyn, "So you do not kill the American. Why you not stay and say so, pliss? You put us to great trouble."

They found her upstairs, as Hollinger had said, behind the locked door, kneeling in death on a satin prayer pillow before a framed photograph of the man Evelyn Brainard had come out to marry. A pitch of incense sent a thread of smoke curling up before it. Her god.

She had toppled forward, as the ritual prescribed, to show she was not afraid of meeting death. Her hands were tucked under her, firmly clasping the hara-kiri knife that had torn her abdomen apart.

She looked pathetic and lovely and small—incapable almost of the act of violence that had been necessary in order to die.

Hollinger looked at the weak mouth and chin on Mallory's photograph inside the frame. Too cowardly to hurt either one, he had hurt both, one unto death. A pair of lovebirds were twittering a scarlet bamboo cage. A bottle of charcoal ink, a writing brush, a long strip of hastily traced characters lay behind her on the floor.

The detective picked it up, began to read.

"I, Yugiri-san, Mist of the Evening, most unworthy of wives, go now to keep my husband's house in the sky, having unwittingly twice failed to carry out my honored husband's wish . . ."

Evelyn had stayed downstairs, and Hollinger was glad now.

"Don't tell her," he said. "She doesn't have to know. Let her go on thinking the woman was the one who tried to get rid of her, through jealousy. Don't tell her the man she came out here to marry hired a murderer to get her out of his way because he didn't have the guts to tell her to her face. It's tough enough as it is. Don't tell her."

It was getting light in Tokyo when they left the police station, walking slowly side by sides. They held hands, walking idly, like two lovers anywhere, anytime.

"I guess," she said ruefully, squeezing his hand a little, "I pretty well messed up your shore leave."

He grinned playfully. "I didn't have anything to do, anyway." He snapped his fingers. "Which reminds me. Keep the night of November third open, will you?"

"November third! But that's six months away."

"I know. But that's when we dock in Frisco Bay."

"I will," she said. "I'll keep November third open. There isn't any night I wouldn't keep for you—ever."

Hollinger looked down at her, at the way her body molded the lines of the dress the police had secured for her. Her eyes were bright, and they met his with unveiled honesty.

"There's a little time yet before I make the ship," he said.

She didn't answer. She gripped his hand more tightly, and they walked slowly down the street, bright now in the morning's sunshine.

PROFESSIONAL MAN

by David Goodis

A t five past five, the elevator operated by Freddy Lamb came
to a stop on the street floor. Freddy smiled courteously
to the departing passengers. As he said good-night to the
office-weary faces of secretaries and bookkeepers and executives,
his voice was soothing and cool-sweet, almost like a caress for the
women and a pat on the shoulders for the men. People were very
fond of Freddy. He was always so pleasant, so polite and quietly
cheerful. Of the five elevator-men in the Chambers Trust Building,
Freddy Lamb was the favorite.

His appearance blended with his voice and manner. He was neat
and clean and his hair was nicely trimmed. He had light brown hair
parted on the side and brushed flat across his head. His eyes were
the same color, focused level when he addressed you, but never
too intent, never probing. He looked at you as though he liked
and trusted you, no matter who you were. When you looked at
him you felt mildly stimulated. He seemed much younger than
his thirty-three years. There were no lines on his face, no sign of
worry or sluggishness or dissipation. The trait that made him an
ideal elevator-man was the fact that he never asked questions and
never talked about himself.

At twenty past five, Freddy got the go-home sign from the starter,
changed places with the night man, and walked down the corridor

to the locker room. Taking off the uniform and putting on his street clothes, he yawned a few times. And while he was sitting on the bench and tying his shoelaces, he closed his eyes for a long moment, as though trying to catch a quick nap. His fingers fell away from the shoelaces and his shoulders drooped and he was in that position when the starter came in.

"Tired?" the starter asked.

"Just a little." Freddy looked up.

"Long day," the starter said. He was always saying that. As though each day was longer than any other.

Freddy finished with the shoelaces. He stood up and said, "You got the dollar-fifty?"

"What dollar-fifty?"

"The loan," Freddy said. He smiled off-handedly. "From last week. You ran short and needed dinner money. Remember?"

The starter's face was black for a moment. Then he snapped his finger and nodded emphatically. "You're absolutely right," he declared. "I'm glad you reminded me."

He handed Freddy a dollar bill and two quarters. Freddy thanked him and said good-night and walked out. The starter stood there, lighting a cigarette and nodding to himself and thinking, *Nice guy, he waited a week before he asked me, and then he asked me so nice, he's really a nice guy.*

At precisely eight-ten, Freddy Lamb climbed out of the bathtub on the third floor of the uptown rooming house in which he lived. In his room, he opened a dresser drawer, took out silk underwear, silk socks, and a silk handkerchief. When he was fully dressed, he wore a pale grey roll-collar shirt that had cost fourteen dollars, a grey silk-gabardine suit costing ninety-seven fifty, and dark grey suede shoes that had set him back twenty-three ninety-five. He broke open a fresh pack of cigarettes and slipped them into a wafer-thin sterling silver case, and then he changed wrist watches. The one he'd been wearing was of mediocre quality and had a steel case. The one he wore now was fourteen karat white-gold. But both kept perfect time. He was very particular about the watches he bought. He wouldn't wear a watch that didn't keep absolutely perfect time.

The white-gold watch showed eight-twenty when Freddy walked out of the rooming house. He walked down Sixteenth to Ontario, then over to Broad and caught a cab. He gave the driver an address downtown. The cab's headlights merged with the flooded glare of southbound traffic. Freddy leaned back and lit a cigarette.

"Nice weather," the driver commented.

"Yes, it certainly is," Freddy said.

"I like it this time of year," the driver said. "It ain't too hot and it ain't too cold. It's just right." He glanced at the rear-view mirror and saw that his passenger was putting on a pair of dark glasses. He said, "You in show business?"

"No," Freddy said.

"What's the glasses for?"

Freddy didn't say anything.

"What's the glasses for?" the driver asked.

"The headlights hurt my eyes," Freddy said. He said it somewhat slowly, his tone indicating that he was rather tired and didn't feel like talking.

The driver shrugged and remained quiet for the rest of the ride. He brought the cab to a stop at the corner of Eleventh and Locust. The fare was a dollar twenty. Freddy gave him two dollars and told him to keep the change. As the cab drove away, Freddy walked west on Locust to Twelfth, walked south on Twelfth, then turned west again, moving through a narrow alley. There were no lights in the alley except for a rectangle of green neon far down toward the other end. The rectangle was a glowing frame for the neon wording, *Billy's Hut.* It was also a beckoning finger for that special type of citizen who was never happy unless he was being taken over in a clipjoint. They'd soon be flocking through the front entrance on Locust Street. But Freddy Lamb, moving toward the back entrance, had it checked in his mind that the place was empty now. The dial of his wrist watch showed eight-fifty-seven, and he knew it was too early for customers. He also knew that Billy Donofrio was sound asleep on a sofa in the back room used as a private office. He knew it because he'd been watching Donofrio for more than two weeks and he was well acquainted with Donofrio's nightly habits.

When Freddy was fifteen yards away from *Billy's Hut,* he reached into his inner jacket pocket and took out a pair of white cotton gloves. When he was five yards away, he came to a stop and stood motionless, listening. There was the sound of a record-player from some upstairs flat on the other side of the alley. From another upstairs flat there was the noise of lesbian voices saying, "You did," and "I didn't," and "You did, you did—"

He listened for other sounds and there were none. He let the tip of his tongue come out just a little to moisten the center of his lower lip. Then he took a few forward steps that brought him to a section of brick wall where the bricks were loose. He counted up from the bottom, the light from the green neon showing him the fourth brick, the fifth, the sixth and the seventh. The eighth brick was the one he wanted. He got a grip on its edges jutting away from the wall, pulled at it very slowly and carefully. Then he held it in one hand

and his other hand reached into the empty space and made contact with the bone handle of a switchblade. It was a six-inch blade and he'd planted it there two nights ago.

He put the brick back in place and walked to the back door of *Billy's Hut*. Bending to the side to see through the window, he caught sight of Billy Donofrio on the sofa. Billy was flat on his back, one short leg dangling over the side of the sofa, one arm also dangling with fat fingers holding the stub of an unlit cigar. Billy was very short and very fat, and in his sleep he breathed as though it was a great effort. Billy was almost completely bald and what hair he had as more white than black. Billy was fifty-three years old and would never get to be fifty-four.

Freddy Lamb used a skeleton key to open the back door. He did it without sound. And then, without sound, he moved toward the sofa, his eyes focused on the crease of flesh between Billy's third chin and Billy's shirt collar. His arm went up and came down and the blade went into the crease, went in deep to cut the jugular vein, moved left, moved right, to widen the cut so that it was almost from ear to ear. Billy opened his eyes and tried to open his mouth but that was as for as he could take it. He tried to breathe and he couldn't breathe. He heard the voice of Freddy Lamb saying very softly, almost gently, "Good night, Billy." Then he heard Freddy's footsteps moving toward the door, and the door opening, and the footsteps walking out.

Billy didn't hear the door as it closed. By that time he was far away from hearing anything.

2

On Freddy's wrist, the hands of the white-gold watch pointed to nine twenty-six. He stood on the sidewalk near the entrance of a night-club called "Yellow Cat." The place was located in a low-rent area of South Philadelphia, and the neighboring structures were mostly tenements and garages and vacant lots heaped with rubbish. The club's exterior complied with the general trend; it was dingy and there was no paint on the wooden walls. But inside it was a different proposition. It was glittering and lavish, the drinks were expensive, and the floor show featured a first-rate orchestra and singers and dancers. It also featured a unique type of strip-tease entertainment, a quintet of young females who took off their clothes while they sat at your tables. For a reasonable bonus they'd let you keep the brassiere or garter or what-not for a souvenir.

The white-gold watch showed nine twenty-eight. Freddy decided to wait another two minutes. His appointment with the owner of "Yellow Cat" had been arranged for nine-thirty. He knew that Herman Charn was waiting anxiously for his arrival, but his personal theory of punctuality stipulated split-second precision, and since they'd made it for nine-thirty he'd see Herman at nine-thirty, not a moment earlier or later.

A taxi pulled up and a blonde stepped out. She paid the driver and walked toward Freddy and he said, "Hello, Pearl."

Pearl smiled at him. "Kiss me hello."

"Not here," he said.

"Later?"

He nodded. He looked her up and down. She was five-five and weighed one-ten and Nature had given her a body that caused men's eyes to bulge. Freddy's eyes didn't bulge, although he told himself she was something to see. He always enjoyed looking at her. He wondered if he still enjoyed the nights with her. He'd been sharing the nights with her for the past several months and it had reached the point where he wasn't seeing any other women and maybe he was missing out on something. For just a moment he gazed past Pearl, telling himself that she needed him more than he needed her, and knowing it wouldn't be easy to get off the hook.

Well, there wasn't any hurry. He hadn't seen anything else around that interested him. But he wished Pearl would let up on the clinging routine. Maybe he'd really go for her if she wasn't so hungry for him all the time.

Pearl stepped closer to him. The hunger showed in her eyes. She said, "Know what I did today? I took a walk in the park."

"You did?"

"Yeah," she said. "I went to Fairmount Park and took a long walk. All by myself."

"That's nice," he said. He wondered what she was getting at.

She said, "Let's do it together sometimes. Let's go for a walk in the park. It's something we ain't never done. All we do is drink and listen to jazz and find all sorts of ways to knock ourselves out."

He gave her a closer look. This was a former call-girl who'd done a stretch for prostitution, a longer stretch for selling cocaine, and had finally decided she'd done enough time and she might as well go legitimate. She'd learned the art of stripping off her clothes before an audience, and now at twenty-six she was earning a hundred-and-a-half a week. It was clean money, as far as the law was concerned, but maybe in her mind it wasn't clean enough. Maybe she was getting funny ideas, like this walk-in-the-park routine. Maybe she'd soon be thinking in terms of a cottage for two and a little lawn in front and shopping for a baby-carriage.

He wondered what she'd look like, wearing an apron and standing at a sink and washing dishes.

For some reason the thought disturbed him. He couldn't understand why it should disturb him. He heard her saying, "Can we do it, Freddy? Let's do it on Sunday. We'll go to Fairmount Park—"

"We'll talk about it," he cut in quickly. He glanced at his wrist watch. "See you after the show."

He hurried through the club entrance, went past the hat-check counter, past the tables and across the dance-floor and toward a door marked "Private." There was a button adjoining the door and he pressed the button one short, two longs, another short and then there was a buzzing sound. He opened the door and walked into the office. It was a large room and the color motif was yellow-and-grey. The walls and ceiling were gray and the thick carpet was pale yellow. The furniture was bright yellow. There was a short skinny man standing near the desk and his face was grey. Seated at the desk was a large men whose face was a mixture of yellow and grey.

Freddy closed the door behind him. He walked toward the desk. He nodded to the short skinny man and then he looked at the large man and said, "Hello, Herman."

Herman glanced at a clock on the desk. He said, "You're right on time."

"He's always on time," said the short skinny man.

Herman looked at Freddy Lamb and said, "You do it?"

Before Freddy could answer, the short skinny man said, "Sure he did it."

"Shut up, Ziggy," Herman said. He had a soft, sort of gooey voice, as though he spoke with a lot of marshmallow in his mouth. He wore a suit of very soft fabric, thick and fleecy, and his thick hands pressed softly on the desk-top. On the little finger of his left hand he wore a large star-emerald that radiated a soft green light. Everything about him was soft, except for his eyes. His eyes were iron.

"You do it?" he repeated softly.

Freddy nodded.

"Any trouble?" Herman asked.

"He never has trouble," Ziggy said.

Herman looked at Ziggy. "I told you to shut up." Then, very softly, "Come here, Ziggy."

Ziggy hesitated. He had a ferret face that always looked sort of worried and now it looked very worried.

"Come here," Herman purred.

Ziggy approached the large man. Ziggy was blinking and swallowing hard. Herman reached out slowly and took hold of Ziggy's hand. Herman's thick fingers closed tightly on Ziggy's bony fingers, gave a yank and a twist and another yank. Ziggy moaned.

"When I tell you to shut up," Herman said, "you'll shut up." He smiled softly and paternally at Ziggy. "Right?"

"Right," Ziggy said. Then he moaned again. His fingers were free now and he looked down at them as an animal gazes sadly at its own crushed paws. He said, "They're all busted."

"They're not busted," Herman said. "They're damaged just enough to let you know your place. That's one thing you must never forget. Every man who works for me has to know his place." He was still smiling at Ziggy. "Right?"

"Right," Ziggy moaned.

Then Herman looked at Freddy Lamb and said, "Right?"

Freddy didn't say anything. He was looking at Ziggy's fingers. Then his gaze climbed to Ziggy's face. The lips quivered, as though Ziggy was trying to hold back sobs. Freddy remembered the time when nothing could hurt Ziggy, when Ziggy and himself were their own bosses and did their engineering on the waterfront. There were a lot of people on the waterfront who were willing to pay good money to have other people placed on stretches or in caskets. In those days the rates had been fifteen dollars for a broken jaw, thirty for a fractured pelvis, and a hundred for the complete job. Ziggy handled the blackjack work and the bullet work and Freddy took care of such special functions as switchblade slicing, lye-in-the-eyes, and various powders and pills slipped into a glass of beer or wine or a cup of coffee. There were orders for all sorts of jobs in those days.

Fifteen months ago, he was thinking. And times had sure changed. The independent operator was swallowed up by the big combines. It was especially true in this line of business, which followed the theory that competition, no matter how small, was not good for the over-all picture. So the moment had come when he and Ziggy had been approached with an offer, and they knew they had to accept, there wasn't any choice, if they didn't accept they'd be erased. They didn't need to be told about that. They just knew. As much as they hated to do it, they had to do it. The proposition was handed to them on a Wednesday afternoon, and that same night they went to work for Herman Charn.

He heard Herman saying, "I'm talking to you, Freddy."

"I hear you," he said.

"You sure?" Herman asked softly. "You sure you hear me?"

Freddy looked at Herman. He said quietly, "I'm on your payroll. I do what you tell me to do. I've done every job exactly the way you wanted it done. Can I do any more than that?"

"Yes," Herman said. His tone was matter-of-fact. He glanced at Ziggy and said, "From here on it's a private discussion. Me and Freddy. Take a walk."

Ziggy's mouth opened just a little. He didn't seem to understand the command. He'd always been included in all the business conferences, and now the look in his eyes was a mixture of puzzlement and injury.

Herman smiled at Ziggy. He pointed to the door. Ziggy bit hard on his lip and moved toward the door and opened it and walked out of the room.

For some moments it was quiet in the room and Freddy had a feeling it was too quiet. He sensed that Herman Charn was aiming something at him, something that had nothing to do with the ordinary run of business.

There was the creaking sound of leather as Herman leaned back in the desk-chair. He folded his big soft fingers across his big soft belly and said, "Sit down, Freddy. Sit down and make yourself comfortable."

Freddy pulled a chair toward the desk. He sat down. He looked at the face of Herman and for just a moment the face became a wall that moved toward him. He winced, his insides quivered. It was a strange sensation, he'd never had it before and he couldn't understand it. But then the moment was gone and he sat there relaxed, his features expressionless, as he waited for Herman to speak.

Herman said, "Want a drink?"

Freddy shook his head.

"Smoke?" Herman lifted the lid of an enamelled cigarette-box.

"I got my own," Freddy murmured. He reached into his pocket and took out the flat silver case.

"Smoke one of mine," Herman said. He paused to signify it wasn't a suggestion, it was an order. And then, as though Freddy was a guest rather than an employee. "These smokes are special-made. Come from Egypt. Cost a dime apiece."

Freddy took one. Herman flicked a table-lighter, applied the flame to Freddy's cigarette, lit one for himself, took a slow soft drag, and let the smoke come out of his nose. Herman waited until all the smoke was out, and then he said, "You didn't like what I did to Ziggy."

It was a flat statement that didn't ask for an answer. Freddy sipped at the cigarette, not looking at Herman.

"You didn't like it," Herman persisted softly. "You never like it when I let Ziggy know who's boss."

Freddy shrugged. "That's between you and Ziggy."

"No," Herman said. And then he spoke very slowly, with a pause between each word. "It isn't that way at all. I don't do it for Ziggy's benefit. He already knows who's top man around here."

Freddy didn't say anything. But he almost winced. And again his insides quivered.

Herman leaned forward. "Do you know who the top man is?"

"You," Freddy said.

Herman smiled. "Thanks, Freddy. Thanks for saying it." Then the smiled vanished and Herman's eyes were hammerheads. "But I'm not sure you mean it."

Freddy took another sip from the Egyptian cigarette. It was strongly flavored tobacco but somehow he wasn't getting any taste from it.

Herman kept leaning forward. "I gotta be sure, Freddy," he said. "You been working for me more than a year. And just like you said, you do all the jobs exactly the way I want them done. You plan them perfect, do them perfect, it's always clean and neat from the start to finish. I don't mind saying you're one of the best. I don't think I've ever seen a cooler head. You're as cool as they come, an icicle on wheels."

"That's plenty cool," Freddy murmured.

"It sure is," Herman said. He let the pause drift in again. Then, his lips scarcely moving. "Maybe it's too cool."

Freddy looked at the hammerhead eyes. He wondered what showed in his own eyes. He wondered what thoughts were burning under the cool surface of his own brain.

He heard Herman saying, "I've done a lot of thinking about you. A lot more than you ever imagine. You're a puzzler, and one thing I always like to do is play stud poker with a puzzler.

Freddy smiled dimly. "Want to play stud poker?"

"We're playing it now. Without cards." Herman gazed down at the desk-top. His right hand was on the desk-top and he flicked his wrist as though he was turning over the hole-card. His voice was very soft as he said, "I want you to break it up with Pearl."

Freddy heard himself saying, "All right, Herman."

It was as though Freddy hadn't spoken. Herman said, "I'm waiting, Freddy."

"Waiting for what?" He told the dim smile to stay on his lips. It stayed there. He murmured, "You tell me to give her up and I say all right. What more do you want me to say?"

"I want you to ask me why. Don't you want to know why?"

Freddy didn't reply. He still wore the dim smile and he was gazing past Herman's head.

"Come on, Freddy. I'm waiting to see your hole-card."

Freddy remained quiet.

"All right," Herman said. "I'll keep on showing you mine. I go for Pearl. I went for her the first time I laid eyes on her. That same night I took her home with me and she stayed over. She did what I wanted her to do but it didn't mean a thing to her, it was just like turning a trick. I thought it wouldn't bother me, once I have them in bed I can put them out of my mind. But this thing with Pearl, it's different. I've had her on my mind and it gets worse all the time and now it's gotten to the point where I have to do something about it. First thing I gotta do is clear the road."

"It's cleared," Freddy said. "I'll tell her tonight I'm not seeing her anymore."

"Just like that?" And Herman snapped his fingers.

"Yes," Freddy said. His fingers made the same sound. "Just like that."

Herman leaned back in the soft leather chair. He looked at the face of Freddy Lamb as though he was trying to solve a cryptogram. Finally he shook his head slowly, and then he gave a heavy sigh and he said, "All right, Freddy. That's all for now."

Freddy stood up. He started toward the door. Half-way across the room he stoped and turned and said, "You promised me a bonus for the Donofrio job."

"This is Monday," Herman said. "I hand out the pay on Friday."

"You said I'd be paid right off."

"Did I?" Herman smiled softly.

"Yes," Freddy said. "You said the deal on Donofrio was something special and the customer was paying fifteen hundred. You told me there was five hundred in it for me and I'd get the bonus the same night I did the job."

Herman opened a desk-drawer and took out a thick roll of bills.

"Can I have it in tens and twenties?" Freddy asked.

Herman lifted his eyebrows. "Why the small change?"

"I'm an elevator man," Freddy said. "The bank would wonder what I was doing with fifties."

"You're right," Herman said. He counted off the five hundred in tens and twenties, and handed the money to Freddy. He leaned back in the chair and watched Freddy folding the bills and pocketing them and walking out of the room. When the door was closed, Herman said aloud to himself, "Don't try to figure him out, he's all ice and no soul, strictly a professional."

3

The white-gold watch showed eleven thirty-five. Freddy sat at a table watching the floor show and drinking from a tall glass of gin-and-ginger ale. The *Yellow Cat* was crowded now and Freddy wore the dark glasses and his table was in a darkly shadowed section of the room. He sat there with Ziggy and some other men who worked for Herman. There was Dino, who did his jobs at long-range and always used a rifle. There was Shikey, six-foot-six and weighing three hundred pounds, an expert at bone-cracking, gouging, and the removing of teeth. There was Riley, another bone-cracker and strangling specialist.

A tall pretty boy stood in front of the orchestra, clutching the mike as though it was the only support he had in the world. He sang with an ache in his voice, begging someone to "—please understand." The audience liked it and he sang it again. Then two colored tap-dancers came out and worked themselves into a sweat and were gasping for breath as they finished the act. The M.C. walked on and motioned the orchestra to quiet down and grinned at ringside faces as he said, "Ready for desserts?"

"Yeah," a man shouted from ringside. "Let's have the dessert."

"All right," the M.C. said. He cupped his hands to his mouth and called off-stage, "Bring it out, we're all starved for that sweetmeat."

The orchestra went into medium tempo, the lights changed from glaring yellow to a soft violet. And then they came out, seven girls wearing horn-rimmed glasses and ultra-conservative costumes. They walked primly, and altogether they resembled the stiff-necked females in a cartoon lampooning the W.C.T.U. It got a big laugh from the audience, and there was some appreciative applause. The young ladies formed a line and slowly waved black parasols as they sang, "—Father, oh father, come home with me now." But then it became, "—Daddy, oh daddy, come home with me now." And they emphasized the daddy angle, they broke up the line and discarded the parasols and took off their ankle-length dark-blue coats. Then, their fingers loosening the buttons of dark-blue dresses, they moved separately toward the ringside tables. The patrons in the back stood up to get a better look and in the balcony the lenses of seven lamps were focused on seven young women getting undressed.

Dino, who had a footwear fetish, said loudly, "I'll pay forty for a high-heeled shoe."

One of the girls took off her shoe and flung it toward Freddy's table. Shikey caught it and handed it to Dino. A waiter came over and Dino handed him four tens and he took the money to the girl. Riley looked puzzledly at Dino and said, "What-cha gonna do with a high-heeled shoe?" And Shikey said, "He boils 'em and eats 'em." But Ziggy had another theory. "He bangs the heel against his head," Ziggy said. "That's the way he gets his kicks." Dino sat there gazing lovingly at the shoe in his land while his other hand caressed the kidskin surface. Then gradually his eyes closed and he murmured, "This is nice, this is so nice."

Riley was watching Dino and saying, "I don't get it."

Ziggy shrugged philosophically. "Some things," he said, "just can't be understood."

"You're so right." It was Freddy talking. He didn't know his lips were making sound. He was looking across the tables at Pearl. She sat with some ringsiders and already she'd taken off considerable clothing, she was half-naked. On her face there was a detached look and he hands moved mechanically as she unbuttoned the buttons and unzipped the zippers. There were three men sitting with her and their eyes feasted on her, they had their mouths open in a sort of mingled fascination and worship. At nearby tables the other strippers were performing but they weren't getting undivided attention. Most of the men were watching Pearl. One of them offered a hundred dollars for her stocking. She took off the stocking and let it dangle from her fingers. In a semi-whisper she asked if there were any higher bids. Freddy told himself that she wasn't happy doing what she was doing. Again he could hear her plaintive voice as she asked him to take her for a walk in the park. Suddenly he knew that he'd like that very much. He wanted to see the sun shining on her hair, instead of the night-club lights. He heard himself saying aloud, "Five hundred."

He didn't shout it, but at the ringside tables they all heard it, and for a moment there was stunned silence. At his own table the silence was very thick. He could feel the pressure of it, and the moment seemed to have substance, something on the order of iron wheels going around and around, making no sound and getting nowhere.

Some things just can't be understood, he thought. He was taking the tens and twenties from his jacket pocket. The five hundred seemed to prove the truth of Ziggy's vague philosophy. Freddy got up from his chairs and moved toward an empty table behind some potted ferns adjacent to the orchestra-stand. He sat down and placed green money on a yellow tablecloth. He wasn't looking at Pearl as she approached the table. From ringside an awed voice was saying, "For one silk stocking she gets half a grand—"

She seated herself at the table. He shoved the money toward her. He said, "There's your cash. Let's have the stocking."

"This a gag?" she asked quietly. Her eyes were somewhat sullen. There was some laughter from the table where Ziggy and the others were seated: they now had the notion it was some sort of joke.

Freddy said, "Take off the stocking."

She looked at the pile of tens and twenties. She said, "Whatcha want the stocking for?"

"Souvenir," he said.

It was the tone of his voice that did it. Her face paled. She started to shake her head very slowly, as though she couldn't believe him.

"Yes," he said, with just the trace of a sigh. "It's all over, Pearl. It's the end of the line."

She went on shaking her head. She couldn't talk.

He said, "I'll hang the stocking in my bedroom."

She was biting her lip. "It's a long time till Christmas."

"For some people it's never Christmas."

"Freddy—" She leaned towards him. "What's it all about? Why're you doing this?"

He shrugged. He didn't say anything.

Her eyes were getting wet. "You won't even give me a reason?"

All he gave her was a cool smile. Then his head was turned and he saw the faces at Ziggy's table and then he focused on the face of the large man who stood behind the table. He saw the iron in the eyes of Herman Charn. He told himself he was doing what Herman had told him to do. And just then he felt the quiver in his insides. It was mostly in the spine, as though his spine was gradually turning to jelly.

He spoke to himself without sound. He said, *No, it isn't that, it can't be that.*

Pearl was saying, "All right, Freddy, if that's the way it is."

He nodded very slowly.

Pearl bent over and took the stocking off her leg. She placed the stocking on the table. She picked up the five hundred, counted it off to make sure it was all there.

Then she stood up and said, "No charge, mister. I'd rather keep the memories."

She put the tens ad twenties on the tablecloth and walked away. Freddy glanced off to the side and saw a soft smile on the face of Herman Charn.

4

The floor-show was ended and Freddy was still sitting there at the table. There was a bottle of bourbon in front of him. It had been there for less than twenty minutes and already it was half-empty.

There was also a pitcher of ice-water and the pitcher was full. He didn't need a chaser because he couldn't taste the whiskey. He was drinking the whiskey from the water-glass.

A voice said, "Freddy—"

And then a hand tugged at his arm. He looked up and saw Ziggy sitting beside him.

He smiled at Ziggy. He motioned toward the bottle and shot-glass and said, "Have a drink."

Ziggy shrugged. "I might as well while I got the chance. At the rate you're going, that bottle'll soon be empty."

"It's very good bourbon," Freddy said.

"Yeah?" Ziggy was pouring a glass for himself. He swished the liquor into his mouth. Then, looking closely at Freddy, "You don't care whether it's good or not. You'd be gulping it if it was shoe-polish."

Freddy was staring at the tablecloth. 'Let's go somewhere and drink some shoe-polish."

Ziggy tugged again at Freddy's arm. He said, "Come out of it."

"Come out of what?"

"The clouds," Ziggy said. "You're in the clouds."

"It's nice in the clouds," Freddy said. "I'm up here having a dandy time. I'm floating."

"Floating? You're drowning." Ziggy pulled urgently at his arm, to get his hand away from a water-glass filled with whiskey. "You're not a drinker, Freddy. What do you want to do, drink yourself into a hospital?"

Freddy grinned. He aimed the grin at nothing in particular. For some moments he sat there motionless. Then he reached into his jacket pocket and took out the silk stocking. He showed it to Ziggy and said, "Look what I got."

"Yeah," Ziggy said. "I seen her give it to you. What's the score on that routine?"

"No score," Freddy said. He went on grinning. "It's a funny way to end a game. Nothing on the score-board. Nothing at all."

Ziggy frowned. "You trying to tell me something?"

Freddy looked at the whiskey in the water-glass. He said, "I packed her in."

"No," Ziggy said. His tone was incredulous. "Not Pearl. Not that pigeon. That ain't no ordinary merchandise. You wouldn't walk out on Pearl unless you had a very special reason."

"It was special, all right."

"Tell me about it, Freddy." There was something plaintive in Ziggy's voice, a certain feeling for Freddy that he couldn't put into words. The closest he could get to it was, "After all, I'm on your side, ain't I?"

"No," Freddy said. The grin was slowly fading. "You're on Herman's side." He gazed past Ziggy's head. "We're all on Herman's side."

"Herman? What's he got to do with it?"

"Everything," Freddy said. "Herman's the boss, remember?" He looked at the swollen fingers of Ziggy's right hand. "Herman wants something done, it's got to be done. He gave me orders to break with Pearl. He's the employer and I'm the hired man, so I did what I had to do. I carried out his orders."

Ziggy was quiet for some moments. Then, very quietly, "Well, it figures he wants her for himself. But it don't seem right. It just ain't fair."

"Don't make me laugh," Freddy said. "Who the hell are we to say what's fair?"

"We're human, aren't we?"

"No," Freddy said. He gazed past Ziggy's head. "I don't know what we are. But I know one thing, we're not human. We can't afford to be human, not in this line of business."

Ziggy didn't get it. It was just a little too deep for him. All he could says was, "You getting funny ideas?"

"I'm not reaching for them, they're just coming to me."

"Take another drink," Ziggy said.

"I'd rather have the laughs." Freddy showed the grin again. "It's really comical, you know? Especially this thing with Pearl. I was thinking of calling it quits anyway. You know how it is with me, Ziggy. I never like to be tied down to one skirt. But tonight Pearl said something that spun me around. We were talking outside the club and she brought it in out of left field. She asked me to take her for a walk in the park."

Ziggy blinked a few times. "What?"

"A walk in the park," Freddy said.

"What for?" Ziggy wanted to know. "She gettin' square all of a sudden? She wanna go around picking flowers?"

"I don't know," Freddy said. "All she said was, it's very nice in Fairmount Park. She asked me to take her there and we'd be together in the park, just taking a walk."

Ziggy pointed to the glass. "You better take that drink."

Freddy reached for the glass. But someone else's hand was there first. He saw the thick soft fingers, the soft green glow of the star-emerald. As the glass of whiskey was shoved out of his reach, he looked up and saw the soft smile on the face of Herman Charn.

"Too much liquor is bad for the kidneys," Herman said. He bent down lower to peer at Freddy's eyes. "You look knocked-out, Freddy. There's a soft couch in the office. Go in there and lie down for awhile."

Freddy got up from the chair. He was somewhat unsteady on his feet. Herman took his arm and helped him make it down the aisle past the tables to the door of the office. He could feel the pressure of Herman's hand on his arm. It was very soft pressure but somehow it felt like a clamp of iron biting into his flesh.

Herman opened the office-door and guided him toward the couch. He fell onto the couch, sent an idiotic grin toward the ceiling, then closed his eyes and went to sleep.

5

He slept until four-forty in the morning. The sound that woke him up was a scream.

At first it was all blurred, there was too much whiskey-fog in his brain, he had no idea where he was or what was happening. He pushed his knuckles against his eyes. Then, sitting up, he focused on the faces in the room. He saw Shikey and Riley and they had girls sitting in their laps. They were on the other couch at the opposite side of the room. He saw Dino standing near the couch with his arm around the waist of a slim brunette. Then he glanced toward the door and he saw Ziggy. That made seven faces for him to look at. He told himself to keep looking at them. If he concentrated on that, maybe he wouldn't hear the screaming.

But he heard it. The scream was an animal sound and yet he recognized the voice. It came from near the desk and he turned his head very slowly, telling himself he didn't want to look but knowing he had to look.

He saw Pearl kneeling on the floor. Herman stood behind her. With one hand he was twisting her arm up high between her shoulder blades. His other hand was on her head and he was pulling her hair so that her face was drawn back, her throat stretched.

Herman spoke very softly. "You make me very unhappy, Pearl. I don't like to be unhappy."

Then Herman gave her arm another upward twist and pulled tighter on her hair and she screamed again.

The girl in Shikey's lap gave Pearl a scornful look and said, "You're a damn fool."

"In spades." It came from the stripper who nestled against Riley. "All he wants her to do is kiss him like she means it."

Freddy told himself to get up and walk out of the room. He lifted himself from the couch and took a few steps toward the door and heard Herman saying, "Not yet, Freddy. I'll tell you when to go."

He went back to the couch and sat down.

Herman said, "Be sensible, Pearl. Why can't you be sensible?"

Pearl opened her mouth to scream again. But no sound came out. There was too much pain and it was choking her.

The brunette who stood with Dino was saying, "It's a waste of time, Herman. She can't give you what she hasn't got. She just don't have it for you, Herman."

"She'll have it for him," Dino said. "Before he's finished, he'll have her crawling on her belly."

Herman looked at Dino. "No," he said. "She won't do that. I wouldn't let her do that." He cast a downward glance at Pearl. His lips shaped a soft smile. There was something tender in the smile and in his voice. "Pearl, tell me something. Why don't you want me?"

He gave her a chance to reply, his fingers slackening the grip on her wrist and her hair. She groaned a few times, and then she said, "You got my body, Herman. You can have my body anytime you want it."

"That isn't enough," Herman said. "I want you all the way, a hundred percent. It's got to be like that, Pearl. You're in me so deep it just can't take any other route. It's gotta be you and me from here on in, you gotta need me just as much as I need you."

"But Herman—" She gave a dry sob. "I can't lie to you. I just don't feel that way."

"You're gonna feel that way," Herman said.

"No." Pearl sobbed again. "No. No."

"Why not?" He was pulling her hair again, twisting her arm. But it seemed he was suffering more than Pearl. The pain wracked his pleading voice. "Why can't you feel something for me?"

Her reply was made without sound. She managed to turn her head just a little, toward the couch. And everyone in the room saw her looking at Freddy.

Herman's face became very pale. His features tightened and twisted and it seemed he was about to burst into tears. He stared up at the ceiling.

Herman shivered. His body shook spasmodically, as though he stood on a vibrating platform. Then all at once the tormented look faded from his eyes, the iron came into his eyes, and the soft smile came onto his lips. He released Pearl, turned away from her, went to the desk and opened the cigarette-box. It was very quiet in the room while Herman stood there lighting the cigarette. He took a slow, easy drag and then he said quietly, "All right, Pearl, you can go home now."

She started to get up from the floor. The brunette came over and helped her up.

"I'll call a cab for you," Herman said. He reached for the telephone and put in the call. As he lowered the phone, he was looking at Pearl and saying, "You want to go home alone?"

Pearl didn't say anything. Her head was lowered and she was leaning against the shoulder of the brunette.

Herman said, "You want Freddy to take you home?"

Pearl raised her head just a little and looked at the face of Freddy Lamb.

Herman laughed softly. "All right," he said. "Freddy'll take you home."

Freddy winced. He sat there staring at the carpet.

Herman told the brunette to fix a drink for Pearl. He said, "Take her to the bar and give her anything she wants." He motioned to the other girls and they got up from the laps of Shikey and Riley. Then all the girls walked out of the room. Herman was quiet for some moments, taking slow drags at the cigarette and looking at the door. Then gradually his head turned and he looked at Freddy. He said, "You're slated, Freddy."

Freddy went on staring at the carpet.

"You're gonna bump her," Herman said.

Freddy closed his eyes.

"Take her somewhere and bump her and bury her," Herman said.

Shikey and Riley looked at each other. Dino had his mouth open and he was staring at Herman. Standing next to the door, Ziggy had his eyes glued to Freddy's face.

"She goes," Herman said. And then, speaking aloud to himself, "She goes because she gives me grief." He hit his hand against his chest. "She hits me here, where I live. Hits me too hard. Hurts me. I don't appreciate getting hurt. Especially here." Again his hand thumped his chest. He said, "You'll do it, Freddy. You'll see to it that I get rid of the hurt."

"Let me do it," Ziggy said.

Herman shook his head. He pointed a finger at Freddy. His finger jabbed empty air, and he said, "Freddy does it. Freddy."

Ziggy opened his mouth, tried to close it, couldn't close it, and blurted, "Why take it out on him?"

"That's a stupid question," Herman said mildly. "I'm not taking it out on anybody. I'm giving the job to Freddy because I know he's dependable. I can always depend on Freddy."

Ziggy made a final frantic try.

"Please, Herman," he said. "Please don't make him do it."

Herman didn't bother to reply. All he did was give Ziggy a slow appraising look up and down. It was like a soundless warning to Ziggy, letting him know he was walking on thin ice and the ice would crack if he opened his mouth again.

Then Herman turned to Freddy and said, "Where's your blade?"

"Stashed," Freddy said. He was still staring at the carpet.

Herman opened a desk-drawer. He took out a black-handled switch-blade. "Use this," he said, coming toward the couch. He handed the knife to Freddy. "Give it a try," he said.

Freddy pressed the button. The blade flicked out. It glimmered blue-white. He pushed the blade into the handle and tried the button again. He went on trying the button and watching the flash of the blade. It was quiet in the room as the blade went in and out, in and out. Then from the street there was the sound of a horn. Herman said, "That's the taxi." Freddy nodded and got up from the sofa and walked out of the room. As he moved toward the girls who stood at the cocktail bar, he could feel the weight of the knife in the inner pocket of his jacket. He was looking at Pearl and saying, "Come on, let's go," and as he said it, the blade seemed to come out of the knife and slice into his own flesh.

6

The taxi was cruising north on Sixteenth Street. On Freddy's wrist the white-gold watch said five-twenty. He was watching the parade of unlit windows along the dark street. Pearl was saying something but he didn't hear. She spoke just a bit louder and he turned and looked at her. He smiled and murmured, "Sorry, I wasn't listening."

"Can't you sit closer?"

He moved closer to her. A mixture of moonlight and streetlamp glow came pouring into the back-seat of the taxi and illuminated her face. He saw something in her eyes that caused him to blink several times.

She noticed the way he was blinking, and she said, "What's the matter?"

He didn't answer. He tried to stop blinking and he couldn't stop.

"Hangover?" Pearl asked.

"No," he said. "I feel all right now. I feel fine."

For some moments she didn't say anything. She was rubbing her sore arm. She tried to stretch it, winced and gasped with pain, and said, "Oh Jesus, it hurts. It really hurts. Maybe it's broken."

"Let me feel it," he said. He put his hand on her arm. He ran his fingers down from above her elbow to her wrist. "It isn't broken," he murmured. "Just a little swollen, that's all. Sprained some ligaments."

She smiled at him. "The hurt goes away when you touch it."

He tried not to look at her, but something fastened his eyes to her face. He kept his hand on her arm. He heard himself saying, "I feel sorry for Herman. If he could see you now, I mean if you'd look at him like you're looking at me—"

"Freddy," she said. "Freddy." Then she leaned toward him. She rested her head on his shoulder.

Then somehow everything was quiet and still and he didn't hear the noise of the taxi's engine, he didn't feel the bumps as the wheels hit the ruts in the cobblestoned surface of Sixteenth Street. But suddenly there was a deep rut and the taxi gave a lurch. He looked up and heard the driver cursing the city engineers. "Goddamit," the driver said. "They got a deal with the tire companies."

Freddy stared past the driver's head, his eyes aimed through the windshield to see the wide intersection where Sixteenth Street met the Parkway. The Parkway was a six-laned drive slanting to the left of the downtown area, going away from the concrete of Philadelphia skyscrapers and pointing toward the green of Fairmount Park.

"Turn left," Freddy said.

They were approaching the intersection, and the driver gave a backward glance. "Left?" the driver asked. "That take us outta the way. You gave me an address on Seventeenth near Lehigh. We gotta hit it from Sixteenth—"

"I know," Freddy said quietly. "But turn left anyway."

The driver shrugged. "You're the captain." He beat the yellow of a traffic-light and the taxi made a left turn onto the Parkway.

Pearl said, "What's this, Freddy? Where're we going?"

"In the park." He wasn't looking at her. "We're gonna do what you said we should do. We're gonna take a walk in the park."

"For real?" Her eyes were lit up. She shook her head, as though she could scarcely believe what he'd just said.

"We'll take a nice walk," he murmured. "Just the two of us. The way you wanted it."

"Oh," she breathed. "Oh, Freddy—"

The driver shrugged again. The taxi went past the big monuments and fountains of Logan Circle, past the Rodin Museum and the Art Museum and onto River Drive. For a mile or so they stayed on the highway bordering the moonlit water of the river and then without being told the driver made a turn off the highway, made a series of turns that took them deep into the park. They came to a section where there were no lights, no movement, no sound except the autumn wind drifting through the trees and bushes and tall grass and flowers.

"Stop here," Freddy said.

The taxi came to a stop. They got out and he paid the driver. The driver gave him a queer look and said, "You sure picked a lonely spot."

Freddy looked at the cabman. He didn't say anything.

The driver said, "You're at least three miles off the highway. It's gonna be a problem getting a ride home."

"Is it your problem?" Freddy asked gently.

"Well, no—"

"Then don't worry about it," Freddy said. He smiled amiably. The driver threw a glance at the blonde, smiled, and told himself that the man might have the right idea, after all. With an item like that, any man would want complete privacy. He thought of the bony, buck-toothed woman who waited for him at home, crinkled his face in a distasteful grimace, put the car in gear and drove away.

"Ain't it nice?" Pearl said. "Ain't it wonderful?"

They were walking through a glade where the moonlight showed the autumn colors of fallen leaves. The night air was fragrant with the blended aromas of wild flowers. He had his arm around her shoulder and he was leading her toward a narrow lane sloping downward through the trees.

She laughed lightly, happily. "It's like as if you know the place. As if you've been here before."

"No," he said. "I've never been here before."

There was the tinkling sound of a nearby brook. A bird chirped in the bushes. Another bird sang a tender reply.

"Listen," Pearl murmured. "Listen to them."

He listened to the singing of the birds. Now he was guiding Pearl down along the slope and seeing the way it levelled at the bottom and then went up again on all sides. It was a tiny valley down there, with the brook running along the edge. He told himself it would happen when they reached the bottom.

He heard Pearl saying, "Wouldn't it be nice if we could stay here?"

He looked at her. "Stay here?"

"Yes," she said. "If we could live here for the rest of our lives. Just be here, away from everything—"

"We'd get lonesome."

"No we wouldn't," she said. "We'd always have company. I'd have you and you'd have me."

They were nearing the bottom of the slope. It was sort of steep now and they had to move slowly. All at once she stumbled and pitched forward and he caught her before she could fall on her face. He steadied her, smiled at her and said, "Okay?"

She nodded. She stood very close to him and gazed into his eyes and said, "You wouldn't let me fall, would you?"

The smile faded. He stared past her. "Not if I could help it."

"I know," she said. "You don't have to tell me."

He went on staring past her. "Tell you what?"

"The situation." She spoke softly, almost in a whisper. "I got it figured, Freddy. It's so easy to figure."

He wanted to close his eyes. He couldn't understand why he wanted to close his eyes.

He heard her saying, "I know why you packed me in tonight. Orders from Herman."

"That's right." He said it automatically, as though the mention of the name was the shifting of a gear.

"And another thing," she said. "I know why you brought me here." There was a pause, and then, very softly, "Herman."

He nodded.

She started to cry. It was quiet weeping and contained no fear, no hysteria. It was the weeping of farewell. She was crying because she was sad. Then, very slowly, she took the few remaining steps going down to the bottom of the slope. He stood there and watched her as she faced about to look up at him.

He walked down to where she stood, smiling at her and trying to pretend his hand was not on the switchblade in his pocket. He tried to make himself believe he wan't going to do it, but he knew that wasn't true. He'd been slated for this job. The combine had him listed as a top-rated operator, one of the best in the business. He'd expended a lot of effort to attain that reputation, to be known as the grade-A expert who'd never muffed an assignment.

He begged himself to stop. He couldn't stop. The knife was open in his hand and his arm flashed out and sideways with the blade sliding in neatly and precisely, cutting the flesh of her throat. She went down very slowly, tried to cough, made a few gurgling sounds, and then rolled over on her back and died, looking up at him.

For a long time he stared at her face. There was no expression on her features now. At first he didn't feel anything, and then he realized she was dead, and he had killed her.

He tried to tell himself there was nothing else he could have done, but even though that was true it didn't do any good. He took his glance away from her face and looked down at the white-gold watch to check the hour and the minute, automatically. But somehow the dial was blurred, as though the hands were spinning like tiny propellers. He had the weird feeling that the watch was showing Time traveling backward, so that he found himself checking it in terms of years and decades. He went all the way back to the day when he was eleven years old and they took him to reform school.

In reform school he was taught a lot of things. The thing he learned best was the way to use a knife. The knife became his profession. But somewhere along the line he caught onto the idea of holding a daytime job to cover his night-time activities. He worked in stockrooms and he did some window-cleaning and drove a truck for a fruit-dealer. And finally he became an elevator operator and that was the job he liked best. He'd never realized why he liked it so much but he realized now. He knew that the elevator was nothing more than a moving cell, that the only place for him was a cell. The passengers were just a lot of friendly visitors walking in and out, saying "Good morning, Freddy," and "Good night, Freddy," and they were such nice people. Just the thought of them brought a tender smile to his lips.

Then he realized he was smiling down at her. He sensed a faint glow coming from somewhere, lighting her face. For an instant he had no idea what it was. Then he realized it came from the sky. It was the first signal of approaching sunrise.

The white-gold watch showed five fifty-three. Freddy Lamb told himself to get moving. For some reason he couldn't move. He was looking down at the dead girl. His hand was still clenched about the switch-blade, and as he tried to relax it he almost dropped the knife. He looked down at it.

The combine was a cell, too, he told himself. The combine was an elevator from which he could never escape. It was going steadily downward and there were no stops until the end. There was no way to get out.

Herman had made him kill the girl. Herman would make him do other things. And there was no getting away from that. If he killed Herman there would be someone else.

The elevator was carrying Freddy steadily downward. Already, he had left Pearl somewhere far above him. He realized it all at once, and an unreasoning terror filled him.

Freddy looked at the white-gold watch again. A minute had passed, and he knew suddenly that he was slated to do a job on someone in exactly three minutes now. The minutes passed and he stood there alone.

At precisely five fifty-seven he said goodbye to his profession and plunged the blade into his heart.

AN INTERVIEW WITH PATRICIA HIGHSMITH

by John Williams

Patricia Highsmith is in London for a few days, visiting old friends in St John's Wood and appearing on a late night chat show. We talk sitting outside as good an approximation of a country pub as London can provide. She is small, dark and intense and comes over as very smart, basically shy and consequently fierce with respect to her privacy. When it comes to providing details of her life she becomes progressively more cagey as we approach the present. It is like drawing teeth to have her admit to living in Switzerland. Going back to the beginning she is a little more forthcoming.

"I was born in Texas and stayed there until the age of six, them my mother and stepfather took me to New York, put me into school". From an early age she was fascinated by life's darker areas; "I used to read books about criminals. When I was about 8 years old I read *The Human* Mind by Carl Menninger, a book about all kinds of mental abberations, people sick in the head and whether they could be cured or not—arsonists, rapists, hallucinators, murderers, alcoholics—case histories".

Later she attended the prestigious Barnard College. After college she remained in New York, determined to be a writer; "I was living on E 56th St. I had a modest but very adequate apartment which I took when I was 22, just after school. In order to earn my living I did comic books, a job I fell into. I answered an advertisement in the paper for 'reporter/rewrite'. I thought this would have something to do with newspapers or magazines, but it had to do with comic books. They used to sell for ten cents and were very popular with teenagers. Some of them were like Superman, some were funny and some were full of death rays. They certainly earned the rent very nicely."

Just in the way Highsmith enunciates the word 'teenagers', as if talking about a race of aliens, one has the sense that she is not a person who has ever fitted in particularly, and is not overly concerned with fitting in either. It is not so much a simple shyness, but a sense of. . . detachment that she exudes. It is precisely this quality of detachment that makes her books so frequently unnerving to read. None more so than her first book, *Strangers On A Train*, started while she was working on the comic books. Its inspiration was 'an idea that popped into my head'—that idea being two strangers meeting on a train, each with family problems, drunkenly they agree to solve them by one killing the other's wife and the other murdering in turn. Next day one man tries to forget it all, but the other is deadly serious. . .

Clearly, however, her detachment was far from terminal as she was able to call on some high-class help when it came to solving the problem of how to find time to write the novel "I met Truman Capote at a party and he said 'Oh, I have a thing about you' and invited me to tea on a Sunday. I said 'I'm working on a book, I always work on Sundays, so I'm sorry but I can't come'. Then Truman needed an apartment so he said he would recommend me to Yaddo if he could take over my apartment for two months. Yaddo is a writers' colony in Saratoga Springs. It cost no money, but you have to produce a sample of the work you were engaged in and recommendations from people in your field. Yaddo was divine, everyone worked seven days a week. There's no telephone, meals are made for you. You can work much more efficiently than at home."

Strangers on A Train was an extraordinary book, a fusion of detective story pace with Dostoyevsky's psychological doominess. Its success, and Hitchcock's decision to film it, ensured that Highsmith was able to give up her job. She has been a full-time writer ever since. She took a trip to Europe, wrote her second novel, *The Blunderer*, returned to

Europe in 1952, and came to Positano, then an unspoilt Italian
resort.

It was in Positano that she came up with her most famous
fictional creation. Early one morning, thirty years old, she was
standing on her hotel terrace. In the distance there was a solitary
figure on the beach. A young man walking, apparently intent. "I
wondered why he was there. One dreams about these things, at
least I do. Weeks later, I made a note in my notebook, *what if
some one had sent him?*" The young man on the beach became Tom
Ripley, one of the most singular characters in modern fiction, first
appearing in *The Talented Mr Ripley,* a book written by Highsmith
'in a dash'. He is a shy, charming, sexually ambivalent, Europhile
psychopath who must inevitably be seen as a kind of alter ego for
Highsmith, a fellow American exile. In *The Talented Mr Ripley* he
is sent out to Italy from the States to bring back an erring son,
Dickie Greenleaf. Tom becomes infatuated with Dickie to such
an extent that he decides to become him, which of course means
getting rid of the original Dickie. The thing is tentatively achieved
and Tom Ripley settles into the life of European sophistication for
which he feels he was born.

Unlike the fictional Ripley, his creator did not immediately decide
to remain in Europe. Instead she returned to the States and her next
novels are set in American suburbia, tales of ordinary atrocities in
the dream-homes of '50s USA. "I lived in Lenox, Massachussets
briefly and became acquainted with the suburban lifestlye, not
socially but the way it looks, the greenery, the private houses."
Typical is the first of these novels, *Deep Water,* the story of
Vic Van Allen, an apparently nice guy bravely putting up with
a flirtatious wife. As the story unfolds it becomes clear that Vic
is a murderous schizophrenic. What is shocking is the degree to
which Highsmith seduces us into seeing his point, siding with him
in his distaste for suburban mediocrity.

Deep Water, like its successors such as *Cry of The Owl,* is a
remarkable dissection not only of suburban life but also of the
American male. It is men that Highsmith is interested in, almost
exclusively so in her early books, but her relationship to them is
that of a spider to a posse of flies. She has a merciless sense of
a the insecurities and inadequacies that underlie the male role in
that ideal suburban family unit. Vic Van Allen refusing to dance
with his skittish wife at a cocktail party is in a situation that is
at once entirely trivial, and a primal battle over mating rights.
In Highsmith's world brutality will win out over urbanity any
day. When asked as to why she picks on men, however, her
answer is typically understated; "I associate men with not being

tied down and maybe I'm quite wrong but I think of women and they either have a boyfriend or a husband and a family and they can't leave the house so easily. And the other aspect is that men can fight, physically, much better, which I sometimes need for my plots." Maybe her approach to men is modelled on that of the aforementioned Dr. Menninger, her novels could be seen as a series of aberrant case histories. Certainly she is not over impressed by the romantic ideal. The only successful relationships in her books tend to be oddly unconvincing, somewhat chocolate box. She is much happier in territory like that of her last novel, *Found In The Street*, a tale of love and death in New York's SoHo, which she describes thus; "I wanted to write something on the theme of people falling in love with a pretty face and having great hopes that may not be fulfilled. It's about the emptiness of love, not the love being empty but the object of it being empty."

She moved to Europe, permanently, in 1962, living first in Positano for a year, then in Suffolk for three years before moving to France. Unsurprisingly her '60s novels tend to have European settings. Particularly there are three further Ripley books. Ripley is depicted as settling in rural France, rich and happily, if somewhat sexlessly, married. Still his mode of supporting this lifestyle does not stay rigorously within the law – murder, fraud and general duplicity being more his style. The amorality, even cynicism of the Ripley books endeared her to a new generation of European readers. She developed a cult following in avant-garde circles which led to the idiosyncratic German film-maked Wim Wenders ('Paris Texas', 'Wings of Desire' et al.) making a movie based on two of the Ripley stories. This movie, 'The American Friend', starring Dennis Hopper as Ripley, provoked a mixed reaction from Highsmith; "I think it has style. I do not think it's much like my book. I do not see Ripley as a bachelor, (grim chuckle) or beatnik or opting out type. The important thing is that it was a good film, a successful film, the critics liked it."

Another novel from this period was *The Tremor of Forgery*, set in Tunisia, and a foretaste of things to come in that there is virtually no element of crime in it, "a man throws a typewriter. That is all". I asked Highsmith how that one came to be written. "I went to Hammamet with a friend —a summer vacation—I had never been to Africa before. It was a different world to me. I also went to Sidi Bou Said, the town where the Israelis just assassinated Abu Jihad. It's a sleepy pleasant town but at the same time they have a very different mentality. I wanted to make a story out of that contrast."

In the late '70s, however, and despite her continued residence in Europe, Highsmith turned her attentions back to America and began to incorporate a political context into her writing. The first evidence of this came with 1977's *Edith's Diary*. This is at once the furthest thing from crime fiction she had yet written and also her most frightening book to date. It's the story of a woman, Edith, part-time journalist, wife and mother, who is divorced by her husband and left with a dying father-in-law and a monstrously slobbish teenage son, Cliffie. Confronted with the awfulness of a life formed out of good intentions, Edith retreats into her diary in which she describes an idealised fantasy life. In the diary Cliffie is successful, marries, has kids; in real life he does little but masturbate and drink beer. Meanwhile the Vietnam war goes on and Edith's political commitment grows and contorts with her repressed despair. Finally it all converges, Watergate, the U.S. withdrawal from Saigon and Edith's final crack-up.

I wondered what had provoked this extraordinary siting of the roots of our contemporary political crises in the bosom of the family. As ever, her answer is somewhat tangential; "It was the time of the Vietnam war which really brought people out in the streets. At the same time I was interested psychologically in some young men who have not found their feet."

The same combination of politics and the family crops up in 1983's *People Who Knock On The Door,* a novel about the effects of the new Evangelists, the 'Moral Majority', on small-town America, and a book in which Highsmith seems to have discovered a new optimism. She explained that she kept up with what is happening in America by irregular visits and a subscription to *Time* magazine; "I had begun to read about this born-again stuff which, in American, is usually attached to right-wingers, and, when one goes to America, it is appalling to find the number of TV stations devoted to this. I associate it with going backwards, looking for security. I associate it with the fundamentalism in the Middle East. Iran specifically. One expects it there because the people there are, *presumably*, more primitive. But now one finds the same thing happening in America, going back to fundamentalism, the Bible's world is definite, they don't want to talk about evolution. It's a security mechanism against the computer age."

Her latest book, *Tales Of Natural And Unnatural Catastrophes,* a collection of short stories, shows that a sense of outrage at what we are allowing to happen to the world is becoming increasingly central to Highsmith's work. Stories cover such issues as the impossibility of finding a safe home for nuclear waste, the possibility of a radical Pope and the anti-abortion movement in the States. So does she see it as the writer's duty to make political points? "I think it is important to speak out and speak up, as Amnesty International have it. I think everyone should do it. However, I find it very hard to attach it to fiction in the way that George Orwell did it. With the Pope story I made three starts and almost gave up because he is not so much a man as an institution and I cannot write about an institution. Finally I had him stub his toe because everyone has a toe, everyone can trip going up some stairs!"

The prospect of a campaigning Pope is still a fantasy, though, and for now she is less than entirely impressed by the Catholic Church; "I think the world would be much better off with birth control—I don't mean abortion, that is a terrible last resort—I think it is absurd that a church as important as the Catholic should oppose it. It makes people poor, lowers education. In the countries the Pope has visited, the land has to redistributed. There's no alternative."

As for how the book came about; "I had written the first two stories and they seemed to have a catastrophic edge to them so I decided to write six more. The nuclear waste one, for instance, was obvious because it is absolutely not solved, what to do with these masses of dangerous garbage. I think I could write a second book of such things".

She is not overawed by the tenor of the times. "I think I do feel optimistic. Things must be talked about. Hardship or injustice must not be concealed. I think again of Amnesty". As well as Amnesty she is also impressed by the European Green movement, "I'm glad it's there. People always laugh at these goody-goody movements, they laughed at the feminist movement. Somebody has to stand up and begin."

A few last details: she lives in Switzerland near the Italian border; "I like the greenery, the quiet"; there is talk of various films being made from her books, *The Blunderer* being a particular prospect, a series is being made by French TV from her short stories. She reads little fiction, though she will admit to a fondness for Margaret Atwood, an apparent influence on the new book. Mainly she reads non-fiction, particularly politics and sociology, often on the subject of the Palestinians, of whose cause she is a passionate supporter. Recently she had been impressed by Pauline Cutting's book on life in the camps of the Lebanon.

We wrap up the interview as she firmly suggests she would like some lunch. While we eat a photographer from a newspaper arrives, throwing her into a state of high nervousness. I feel like a dentist who on completing a moderately unpleasant session then watches the hapless patient taken off to have their tonsils removed. I make my excuses and leave.

THE MAKING OF TROUBLE IS THEIR BUSINESS

by John Conquest

I
t started out harmlessly enough as check lists of the private eye novels I already had and those I wanted to get. It ended up as a 500-page book, *Trouble Is Their Business*, listing and commenting on over 4,000 titles by 926 authors, 175 feature films, 162 television programmes, 56 radio shows and a grand total of 1,530 Private Eyes, with more to come in the 2nd edition!

Along the way I found some remarkable, and virtually unknown, books such as James Reasoner's *Texas Wind* and Louis Williams' *Tropical Murder* or, frustratingly, read about novels that sounded fascinating but were impossible to locate. Equally I was often forced to mourn the waste of trees and paper involved in publishing unreadable trash.

An overview of the material revealed certain oddities, such as the complete disappearance of women PIs in the 1960s and a two year period in which PIs vanished from television, as well as patterns and sub-genres. More detailed analyses of the following themes, and various others of more technical interest, can be found in *TITB*, but, condensed to their essence, these were some of the observations

I made on what, for better or worse, is a mass of information on a specific genre that I am confident is unique.

ETHNIC DETECTIVES

Of my 1,530 PIs, a mere 44 are non-white. The first black, by many years, was Ed Lacy's Toussaint Moore who first appeared in 1957. Lacy (Leonard Zinberg) was himself white but married to a black woman. It was not until 1970 that a black writer, Ernest Tidyman, created a black hero, but since then there have been a number of black PIs, from the pens of Ishmael Reed, Percy Spurlark Parker, J.F. Burke, Nat Richards, Eric Corder, Kenn Davis, Clifford Mason, Richard Hilary and Gar Anthony Haywood, whose debut won the second PWA Best First Novel contest. One notable black author, John B. West, had a white hero. The only fictional black PI to live and work in the South (Atlanta, Georgia) co-stars in Ralph Dennis' books.

There are also two and a half black women PIs of whom the earliest, James Lawrence's unspeakably sexist creation, reflects little credit on either her sex or her race. However, Dolores Komo, a woman writer published by a feminist publisher, begins to redress the balance. Hosanna Brown's mulatto heroine is, unfortunately, a lightweight.

Television adds only five more to the roster of black PIs, two of them from short-lived series and two more from failed pilots, with cinema adding only another three.

Native American Indians have a longer, if briefer, history in the genre but it is striking how seldom they are pure blooded. In fact there is only one full Indian, Gilbert Ralston's half Shoshone, half Piegan PI, though a junior partner in a novel by William Babula is a Seminole.

Of the 'half-breeds,' the first (1938) was Geoffrey Homes' part-Piute Humphrey Campbell. One of Hugh Lawrence Nelson's Denver PIs is part Indian, though of what nation I have been unable to determine. James Moffatt's Canadian is only a quarter Sioux, but the blood manifests itself in stereotyped ways. Allan Nixon's appalling novels had a half Aztec hero, while the lame L.V. Roper made much of his half Cherokee hero's heritage. M.K. Wren's hero is half Nez Percé, but more sympathetically treated as is Marcia Muller's Scotch-Irish–Shoshone woman PI. Warwick Downing's Joe Reddman was raised by a Cheyenne foster mother but is not himself of Indian blood.

Hispanic Americans have an even shorter record. In the 30s,

Cleve F. Adams wrote short stories narrated by assistant PI Nevada Alvarado. In 1977 M (ary) F. Beal featured a Chicana women's movement activist in one novel. In 1987, Rider McDowell created a Spanish Harlem PI, while Peter Israel's Pablo Rivera, in the same year, went by the waspische name of Philip Revere, betraying a certain detachment from his roots. The latest addition is Bruce Cook's Los Angeleno, though a forthcoming Ron Goulart novel features the likely sounding Rudy Navarro.

The rest of the world is represented in novels by a Norwegian-Japanese-Hawaiian from Poul Anderson, a half-Chinese, half-White Russian from Owen Park and an Irish-Hawaiian from Day Keene. San Francisco's Chinatown was home to Khan in a TV series cancelled after four episodes, and Hong Kong to Joseph in a Cantonese comedy film, "The Private Eyes."

HOMOSEXUAL DETECTIVES

The predominant gay PI is, of course, Joseph Hansen's Dave Brandstetter, a purposefully didactic figure who first appeared in 1970 and was designed both to entertain in good stories and enlighten on the realities of homosexual life. The earliest gay PI novel seems to have been by Lou Rand in 1961, though I have been unable to confirm this. Following very much in Hansen's footsteps, Richard Stevenson has broken into the mainstream market, while Stephen Lewis, published by a gay publishing house, aimed at a more specific audience, though his one novel is by no means overtly sexual. A gay San Francisco PI stars in a book by Kelly Bradford put out by a small feminist house. The most aggressive lifestyle among gay PIs is that of Dan Kavanagh's British bisexual PI, Kavanagh being a pen name of Julian Barnes.

There are, in fact, rather more lesbians in the literature, though one of them, was the creation of a male writer, David Galloway, while another takes only a secondary role in Shelley Singer's novels. M(ary) F. Beal's Chicana revolutionary was a bisexual who preferred female partners while Eve Zaremba's heroine is a member of three different PI minority groups—a woman, a lesbian and a Canadian—but her sexuality is so low key that it's known from an author interview rather than from the text. New books by Dolores Klaich and Diana McRae have lesbian heroines and a short story in Zahava's Woman Sleuth Anthology may be a debut for another. Knowledgeable readers could infer the sexual orientation of Nancy Spain's subversive duo but it is never explicitly stated.

On the subject of homosexuality, a minor oddity is the genre's common and continuing misuse of the word "gunsel," which means a boy kept for immoral purposes. Joseph Shaw, editing *The Maltese Falcon* for serialization in *Black Mask*, misunderstood it as a variation of gunman (or he would have cut it out), in which error he has been followed by dozens of writers.

MEAN STREETS OR MEMORY LANE?

Since the mid-1970s, a number of writers have set PI books in the past, often over-parading their research and displaying a marked weakness for dragging in famous, but now safely dead, real-life personalities. The most articulate spokesman of this tendency is Max Allan Collins who commented (in Reilly's *20th Century Crime Writers*), "I rejected the private eye because I could not find a way to write about him in the 1970s that didn't seem foolish to me—the private eye in the 1970s (and now 1980s) seemed an anachronism. Then it occured to me that the private eye now existed in *history*—That Hammett had created archetypical P.I. Sam Spade in 1929—making Spade a contemporary of Al Capone's. From this starting point I developed the historical private-eye novel. . ."

Collins, despite his epochal claims, was a relative latecomer to his sub-genre, starting in 1983, some years after Andrew Bergman and Stuart Kaminsky first charted the territory.

However, there is considerable disagreement as to exactly when the Golden Age was; the 1920s, 30s, 40s and 50s are all supported by different writers. To what extent Collins reflects their thinking is open to question, Kaminsky at least is less pretentious on the subject, but they too must have their reasons. The obvious flaw in Collins' reasoning is that other, and better, writers, James Crumley, Loren D. Estleman, Sara Paretsky and Andrew Vachss to name only four who would not be called "foolish" by their harshest critics, are creating, and sustaining, 80s PIs in a genre that shows no sign of coming to a standstill. Indeed, the 80s are as much a PI 'Golden Age' as any period since 1927.

The historical PI novel, in my view, sabotages the PI's historic, still relevant, mission of social comment, and denies the continued existence of "mean streets." As David Geherin remarks in *The American Private Eye*, "Writers in the genre have aimed at depicting realistically the society in which they lived rather than follow the example of the classic whodunit tradition they rejected and create a safe cozy world that offers a temporary escape from reality and its actual concerns and problems." By retreating into the past, writers precisely avoid the present's "actual concerns and problems," and mutate the PI novel into its antithesis, the cozy mystery. It is perhaps, not going too far to query Collins' motives in waving the white flag on behalf of an entire genre. He is, after all, an outspoken admirer of Mickey Spillane.

Readers would be better served by reprinting the all but unobtainable work of 20s, 30s and 40s writers rather than publishing what must be, in the very nature of things, inevitably ersatz recreations. British and Australian ersatz authors could at least visit the America in which they laid their novels, but the past is a country to which modern writers can never go. PI history is better served by writers like Mark Schorr, who acknowledge it without trying to reproduce it.

REVIEWS & REVIEWERS

In compiling *TITB* I read thousands of reviews spanning sixty years which revealed countless PIs I was not aware of, either directly or from critical literature; sleuths whose stories had appeared, sometimes to considerable acclaim, only to vanish from secondhand bookstores and, as it were, the collective consciousness of the genre.

The most famous mystery critic was, of course, Anthony Boucher—*San Francisco Chronicle* 1942–47, *Ellery Queen's Mystery Magazine* 1948–50 and 1957–68, and *New York Times Book Review* 1951–68. But, for all his undoubted merits, Boucher's exaggerated reverence for British mysteries and ingrained aversion to sex and violence, taken in concentrated doses, become extremely tedious. Also he developed a hardline attitude to what he condemned, without specifics, as the clichés of PI literature which he reviewed less and less towards the end of his life.

However, Isaac Anderson, his predecessor at the *New York Times*, manifested the same prejudices in far greater degree. While capable on occasion of pithy, revealing comments, Anderson regularly summarized plots while, in common with many of his contemporaries, being more likely to damn with faint praise than offer firm opinions.

After Boucher's death, Allen J. Hubin maintained his standards for three years, but thereafter, under the aegis of Newgate Callendar, the *New York Times* lost its commanding position in mystery criticism. Where Boucher and Hubin's reviews are, by and large, able to stand the best of time, Newgate Callendar's are revealed to be inept.

Far and away the most reliable, not to say pungent, source for the 30s, 40s and 50s is the uncredited Criminal Record column of *Saturday Review of Literature* (from 1951 it carried the name of "Sergeant Cluff", actually 1966 Edgar winner John Winterich). Highly compressed, *SR*'s capsule reviews invariably convey more in 50 words than other critics including, it must be said, Boucher, in four or five times that many. Over the years, however, the magazine showed less and less interest in crime fiction, dropping the column for weeks at a time and then completely.

In modern times, reviewers I found consistently useful and credible were the late Charles Willeford (*Mystery Scene*), virtually all the critics associated with *Drood Review*, Francis M. Nevins Jr and the mystery reviewers of *Publisher's Weekly*.

UNAMERICAN ACTIVITIES

While there are some very competent non-American writers of PI novels, a number wrote, and still write, books set in the US that range from the laughably inept to clever pastiche. It is not simply problems of language and geography; the fact is that the British and American experiences are so different that writing meaningful, even readable, fiction about America is, if not impossible, beyond the competence of most writers of any kind. It can be argued that ersatz novels are simply entertainments, with no literary presumptions, aspiring to, though rarely achieving, mediocrity, but I fail to see why 'mere' PI novels should be a license for third-rate hack work.

After lack of talent, language is usually the most obvious pitfall. Writers like Carter Brown and James Hadley Chase relied on colloquial dictionaries, neither reliable nor current sources for American slang, and such artificial writing would occasionally supply outright *Gun in Cheek* gems such as Peter Cheyney's classic line "Lay the gat on the bonnet." Perhaps the absolute worst of the ersatz writer, (there are many contenders) is W.B.M. Ferguson, but all are, at best, undistinguished.

A very striking feature of the ersatz is the fecundity of its main exponents. In *TITB* will be found one Australian and seven British authors who, between them, have written at least 421 PI novels—a brilliant illustration of the maxim "More means worse." Leading the field is, of course, Carter Brown (78), trailed by Harry Carmichael (65), Neill Graham (65), Basil Copper (62), Bevis Winter (44), Peter Chambers (34), Hugh Desmond (33), and Mark Corrigan (30). A truly depressing thought is that Cooper and Chambers are still active and the total has almost certainly risen already. Mercifully, John Creasey devoted little energy to his Robert Caine Frazer PI series.

However, there are also some very fine writers in the field outside America who, it is very noticeable, chose without exception to write about their home ground. Britain is, obviously, the second largest producer of PI fiction in the world, with Canada and Australia far behind and, while the non-English-speaking world may well teem with unstranslated PI writers, so far only two Spanish, one Italian and one French author have surfaced in translation.

In my opinion, the 10 best non-American PI Writers are, in chronological order:

1 Nancy Spain (UK)
2 Kevin O'Hara (UK)
3 P.B. Yuill (UK)
4 Manuel Vazquez Montalban (Spain)
5 Liza Cody (UK)
6 Peter Corris (Australia)
7 Howard Engel (Canada)
8 Dan Kavanagh (UK)
9 John Milne (UK)
10 Peter Whalley (UK)

WOMEN DETECTIVES

Of the 1,530 PIs listed in *TITB*, 165 are women though 18 feature only as adjuncts to husbands and 13 appear only in anthologized short stories. This may well, of course, reflect the real world of private detection. In fact there are fewer female PI writers—116 at the most generous count, including co-writers and two dubious pseudonyms—than there are female PIs and many women writers in the genre, including such illustrious names as Leigh Brackett, Dolores Hitchens, Margaret Millar and Hilda Lawrence, wrote about male PIs. Many women, indeed, not only write about men but conceal their own sex, even in modern times, behind male pseudonyms or ambiguous initials—Jack Early (Sandra Scoppettone), M.V. Heberden, who also wrote as Charles L. Leonard, Paul Kruger (Roberta Sebenthal), M.R.D. Meek, J.M.T. Miller, Joe Rayter (Mary McChesney), L.J. Washburn and M.K. Wren (Martha Renfroe).

All but four of the '&' women (as in Nick & Nora) were the creation of male authors, but, regardless of the sex of the author, in each case the female partner is, in James M. Fox's phrase, "the little woman," with the male taking the initiatives and the woman making herself available for plot devices. They are all too often given to intuition and while sometimes secretly smarter than their partners, rarely get the credit.

Of the "real" women PIs, almost half of those in fiction were created by male authors, 57 to the women's 59. One author, Ron S. Miller, adopted a female pseudonym, Fran Huston, two, Victor B. Miller and Jim Conaway, had supposedly "liberated" heroines, while David Galloway had the temerity to create a lesbian PI, though at least one female commentator thought quite highly of the result. Of male authors, W.R. Philbrick is almost alone in being praised by a female critic.

Women PIs created by women date from 1928, but, while they were by no means numerous in the 30s, 40s, and 50s, they disappeared completely, as far as I can see, between 1957 and 1972. The modern era of female PI opened in 1977 with Marcia Muller's first book, gathering strength in 1982 when the twin talents of Sara Paretsky and Sue Grafton entered the field. Since then the female PI has prospered as never before.

The balance of the numbers is made up by television, film and radio. Women PIs did relatively better on radio that in any other medium but, while they have been reasonably, if not equally, represented on TV, the female PI in film is an extreme rarity.

Kathleen Gregory Klein's feminist critique of the female PI in fiction, *The Woman Detective* (1988), is interesting, indeed fascinating, on the genre's consistent unwillingness, in both male and female hands, to allow female PIs to succeed both as women and detectives, though I would like to think that she is over-pessimistic about future possibilities. PI fiction is, I hope, dynamic enough to respond to her call, echoing Carolyn Heilbrun on science fiction, to "deconstruct . . . the structures of the patriarchy." As things stand, Sara Paretsky is the only currently active PI writer of whom she approves in both genre and feminist terms.

WOUNDED HEROES

One can hope that heroes or heroines of PI novels will have some individuality, an expectation not always rewarded, but many have a problem that dominates their entire persona, sometimes complementing personality, but all too often substituting for it.

Gary Hoppenstand and Ray Browne call them Defective Detectives, but it is more positive to think of them as wounded heroes, a literary usage with a respectable history, though, like any other usage, open to sensationalizing abuse or simplistic misuse.

The most exotic problems are, in fact, to be found in Hoppenstand and Browne's collections which include a haemophilic, a glaucoma victim, an amnesiac, a stone-deaf PI, another with hyperacute hearing, another stunted by childhood polio and one whose hideously mutilated face is hidden behind a plastic shield. Even in shudder pulps such as *Dime Mystery* these unfortunates would seem eminently unsuited to the life of PI.

But the more respectable world of the PI novel can offer many equally unlikely heroes (well, almost). Of the physically handicapped PIs, two are missing an arm, another two have lost a hand, one has an artificial leg, another lost a foot and the hearing in one ear in a bomb outrage, yet another left a foot and a testicle in Vietnam, and three were effectively crippled by being shot in the knee.

The two real sensory handicaps on record belong to a blind PI and a dead one. Perhaps the most effective defect is the permanent insomniac who perpetually roams the streets of Los Angeles with no home, nor car and no office.

There is, I think only one, dwarf PI in fiction, with two more appearing on TV, thought at least two others are only 5'1". The oldest PI I found was over 100 years old, followed at a distance by 85 and 78.

On the psychological side, there are several traumatized women, two obsessed by their husbands' murders, two others both frigid as a result of rapes.

There *are* abstemious PIs but most can deal with a bottle. The most extreme case is an alcoholic who pistol-whipped his adulterous wife and best friend, lost his license, and became a homeless derelict. Several manage to combine steady drinking with a kind of quasi-respectable life, though at least one thinks of chucking PI work because it interferes with his drinking.

The drinkers are often consumed by guilt, existential or induced by real events, but others deal with it in other ways, most conspicuously one who obsessively builds a high wall around his house. Fear haunts another who consumes handfuls of antacid tablets to try and calm his panic about almost everything while there is a hardboiled PI who, rather curiously, is terrified of guns.

One PI's hyprochondria is brought on by meeting strangers, so his assistant has to carry a pharmacy with him, but while his weakness is for prescription drugs, there are several notable drug abusers, one of whom who can virtually give the reader a contact cocaine high.

The extreme psychological problems are those of two suicidal PIs. One went so far as to put a gun to his head and pull the trigger but his skull was so thick that the bullet bounced off. The other plays Russian Roulette and will, presumably, lose (or win, depending on the point of view) some day.

In the gimmicky world of television, the most outstanding problem of all must be that of a dead PI who features as a ghost.